A Pennine Dynasty

Lawrence Alderson

A novel following the contrasting careers of two brothers and the impact of women on their lives

HAYLOFT PUBLISHING LTD
KIRKBY STEPHEN

First published by Hayloft 2009

Hayloft Publishing Ltd, South Stainmore,
Kirkby Stephen, Cumbria, CA17 4DJ

tel: 017683 42300
email: books@hayloft.eu
web: www.hayloft.eu

ISBN 1 904524 67 2

CAP data for this title are available from the British Library

Designed, printed and bound in the EU

Papers used by Hayloft are natural, recyclable products made from wood grown in sustainable forest. The manufacturing processes conform to the environmental regulations of the country of origin.

This book is dedicated to my father and mother who would have understood completely both the affinity with their environment that prompts some to remain securely within their heritage of the glorious Pennine Dales, and the desire that drives others to escape from the hardship of hill farming.

Acknowledgements

The inspiration for this book came from my friends and colleagues in many walks of life, and I owe a debt of gratitude to them for their unconscious contribution. More particularly, I must make special mention of my cousin, John Hastings Dent, who refreshed my memory on many aspects of Dales life, and his wife, Ruth Harrison Dent, whose unrivalled expertise was invaluable in refining the passages of Yorkshire dialect. Finally, I have been very fortunate that my ambition as an aspiring author of fiction has been eased and encouraged by Dawn Robertson and the team at Hayloft, which ensured that the manuscript did not remain hidden on a remote shelf.

All the characters in this book are fictitious, and any resemblance to actual persons, living or dead, is purely coincidental.

CONTENTS

Part I

THE ENGLISH OAK

RECOGNITION

The gates of Buckingham Palace were bathed in the watery sunshine of an October day as a photographer marshalled four members of a family into position. The oldest man, in formal Morning Dress, was tall and broad like an English oak in mature dignity. His dark curly hair betrayed a hint of grey but showed no sign of thinning, and the quiet smile on his tanned face matched the calmness of his blue-grey eyes. His wife, standing proudly at his side, was less comfortable in designer-labelled finery than her normal rural attire, but that was forgotten in the significance of the moment. They were flanked by his two sons, strong men of the soil like their father.

The cause of their pride was the CBE Insignia which Dick Bainbridge held in his hand. The smile on his face might justifiably have been an afterglow of the pomp and grandeur of the ceremony that he had recently endured. But that would not have been a true reflection of his character and, in truth, the whole affair had scarcely made any impression on him. The entrance up The Grand Staircase, and the briefing in The Green Drawing Room with other recipients, before his stately progress along The East Gallery to The Ballroom for the Investiture, and finally the departure of the family together along The East Gallery, to their appointment with the photographer – he could not understand why such a performance had been necessary.

His smile expressed rather the recall of more significant memories as they flooded into his thoughts.

He had heard the news of his award with mixed feelings. Of course it was an honour, but he was sceptical of a tarnished honours system which rewarded political cronies and targeted self-interested benefactors, and he had never shaken off the memories of the abject conduct of officialdom during the foot-and-mouth disease epidemic. He only had been persuaded eventually to accept the award by his wife's strong and insistent reassurance that in his case it was genuinely deserved. The letter, signed by the Secretary for Appointments from the Cabinet Office, had arrived in early May, addressed to R. M. Bainbridge Esq., and marked 'IN CONFIDENCE'.

> Dear Sir,
> The Prime Minister has asked me to inform you, in strict confidence, that he has it in mind, on the occasion of the forthcoming list of Birthday Honours, to submit your name to The Queen with a recommendation that Her Majesty may be graciously pleased to approve that you be appointed a Commander of the Order of the British Empire.

Three months later another letter arrived; this time from the Secretary of the Central Chancery of the Orders of Knighthood, and addressed to Richard Matthew Bainbridge, Esq., CBE.

> Sir,
> I am commanded to inform you that an Investiture will be held at Buckingham Palace – You are asked to arrive at the Palace between the hours of 10.00 and 10.30am – You may bring with you THREE guests to watch the Ceremony

Also enclosed was a car park ticket for admittance by the South Centre Gate to the inner Quadrangle of the Palace, and instructions for all recipients and guests to bring photographic proof of identity.

Dick was a down-to-earth honest Yorkshireman. He was not attracted by the thought of such convoluted procedures and almost backed out of the whole idea. It smacked too much of personal and institutional glorification. In the end he had agreed because he could see that it would give wider recognition to the causes he had espoused, and he accepted that was the way things were done at the Palace. Susan had not experienced any inhibitions about acceptance. She knew that his life's work had made a real difference to his colleagues, to his community, and ultimately to the British public. He had made things change, not for self-interest, but for the benefit of others.

Dick valued the support of his family. Susan was the sheet-anchor that held him safe in times of trouble, and in his mind the CBE belonged as much to her as to him. Ralph, his elder son, stood beside Susan, while the younger sibling, Simon, stood beside Dick. Ralph was a young oak – almost as tall and strong as his father, but Simon was two or three inches shorter and more slightly built – not an oak, rather an English elm. They were very different characters, but Dick loved them both.

"You must be happy. Smile to the camera. Thank you. Now perhaps a shot of Mr and Mrs Bainbridge together." The photographer followed his tested routine, and as he arranged and rearranged the group, one thought was uppermost in Dick's mind. *"It's taken me a long time, Harry, but at last I know my own worth. For almost 60 years I've lived with the feeling that I was in your shadow, but not any more. Neither your lack of recognition nor your absence has any significance today."*

Dick's elder brother, Harry, had been a major influence on his life, directly by his presence in their early years, and indirectly by his absence thereafter.

Dick's life may have seemed uneventful in comparison with the roller-coaster international itinerary that had typified Harry's, but eventually he had made his mark. He started as a humble farmer in northern England, but had spread his wings and earned his reputation through hard work and commitment. The citation under CBE in the *London Gazette*, 'Richard Matthew BAINBRIDGE, Trustee, Ridings Conservation Trust and Chair, Richmond Diversification Developments. For services to conservation and agriculture', was a glowing tribute, but it scarcely did justice to his outstanding achievements and wide-ranging work with breed improvement, exports and fund-raising for good causes in the local community.

Harry had been the golden boy, a high-flyer, a flamboyant charismatic risk-taker. He had indulged in extravagant luxuries and all his childhood friends were envious of his high living as stories of his progress filtered back to them. But Harry's qualities were alloyed by an egotistical arrogance, which had allowed him to ignore his family and insult his geographical roots with reckless indifference. As a youngster Dick had adored his brother, and later admired his prowess. With maturity, he recognised the need to break out of the overpowering desire to emulate him, until finally he had come to recognise the fatal flaws in his brother's character. Now, at last, he was free of his influence. The CBE could claim credit for the final break. Henceforth, maybe rather late in life, Dick could relax in the confidence of a man who believes in himself.

1
LAKELAND SPORTS 1962

The slow process of breaking free from Harry had started 42 years previously, when Dick was approaching his twentieth birthday.

He was stretched out on the grass at Langthwaite in Westmorland on a fine summer day in early August. He wore a costume of white vest, black cutaway velvet shorts, white tights and black calf-length socks. The vest and shorts were embroidered with colourful motifs in the custom of Lakeland wrestlers. He lay back and relaxed; his eyes closed as the sun warmed his face.

"Fred Burlinson and Dick Bainbridge, final of the heavyweight contest," called an official from the nearby square of grass surrounded by a crowd of onlookers.

Dick sprang to his feet, easily and athletically, and approached the ring. His opponent advanced from the other side. They were an evenly matched pair – both well over six feet in height and maybe fourteen stone in weight. Dick had the brash vigour of youth, but at 34 years of age Fred Burlinson had experience and an unequalled record of success in his chosen sport. They reached the centre of the ring, which was roughly ten to fifteen yards in diameter, shook hands, and the referee called "Take hold."

The rules governing the Cumberland and Westmorland style of wrestling had been ingrained on Dick's subconscious through years of watching, discussing and competing. He had learned them by practice in the ring, but he also had taken the trouble to read and understand them to ensure that he did not lose by default.

The sport demanded strength, agility, skill and courtesy. Rule 8 states that competitors shall shake hands on entering and leaving the ring, but no talking whatever shall be allowed during the contest. A contest is won when the opponent touches the ground with any part of his body except his feet, or when his hold is broken. Play commences on the word of the referee when both men have got hold and are fairly on their guard, and, with the exception of kicking, the wrestlers are allowed to use every legitimate means to throw each other, including striking with the side of the foot.

Dick had missed the early part of the season, which started each year on Whit Monday at Pooley Bridge on the shores of Ullswater. He had been in Canada, but had asked his father, Ralph, to enter him for Langthwaite in early August, and for Grasmere later in the same month. To be Champion at Grasmere was the pinnacle of achievement, and Langthwaite would be a useful warm-up event.

Grasmere was a sporting mecca, and outstanding athletes achieved legendary status in Lakeland. Bryce Scott came down from Loch Lomond in 1910 and, in a primitive sandpit, set a record of 22 feet 7 inches for the long leap. Gilpin Bland dominated middleweight wrestling from 1923 to 1938 and created a dynasty of champions, while the wiry five foot three inch figure of Bill Teasdale of Caldbeck had been equally dominant in fell racing since 1950. But the champion who stood above all others in Dick's eyes was George Steadman. He was a bulky powerful figure, just short of six feet in height, and first won the heavyweight wrestling championship in 1872. He still was winning at 46 years of age at the turn of the century, when he weighed a deceptively nimble eighteen and a half stone. Dick believed that he was related by marriage to Steadman, who had been born in Brough-under-Stainmore, and had dreamed since he started wrestling of emulating his achievements.

At the call "Take hold," Dick and his opponent leaned forward, each with his chin on the other's right shoulder, arms encircling the other's torso, fingers locked in a firm hold. Dick felt the power of Fred's grip, but it was the difference in experience which without doubt would be the main threat. Fred had won more than four hundred championships in the last fourteen years, and Dick knew he had to be on his guard against any of the ingenious throws that Fred could execute with lightning precision – the hype, the hank, the cross buttock. On the other hand, Dick was a left-hander – a 'cuddy wifter' – and that gave him the advantage of unorthodoxy.

The referee called "Both hold," and the contest began. Fred tried a couple of feints to test the younger man, but Dick was alert to the danger and countered with his own attempted back heel. Fred matched

Dick for height and weight, and was infinitely more experienced, but Dick's strength was phenomenal. As he successfully resisted Fred's attacks, his confidence grew, and with a sudden rib-crushing grip, he lifted his opponent off the ground and felled him with a swinging hype. Fred lay on the ground, his pride hurting as much as his ribs. Masking the pain, he climbed to his feet. Dick was standing nearby, apparently calm, but adrenaline surged through him. He had felled the undisputed champion of Cumberland and Westmorland wrestling.

They shook hands and prepared for the next hold.

The final was best of three falls. Dick now was confident he had the measure of his man, although he knew he must not be tempted into rash mistakes. Fred's composure had been ruined. He had been felled by an unknown novice. He had never heard of Dick Bainbridge. They were called again by the referee. Now the psychological advantage lay with Dick, and this time he went straight to the attack. A feint, a lift, a left-foot hank as his powerful arms tightened again on Ted's ribs, and he was champion. He reached down, grasped Fred's hand and pulled him to his feet.

"Well done, lad," said Fred, and retreated to lick his wounded pride.

Dick had beaten the undisputed world champion by two straight decisive falls, and he still was three weeks short of his twentieth birthday – the youngest ever winner of the heavyweight class. The treasured prize was not the few paltry pounds for the winner, although that made him a professional; rather it was the achievement and the glory that really mattered. Other wrestlers came up and congratulated him, keen to get a closer view of the newcomer. Some had met Dick in earlier rounds of the contest, and already had a fair appreciation of his ability. They sensed a change in the order of the sport, and Dick sensed that Grasmere was his for the taking.

Dick was bursting with pride, and he wished that his father had been there to see him. Ralph had wanted to go to support his son, but he had just moved to Deep Ghyll, a new farm four or five miles lower down the valley in Teesdale, and there was urgent work to be done. It was an unusual time to take possession of a new farm, and the previous owner had left the hay meadows in disarray. It was too late for silage, and there would be a problem gathering enough hay for the winter.

When Dick arrived home and announced his news, Ralph was thrilled. "Ah's prood o' tha, lad. Thoo's a reet credit ti t'family. Bah

Jove, thi gran'father would ha' bin reet set up an' all. Noo, wheear's next? Grasmere?"

Ralph was not a tactilely demonstrative man, but his words carried all the praise and approval that Dick needed. "Thanks, Dad. It was grand. I wish you could've seen it. I never thought I'd beat Fred Burlinson, but I'm really looking forward to Grasmere now." That was all they said, and Dick changed the subject. "How about the farm? Are you getting it sorted out?"

"Nay, lad, it's a mess, a reet scrow," replied Ralph, lifting his cap to scratch his greying hair, "Yon chap left it i' bad shape. We'll hev a job ti git eneeaf decent hay fer t'winter."

Dick saw the concern on his father's face. "I shouldn't have gone to Langthwaite," he exclaimed. "You need all of us here. Never mind, if we get stuck in we can get enough before the end of the month. We don't want to be haymaking in September. I'll give Grasmere a miss. Fred Burlinson probably will be pleased!"

"Nay, Dick, thoo can't miss Grasmere. Ah'd nivver fergive misel' if thoo stayed at yam. We can spare tha fer summat as special as that. Thoo'd bi t'youngest winner of t'main wrestlin event in t'calendar."

Despite his father's pleas, Dick was adamant. He knew his priorities. "I'll have plenty of other chances, Dad. I'm needed here, and that's where I'll be. Yes, I want to win Grasmere, but family comes first."

Nothing would change Dick's mind. Ralph tried to persuade him, and urged his wife to add her voice. Where Ralph was sentimental, Annie was pragmatic. She was loath to see her son miss his deserved success, but she knew how essential it was to get the farm into effective working order. Dick saw her hesitation, and it reinforced his decision to miss Grasmere.

Fred Burlinson went on to win at Grasmere later in the month in Dick's absence, but his former invincibility now was tinged with apprehension, and even a suggestion of fear. He had felt the young man's strength, and he knew that Dick would improve with age, while he was almost past his peak. He was right to fear Dick's strength; it was a genetic trait. Stories of his great-uncle Will, who would carry a three-hundredweight sack on his back from the railway station at Bowes to the Unicorn Hotel, a distance of eleven hundred yards, without stopping for breath, had been passed down to him in family legend.

2
GROWING UP

The Younger Sibling

Family was an essential cornerstone of Ralph Bainbridge's life. His ancestors had lived in the Pennine area of North Yorkshire and Westmorland for generations, and a network of siblings, uncles and aunts, cousins and half-cousins, populated Swaledale, Arkengarthdale, Stainmore and Teesdale. The Norwegian element of Viking culture, pouring in from the Irish Sea across the Lakeland mountains and Eden valley to the Pennines, surged through the Stainmore Gap and settled in the rugged hills, reassured by the familiarity of upland heath. The legacy of their genes has persisted for more than a thousand years, reinforced by Scandinavian place-names, dialect and architecture. Their ancient culture resonates in Baldersdale and Woden's Croft near Cotherstone, and in farmyards built on old Viking thwaites. Even Ralph's speech echoed the vocabulary of his Scandinavian ancestors. Ralph had few written records of his antecedents, but an oral tradition prevailed and he regaled his sons with stories of the exploits of their relatives – the size of their families, the great weights they could carry, and the speed of their ponies. His elder son, Harry, showed little interest, but the younger sibling was engrossed by family history.

Dick was a wartime baby, born on 30 August 1942 while his parents were farming at Ellerbeck, a small hill farm in the Pennines several miles from Barnard Castle. Although he was born into a strong Primitive Methodist tradition, his mother had him baptised into the Church of England. He was christened Richard Matthew Bainbridge, named after Matthew Metcalfe, his maternal grandfather. Annie's late pregnancy had coincided with haymaking, a critical time on a hill farm, and it had made life difficult, but John Joyce, a pleasant hard-working itinerant Irishman, had been employed for the summer to augment the work force, and ensured that Dick's birth did not disturb the progress of the summer harvest.

Harry, already two-and-a-half years old, soon exhibited the petulant signs of jealousy as parental attention was accorded to the new arrival, and became closer to his grandparents. He competed unsuccessfully for a greater share of Annie's limited time, and his failure at that early age to keep himself in the forefront of attention weakened the mother-son bond and stored up psychological insecurities. An underlying foundation of resentment was a hidden but de-stabilising influence as Harry built his life.

Dick started at the local village school in 1947. It should have been an advantage that Harry was there already, but his elder brother ignored him. For the next two years the blonde curly-haired brothers lived at home together, and travelled to school together, but at school they followed a separate existence. Harry never lifted a finger to help Dick, even when school bullies were abusing him. He was a shy boy, and held back when Harry and the others were tearing riotously around the schoolyard, or trying to steal a precocious kiss from pretty little Phyllis Close. Dick was not aware of anything unusual in this state of affairs. His elder brother was a leader, and Dick was happy to follow in his shadow.

Ralph and Annie were aware of the limitations of the village school, and they agreed that their sons were above average – maybe even exceptional – both on the sports field and in the classroom. They did not have any significant financial assets, but they were determined to give their children the opportunities which they had been denied. Ralph had never enjoyed school. He was a natural rebel, and his posterior had been in regular contact with the cane of authority. Annie, in contrast, had shown remarkable academic inclination and ability. She could have gained admittance to university, but lack of funds had not allowed the opportunity and, in any case, girls as well as boys were needed on the family farm. She had duly left school at the age of fourteen.

When Harry was nine he was sent to Barnard Castle Preparatory School, nestling behind a protective belt of trees in the triangle of land between Westwick Road and Mount Eff Lane at the eastern edge of the town. His initiation quickly disabused him of any notion that it was only on the hills that life was hard. On his first day, standing uncertainly in the playground, he was pushed roughly by a large boy. He did not react immediately, but when the treatment was repeated with greater vigour, he hit out angrily. Adrian Blackthorn, the school bully, was accustomed to meek acquiescence by his victims, and the glancing blow of Harry's hand on his arm enraged him. He launched himself at the smaller boy, and knocked him to the ground. The injustice of the attack obliterated the sense of apprehension that Harry had felt as a new boy, and he responded to his basic instinct to fight to defend himself. The other pupils gathered round, and their murmurs of surprise grew to cheers of support as the protagonists wrestled on the ground. When finally Harry pinned down Blackthorn with his face in the dirt until he submitted, the new boy was a hero. The bully slunk away, and Harry's reputation was established. Despite the ignominious consequences, when the headmaster's cane descended with painful accuracy on his exposed buttocks, he had earned the respect of his peers. He flourished and quickly distinguished himself, which softened the hardship of the sacrifices made by Ralph and Annie to afford the fees of private education.

Dick was bursting with eagerness to follow Harry to the new school. He listened to Harry's exciting stories of life in a boarding school, and longed to join him. Ralph and Annie watched his excitement with increasing sadness. They knew they could not afford a second tranche of fees.

One day when Dick returned from school and was sitting in the kitchen by the big black range as his mother was baking bread, Annie asked him softly, "Are you looking forward to being in the school football team?" Dick had shown an aptitude for games, and had been selected for the junior team.

"Aye, Ah's gaan ti play centre hauf, bud Ah'll like it better when Ah's off ti Barney ti play rugby."

Annie's heart sank. How was she going to tell him? "Dick," she started tentatively and with a sorrowful spirit, brushing the flour from her hands, "you know how hard farming is, and we do not have much money. I'm not sure we'll be able to afford to send you to Barney." She stopped as the tears sprang to Dick's eyes.

"Bud Harry's theer. Why can't Ah gan? Ah want ti gan ti Barney."

Annie tried to reason with him. She saw the hurt in his eyes, and his inability to comprehend the situation. She felt infinitely sad for her son, but what could she do? She tried to give him a hug, but he pushed her away and rushed to his room – the room he had shared with Harry until a couple of years ago. Resentment filled him. *'It was favouritism. Why did his Mam favour Harry? Was he not as good? His Mam and Dad must think Harry was better than him.'*

A sense of inferiority overwhelmed him. He became difficult and unco-operative. His natural shyness was accentuated and drove him to spend time by himself, wandering by the river or riding his bicycle in the old quarry up the road – lonely and confused in his isolation.

In February 1951, when Harry was a month short of his eleventh birthday, he won a Flounders Scholarship to Barnard Castle main school, an imposing facade looking across the valley alongside the even more imposing Bowes Museum. It was a great relief to Ralph and Annie, because now they could afford to pay fees for Dick. But Dick's resentment after learning that he could not go to Barney had made him perverse, and he insisted that he preferred the village school. In the end they allowed him to stay there rather than risk another damaging emotional confrontation.

Ellerbeck – a Hill Farm

Dick had been born into a harsh environment. The northern climate was cold and damp. Upland summers could be warm and pleasant, except when clouds of biting midges descended at the end of an exhausting day of haymaking. The air was fresh, and the breeze sweet with the scent of upland meadows. But the long Pennine winters were harsh on all living creatures. The icy winds howling down from the hills bit into numbed flesh, and even the toughest body was chilled to the bone. When Dick was only four years old the winter storms of 1947 broke over the hills in February. The swirling snow was sculpted into fantastic shapes, and piled in drifts so deep that they hid from view the stone walls in the fields and reached the eaves of the buildings in the farmyard.

Ralph cut steps in the snow from the doors of the cow byres to enable the cattle to be unchained every day and climb up to cross the fields to the only spring where water still was running. More than half the sheep flock perished. Many were buried under snow – although Tess and Rex, the Border Collies, detected many by tracing their scent and alerting Ralph – and others died at the end of the winter through weakness and exhaustion. Feeding stuffs for the animals were in short supply, and it was not until late in the storm that extra hay was airlifted to the stricken areas. The school bus could not negotiate the roads, and Harry missed school for six weeks. The upper Dale was blotted out by repeated blizzards, and trains on the Barnard Castle to Brough line were engulfed by snowdrifts on Stainmore Summit.

The conditions of 1947 were extreme, but every year was hard. The total regular work force on the farm consisted of Ralph and Annie, two sturdy black Dales Ponies, Sapphire and Black Diamond, and Tess and Rex. Temporary labour was recruited at times of peak demand, and a girl helped in the house, but mostly it was lonely back-breaking toil. If thoughts of the missed opportunity of university ever entered Annie's mind, she had little time to dwell on them.

Petty jealousies penetrated even to this corner of rural England. The hefted curly-horned black-faced Swaledale sheep ran on the moor, and the size of the flock was determined by the number of stints allocated by the Lords of the Manor. This led to bitter feuds among the Field Reeves who administered the system, but among the farmers usually there was neighbourly communal effort for the major seasonal tasks. After lambing in April the ewes were turned back onto the fell, drafted out in groups of twenty by the old Celtic tally of counting – yan, tean, tethera, methera, pip, razer, seazar, catrah, horna, dik. Later they were sheared, and their male lambs castrated. The sweetbreads – genuine sweetbreads, not pseudo pancreatic imitations – provided a tasty extra for several breakfasts. The ewes were dipped in noxious liquid to destroy biting and blood-sucking parasites, and in the autumn the lambs were spained (weaned). The gimmer (female) lambs were sent off to kinder land for winter, while wether (castrated male) lambs were sold, although one or two were kept back for a supply of hogget in the following year. No self-respecting hill farmer would eat lamb when there was the chance of hogget or mutton.

A few hens scratched around the farmyard, and provided an adequate supply of eggs. One of Dick's duties was to keep watch where the hens were making nests – usually in the corner of the calf shed or an old building in the back paddock – and collect the eggs, always making sure to leave a pot egg in the nest. The breeding flock of white

Embden geese reared broods of goslings each year to be ploated (plucked) for the Christmas market, but one was kept for the traditional family celebrations.

Each spring a young pig was bought, and reared largely on household scraps supplemented by a little gruel until the autumn, when it was killed on the farm. That was a time of relative plenty. There were black puddings and spare ribs to break the monotony of the usual plain wholesome fare. Long strings of sausages, encased in the cleaned intestines, were forced out of the hand-turned mincing machine, and Dick played football with the blown-up bladder. Sides and hams were brine-cured and hung from rafters in the corner of the kitchen for use during the year ahead.

It approached self-sufficiency more nearly than any other system of farming. It was based on practices which had been evolved by necessity, and passed by example down the generations, rather than selected by choice. Peat for fuel was cut on the moor and stacked to dry, bracken and rushes were cut and hauled for bedding for the winter-housed cattle, and even heather was gathered occasionally to thatch one of the sheep houses down by the river. Indoors, milk was churned into butter, or processed into Cotherstone cheese redolent with the flavour of herb-rich pastures. Bread was baked, wool was spun and knitted, and old clothes were recycled as prodded mats which were the only floor covering. The weekly visits to market in Barnard Castle replenished the stocks of necessary basic supplies such as flour, sugar, soap, fruit and vegetables, plus rarely shoes and clothes, but the shopping list was very short.

The low-ceilinged, damp dwellinghouse at Ellerbeck stood at the top of the sloping farmyard, sparsely furnished and typical of the upper Dale. The stone-flagged kitchen, immediately inside the front door, was the hub of the house. It was dominated by the old black range, which contained the fire, oven and water boiler. A large black kettle was suspended from the reckan-crook over the fire, and several small items stood on the mantelpiece above. A press, holding all the crockery and breakable items in the upper shelves and more solid items in the cupboard below, stood against the back wall. Nearby was Annie's sewing-machine, on which new clothes were made and old repaired. It had a treadle action which freed both hands to manoeuvre the cloth.

A door on the left, immediately inside the front door, opened into the parlour, which was used only on very special occasions, and where the old grandfather clock ticked with emphatic solemnity. A door at the back of the kitchen led into the stairwell, with the larder to the right and the back kitchen at the left with a door opening directly into the outbuildings of the farm. Upstairs there were two bedrooms at the front, and two small rooms under the eaves at the back. There was no bathroom. A tin bath, brought out when necessary in front of the black range, chamber pots under the bed, and an earth closet at the bottom of the yard sufficed. Water was pumped up to the house from a stream by a hydraulic ram – except when it froze. Candles and spirit lamps provided light indoors, and storm lanterns outdoors. Hardiness was an essential attribute that the Pennine hill farmer shared with his animals.

Each week was ordered to a set pattern. On Monday, Annie washed clothes in the back kitchen with the possen tub and mangle; Tuesday she cleaned downstairs and polished the black range; Wednesday was market day – an opportunity for the rural residents in the Dale to exchange the latest news; Thursday she baked bread, scones, pies and cakes on the black range; Friday she cleaned upstairs; some Saturdays she churned butter and pressed cheese to store on the cool stone shelves in the larder, and remembered how a decade previously she took them to sell at the Market Cross in Barnard Castle. In the intervals between she sortied outside to help Ralph on the farm during the day, and in the evening knitted or looped strips of material gleaned from worn-out clothes through frame-stretched hessian in patterns that emerged as prodded mats.

The seventh day was the Sabbath, for "six days thou shalt do thy work, and on the seventh day thou shalt rest." The Bainbridge family knew and faithfully observed that commandment. They were God-fearing and devout and, apart from essential tasks, the seventh day was devoted to Sunday School, chapel and reading of the Bible. There were few books in the house; mostly they were kept in the press in the kitchen, but the two most important volumes – the massive Bainbridge family Bible dating from the early nineteenth century, and a large copy of *Pilgrim's Progress* with coloured illustrations – had pride of place in the parlour.

Life outside on the farm was equally hard. Every day, even in winter when the first glimmer of daylight had scarcely begun to penetrate the blanket blackness of the frozen morning, Ralph tied the laces on his hobnailed boots, pulled on his jacket, and paused by the door to tap the weatherglass, murmuring 'T'glass is gaan up. Mightn't be a bad day if t'fog lifts', as he and Annie went out into the raw bone-chilling gloom to milk the small herd of cows before breakfast. Ralph's collarless shirt was open at the neck, but with the addition of studs and a collar would accept a tie in readiness for chapel or any official event, which would also demand the attention of his cut-throat razor to remove the whiskers that had grown since market day. Annie was encased in a stout apron, but her metal-shod wooden clogs of earlier years now had been replaced by strong shoes or Wellington boots.

After breakfast Ralph went up onto the unfenced fell for a walk of many miles over rough heather and bog, to shepherd the flock of Swaledale sheep and inspect the Blue-grey cows and calves on the way home. After dinner at midday there was any one of a myriad of tasks to be completed – drystone walling, muck carting and spreading, and cutting peat. Then, as Ralph went in for his tea, a whistle and a wave of his hand dispatched Tess – his faithful old Border Collie – to bring the cows from the bottom pasture, and they were always waiting ready for afternoon milking when he emerged from the house.

The year was regulated by the rhythm of the seasons – lambing time in spring, haytime and sheep shearing in summer, tupping in autumn. Winter was remarkable only for the grinding monotony of mind-numbing toil in atrocious conditions. Cattle were housed in the lower level of field barns set into sloping meadows in the style of the Vikings. They received their daily ration of hay, thrown down from the upper level that opened onto the upper meadow through wide double doors. Repairing drystone walls was often a winter task, as gaps frequently fell in the thaw after a hard spell of weather. Walling was a skilled craft, and the selection of the right stone was an art form in the hands of an expert. The tapered wall, constructed to a standard pattern by the use of different stones – flat walling stones, large thruffs, small fillers and rounded capes at the top – was about five feet in height, and almost three feet in width at the bottom. A smout hole, maybe two feet square, was left in each wall to enable sheep to be moved from one field to another when required. Walling was an art that inspired wonder in the spectator, but was a thankless bone-chilling task for the waller, and his frozen fingers would still be numb long after he reached the warmth of the farmhouse kitchen.

Initially, the Dales Ponies were the only source of power, and their contribution was essential, especially in haytime. The tempo and urgency of work was often particularly notable on a Saturday evening, when ponies and humans alike were sweating profusely as another day of toil drew to a close. The muggy, humid atmosphere, with its threat of rain overnight, brought greater urgency to the work. Ralph forked hay onto the stack with such vigour that Annie struggled to keep pace as she built the overlapping layers. Harry and Dick played by the dry-stone wall, while their grandfather refilled his pipe with black plug tobacco and blew smoke to keep the swarming clouds of predatory midges at bay.

The horses stood by, still breathing heavily. They had gathered all the hay from the meadow with the wooden sweep, and now swished their tails and kicked their bellies as slow-witted clumsy klegs homed in on their soft underparts. In the end, they might have to admit defeat, even though the relentless blood-sucking insects had retired, as dusk turned to dark and it was long past the boys' bedtime. The remaining hay was piled into a heap, a sheet was thrown over the stack, and they all trooped up the fields to the farmyard, weary and disappointed they had not completed the task. Tomorrow, the Sabbath, would be devoted to worship, and the hay must lie unprotected until Monday morning whatever the weather.

Mechanisation did not penetrate the isolated northern Dales for some time. A small Morris 8 car had arrived at the beginning of the War, and took them on their weekly visit to market in Barnard Castle – arriving in style over the County bridge, and past the old women leaning over half-doors in Bridgegate. It struggled in low gear up the bank, as Annie wondered each time at Blagraves with its projecting gable and mysterious stone-carved figures, until they reached the Market Cross and the cobbled familiarity of Market Place and Horsemarket. Just after the end of the War a tractor arrived at Ellerbeck. Soon after, hand-milking the Northern Dairy Shorthorn cows gave way to machine-milking, and the lorry came early each morning to collect the churns of milk for the dairy. That removed the need to make butter and cheese for sale, but it also deprived Annie of regular cash on market day. Administration of the bank account assumed greater importance, and the simple systems of hill farming began to be burdened with the accumulation of bureaucracy. The harbingers of modernisation had arrived.

Gamekeeping

The hardships and the pleasures of life at Ellerbeck all seemed very normal to Dick. He had grown up on the farm, and knew nothing different. His chronic early shyness persisted, and he spent much time by himself. He was happy with his own company, and had a natural affinity for the remote area in which he lived – an ingrained understanding of animals, both domestic and wild.

Bob Johnson, the local gamekeeper, with two black Labradors at his heels and his twelve bore shotgun seemingly an essential extension of his anatomy, usually called at the farm when he was passing. He often saw Dick playing on his own. Sometimes he was with his pigeons at the top of the stone steps that led to the loft over the stable. They had been a present from his great-uncle Tom from Crook, who had given him advice on breeding good birds. At other times he was down by the beck with Rex, the black-and-tan Border Collie. Rex tried to catch the eddies in the rushing water, while Dick built stone dams and made mud pies, or later tickled small trout which he cooked on the bank. Bob thought it not good for a young lad to be on his own so much.

"Now Ralph," he said one morning, "What fettle? Ah's off up ti t'Bog Moss today. Ah can tek young Dick wi mi if he fancies a bit o'exercise."

Dick had already learned from his father the importance of pest control. Rabbits bared the upland sward to its roots, competing with the cattle and sheep for limited grazing. Pastures pock-marked with mounds of earth betrayed the industry of moles, which further reduced the grazing for livestock. The rabbits found sanctuary in their warrens in the railway embankment, to which they retreated with a bobbing white warning at any sign of danger. Ralph flushed them out with ferrets into nets placed at the mouth of each hole, and any which circumvented that hazard rarely escaped the combined effect of Ralph's keen eye and shotgun. Moles were trapped in their tunnelled labyrinth, detected by Ralph from the pattern of molehills on the surface.

Previous generations had skinned them to manufacture moleskin waistcoats, but time now was too precious to devote to such antiquated rural crafts.

Mindful of the excitement of earlier excursions with his father, Dick thought it would be very grand to accompany the gamekeeper. He felt grown-up, and was keen to go. Ralph agreed readily. It might bring Dick out of himself. Bob opened Dick's eyes to a new world. He had grown up in the country, but the gamekeeper added specific knowledge to his generality. They walked past colonies of gulls nesting on the fringes of moorland tarns, and sometimes found a curlew's nest with four speckled eggs. He watched the peewits wheeling overhead in their aerobatic display, and learned that they helped farmers by devouring insect pests but that gourmets considered their eggs a great delicacy and raided their nests.

He learned how to use his understanding of the behaviour of each species to best advantage. He could build tunnels of flat stones that never failed to attract the stoat's inquisitive aggression, or suspend the carcase of a dead ewe over a peat hag knowing that crows find sheep's eyes irresistible. A well-placed trap then delivered the *coup de grace*. He learned how areas of old heather should be burned in a rotation of ten years to stimulate regeneration and provide fresh nutritious shoots, and the problems of selecting the correct day for burning. The season allowed was October to mid-April, but if conditions were too dry the peat could be set alight and burn with intensity to a great depth. When snow was lying, or there had been heavy rain, it was too wet, and often the burning was done in March by default. The purpose of the application of all this knowledge was the conservation of grouse stocks to provide good sport for the shooting parties arriving from the affluent south, resplendently superior in deer-stalkers and plus-fours, for the opening of the season on the Glorious Twelfth.

Sometimes he was allowed to go with Bob when a shoot was in progress. That was a privilege not usually afforded to young boys, and it boosted his ego. He puffed out his chest with pride.

The season for grouse shooting opened on the 12 August and closed officially on the 10 December, although in a poor season a halt may be called well in advance of this deadline. Lines of eight to ten shooting butts, located at strategic points on the moor, were the focus of the sport. The butts, roughly 50 yards apart, were circular open-topped constructions, five or six feet in diameter, and camouflaged with turf. Dick did not miss a detail: each butt was occupied by a plus-foured 'gun' and his loader, and he asked why there were two men in each butt, and why one carried two guns. Bob explained that as the 'gun' fired one of the matched pair of 12-bore double-barrelled shotguns, his assistant loaded the other so that one was always ready to use.

Bob had recruited a dozen or so local lads and men to act as beaters, and they were set out by the senior beater in a large semi-circle which converged on the line of butts, driving the grouse before it. In the early season, when the birds were still in family groups, they flew low and fast, close to the natural contours of the purple-heathered moor. As autumn approached the groups of hens and young amalgamated into larger flocks, while the old cock birds tired of family responsibility and pursued a more solitary existence. Their abdication of duty would earn an appropriate reward. Individual birds were targeted more easily by the guns, and many cock birds, resplendent in their crimson combs and their sheen of rufous-brown plumage, left the moor destined for the dinner table.

Dick was swept along in the excitement of a shoot, but the dead birds – piled in limp heaps ready for removal – left him with a sense of loss. He remembered their bold staccato territorial call – 'go-bak go-bak go-bak' – when he had walked across the moor, and the power of their rapid whirring flight. Although he had grown up to accept grouse-shooting as part of the natural order of the moor, his sympathies tended more to healing than killing. Conservation rather then destruction lit his imagination.

Homeopathy

His paternal grandfather, George Bainbridge, had died during the great storm of 1947 when Dick was only four years old. Dick had been too young to remember him clearly, and he had forgotten the two books which his grandfather had given him. One, small and almost pocket-sized, was titled 'The Pocket Manual of Veterinary Homeopathy', while the other had several pages missing front and back and had been given a makeshift cover of brown paper. Annie had put the books away carefully until Dick was old enough to value them. One day, when he was rummaging about on the shelves in the bottom of the kitchen press, he discovered the hard-backed book with his name written in it.

"Mam," he shouted, taking it across to his mother, "this beuk 'as mi neeame in't. Is't mine?"

Annie took the last batch of bread out of the oven and set it to rest, wiped her hands on her apron, and sat Dick down. She went to the press and brought out the other tattered volume. She had been very fond of her father-in-law – a quiet, kindly man, who had made her feel very welcome in the Bainbridge family. It was important that Dick understood at an early age the high respect in which his grandfather had been held, and she talked to her son for more than an hour before she realised it was getting towards dusk, and it was time the hens and geese were fastened up safe from the fox.

Dick had listened to his mother with scarcely an interruption. Often, since learning that he could not go to Barney, he had been stubborn, sulky and difficult, but Annie's description of his grandfather held him spellbound. George had been a celebrated animal doctor, his reputation spreading far afield and earning calls from distant clients. His expertise was given for no more than the expenses he incurred. He had no qualifications and had been dismissed contemptuously by the local veterinary surgeons as a charlatan, but he often was called in to effect a cure when their ministration had failed. He had learned the skills from his father – Dick's great-grandfather – who also passed down an old wooden box divided into compartments, each of which contained a small green bottle with a grooved lip and a named label on the side. It was part of the Bainbridge heritage.

Annie went and fetched the box. Dick was fascinated. He looked at the names on the bottles and, turning the pages of the books, saw the same names. Some were familiar to him, even though they were Latin. He often had heard Ralph use them. He began to match the names of medicines to those of plants – aconite and monkshood, belladonna and deadly nightshade, digitalis and foxglove – and started to pester his parents with questions about them. He knew that the plants were poisonous, but that the medicines could cure disease when used as a homeopathic. Ralph would recall how his father would cure his mother's headaches with two drops of belladonna, but he regularly impressed on Dick that they were poisons and needed to be handled only by an expert.

Some of old George Bainbridge's remedies would have seemed archaic – even heathen – to university-educated veterinarians. If a cow had Johnes disease she was dosed with a mixture of goose droppings, soot and arsenicum album, using a hollow horn to deliver the drench. When the tail of a young horse was docked, a ripe puffball was placed over the wound, and the fungus acted as a bactericide in the same way as penicillin. George had worked with the ingredients available to him, and trusted his reputation to their efficacy.

Ralph came into the house one day and said to Annie, "Ah's nut seur aboot t'red coo. She's thrivin badly. Mebbe Ah'll gie 'er a seton."

Dick was sitting reading his grandfather's book, but looked up when Ralph came in. "Ah've nivver heeard of a seton, Dad. What is't?"

Ralph was encouraged that Dick was showing an interest in homeopathics, and was happy to explain even though he was in a hurry. "Whya noo, if a coo hez an infection, an' she's nut thriving, we mun thread a bit o' felon grass on a seton soaked i' turpentine throo t'brisket o' t'coo wi' a rewel. A laal bit o' leather at either end o' t'seton hods it i' pleace, an' then we pull it fra yan side t' t'other an' draw t'infection oot." Ralph paused, as Dick sat listening intently to the strange story.

"What's felon grass, an' a seton, an' a rewel?" Dick was bursting with questions.

"Bah lad thoo's full o' questions. Whya, thoo knaws t'stuff that grows on top o' t'lavatory, on t'slates? That's felon grass. A seton's lahke a thin bit o' rope, an' a rewel's a needle." He got to his feet, took the rewel from the drawer of the press and gave it to Dick to examine. It resembled a large packing needle, with a sharp flat blade at one end and a small loop at the other.

Dick's interest was well and truly stimulated. He already had started at the beginning of the alphabet and learned that arnica reduced pain and aconite reduced inflammation, but today he had learned much more from Ralph's direct tutelage.

Cock o' t'middin

When Dick was in his eleventh year, his parents again broached the possibility that he should go to Barney. Although he enjoyed being involved with animals on the farm, and with Bob Johnson's gamekeeping excursions, he was becoming bored with the village school. It did not provide enough excitement – no opportunity to stretch his potential – and he was looking increasingly for extra interests. There was little stimulating activity up the Dale, and this time the thought of Barney struck a chord. He willingly agreed to go, but failed to get a scholarship and Ralph and Annie were locked into fees again.

Dick's time at Barney mirrored exactly the relationship with his brother at the village school. They were both in York House, which dominated inter-House sport, but Harry ignored his brother. Harry already was becoming a star. He had won a scholarship, he was in the top academic stream, and he was an inspirational leader in the school colours of chocolate and blue as captain of Under-15s rugby.

Dick basked in some reflected glory but sensed that he could not emulate him, and meandered through school in a mix of mediocrity. He took full advantage of exeats to go home at weekends when permitted. Otherwise, he went into town on Wednesday afternoons and weekends with a group of similarly disaffected friends, following Crook Lane, the old unmetalled back lane behind the Museum. Frequently they encountered the gang of rough local lads from the council houses in Dawson Road, wielding sticks and stones. Their running battles took them past the cemetery and allotments, and down the narrow path by the foundry. If retreat was necessary, they escaped down Hall Street and emerged near the Witham Hall in Horsemarket, or through the Hole-in-the-Wall from Queen Street to Newgate beside the Primitive Methodist chapel. Barney was a labyrinth of old passageways, and the local lads knew every twist and turn. Sometimes Dick and his friends were ambushed in the Museum grounds, and returned to school with bruises and muddied uniforms, as part of their initiation into class warfare.

Henry Brock was one of the colourful characters on the staff at Barney. His gruff demeanour masked a strong sense of public spiritedness and inventiveness. He lived in Corn Close, a spacious and elegant house in Flatts Road, with turrets, leaded panes, a stained glass window at the turn of the broad stairway, and uninterrupted views across the river to the Pennines hills beyond. He practised a philosophy of reward for achievement and in the autumn enlisted the help of groups of pupils to gather logs from Flatts Woods for winter fires. This activity appealed to Dick – he was part of an extra-curricula group, doing something active and enjoying scones and jam afterwards in front of a blazing fire.

But it was symptomatic of his unorthodoxy. He did not attempt to win a place in the rugby team; instead he played unofficial soccer, which was frowned upon. He took 'O' levels without any great enthusiasm, and the results confirmed his expectations. Ralph and Annie were very disappointed, but did not resist when he announced that he wanted to leave as soon as possible after his sixteenth birthday.

Barney had one last trial for him before he departed. The Asian flu epidemic struck in the autumn term of the last year he and Harry were at Barney. The vicious plague brought the school to a halt during the first two weeks of term, and Dick was one of only three boarders in the whole school who did not succumb at some stage. The York dormitories became an extension of the sanatorium, and Dick was delegated to look after the sick pupils. It was a valuable learning experience in social responsibility, but it also demonstrated an innate mental toughness that had not been tested previously, and a level of immunity to infection that even his brother appeared to lack.

Perhaps the most noticeable effect of his time at Barney was the suppression of his Yorkshire dialect. In his first year, his classmates had laughed at his broad rural vowels when he was asked to answer questions. They soon desisted after a bloody nose or two, but public school enforced a conformity which ensured that he emerged as a reasonable practitioner of standard spoken English, and with some understanding of upper-middle class behaviour.

Dick was vaguely aware that he had failed his parents. They had paid for his time at Barney and he had not realised their hopes. Harry now was head of York House, had played rugby for the county, and had won a place at Cambridge, while he was leaving school at sixteen. Harry's VALETE in the Barnardian extended to more than nine lines; Dick's was a paltry single-line entry near the bottom of the list. He experienced an undercurrent of shame, and felt an urge to redeem himself somehow.

He may have been unable to follow in his brother's footsteps as a sportsman at Barney, but he determined he would prove himself elsewhere. He went to work as a pre-college student on an estate in Derbyshire. It was a new experience, and he knew homesickness for the first time. He invariably came back to Ellerbeck on his free weekends, and went out with his friends to see a film in Barnard Castle –

sometimes at the Scala Cinema in broad tree-lined Galgate, or more often at the Victoria Hall down narrow Birch Street – followed by the inevitable ritual of fish and chips from the chippie in Galgate just below Marshall Street. The routine was broken occasionally by a dance at one of the villages up the Dale, or maybe at Marwood or Bowes. The young men stood on one side of the village hall laughing and jostling with self-conscious bravado, casting sidelong glances at the girls sitting opposite with demure intent. By the end of the evening, some individuals had become couples, but Dick's natural reticence precluded such a conclusion for him.

The local agricultural show in early September traditionally was a venue for wrestling and a quoits tournament, but more recently had included a series of athletic events, and Dick decided to compete. It was not an event that Harry would deign to frequent, and that was an added incentive for Dick. He entered for the 100 yards, the quarter-mile, half-mile and wrestling. His pedigree was promising. Annie had been a noted sprinter in the Dales as a girl and young woman, and had been unbeaten in the 100 yards sprint during a long racing career. Ralph had done some wrestling without particular success – quoits was his forte – but there was a strong wrestling tradition further back in the family, and all village boys wrestled in play as soon as they wore trousers.

Ralph was at the show with Swaledale sheep and Northern Dairy Shorthorn cattle. Annie had entered cakes and jam in the home produce section. As they compared notes that evening, they all could record some success. It was a high achievement for Ralph's shearling tup to stand reserve for the Swaledale Championship, and Annie was quietly pleased that her raspberry jam was highly commended, but they both were overjoyed to see once again a look of enthusiasm and eagerness in Dick's eyes. He had won the half-mile race and reached the final of the Cumberland and Westmorland wrestling. The latter excited him. He had been competing as a sixteen-year-old against mature men, and had found a metier which appealed to him. He took particular satisfaction from beating George Hastings, who came with a reputation and would wrestle at Grasmere with considerable success the following year.

He returned to the show during the next two years. He repeated his initial success in the half-mile race, and also added the first prize card for the quarter-mile. He had a very public confrontation before the hundred yards race with Sergeant Garforth, the portly local policeman who was officiating, because he disagreed with the handicaps. He was started three yards behind Stanley Guy, who had won the event the previous year, and made his objection in very plain language. His mother had sought to instil in him the sentiment that it is better to have played and lost than never to have played, and had quoted him verse, especially the lines:

The throng loves a winner, whatever the test.
The crowd likes a man who has proved he's the best.
But cheers for the victor would seldom be heard
Were it not for the boys who run second and third.

However, Dick had discovered that nothing short of victory gave him satisfaction, and particularly it was the wrestling that continued to catch his imagination. At the relatively tender age of seventeen and eighteen years, he demolished the mature opposition and walked away as All Weights Champion each year. Even when he conceded considerable weight to his opponents, they were unable to cope with his speed and strength. The village Show might be a relatively small pool, but he was a big fish in that pool! An upwelling of confidence began to push aside his shyness and his inhibitions.

"Thoo's cock o' t'middin noo!" Ralph jokingly said to him after his latest triumph.

He had become aware gradually of his natural strength. One of the temporary workers at Ellerbeck had been a devotee of Eugene Sandow, the renowned strong man. He boasted of his strength, and made foolish attempts to lift objects of excessive weight. Dick joined in during one of his weekends at home and was surprised to find, despite being only sixteen, he could lift a 120 lb crowbar over his head with one hand.

"Thoo'll do thisel' some damage laykin' aboot wi' that gavelick," said Ralph, "Better stick ti spreadin' muck." But secretly he was proud of his younger son. His strength and wrestling prowess marked him out as a true Bainbridge.

In the autumn of 1960, when he was eighteen, Dick went to the local agricultural college at Houghall and enrolled for the sandwich course. During the first year he would study for the National Certificate of

Agriculture, followed by a year's practical experience, then a final year at college for an advanced certificate in Animal Breeding and Production.

College was not too far from home, and he would be able to help on the farm at peak times of demand, although now it was some time since the small Fordson tractor had broken the monopoly of four-legged horsepower, and the soothing liquid purr of hand-milking had given way to the loud throb of milking machines. He would be happy to maintain close contact with his village friends, and continue to enjoy his walks over the fells and pastures with Bob Johnson. He ventured out into the wider world with a growing spirit of adventure and anticipation.

He often wished to tell Harry of his achievements and his hopes. Harry still remained psychologically the dominant sibling, and a natural desire persisted in Dick to report success to him, but Harry had pitched his tent securely in Cambridge life and Teesdale lay outside his sphere of interest. His letters home were infrequent at first and rapidly dwindled to near absence. His visits home in vacations were fleeting calls between other more glamorous activities. Ralph and Annie never complained about his brother, and they were proud of his achievements, but Dick could feel their keen disappointment in Harry's cavalier behaviour. He knew that he also had disappointed them in the past, and he resolved that in future they would be proud of him.

Travels Abroad 1961-1962

Ralph was pleased with the price for Phoebe, the cocky-horned light-roan cow he had brought to the Wednesday auction mart in Vere Road at Barnard Castle. Buyers had been keen to purchase such a quality animal, and conveyed their bids with half winks or the twitch of a finger familiar to the practised eye of the auctioneer. From his elevated position above the ring, he attempted to fire the enthusiasm of the dour farmers and dealers leaning over the metal rails in the cold atmosphere of the bare brick walls and corrugated metal roof of the mart. With a smart crack of his short stick on the front of the rostrum, he declared "You're all out at the front. Going, going, gone to Jack Elwood."

The successful bidder, a florid man in flat cap and brown leather leggings, came over to Ralph in the cow byre afterwards.

"Ah paid ower much fer t'cow", he said. "There'll be some luck money."

Luck money was an established custom, and Ralph complied willingly, although with a ritual show of reluctance, before going down to the market café in Commercial Yard for the standard dinner of meat pie and mushy peas with gravy.

In the afternoon Ralph had a meeting with his accountant, Nicholas Parkin, in the office looking out over Galgate. Like its occupant, the office exuded a sense of efficiency and frugality – functional furniture, with no concessions to luxury. Having dealt with the business of farm profits and annual accounts, they fell into a discussion of the progress of their respective children.

"Aye, t'bairns are off afoor ye ken. 'Ow's thi laal Judith gittin on?" he asked. "She's a bonny lass a' reet."

"She's very well, thank you" replied Nicholas, "we're sending her to the Convent School in Richmond next year. What about Harry and Dick?"

"Whya noo, Harry's off at Cambridge, an' we see varra laal of 'im. Dick wasna doin' si weel until a couple o'yeear ago, bud 'e's cumin on weel noo. College 'as sorted 'im oot, an' 'e's leukin aboot fer somewheer te wark next yeear."

"How about a year abroad, Ralph? It might be a great experience for him. I've a friend in Wyoming, Sam Forbes. He owns the Dickie Ranch – an appropriate name for Dick – and I'm sure he'd love to have him there for a year."

Nicholas was not noted for unsolicited generosity, and Ralph was grateful to him for his interest. He thought that America was a great distance away and pondered whether it was a good idea. He decided that it was a chance that might not come again, and mentioned it to Dick on his next visit home. He was taken aback by the enthusiasm with which Dick accepted the proposal, and a little sad at the thought of losing him for a year. Ralph's pride in his younger son had grown by leaps and bounds in the last two or three years.

The itinerary was planned, and Dick flew to the United States in July. After the transatlantic flight, he transferred to a smaller plane for the final leg to Billings on the Yellowstone River. Sam Forbes was there to meet him in a large station wagon, and they chatted freely during the 250 mile journey to Worland. Sam was a portly, kindly man whose baldness was permanently hidden by a broad-brimmed Stetson. He suggested that after a week or two, when Dick had recovered from his inevitable jet-lag, he should take out a couple of months to travel before settling down to work on the Dickie Ranch. It was a surprising and very generous suggestion, and Dick accepted readily.

He borrowed an old truck from Sam and drove eastwards from Wyoming through the plains of Nebraska, where he fell in and out of love with a pretty drum majorette, and on through Iowa to Virginia. He was amused to find they still were fighting the Civil War, and flew the Yankee flag to acknowledge American history. His intent was well received until he reached Harpers Ferry and discovered that he should rapidly assume Confederate sympathies. Here he turned and crossed the Appalachian Mountains into Tennessee and arrived in Nashville, where he avoided the race riots, and ignored prohibition with some moonshine and an attractive older girl. America introduced him gently to female allure.

Back in Wyoming in late September, it had been decided he should divide his time between the Dickie Ranch under the supervision of the ranch foreman, and Sheridan Stock Farm with Mrs Mo Healy. The Dickie Ranch, nestling in the foothills of the Bighorn Mountains, was noted for its special breed of sheep. The Warhill had been developed by Sam Forbes to combine adaptation to the dry summers and cold winters of Wyoming with higher production of wool than other local breeds. Sam explained his philosophy of livestock breeding to Dick, who quickly grasped the principles of the selection index on which the choice of breeding animals was based.

Sheridan Stock Farm was noted for its herd of pedigree Red Angus cattle, and Mo Healy had developed a performance-recording system. All the young bulls were weighed and measured, rather than simply evaluated by eye. Each year she held a three-day event on the ranch for the sale of bulls. It included lectures in the barn by noted breeders and scientists, and a barbeque of Red Angus beef in the adjacent paddock, and gave Dick a unique opportunity to meet many other pedigree breeders.

Dick stayed in Wyoming until May the following year. During autumn and spring he spent a good deal of time in his high-pommeled saddle astride a strong Quarter Horse – the cowboy's cutting horse *par excellence* – rounding up the range cattle or simply riding out into the Bighorn Mountains. During the continental winter, when the temperature fell to an average of 20 centigrade below freezing in the upper reaches of the Mississippi tributaries, work was concentrated around the ranch, and he often sat late into the night discussing livestock with both Sam and Mo. He absorbed sponge-like all he saw and heard, and accumulated a reservoir of knowledge that would serve him well. Genetics and animal breeding struck a chord of deep-seated interest, and he looked forward to the second year of his college course when he would major on those subjects.

Although he derived great enjoyment from their long discussions, Sam now thought that some wider experience might be sensible, and suggested that a spell as a lumberjack might provide a new and very different challenge. He knew a Director of Anglo-Canadian Pulp and Paper Mills which had a logging operation at Forestville in Canada, two hundred miles downriver from Quebec.

"I guess it's pretty wild and uncivilised, but you'll soon discover what you're made of in the middle of nowhere!" He smiled as Dick raised his eyebrow. "You'll be just fine. You've been up in the Bighorn in the last few months and that's tough country."

After a journey by air to Quebec, by boat down the broad St Lawrence River and a bone-jarring suspension-grinding finale on *terra firma* one hundred miles inland, Dick arrived in a desolate place surrounded by millions of acres of trees. The forests were very different to the moors among which Dick had grown up, but they had the same feeling of endlessness. The blanket of trees was pierced only by two large bunkhouses and the chuckhouse which stood in a clearing on the shore of a small lake. The nearest village – and the nearest social life – was on the St Lawrence River back down the rough pot-holed dirt road. The resident lumberjacks were French-speaking, albeit with a marked North American pronunciation, but they were cheerful and helpful workmates.

Dick's initiation was uncompromising. He was pitched straight into muscle-wrenching work, swinging a heavy axe for several hours each day. He was allocated to a gang which was felling small trees and building bridges to permit vehicular access to the virgin forest.

Summer temperatures were high, but his collar was fastened and his clothing buttoned at the wrists and tied at the ankles to protect him against mosquitoes from the lake and black fly in the forests. Despite these precautions they still discovered unguarded gaps to his susceptible flesh, and the nibbling of the Yorkshire midges in his youth was insignificant in comparison with the predation of their American cousins. Even the barrier of his newly-cultivated beard failed to deter them.

But there were many compensations. The fleeting glimpse of moose at the end of a track-way, the melancholy howling of wolves at night, and the elaborate construction work of the busy beavers, all were memories he would carry away with him.

He had been blessed already with above average strength when he arrived, but the effects of two months of hard physical labour were clearly evident when he left in early July. Maybe the gargantuan breakfasts of porridge, maple syrup and cream, and mounds of egg and bacon, played some part, but he now was a powerful physical specimen of manhood by any standards.

He returned home in July 1962, wiser, stronger and a fuller personality in every way. He did not realise how much he had missed Ralph and Annie until he saw them waiting anxiously at Darlington railway station. He had enjoyed an unforgettable experience, but he was glad to be home. Now he looked forward to completing his final year at college, and resuming his wrestling career.

3
A FALSE START

Getting Started, 1963

America had exposed Dick to a new environment with experiences and challenges which developed his physique and his character. His homecoming, to a tearfully happy Annie and stoically proud Ralph, was an emotional time for him and a subconscious confirmation of the importance of family. His wrestling success at Langthwaite had served only to intensify further the charged atmosphere, and he felt a powerful sense of elation and wellbeing.

Now, after his final year at college, reality reeled him in. The Cheldale estate in Derbyshire needed a new assistant manager, and the position had been offered to Dick. It was not an invitation to make an application; it was a firm offer. He had proved a star student at college, and the initiative demonstrated by his American venture had added to his reputation. If he accepted the offer, he was asked to report for duty immediately on leaving college as they were short-staffed.

It was an opportunity that could launch him on a successful career. Lt. Col. Sir Jacob Milner ran an exemplary estate. It was a blueprint on which other estate owners modelled their properties; it had won the prestigious Sledisham Award, and was a preferred venue for game fairs and equine events. First impressions of Sir Jacob did not inspire great confidence. He was small and stooping, with thinning grey hair and a narrow unsmiling face punctuated by a trim grey moustache. His wrist-limp, damp handshake brought to mind images of wet cabbage, and his tortured aristocratic vowels were scarcely intelligible to the ears of a country boy. But he had a shrewd mind, an impeccable military record, and an uncanny ability to assess the potential of employees. Dick would come to understand and appreciate the qualities that lay beneath his employer's unimpressive exterior.

Dick was glad to start in the summer of 1963. The storms of the previous winter had been some of the worst in living memory. Perhaps not as severe as 1947 in the north of England, but a test of man and beast nevertheless. Even when Dick arrived on the estate in July, they still were dealing with the legacy of the damage – both financial and physical.

He had not gone home to Deep Ghyll when he left college, although Ralph would have welcomed his support, as it could not yet sustain the cost of two full-time men. Annie had been hoping to arrange a 21st birthday party for him, but that now was not possible. His immediate start at Cheldale also meant that he would miss Grasmere. He had neither time to train nor travel to Lakeland, and his budding sporting career had to be put on hold. He was a working man with a responsible position, and that took priority.

The Cheldale estate was not new to him. During the two years after he left school and before he started college, he had gone to work on the estate as a farmhand. Initially he had been an unremarkable employee but, as he started to find his feet, first the farm foreman and then Arthur Burns, the lugubrious manager, had noticed his potential. Some rough edges were smoothed away, and by the time he departed to begin his college course in 1960, Sir Jacob had been made aware of the young fellow's possibilities as management potential in the future.

The estate was divided into four departments – farm, equine, forestry and sporting – but Sir Jacob also had property interests in the old spa town of Buxton. As a student, Dick had been employed in the farming department working mainly with the shepherd, but from time to time was deputed to other departments. The time he had spent with Bob Johnson proved invaluable when he was required to help with the control of vermin for the shoots. He also occasionally brought a horse and cart to collect the dead birds, but he could not come to terms with driven pheasant shooting. He could tolerate rough shooting, where the game is wary and the odds are even, when a pheasant flies high and wild, or a rabbit breaks cover from a tussock of grass. He had been used to grouse shooting, where birds come storming down the wind and present a real challenge to the guns.

Rearing pheasants by the thousand, protected in wired cages, and fed until they were almost too cumbersome to fly – more like heavy bombers than sleek fighters – did not fit Dick's concept of sport. Tame birds, ushered by beaters towards the guns for point-blank target practice, was no contest – more akin to ritualised slaughter, and reports of boasting of excessive mass destruction on estates like Sandringham served only to heighten his disgust.

He felt more comfortable in the equine department. His interest in horses and ponies, and especially his experience of harnessing and handling Sapphire and Black Diamond at Ellerbeck, stood him in good stead. When work on the farm was slack, he often was asked to go and help with the horses, and quickly acquired a reputation. He had an early opportunity to put his grandfather's arts into practice when one of the horses wrenched a ligament and failed to respond to standard veterinary treatment. Dick persuaded the groom to let him try the homeopathic remedy. It was a serious injury, but Dick's application of a combination of arnica lotion, alternated with aconitum and Rhus Toxicodendron, successfully removed the pain and inflammation, and reduced the swelling. On another occasion, one of the horses, when left unattended in the yard for a short while on returning from a hard day's work, had gulped copious draughts of cold water from the trough, and had developed rapid laboured breathing and a critically high pulse rate. It was saved only by Dick's urgent treatment with ammonium causticum, which brought it back to normal within a few hours. His willingness to grasp opportunities and accept responsibility was noted.

Sir Jacob kept four breeds, Irish Draught horses for breeding hunters, Fell and Dales ponies for forestry work, and Yomut horses because there had been talk of interest in them at the Royal Mews at Windsor. Dick was impressed by the Irish Draught horses. They were big and athletic, but he thought they had too much 'hot blood' in them. They wouldn't have lasted long at Ellerbeck. He could talk at length, and almost as an equal, with the forestry workers about the Dales and Fell Ponies. They were marvellously versatile animals that were as effective in carriage driving as they were hauling logs or pulling farm carts.

The traces were much simpler than the harness for the farm horses that Dick had used, but the basic principle of power transfer was the same. The neck collar – braffin and heeames – provided the attachment for either chains or shafts. Dick's adroitness at harnessing earned him praise: the pony's head threaded through the upside-down braffin, which was revolved on the narrow part of the neck and slipped back to fit snugly on the shoulders; the shaped iron heeames clasped around the braffin in the moulded grooves, and the two projecting arms at the top secured firmly together – all done in less than a minute!

The Yomut intrigued him. They were pony-sized, but called horses because of their conformation. Originally from Turkmenistan in the USSR, a few had found their way to England and onto the Cheldale estate. Sir Jacob treasured them, and was in regular contact with the Crown Equerry. Dick was fascinated by their story, but doubted whether they would make any impact on the British equine scene. They were narrow, sickle-hocked, and too upright in the shoulder for his liking.

Camilla Leyland, the girl groom in charge of the Yomut when he returned as assistant manager, recounted their background. "They are a rare and ancient breed, associated originally with the Scythians as early as 3,000 BC. They pre-date the Arab, and closely resemble the horses in the Pazyryk burial mounds in the Altai Mountains. Their thin skin is typical of desert horses, and their fine hair has a metallic sheen."

Dick smiled at her stilted prose. She clearly had learned the script by rote. She agreed it was too early to determine their likely use in Britain, but she was attached to them. However, her main equine interest was riding in the Ladies race at various point-to-point meetings from March to May each year, and she hunted a couple of horses to qualify for the season.

Dick had made many friends in all departments on the estate during those two pre-college years, and it was not surprising that Sir Jacob had been keen to recruit him to the staff when he completed his college course. The final year had been primarily Animal Breeding and Production, but it had included the City & Guilds 278 Business Management course, and was an excellent foundation for a budding management employee. Even so, appointment as assistant manager for the whole estate at the age of 21 was a strong statement of Sir Jacob's faith in him.

Sir Jacob was looking continually for new opportunities. He held regular management meetings with Arthur Burns and Dick, and encouraged them to propose new ideas. At first, Dick was content to listen, but before long he was an active participant in the discussions. Soon after Dick's arrival, Sir Jacob opened a shop on the estate to sell home-grown farm produce. The shelves were stacked with eggs, and locally-made jam and chutney. Shepherd's crooks stood in the corner.

Vegetables from the more fertile part of the estate were sold from the grocer's section when they were in season, and the butcher's counter on the opposite side of the shop displayed a mouth-watering range of fresh meats, cooked meats, sausages and a range of joints from cattle, sheep and pigs. It was a novel development.

When Dick had been at Cheldale for rather more than three years, Arthur arrived at a management meeting with proposals for improvements. He had begun to feel uncomfortable because of the strong impression that Dick appeared to be making, not only by his work around the estate, but mainly by the impact of his discussion in business meetings. He felt he was being overshadowed by a youngster, and needed to impose his authority. It was a needless worry. Dick had great respect for the ability of his immediate boss, and willingly gave him support at all times, but Arthur could only see the threat posed by his assistant.

Arthur's proposals centred around three main items. He wanted to establish a pedigree herd of the newly-imported French Charolais cattle noted for their high rate of growth; to mate the draft Derbyshire Gritstone ewes off the hills with Suffolk tups; and to mechanise the forestry operations. He praised Charolais cattle for the high weight of lean meat they produced, and predicted they would become very popular and profitable for those who were sufficiently astute to get in on the ground floor of the importation. He advised that the weight of pure Derbyshire Gritstone lambs was too low, and that a cross with the Suffolk would remedy that problem. He dismissed the continuing use of ponies in forestry work.

"Ponies haven't enough power. A couple of tractors with a grab and a trailer will shift far more timber in half the time." Arthur's long face was expressionless as he finished his presentation.

Sir Jacob and Dick attempted to evaluate the proposals while the manager talked. He had caught them cold, and hoped to get rapid agreement for his plans. Dick quickly saw the general drift of the proposals, and could see the logic, but some elements did not fit with his philosophy. Sir Jacob looked at him with a raised eyebrow, and Dick understood that he was expected to make the first response.

"Well, it's a lot to take in all at once," he began, "but I can see the direction that Arthur wants to go, and I agree that we need to keep up to date. Putting the Suffolk on our own ewes will enable us to sell native lamb as well as hogget through the shop, but we must be sure that we maintain the flock of Gritstones on the moor. I can't quite see how the Charolais cattle would fit in. They're a foreign breed, and we wouldn't be able to sell the beef as native breed product. And one of the lessons I learned in Wyoming was the importance of using breeds that are adapted to local conditions; the South Devon would be a better bet if we have to use a big breed. But with our speciality marketing, shouldn't we be looking for quality rather than quantity? As far as the ponies are concerned, I'm sure some degree of mechanisation of the forestry could help, but machines will break up the land surface in the woodland and cause significant damage. I'd prefer to keep the ponies to snig most of the smaller timber."

Arthur bristled. Dick had not attacked his ideas head-on, but had given a balanced response that made his presentation seem rather immature in comparison. "Ponies are out of date. You might still use them further north, but we can't be held back by sentiment down here. As for the Charolais, you mark my words, they'll be the breed of the future."

The discussion continued for a while until Sir Jacob intervened.

"I think I'm extremely fortunate to have management of such high calibre." He addressed both of them equally. "Your ideas are excellent, and I think we all agree we must move forward."

He gave his public support to Arthur, but privately knew that Dick's arguments were sound. While apparently accepting Arthur's proposals, he agreed that the ponies should be retained in the forestry, and manipulated a compromise on the cattle by accepting a trial of foreign cattle with the use of a Charolais bull on the crossbred Hereford-Friesian suckler cows. Sir Jacob's diplomacy had saved Arthur's face, but the manager was not pleased. He now perceived Dick as a 'bloody upstart', and the relationship between them deteriorated.

They continued in this manner for a year or so. Dick never challenged Arthur's authority but regularly held the advantage in discussion during policy meetings. The manager was too proud to suffer such indignity for long, and Sir Jacob was not surprised when he handed in his notice in the summer of 1967. The loss of senior staff was not a desirable occurrence, but in this case Sir Jacob was not particularly disappointed. It had been four years since Dick had arrived as assistant manager, and he had proved his mettle. He was not yet 25 years of age, but Sir Jacob was confident in his ability and prepared to take a chance and appoint the young man as his estate manager.

The girl groom responsible for the Yomut horses was still on the estate. She was not an employee, and enjoyed an unusual status by virtue of Sir Jacob's friendship with her aunt who was Joint-Master of the Cottesmore. Dick saw her routinely in the course of his duties, but rarely for more than a cursory greeting. Camilla Leyland was concerned mainly with the sport horses, and was an accomplished performer in both show-jumping and point-to-point races. She was a flashy, busty girl, with eye-catching bottle-blonde hair. Her brown eyes and ready smile were a siren invitation for any suitable suitor, and there was no shortage at her 21st birthday celebrations in Buckinghamshire in February 1967.

Dick was not invited to her party, but when he was appointed manager, Camilla took a sudden interest in him. He had moved up a step in the eligibility stakes.

Camilla

Camilla lost no time in cultivating Dick's interest. She was aware that many local girls would be attracted by the status of the manager of the Cheldale estate. He had not entered her reckoning originally when he arrived as a raw young man from the north, fresh out of college, and seemingly somewhat naive from her seventeen-year-old perspective. She moved in more elevated circles. Now, four years later, the balance had changed. Her social circle still had cachet. She was embedded firmly in the glamour of the equine world; her friends from the Home Counties frequented the London theatre scene, and others had contacts on the motor-racing circuit. But his prospects now were significant, and he was altogether a more desirable catch.

She invited Dick to London for an opening night at the Mermaid Theatre, and then to Northamptonshire for a race meeting at Silverstone. It was a strong opening gambit, and Dick was not well versed in the arts of the fairer sex. She swept him through a panoply of parties with her glossy friends and then her parents. They all cooed over Camilla's tall new escort, and thought he was rather quaint. Dick was flattered by the attention he received, and somewhat intoxicated by the heady progress of the romance.

When Camilla suggested they should go shopping, he thought it was an unusual idea, but was not aware of any significance behind the suggestion. When she manoeuvred him into the jewellers to choose an engagement ring, he quickly discovered the meaning. In that predicament he did not wish to appear a fool, and was too embarrassed to admit that he had misunderstood her intention. A ring was chosen, and as soon as they emerged from the shop Camilla rushed to a telephone box to ring her parents and thereby seal the arrangement. The unsuspecting victim had taken the bait. The trap was sprung, and the capture was complete. Camilla expected that it would make little change to her life – her priorities would continue as before – but a handsome and upwardly mobile husband definitely would add to her status.

Sir Jacob watched with some interest and amusement. He wondered how it would develop. He was a good friend of Camilla's parents, who came from good stock but had fallen on harder times, but had noted some of her wilder escapades with considerable concern. Maybe Dick would calm her down.

If Sir Jacob had been aware of all Camilla's escapades, he might have viewed the future with significantly greater alarm. Meanwhile, Dick had recovered from the shock of the initial frontal assault, and thought maybe it would be sensible for the manager of a big estate to be married. He had no reason to suspect any fundamental problem. He had not considered the qualities that might be necessary for a young woman in that position, or the qualities that he might desire in his wife, but Camilla was a lively, attractive girl, and a lot of fun. She insisted he rang to tell his parents about the engagement, and that turned the final key in the lock of their contract.

Another factor had played a part. Harry had married quickly and quietly in October that year. Ralph and Annie had been desperately disappointed that they had not been invited, and hurt that their son could behave in such a discourteous and insulting manner. Dick determined that he could make some amends to his parents for his elder brother's unforgivable behaviour. Subconsciously, he still was trying to prove himself and move out of Harry's shadow.

Dick sometimes thought back to his parents' lengthy courtship, and wondered if he should not slow down the mad stampede in which he now found himself. They had been together for seven years before they married. He had been engaged to Camilla after less than two months! But he felt himself wedged into the situation, and the passage of time locked him in more securely. The wedding date was set for June. Ideally, Camilla would have liked it earlier, but she was not prepared to interrupt her programme of point-to-point races.

Serious conversation was not a high priority for Camilla; she was more at home astride a horse or between the sheets of a bed. She excelled in superficial inconsequential chatter. Her attention quickly wandered from meaningful discussion, and Dick rarely could persuade her to delve into deeper feelings or the responsibilities of marriage. It all seemed a game. Camilla talked endlessly of her 'horsey' world, and occasionally in a relaxed state of conjugal satisfaction divulged stories that filled Dick with alarm, although he was too reticent to enquire more deeply. She told him of famous jockeys that she knew, and how they expected their young female camp followers to attend to all their needs; of the goings-on in horse boxes at Hunt meets; of stable girls exercising horses on country rides and clandestine meetings with landowners who divested them of their jodhpurs while declaring simultaneously their undying love and the obstacle of a Catholic wife who would not release them. Dick was not entirely unaware of the ways of the world, but all this lay outside the bounds of his comprehension.

The stories all related ostensibly to Camilla's friends, but gradually the awful realisation began to dawn on Dick that, actually, she was recounting her own experiences. The thought horrified him, but what could he do! He had been trapped and shackled. By the time he realised fully the meaning of her stories, arrangements for the wedding were in place at considerable expense to his prospective in-laws, and his parents were thrilled by the prospect of their son settling down to married life. He was cornered. His only escape would expose him as a fool, and bring further heartache to his parents.

Dick stood in the church at Little Blessingham with his best man, Frank Stoddart, a friend from agricultural college. As they waited for his fiancée to arrive, he turned to Frank and said, "What the hell am I doing here! Am I doing the right thing?"

He desperately wanted his best man to give him a cue – the incentive to abandon the ceremony, but Frank Stoddart was not noted for either perception or intelligence, and he was out of his depth – overawed by the cohort of upper-class guests. "Got a touch of nerves? You'll be alright, Dick," he replied, and nudged the groom knowingly. "Soon be over and then you can get down to real business."

Dick looked away with disappointment and a rising feeling of desperation. His gut feeling told him to get out of the church immediately. He knew that Camilla was the wrong girl for him, but the thought of walking out past all the guests, and his smiling parents, rooted him to the spot. He might be a powerful voice on the estate, but he hadn't the courage of his convictions when it really mattered in his private life. Within a few minutes Camilla arrived at the church door on the arm of her father and it was too late. Their slow advance towards him heightened his panic, and the panic rooted him to the spot. As she arrived at his side, Dick gave her a quick wan smile, and resigned himself to his fate. Camilla emerged on her husband's arm as Mrs Richard Bainbridge, looking radiant with her flowing white train and her carefully coiffured hair blonde to the roots.

The reception had been organised by Sir Geoffrey de Courcy and his wife Violet, friends of Camilla's parents. They had erected a magnificent marquee on the lawn of their Buckinghamshire mansion. There was an abundance of superficial gaiety, and the bride was bursting with satisfaction, but the negative undercurrent was tangible. Dick was subdued, and Frank Stoddart, who was not verbose at any time, was supremely inarticulate.

Dick's speech was brief. He observed the proper courtesies, and particularly thanked Sir Geoffrey and Lady Violet for their kindness and generosity. He also mentioned Sir Jacob, his work and his ambition for his future career, and he expressed sincere and loving thanks to his parents. This was too soft and sentimental for some of horsey set and excited them to sarcastic 'oohs' and 'aahs'. The latter completely unnerved Frank Stoddart. His dry throat and hoarse voice provided Camilla's friends with great merriment. His speech was littered liberally with risqué jokes – many too near the knuckle for even a rural gathering – which served to offend both the religious element of the groom's guests and the snobbish portion of the bride's entourage. Sir Geoffrey was politely non-committal, but the Leylands did not trouble to hide their displeasure.

Dick escaped as quickly as was seemly. He said his farewells to Ralph and Annie, and only then realised that Harry had not been at the wedding. The honeymoon in Dorset was spent around the Purbeck Hills, in Lulworth Cove or visiting Corfe Castle. Work on the estate did not allow a lengthy absence, but Dick was determined to get to the bottom of Camilla's past before they returned, and by the end of a fraught honeymoon he could discern a reasonably accurate picture. It seemed to Dick she had slept with almost as many men as she had met and now, when she had a wedding ring on her finger, she was neither reticent nor apologetic. She simply smiled at Dick's disgust and said it happened all the time in her circle of friends.

As they walked near Corfe Castle, Dick was reminded that King John had incarcerated his niece, Eleanor, first in Bowes Castle in Teesdale and later in Corfe Castle. He wished he could find a way to rid himself of Camilla so easily. Of one thing he was certain. No child of his would ever spring from the loins of such a woman. Camilla was of the same opinion for the time being. Family matters would be on hold until her point-to-point ambitions were realised. She was not yet the leading Lady jockey, and that was her immediate target.

Even if Dick had been able to accept Camilla's promiscuity, there were too many other conflicts to presage a happy marriage. He opposed hunting, but she hunted regularly. She associated with a circle of class-ridden friends and acquaintances who dreamed of a return to feudal times, while he had an inherent loathing for 'chinless wonders'. He had been raised in an austere Primitive Methodist family, and now discovered that Camilla – his newly-wed wife – had been taken willingly by jockeys, landowners, Hunt Masters, huntsmen, and goodness knows who else! He should have found out more before he married!

He was in despair, and could see no avenue of escape.

Dick could not erase the image from his mind. It was a recurring nightmare. He was standing at the altar before the wedding, trying to run, but his feet would not move. He cursed himself for his weakness. He threw himself into his work and tried to shut out the image. Now the disadvantages of a sheltered youth began to emerge. Dick had never been groomed in the intricacies of relationships. His encounters with girls had been brief and superficial. He did not know how to raise the issues with Camilla, and when he attempted to express his worries, she laughed in his face. Neither of them were capable of reasoned discussion.

In the end, he abandoned attempts at rational discussion. He cut straight to the endpoint and summoned up the courage to deliver an ultimatum. He announced that he did not love her, that he should never have married her, and that the marriage was over.

She stared at him in disbelief. She knew he had been surprised by her earlier life, but it never occurred to her that he would take such severe objection to it, or dare to take any effective action. Suddenly, her capture was trying to escape, and her *coup* was crumbling. She swore at him volubly and comprehensively, with obscene blasphemies that catapulted Dick into a new comprehension of vocabulary. She complained to Sir Jacob, and trashed her husband's reputation in front of estate workers, claiming he was naive and ignorant in bed and neglectful out of it. He refrained from retaliation, but his mind was set. Her conduct served only to confirm his decision and his conviction that she had no part in his life.

Sensing that his stubborn determination would not be turned, she took her revenge on him with a former boyfriend whenever he was away from the estate. For a while Dick was unaware he was being cuckolded in his own bed, until the farrier felt impelled to warn him. Dick had lodged with the farrier and his wife during his pre-college years on the estate, and they still felt protective towards him.

That week, instead of making his usual visit to market, Dick returned to the house and caught her *in flagrante delicto*. He ordered her leave that day; she took anything of value she could find, and returned to her parents in Buckinghamshire. They had been married for less than four months. A new Divorce Reform Act was anticipated the following year, but Dick was not prepared to wait for more rational legislation and he had all the evidence necessary to set in motion without delay the proceedings for divorce on the grounds of adultery. He then tried to summon up courage yet again this time to tell his parents they were about to witness the first divorce in the Bainbridge family.

Sir Jacob had lost an important member of his equine team. He guessed that Camilla's lifestyle might have played some part in the outcome, although the gossip had not yet brought the full truth to his ears, but he felt that Dick could not be entirely blameless. Dick was conscious thereafter of a degree of tension between them.

Estate Manager, 1967-1971

Dick's promotion to estate manager at 25 years of age had been a major step upwards on his career ladder. He accepted his increased responsibility with enthusiasm and vigour. The farm shop was reorganised and expanded to include a range of craft goods from the village. A programme of publicity and promotion for the shop produced an unexpected side-benefit through an increased demand for pedigree breeding animals from the estate, and Dick was able to apply his knowledge of genetics and animal breeding to the development of various herds and flocks of Cheldale pedigree livestock.

He continued to work with Sir Jacob in the efficient management of the estate, but the strictly businesslike nature of their weekly meetings disappointed him. There was an absence of informal conversation, and greater reliance on departmental reports. Dick had valued the friendly atmosphere that previously pervaded the whole estate. It had been disturbed slightly in the final months of Arthur Burns' tenure, but that had been remedied almost immediately. This time the inhibition came from the top tier – from Sir Jacob himself. The Camilla episode had taken a severe toll.

The slim package that arrived soon after his promotion carried a postmark from Sheridan in Wyoming. Inside Dick discovered a book *Wortham Lectures in Animal Science* by Jan C. Bonsma, sent to him by Mo Healy, and she wrote:

> *Maybe this review will intrigue you. I know of no single person who has had such a constructive impact on the beef industry – painful as it may be for all of us to face truths. Dr Bonsma is far more than an expert on functional efficiency and livestock ecology, he's a real teacher and philosopher – though many of his audience may not admit how accurately he is pinpointing problems.*

Jan Bonsma had been the guest speaker at one of Mo's pedigree stock sales, and clearly had made a powerful impression. Dick had heard of him with regard to the creation of a new breed of cattle, the Bonsmara, in South Africa during the 1940s and 1950s, and determined to contact him, and obtain his advice on livestock breeding and management.

Jan Bonsma had mixed the genetics of native Afrikaner Boer-trek cattle with those of imported Hereford and Shorthorn cattle to combine local adaptation with exotic performance, but he was insistent that adaptation to local conditions was the most important criterion. He also impressed on Dick that he had developed the new breed on the basis of objectively recorded performance data, rather than subjective visual assessment. Dick felt privileged that Jan showed so much interest in his questions, and gratified that their philosophies of livestock breeding and production seemed to agree so closely.

Dick's reputation was beginning to spread. He had been noticed initially because of his business management skills in developing the concept of added-value for estate products by marketing though the farm shop. Subsequently, his success with breeding pedigree livestock brought his name to a much wider audience. He received regular invitations to address farmers' meetings, and these served to enhance his reputation further. In January 1970 an invitation arrived which particularly excited him.

Each year the Government advisory body for agriculture organised a major conference in the north of England. It was an opportunity to draw together leading practitioners and innovators to generate new ideas for British farming. The next conference would be held at the Scotch Corner Hotel on the Great North Road on Wednesday 25 February. The invitation requested Dick to give a talk on 'Livestock breeding and production for new markets', and asked him to indicate his acceptance as soon as possible to Miss J. Parkin, Secretary to the Organising Committee at York. Dick considered the short notice with a wry smile. Obviously, a speaker had dropped out, and he had been invited as a last-minute replacement, but that did not detract from the opportunity it presented. It had the added advantage that he would be going back to his roots near Teesdale, and he hoped he would not be a prophet without honour in his own land.

He replied immediately in the affirmative, and received a note by return with thanks for his prompt response. The note was signed 'Judith' and there was a hand-written post-script:

> *You probably won't remember me, but my father is your father's accountant, and he used to talk about you and your visit to America. Look forward to meeting you at the conference.*

Dick knew that Nicholas Parkin had been responsible for his opportunity to work in America, but he could not remember Judith. He surmised she must have been much younger, and this opinion was confirmed when they met at the conference a few weeks later. Dick found himself in the company of a vivacious eighteen-year-old, bubbling over with fun and *joie de vivre*. She was not tall, maybe 5' 5" or 5' 6" Dick estimated, and the shapely curves of womanhood accentuated her willowy teenage slimness. Her long dark hair hung over her shoulders and in a light fringe over her brow, but as Dick looked down from his 6' 2" advantage, it was her sparkling brown eyes that held his gaze, and they both felt an immediate emotional surge that was deeper than simple physical attraction. It was sixteen months since Camilla had walked out of his life, and he was ready to test the temperature of his emotions again.

The conference was an unqualified success. Sir Jacob had expressed his hope that the talk would be well received, and congratulated him on his return. The grapevine had worked smoothly, and news of his stimulating presentation had preceded his return to Derbyshire. Sir Jacob was aware that the burgeoning reputation of his young manager would make him a prime target for attractive offers from other hopeful employers. He appreciated fully the value of Dick to the Cheldale estate, and made a generous increase to his salary and benefits. It gave Dick renewed assurance that his employer valued him, but there still remained an uneasiness between them. It blighted a potentially outstanding partnership.

Sir Jacob kept his ear to the ground to warn him of possible approaches to Dick from elsewhere, and endeavoured to bind him to Cheldale by close association with special projects. In the end, the danger came from an unexpected quarter.

"Noo Dick, what fettle?" Ralph's distinctive voice came down the telephone wires. "Thou 'asna bin ti see us fer a bit. Is'ta a' reet?"

"Not too bad," replied Dick, lying through his teeth, "How are you and Mam?"

"Nobbut fair ti middlin'. Ay man, we're fair worried aboot thee an' Camilla. Ah can't think what fooaks roond 'ere'll say when they find oot. It'll bi varra awkerd. Onny rooad, nivver mind that, Ah's gannin t'give up t'farm i' t'backend, an' we want to knaw if thoo's minded to cum yam an' tak ower. Thoo hez a grand job doon theer, bud Ah thowt Ah'd ask afoor Ah did owt."

Ralph's first comment rubbed salt in a still sore wound. He knew his parents were unhappy about his marital problems, and would be devastated when they understood that the first divorce in the family was inevitable and imminent – that was one milestone he would reach before Harry! But Ralph's other announcement took Dick completely by surprise. He had expected his father to carry on farming at Deep Ghyll for at least six or seven more years, and had given no thought to the options. Ralph had been at Deep Ghyll for ten years, and the sudden declaration of his intention to give up farming and follow other interests was a brave move for a man of 59 years who had known nothing but hill farming.

Dick quickly turned over the arguments in his mind – it would be a heaven-sent opportunity to escape from the pall of Sir Jacob's disapproval which he felt keenly; it gave him the chance to farm on his own account on the family farm; and, perhaps the most important factor at that moment, he would be twenty miles closer to Judith. The road between Cheldale and York had become well trodden by Dick since the conference at Scotch Corner, but it was a tortuous route compared with the directness of the Great North Road built on the old Roman Ermine Street from Teesdale to York.

"Dad, it would be grand to come and farm at Deep Ghyll. It's been a great experience here on the estate, but it can't compare with farming on my own account. Anyway, you've done so much there, and it needs to be built on by the family."

It was agreed that Dick would hand in his notice to Sir Jacob for Michaelmas 1971, and return to Teesdale as his father's tenant at Deep Ghyll. Ralph had completed arrangements to set up a livestock haulage business with a former driver from Dalton, and would move to live in Barnard Castle. Ralph knew that Dick and Camilla were not together, but he did not allow his mind to entertain thoughts of divorce, or dwell on the possibility that Dick would occupy Deep Ghyll farmhouse alone.

4
FULL STEAM AHEAD

Judith

Judith Parkin lived with her parents, Nicholas and Evelyn, on the Yorkshire side of the Tees, in a well-appointed house which stood on higher ground looking over the river some miles below Barnard Castle. Her horse, an elegant chestnut Thoroughbred cross Cleveland Bay, grazed the paddock behind the house. Her father had moved into the district as a young qualified accountant, and created a thriving and profitable business. He was precise and well-ordered; he believed in the value of good organisation, and the year ahead always was planned in detail before business was suspended for the Christmas festivities. He was a lean, active man. His stern expression and pale features, accentuated by a narrow face and thin lips, belied a sense of humour which broke out at intervals in a quick smile. He made careful notes of his business discussions, peering at clients from time to time over the glasses perched on his aquiline nose.

He had married soon after his arrival in the district to a local girl who was noted for her beauty, but whose homely inclinations would ensure that his household was maintained to the standard he required. Evelyn was the daughter of a farmer of substantial means, and the wedding took place in the historic setting of Wycliffe Church. A son was born the following year, and a daughter two years later. The high standards of achievement that Nicholas set for his son proved too onerous. He was dispatched at an early age to a boarding school of stern reputation, but proved incompatible with its rigorous regimes, and the subsequent disappointment and ultimate estrangement from his father were inevitable.

In contrast, his daughter was his pride and joy. Judith flourished under her father's watchful protection, although occasionally it proved more irksome as she passed into adolescence. He espoused the principle of female equality and had planned her education with a career in mind. He had focused his attention on two schools, Polam Hall in Darlington and the Convent school in Richmond, and chose the latter as he was persuaded it would provide a stricter and more disciplined regime.

Judith entered the first form in 1962. The thought of attending a Convent school filled her with some apprehension, but she soon discovered it differed very little from other schools. She was a friendly, open girl, who had inherited her father's sharp mind and her mother's quiet beauty. She enjoyed a wide circle of friends who were regular guests at her parties. There was a smaller group of more intimate friends from the Convent school who were her special confidantes – Rosemary Paulie, Josie Mortham, Susan Alderson and Shirley Nicholls – nicknamed 'The Famous Five'. Susan held the intellectual advantage, and Josie was the fashion trend setter, but Judith was the undisputed leader.

In her mid-teens she joined the local Young Farmers Club. Half her family were farmers, and the YFC movement offered a full and vigorous social life. It also pitched her unceremoniously into public speaking competitions, and she discovered a talent that previously had been hidden under her excitable spontaneity. She began to emerge as a girl of considerable ability, and Nicholas dreamed of a glittering future for her. The Famous Five all enjoyed commendable success in their 'O' level examinations, and seemed set fair for academic careers as they embarked on their 'A' level courses.

The following year Sister Theresa, Careers Mistress at the Convent school, began to pencil names of promising pupils against selected universities. She immediately noted two pupils – Susan Alderson for veterinary science or agriculture at Cambridge, and Judith Parkin for history at Oxford. She marked several pupils for Durham University, including Rosemary Paulie and Shirley Nicholls. Creativity was Josie Mortham's forté and her chosen destination was the Royal College of Art in London. Initially, all the girls were thrilled by the prospect of university, but inexplicably Judith began to harbour doubts. She felt a desire to get out into the real world and be involved in real work.

She informed Sister Theresa of her decision not to progress her university application, and she immediately shared her horrified reaction with Judith's father. Nicholas would stand for no nonsense, and ordered his daughter to leave her application in place and concentrate on her studies. It was only then he discovered that Judith was blessed with a degree of stubbornness which was more than a match for his autocratic authority.

Judith obtained excellent grades in her 'A' level examinations, which caused the school and her father even greater grief at the lost opportunity. Her mother was more sympathetic, and reassured Judith that it was important to follow a career in which she felt happy. She applied successfully to join the York office of a firm which specialised in organising conferences and major events, and started work after a short holiday with the other members of the Famous Five.

One of her early assignments was a conference at Scotch Corner in February 1970. The late withdrawal of a key speaker caused last-minute consternation among the members of the organising committee, until one of them mentioned Dick Bainbridge.

"I've been hearing a good deal about him recently. Seems to be making a name for himself in the Midlands. Could solve our problem – we could bill him as 'local lad made good'."

Judith remembered her father talking about Dick Bainbridge several years previously when she was a small schoolgirl. He had gone on an exciting visit to North America – and such a spirit of adventure left a lasting impression on Judith. She was intrigued by Dick's reputation. Obviously he was held in high regard. She was acting as Secretary to the Committee, and ventured to express her opinion.

"I don't wish to sound presumptuous, but maybe I can help. I – well, my father really, knows Mr Bainbridge, and I could contact him if that would be helpful."

The Chairman welcomed the intervention of the attractive young woman who had been delegated to assist with organisation of the event. "My dear girl, far from it. Your suggestion is very timely. Please do exert your best efforts to persuade him."

Dick's prompt acceptance of the invitation raised Judith's stock immeasurably within the committee and with her employers, and Dick rose even further in Judith's eyes because he had responded so quickly and so positively. She allowed herself to fantasise about him, and imagine their meeting. If he had not already exerted a powerful attraction before, he became a figure of desire when they met. The tall Adonis-like young man, with eyes so blue – at once both kind and challenging – captured her heart as soon as she came face to face with him in the foyer at Scotch Corner. She sat at the back of the hall during his talk, and was thrilled by his strong, authoritative delivery.

At the close of the conference, Judith was involved necessarily in dealing with queries from delegates, and with hotel arrangements. Members of the committee locked her in conversation to thank her and congratulate her on her role in the success of the event. She was polite and friendly, but she was aching to escape and find Dick. She was sure he must have gone.

It was late when she had dealt with the last query, and tears of disappointment filled her eyes when she could see no sign of him. Despondent, she collected her briefcase and coat, looked at her watch, and decided she could reach York before the worst of the traffic.

"You weren't going to leave without saying goodbye?" The deep gentle voice brought her to a standstill. She turned, and he was standing waiting for her.

She dropped her case and coat, and ran to him, throwing her arms around his neck.

"I thought you must have gone," she whispered.

He brushed a tear from her cheek. "Gone! Without saying goodbye to the most beautiful girl I've ever seen? I don't want to say goodbye – we've only just said hello."

Dick was staying overnight at the hotel, but Judith had to travel back to York. He did not want her to travel too late, but she argued it was only a journey of an hour or so, and that she had no intention of leaving for a long time. The hours flew by as they sat and talked, immersed in the joy of each other. Judith felt a deep desire to be with him – close to him. If he had asked her to go to his room, she would have gone, but he did not. The thought occurred to him, but he respected this beautiful girl too much to spoil the joyous spontaneity of this first meeting. As it grew late, he insisted that she should leave.

"I'd never forgive myself if anything should happen to you. Please take care Judith, and call me as soon as you arrive home."

"Dick, I can't describe how happy I feel. I've been so excited waiting for today, and it's been as fabulous as I expected. You will come and see me at the weekend, won't you? I can't wait to see you again;

it's almost as if you're already part of me."

He melted in the soft appeal of her brown eyes. "If I have my way I'll never leave you."

They kissed with an intensity and passion that neither had experienced before, and he waved her on her journey home. Neither minded their sleeplessness that night. Their thoughts were full of joy and expectation.

❁ ❁ ❁ ❁ ❁ ❁ ❁ ❁ ❁ ❁ ❁ ❁

Dick's mind was full of the girl who had bewitched him. Judith Parkin – a revelation from his own backyard – how had such a beautiful flower bloomed in Teesdale without him noticing? The broad forehead and wide cheekbones, large brown eyes that laughed and flirted, small straight nose, full lips smiling with just a hint of sensuousness, a square jaw and a chin of firm delicacy that unmistakably signalled defiance. Every detail of her was imprinted on his inner eye, and he could not wait to refresh the image with reality.

The days until the weekend were taut with expectation. It was their first chance to be alone and let their lives begin to intertwine. Dick wished it could be so simple and carefree, but there was a problem he could not keep from her. They drove up to the North Yorkshire Moors and Dick pulled into a space at the top of Sutton Bank. He parked with the vale spread out below them, and Wensleydale beyond in its winter bleakness. He held her in his arms and kissed her, and then sat quiet for a moment.

"Whenever I feel depressed or worried, I only need to see those hills to lift my mood." He pointed at the Pennines in the distance. "They recharge my batteries. Until today I thought they were my inspiration, but now I've met you, and it's impossible to say how much you mean to me already. I know it's only been a day or two since we met, but I haven't stopped thinking about you. You've brought a new meaning into my life, and I want you to stay with me."

"Dick, darling Dick," she exclaimed, "all I want is to be with you. Just hold me close, and I'll feel safe."

"I never want to let you go, but I've done things in the past that I regret, and you may feel different when you know me better."

"We've all done little things that we regret. I'm sure I have."

Dick saw there was no easy way to break the news to her. "My mistakes are not so small. Judith, my darling, I've been married – in fact, I am married!"

She gave a cry, and turned to look at him with disbelief. "No, oh no." Her voice broke as she realised he was speaking the truth.

"Please let me explain, before you decide what to do." His heart was pounding, and his mouth felt dry. The thought of losing her filled him with an awful dread. "It may not be as bad as it sounds. I'm waiting for my divorce, and that will be some consolation, but I wish it had never happened. I can only be honest with you and let you decide my fate. It was a girl from the estate in Derbyshire – I was dazzled by the bright lights and the social whirl – it was outside my understanding and it turned my head. I knew it wasn't my style of life, and I'll never forgive myself for letting it continue. I was a fool. But everybody wanted it to happen – my parents were over the moon – and I was carried along. On the day of the wedding I stood in the church knowing that I couldn't marry the girl, and yet I hadn't the courage to say so and leave. We stayed together for less than four months. How can you love such a fool and a coward? I would understand if you never wished to see me again."

He had been looking straight ahead while he spoke. Now he turned to her, his eyes full of tears, and saw that she was crying quietly. She met his gaze, and when he reached across to hold her hand she did not pull away.

She did not speak for a while. There were too many thoughts rushing round her mind. She would not have chosen to be with a married man; her immediate reaction was to flee; her friends would be quizzically intrigued; her mother would be quietly sad; her most ominous foreboding was the reaction of her father. But as her thoughts cleared, she knew one thing – she loved Dick Bainbridge. She admired him for being so honest; she admired his courage for telling her. She loved him for the tears in his eyes – he surely loved her.

"Oh Dick, it's not what I expected. It will make things very difficult, but we can't change it – it's done and gone. I only know I want to be with you."

He gasped with relief, and hugged her as if he would never stop. They both shed tears that sealed their common destiny.

In the weeks that followed, Dick came to know the road between Cheldale and York in intimate detail. Every twist and turn of the 88 miles was imprinted on his mind like a map. He counted every minute of the journey to reach his love – almost exactly 90 minutes from the moment he turned the key in his sleek new convertible to his arrival at Judith's door. They lost money on the horses at Wetherby, and later at Ripon and York in April and May. Enthused by Judith's love of history, they explored the nooks and crannies of York's ancient lanes and walked in wonder through the atmospheric ruins of famous Yorkshire abbeys – Fountains, Byland and Rievaulx.

Fountains Abbey was a favourite haunt, and they returned often, entering the private estate of Studley Hall along a road bordered by rows of majestic oaks already gnarled with age. In the Abbey grounds, with their ornamental lakes, graceful statues and a bubbling stream, they followed a path hedged by yew while a rare Chilean pine towered above them, until suddenly, rounding a bend in the path, the ruins of the Cistercian Abbey – ruins standing in awe-inspiring defiance of eight centuries of depredation – appeared at the farther end of an avenue of waving trees. Approaching on the springy turf, they were absorbed into the mediaeval atmosphere, imagining the orderly procession of monks and their monotonous chanting. Under the endless geometric vaults of the refectory and in the ruined cloisters and they felt a mutual spiritual bond, their hands clasped in an understanding that needed no verbal confirmation.

They experienced the same feelings when they escaped into the uplands and walked hand-in-hand on the Hambleton Hills looking across the Vale of York to the bleak majesty of the Pennine range in which they had been born, and to which inevitably they would return. They became lovers on a secluded sun-warmed hill in early summer shortly before Judith reached her nineteenth birthday, and both knew they had reached a point of no return. Dick's divorce would not be finalised until December, but breaking the news to Judith's father could be delayed no longer.

Dick wanted to be with Judith when she told her parents, but she thought it better for her to go alone. On her birthday, she drove from York to Wycliffe after work on Friday evening. She hoped that a birthday visit might assuage her father's anticipated wrath. She was uplifted by the joy of her love for Dick, despite her apprehension for the reaction she might expect from her father. Her parents were overjoyed that she had chosen to celebrate with them, and Evelyn had prepared a special dinner and a be-candled cake. They all relaxed in familial contentment – the calm before the storm.

Her news fell like a bombshell. They were sitting in the conservatory after lunch the following day, proudly chatting about the success of Judith's career, when she broke the news.

"I've got something very exciting to tell you," she began. Her parents looked up with immediate interest. "I've met an absolutely wonderful man and... well, we're in love, and I'm so happy."

"Oh Judith, that's wonderful." Evelyn leaned over and kissed her. "When will we...?"

"This is very sudden. Who is this man?" Nicholas cut in sharply. "I assume he has a name and a job." The thought of his daughter being attached emotionally to an unknown man – or indeed, any man – incited his abrupt response.

"Yes," replied Judith, her confidence faltering in the face of her father's stern gaze. "He's Dick Bainbridge, and he manages an estate in Derbyshire."

"Dick Bainbridge!" Nicholas exploded. "You mean Dick Bainbridge from Deep Ghyll?" Judith nodded. "He's a married man. This is impossible. I will not allow it! Remember you're not yet 21."

Evelyn looked from father to daughter, and put her arm round Judith. "Darling, maybe it is unwise to go out with a married man. Have..."

"There is no maybe about it." Nicholas was furious. His eyes were piercing, and a flush of colour suffused his pallor. "It is unforgivable. Is this the result of your Convent school education? Is this the thanks we get for the care and affection we give you? You'll finish up like one of those unmarried mothers from the bottom end of Barnard Castle in Bridgegate." He stormed out and went into his study, closing the door firmly behind him.

Judith burst into tears, and her mother sought to comfort her. "Please don't cry. Your father is upset, and maybe spoke more harshly than he intended. It was rather unexpected news. I'm sure he'll calm down in a while. We thought you would find a nice suitable young man in a year or two. Are you sure you're doing the right thing?"

"Oh Mummy, he is the most wonderful man. He's loving and gentle, and everything I want." She dried her eyes, and sat up straight. "He is married, but separated from his wife. He'll be divorced before the end of the year, and I do want to marry him."

"There can be no white wedding if he's a divorced man." Evelyn saw her dreams disappearing.

When they re-engaged a little later in the day, the balance of advantage had shifted. Nicholas was unmoving in his determination. He would not tolerate the relationship, far less give his approval to such a marriage, but his authority rested only on the intensity of his objection. The Family Reform Act, which had come into force six months previously, reduced the age of majority to eighteen years, and Judith was a free agent. Judith, having recovered her composure, was equally determined not to relinquish the love of her life. She continued to be motivated by family values that had been applied previously, but she also was aware of her rights in the last resort. Evelyn was lost in the neutral ground between the warring factions, buffeted by the angry exchanges.

Nicholas reminded Judith of her responsibility to the reputation of the family, and recommended the virtue of three qualities, recounted to him by a Catholic acquaintance, which perhaps should have dictated her actions – discipline, self-denial and delayed gratification. Maybe less impetuous behaviour would have served her better.

When he observed that the acuteness of his initial displeasure had no effect, Nicholas remembered the earlier confrontation with Judith regarding university, and began to appreciate it might not be so straightforward to impose his will. He perceived that she would not be amenable to instruction, and decided to employ a less confrontational strategy. He would arrange for her to be transferred out of the reach of Dick Bainbridge.

"I'm far from happy with the situation; I'm sure it will end in tears, but I can see you are determined. I think both your mother and I want to be reassured that you'll make a sensible choice and not do anything foolish. A period of separation from Dick Bainbridge will enable us all to see if your feelings – and his – are strong enough. I think a year in London would be good for you. Your firm has a London office; we'll see if a transfer can be arranged – it might also be useful for your career." He paused, and looked directly at her. "You'll avoid great distress to us all by agreeing to this."

It seemed to Judith more like a business contract than a family discussion. Her immediate reaction was to reject any attempt to control her actions or to prevent her seeing Dick, but she did not wish to upset her parents or cause them unnecessary pain. On further thought she agreed to her father's suggestion in the secure knowledge that Dick would travel anywhere to see her. Everyone appeared satisfied with the outcome.

Judith's removal to London doubled Dick's travelling distance and journey time, but it did nothing to dent their ardour. They simply changed the location of their exploration from Yorkshire to London and more exotic destinations. One of the Famous Five, Josie Mortham, was still in London at the Royal College of Art, and found suitable accommodation for Judith near to her own bed-sitter.

It was fortunate that Nicholas's sanity was protected by ignorance of the romantic liaisons that punctuated the following months. They celebrated Dick's divorce with champagne at Pomegranates by Lambeth Bridge in December. They used the Paris Livestock Show in March as an excuse to visit Paris. They saw the spring sunlight burnishing the soaring domes of Sacre Coeur and filtering through the intense colour of the great circled window of Notre Dame; they drank thick sweet coffee at street-side cafés, and savoured the delicacy of Gallic cuisine with new French acquaintances at Les Trois Moutons and Caveau des Chevillards.

Midsummer was a special time. Two hundred and fifty miles from Derbyshire and almost as far from London, they were greeted at their chosen destination in Lympstone by four West Highland terriers that preceded their owners to the door. Dick had determined that a long weekend in Devon would be a fitting celebration of Judith's twentieth birthday, and The River House had established an impeccable reputation for its cuisine and discreet hospitality.

The restaurant upstairs looked out across the estuary of the River Exe to Powderham and Dartmoor beyond, and their table was beside the window. The first evening during dinner, the guests were surprised when the lights in the restaurant were turned out, and even moreso when their hosts, having earlier gleaned the reason for their visit, entered with twenty candles flickering on a hastily prepared cake for Judith. Everyone sang *Happy Birthday* and offered their congratulations. The next evening they felt almost one of the family. Their hosts were informally attentive, and once again the exquisite cuisine did not belie their reputation. The restaurant was full, but Dick and Judith were completely engrossed in each other, and still were talking after all the other guests had left.

As the sun dropped down behind the western horizon of the moor and darkness fell, and the twinkling lights on the farther shore were reflected in the water of the estuary, Dick leaned across and took both of Judith's hands in his.

"My darling, I've been very remiss." His words might have been cause for alarm in other circumstances, and maybe momentarily Judith remembered his confession on their first date, but the kindness in his eyes gave any reassurance she may have needed. "It's sixteen months since I fell in love with you at first sight – the most beautiful girl I've ever seen – and I still hate to be apart from you. It's a year since we lay on a hillside together, and then you faced your father's wrath by yourself – if I ever needed proof you love me, that was it. We've both taken it for granted that we'll be married, but I've never asked you."

He rose from his seat, went round the table and kneeled beside her. Taking a velvet box from his pocket, he continued, "Darling Judith, I love you more than I ever thought possible. Will you marry me?"

She nodded her head, too overcome to speak, and held him against her breast, her dark hair falling over his head. He took a ring from its box, an intense purple sapphire with two opposing diamonds, and placed it on her finger.

"Dick, it's beautiful, so beautiful. I shall wear it for ever." She brushed the tears from her face and kissed him. "You know how much I love you. Isn't it wonderful to be so happy together?"

The simultaneous return of Dick and Judith to Teesdale three months later did not fail to excite the suspicions of her zealous father. He had learned from Ralph that Dick was coming home to farm at Deep Ghyll, but Judith's reappearance took him by surprise. She had handed in her notice to her employers, and returned to the family fold wearing an engagement ring. She saw the look of reprimand forming on her father's face, and anticipated the potential quarrel by quietly proposing that, if he found it was not acceptable for her to live at home, she could go and live with Dick. It was an ultimatum, couched in the form of a concession, that left no room for argument. Nicholas saw that his stratagem to separate the couple had failed. He fumed privately, but had the good grace to accept that he was beaten, and stiffly granted Dick's formal request for his daughter's hand in marriage, on the condition that the wedding should not take place until she had passed her 21st birthday. The condition carried no legal weight, but Dick and Judith complied in the interests of family harmony, secure in their mutual love.

Mistress of the House 1971-1972

Ralph and Nicholas could not decide what to do about the dilemma. Judith spent most of her time at Deep Ghyll, and effectively was mistress of the house for the next year. It was not total cohabitation, but it was not far removed. She and Dick were discreet, and she lived with her parents, but she made sure that Deep Ghyll was a comfortable home for Dick. Ralph's fundamental Methodism could easily have been offended, but Judith's bright and loving disposition soon won him round. Nicholas was aware he had been out-manoeuvred, but it was too late to retrieve the situation, although he still felt an underlying irritation that Dick should repay his earlier kindness by denying his daughter a white wedding.

Nicholas may have lost the battle, but he would not subside without a flourish. He determined that his daughter's 21st birthday would be an occasion to remember. The imminence of her wedding, and the contrast with the anticlimactic plainness of the register office with Dick, may have provided some motivation for his ambition. Until she was married he could orchestrate a memorable symphony of celebration, for which the wedding could never aspire to be an encore, and 25 June 1972 would be the talk of the Dale for many months to come.

He decided that the party would be held at their home. There were clients who would willingly have made their country mansion available to him, but he wanted this to be seen without question as his event. As her birthday fell on a Sunday, the celebration was brought forward to Midsummer Day. Cars were parked at the lower end of the paddock adjacent to the house, and a covered wooden walkway led up to a marquee of truly magnificent proportions erected at the upper end. Guests were greeted and served with champagne by servants in Eastern dress, and mingled among potted palms and oriental decorations. At 8.30pm a trumpet sounded, and dinner was announced. Curtains were pulled back with a flourish to reveal the larger half of the marquee with tables set on three sides of a dance floor, while the band occupied the fourth side.

Judith was placed carefully between her parents on the central table, with Dick facing her, out of conversation distance. Many relatives – mostly strangers to Dick – had come for such a special event, but Judith's brother, Gilbert, was absent. Dick could not avoid speculating on family feuds. Harry had not even had the courtesy to reply to invitations to Bainbridge celebrations, but in this case he thought that it was the son who had been disowned by his father. Gilbert's failure to match his father's expectations had made him a 23-year-old exile. As he sipped his coffee, Dick looked across at Nicholas. It was difficult to reconcile the overt affection of his attention to his daughter with the harshness that excluded his son.

Dick's reverie was broken by the announcement of the speeches. Nicholas took the prime spot, followed by Judith's godfather, whom Dick had never met, with a final response by Judith. She was a picture, her brown eyes dancing, her long dark hair waving as she took the microphone. Dick could not take his eyes from her, and was blushingly proud as she introduced him to the assembled guests – and in just three months she would be his wife.

Nicholas had extra treats in store. A further blast on the trumpet heralded an announcement that the guests should take up their position outside the marquee, and immediately the sky was filled with explosive showers of pyrotechnic colour. When they returned to their seats, the band struck up and dancing began. Dick was not a keen dancer, and spent much of the remainder of the evening watching Judith whirling round the floor with a succession of partners. Her dark beauty dramatised by her choice of a daring red off-the-shoulder dress, close-fitting from bust to hips to reveal her curvaceous femininity, and swirling below as she abandoned herself to the rhythm of the dance. Nicholas derived some consolation that his triumph was proving a little uncomfortable for Dick. Nor was he disappointed when Judith's birthday party became a focus of conversation throughout the Dale.

Three months later, the wedding passed relatively unnoticed. It was a low-key occasion, but for both Judith and Dick it held infinitely more significance. It was the culmination of more than three years of loving and waiting, and their patience now was rewarded. They were married on Saturday 30 September and, if Judith had any regrets that it was not a white wedding with all the finery of silk and lace, she showed no sign of it. She looked radiantly happy. A small reception was held at the Morrit Arms, restricted to family and a few close friends. The Famous Five were represented only by Josie Mortham and Shirley Nicholls, as Susan Alderson had gone to work at university in Canada and Rosemary Paulie was in Africa married already to a photo-journalist.

Ralph and Annie hoped this marriage would last; Evelyn was just happy for her lovely daughter; Nicholas was thankful that, at least, she was not pregnant on her wedding day.

Although Judith's father had a successful practice, and was comparatively wealthy, the family had not travelled far beyond the shores of Britain. An occasional skiing holiday, or a walking tour in the Pyrenees, but nothing particularly adventurous. Dick determined to give Judith a honeymoon to remember – nothing was too good for her. During his year in North America he had heard much of the amazing fall colours in many areas, but he understood that those in New England in early October were the best. That was the destination he selected. They would be away for twelve days, and they departed, leaving Deep Ghyll in the capable hands of Ralph and Annie.

The fall colours had not reached their full glory as they drove northwards up the broad sparsely trafficked highway from Boston to Maine. They would catch the colours in northern Maine and follow their progress back down the White Mountains through Vermont and Massachusetts. They stopped first in Brunswick and drove down a narrow peninsular of woodland and over a wooden causeway to the edge of Casco Bay for their introduction to the culinary arts of New England at the Lobster House. The taste of seafood, especially chowder and lobster, seemed enhanced in the simple restaurant where food was the priority and décor a distraction. The next day, on the road to Farmington, they called by chance at Pam's Place and savoured the epitome of crisp-based quality pizza.

They turned westwards at Moosehead Lake and relaxed for a

couple of days in a quaint old hotel where moose heads peered from the walls, and skins were spread on the floor. A Victorian, colonial atmosphere pervaded its log-blazing rooms and long corridors. As they set their faces towards Boston, the maples and the forests stretching into the far distance were ablaze with colour – iridescent reds and oranges and yellows – sometimes with the deep intensity of shade, sometimes translucent in the bright autumn sun. This corner of America had a special character, and a special meaning for Dick and Judith as it launched them on their joint venture in life.

❋ ❋ ❋ ❋ ❋ ❋ ❋ ❋ ❋ ❋ ❋ ❋

Dick and Judith were sitting close together in front of the fire at Deep Ghyll, his arm around her, and his feet on the Idi Amin stool that Annie's cousin had brought back from Africa many years ago. It was six months after their return from New England, and still they wondered at the sights they had seen. It was the start of lambing time, and they knew they could expect some sleepless nights in the next three or four weeks as the flocks proved their fecundity again. The couple were in reflective mood.

"Isn't it lovely now that Daddy has relaxed and really accepted us as a couple?" Judith sighed contentedly. "He was so very angry at first when he discovered I was going out with you. He can be rather fierce, but he's a softie underneath."

Dick's experience was a variance with Judith's perception of her father's state of mind, but he did not interrupt or contradict his wife. He had attempted – with limited success – to mend fences with his father-in-law, who adopted a more benevolent demeanour when his daughter was present. Knowing that Nicholas had an interest in cricket, Dick had commented on the results of Yorkshire players in the previous year – the outstanding batting average of Boycott, the bowling of Old and the captaincy of Close. He congratulated himself on memorising their performances, but discovered that Nicholas supported Warwickshire and detested Close for his opposition to Smith, the Warwickshire captain. His good intention served only to perpetuate the rift.

Judith was oblivious to his thoughts and continued. "You know, Mummy always liked you. I'm sure she persuaded Daddy that you would be a suitable son-in-law. She's very special – so very warm and cuddly."

"That must be where you got it from," replied Dick, "you're the most cuddlesome girl I know."

"Don't you mean the only cuddlesome girl you know," she teased. "How many girls do you cuddle?"

"About the same as the men you snuggle with!" He laughed, then continued more seriously. "My parents and grandparents were not cuddly at all; I would sit on someone's knee occasionally, but generally it was very undemonstrative. And nobody ever said they loved you. I grew up to accept that was normal. But I always felt secure. Oh, I had spells when I thought that Harry was their favourite, but underneath I knew they were there for me. I felt loved and wanted despite the lack of hugs. Then you came along, and suddenly hugs were as natural as breathing, and feeling close to you the most important thing to me. I love you." He held her closer and kissed her.

Ralph Nicholas Bainbridge was born that year on 16 December. His arrival was the cause of much rejoicing in the Bainbridge and Parkin households. Both grandfathers were gratified to have their names passed down to the next generation, and they reminisced after the christening about their conversations more than a decade earlier comparing notes about their children. Now their blood had been joined. Judith, as a former student of history, joked that Ralph's birth exactly on the two hundredth anniversary of the Boston Tea Party must have some particular significance, maybe linked to their honeymoon in New England! Annie was more concerned with the present, and brought out the family heirloom robes for the christening ceremony. They were not sumptuous or spectacular, but they carried family history. The white silk, defined by two narrow vertical panels of lace, showed a slight tarnish of age; the collar, sleeves and hem were trimmed with lace; and flower motifs in white and blue were embroidered on the front. Dick looked at the tiny garments, and marvelled that he had been christened in them. It gave him acute joy and pride to know that they would do the same service for his son. Dick's heir quickly became 'young Ralph', while his father gradually assumed the name of 'old Ralph'.

Grasmere Revisited 1974

Dick never talked much about the wrestling exploits of his youth. It was perhaps one of his main regrets that he had not been able to test himself against the best over a longer career. Judith understood his feelings, and thought that a visit to Grasmere Sports might be a good idea. It might provide the cathartic effect to remove Dick's lingering regrets but, if not, it would still be an enjoyable family visit with baby Ralph. On 17 August 1974 they packed a picnic, rugs and Ralph's baby chair into the Volvo estate car, and set out for the Lake District.

They made a detour southwards through Windermere, and as they approached Rydal Water the volume of traffic started to increase noticeably. By the time they reached Grasmere it was congested and parking was a problem, but despite the aggravation the atmosphere of the event immediately permeated Dick's senses. He looked around. The green arena nestled in a hollow of the brown dark hills. To the north lay the vast forbidding bulk of Helm Crag, while eastwards Butter Crag towered 750 feet above the sports field. Only the southern aspect was flat, where the outlet from Grasmere flowed towards Windermere through the narrow valley impregnated with Wordsworthian romanticism.

Dick went to buy a programme which would list all the entries. "The fell race and the heavyweight wrestling aren't until this afternoon," he said to Judith. "Why don't we take Ralph for a walk and have the picnic before they start? The Men's Guide Race goes to the top of that mountain." He pointed to Butter Crag. "I hope for their sakes it isn't too hot when they run."

They walked into the village and down to the lake, before returning and unpacking the picnic. They spread out a rug and lay on the ground, with Ralph between them, and basked in warm contentment.

"How d'you feel, now you're here?" asked Judith. "Must be nostalgic for you."

"No, I'm fine," he replied. "I recognise some names from my time, but there's a lot of new ones. The chap I beat in the final at Langthwaite in 1962 is still wrestling. He must be well over 40 by now." He fell silent for a while, then mused aloud, "I'm only 32 – still a youngster in wrestling. Ah, but that's daft thinking; I haven't trained or wrestled in twelve years. These chaps would make mincemeat of me."

Judith leaned over and kissed him. "You'll always be my

Champion," she said softly, "and I know you'd have been the greatest if you'd been able to carry on wrestling." It distressed her when he was not happy.

The competitors were lining up for the senior fell race, and Dick scanned the programme. "I see that Bill Teasdale set the record in 1965. He must have been about 40 then. Thirteen minutes five seconds – they breed them tough up here."

The runners were off. The competitor with number 1 on his vest – Fred Reeves – took an early lead and was never headed. Up the steep slope the runners were slowed to walking pace for much of the ascent, almost to crawling on hands and knees at one point, before turning at the summit and descending in huge stag-like bounds.

"That was fast," declared Dick, who had his stopwatch running. "I make it under thirteen minutes, which would give him the record. Up in ten minutes, and down in three."

They then turned their attention to the heavyweight wrestling, and Judith could see the intensity with which Dick followed each move and throw. He had been talking to one or two other spectators to be updated on current form, and watched the favourites intently. The heavyweight championship eventually was won by the bulk of Wilf Brocklebank. He had been beaten the previous year in the final by Alan Davidson, who weighed in at only fourteen stone – Dick's old wrestling weight

"Well, they tell me he's 46!" exclaimed Dick. "Why am I not out there with them!" His frustration now was evident. Judith took his hand, tears rising in her eyes, and he calmed down as he looked at her. "Ah, I'm upsetting you. I'm sorry, just getting a bit carried away. That chap Brocklebank, I'm sure I could beat him. He's a big fellow though, weighs about nineteen stone – he's a bit like George Steadman – you remember the wrestler from Stainmore who we think might have been related – he was 46 when he won his last championship at Grasmere." He looked down at young Ralph. "What about you my little acorn. Mebbe you'll be the Champion, and do all the things I should've done."

Judith loved her man dearly, and at that moment she knew he was all she ever wanted. That and their children, and the following year she gave birth to a young brother for Ralph. They christened him Simon, after Judith's grandfather.

Deep Ghyll

The garden at Deep Ghyll sloped gently away from the south-facing house. It caught the sun through the main part of the day, and would be a perfect playground for a young family. It was protected from the prevailing westerly wind by a high ivy-clad wall, through which a door led to an outside earth closet. Not an ordinary model, to which the Bainbridges had been accustomed at Ellerbeck, but a deluxe two-seater!

Deep Ghyll house was an old seventeenth century building – the lintel over the front door carried the inscription 'EB 1681'. Dick guessed that EB was the builder, but beyond that could only speculate on his identity. He doubted he had been a Bainbridge. The front door opened into the hall and the main stairs ascending to three bedrooms. There were three downstairs rooms at the front, and a kitchen and large larder behind in a single-storey extension. The family habitually entered the house by the back door into a small extra extension at the rear which stood over the well and housed the water pump. The oldest part of the house at the west end had stone stairs curving within a half-circle that protruded at the back of the house. At the east end external stone steps led up to the door to a loft, under which was a storeroom.

Ralph and Annie had incorporated the storeroom into the house as a new kitchen, and opened a new entrance door at the east end. They converted part of the old kitchen into a bathroom, making the old outside closet redundant. That was real luxury, but water for the house still came from the well, drawn up by the hand-pump.

The house was approached from the main road by a long farm track which curved and dipped into the little valley where a narrow bridge crossed the beck from which the house took its name. A small dam formed a miniature reservoir from which water was pumped up for the livestock in winter, and to keep the milk cool in summer while it waited for collection. The valley was wooded, with oak and ash and sycamore. Copses were decorated with hazel catkins, swaying in the spring breeze; the damp of autumn was bejewelled by the bright red fruit of the rowan, and evident everywhere was the slender grace of the silver birch and the fragile delicacy of its wafer-thin curling white bark.

Electricity and telephone had been installed before Ralph and Annie purchased the property, and they often thought back to the primitive conditions when they had first started to farm at Ellerbeck – but Ellerbeck had been their launch pad and it always would have a special place in their hearts. The land at Deep Ghyll lay behind the house and buildings, sloping down to the river, of which Deep Ghyll beck was a tributary. The field immediately behind the house was undisturbed rig and furrow, and Dick discovered that several other fields were virgin pasture, untouched by plough or seed-drill, at least for many generations. They were rich in herbs and flowers, much as had been the case at Ellerbeck.

Judith had taken another temporary job on her return from London, but she handed in her notice when she married Dick, and became a full and active partner on the farm. They knew that Deep Ghyll now was the sole source of their income, and that its success depended entirely on them. They had a jaundiced opinion of political commitment to farming. The voting power of a shrinking rural population was reflected in the growing disinterest of both executive and legislature at Westminster. Their local Member of Parliament had farming interests, as did the Minister for Agriculture, Fisheries and Food, but the former had no office and the latter was an East Anglian arable farmer. Although the heavy subsidisation of farming continued, Dick and Judith were not confidant to rely on fickle Governmental policy and discussed new projects which would give their business greater security and buffer it against the whims of political inconsistency.

Dick had spotted a gap in the market. The common lowland sheep in England was a relatively unproductive creature, producing on average little more than one lamb each year. He had realised some time ago that the ideal would be two lambs from each ewe – an increase in productivity of 50 per cent. He already had been working with Ralph since the mid-1960s while he was at Cheldale to record the performance of ewes at Deep Ghyll and identify superior animals, and the flock was approaching their production targets. Now his thoughts went a step fur ther. He saw the marketing opportunity for a recognised breed of sheep that would be guaranteed to achieve a high level of productivity.

He augmented the flock with purchases of one or two selected animals from other flocks which maintained records, and applied his knowledge of genetics to fix the qualities he desired in the new breed. He used the knowledge he had gained from Sam Forbes, Mo Healy and

Jan Bonsma, and his experience with the pedigree livestock at Cheldale. He christened it the Ravock breed. Judith had discovered that the earliest evidence of farming activity in Teesdale was found in Bronze Age field boundaries at Ravock, a remote site between the River Greta and Deepdale, and they deemed it a suitable name for a pioneering breeding project.

The application of genetics to create a new breed had been successful and relatively pain free. Marketing the new product was a different challenge, which demanded a steep learning curve from both of them. They mounted a major publicity campaign, both in Britain and abroad. They had been to the SIMA Show in Paris in 1971, and made contact with the export company who welcomed enthusiastically their offer to supply breeding animals for the British display. At home they targeted the farming press, and the resulting high profile created an increasingly strong demand.

They devised an ingenious marketing ploy. Initially, they sold only rams so that purchasers were able to experience and appreciate the level of performance of their crossbred progeny, but no one was able to breed pure Ravock sheep. Sales of females were withheld until 1981 when the demand had reached fever pitch, and they were advertised in specific lots of five ewes and one ram at a stated price – first come, first served. The sale realised a substantial sum, most of which was invested in a trust fund to meet future education costs for Ralph and Simon. The elite nucleus flock, retained at Deep Ghyll, continued to thrive and the early publicity at the Paris Show ensured a profitable ongoing export market for the breed.

The other important initiative was a joint effort. Judith's upbringing had given her no understanding of life on a hill farm in the upper Dale at the end of the War, and she often asked Dick about his childhood. As he described the routine of meals during the day – breakfast, dinner, tea and supper – she realised that there was a speciality up-market outlet for the traditional products. The big stores were taking an increasing share of the market, but she felt sure there was potential for a niche market of discerning consumers. Her comments triggered Dick's mind back to the marketing enterprise on the Cheldale estate, and together they developed her concept like a couple of excited schoolchildren.

"Now Dick, let's go through the items one at a time, and see how each might fit into our system." He acted the role of the producer, and she the consumer.

As he recited each item, she compiled a list – porridge oats, cream, black treacle, bacon (from hams and rolled sides hanging in kitchen), eggs, bread, dripping (occasionally butter), mutton, potatoes, tea, milk, ham, scones, butter, jam, cakes, cheese.

Dick looked at the list. "That's quite a selection. Should be enough to get our teeth into. But maybe some of them are a bit ambitious. You don't really want to spend time baking bread and cakes, do you? The marketing boards will make it difficult to sell milk and dairy products privately – same for wool, if you were having thoughts of knitting! It seems to me that meat marketing is the main opportunity."

"Well, maybe I agree with you for starters, but let's not close our minds to a wider selection later. Think of the opportunities for Dales butter and Cotherstone cheese, just as your mother used to make them."

"It's possible, but small independent businesses have been discouraged ever since the creation of the Milk Marketing Board in the 1930s."

"OK, but we have two basic advantages. We can cut out the middlemen, and our products will be much better quality than the big stores can supply. But I think the real secret of our project will be branded products." Judith stopped, and waited for Dick to comment, but he was listening intently, his eyes opening to the unfolding abilities of his wife, and she continued. "Local branded 'Deep Ghyll' products – beef, lamb, pork – produced non-intensively on unimproved natural pastures and traceable to farm of origin, would give consumers huge confidence, and once they had experienced the quality – well, there would be no stopping them. Oh, I've forgotten eggs – they would be very popular."

"You're a genius," said Dick with real admiration. "That's a gem of an idea, and I think we should include eggs. There's a lot of interest in poultry at present. I was talking to Willie Bousefield the other day, and he's just signed a contract with one of those big American poultry companies – Arbor Acres I think – to keep nucleus breeding stock and produce eggs for hatching. And just across the valley, Colin Richardson has a huge battery unit producing eggs for the Galgate packing station in Barney..."

"Oh, Dick," exclaimed Judith, "I wouldn't want to do anything like that. I can think of nothing worse than laying hens crammed into battery cages, or even breeding birds almost living on top of one another, and the buildings look like factory units with feed hoppers perched above them. They ruin the whole character of the Dale. We could keep our hens in mobile housing in the fields, so that they can range and forage on grass – that would give us eggs of real quality and a marketing advantage."

They started by word of mouth through friends and contacts in the Dale and in town, with a weekly delivery service. It was a concept ahead of its time. Selling branded products direct from farm was a pioneering development that appealed more to urban than rural customers, but their clientele expanded throughout the Dale. The volume of business quickly outgrew their initial forecasts, and in 1976 they opened a shop in Horsemarket in Barnard Castle trading as Deep Ghyll Farm Produce.

Now they were a force to be reckoned with. Dick and Judith were not only a secure married couple; they also were a formidable business partnership.

5
A BACKWARD STEP

Metropolitan Temptation

Dick had begun to involve himself in the National Farmers' Union. He was not a union man by natural inclination, but he saw the need to fight for farmers' rights and interests. He had noted with concern the march of the supermarkets on their ascent to a dominant market position, which threatened to squeeze out smaller speciality competitors, and placed a higher priority on cheapness rather than quality. NFU work inevitably brought him into confrontation with Government on controversial issues. He tried to steer clear of national politics, but, if pressed, classed himself as a liberal conservative. He bitterly opposed integration with Europe and accession to the EEC in February 1973, and had no sympathy for Edward Heath.

If he had a favourite politician, it would be Benjamin Disraeli. Apart from his political persuasion, Dick admired his eloquence, and one of the few things he remembered from history lessons at Barney school was Disraeli's description of Gladstone as "a sophisticated rhetorician inebriated by the exuberance of his own verbosity". It had stuck in his mind, although he knew it would not have amused his grandfather, Matthew Metcalfe, who had been a strong supporter of Gladstone.

After he had overcome his early shyness, public speaking came naturally to Dick – an ability he shared with Judith – and doubtless it was a talent inherited from Annie who was famed for the monologues and lengthy poems she had committed to memory. He particularly noted a line from one of her recitations, with a message which she failed to observe but which he applied to great effect:

> *Keep my mind free from the recital of endless details;*
> *give me wings to get to the point.*

Dick's adherence to this dictum, together with his admiration for Disraeli's eloquence, was evident in the forthright expression of his views at NFU meetings, and probably was a significant factor in his election to representative office. In 1977 he became a delegate of the regional NFU to headquarters in London, and the following year was appointed to a NFU committee to report on opportunities for the livestock sector. The Committee comprised John Allen from Lincolnshire, Ivor Fane from Worcestershire, Julian Richards from Devon, Dick Bainbridge from Durham and the Chairman, Jack Merchant from Kent. A public relations company, Triple A, was appointed and Toni Griffin attended as their representative. Dick was very conscious that he was the only member from the north, and the only representative of upland and mountain livestock farming, and how he hated his Durham tag – he was a Yorkshireman!

Dick attended meetings conscientiously, travelling by car to Darlington and from thence by train to King's Cross. He started very early, and returned very late – sometimes after midnight, but it was a priority to get home to his family. He felt a sense of isolation when he was away from Judith and his young sons. The winter of 1979 was severe and Judith called during one meeting to advise him not to return that evening as the road conditions were too treacherous. Reluctantly he agreed, and was able to obtain a room at the Farmers Club in Whitehall Court. When he returned the next day, Judith insisted that in future he should always stay in London after a meeting rather than arriving home in the middle of the night. He resisted, but she was adamant, and finally he agreed.

It had been a long session for the NFU Committee in the Oak Room at the Farmers Club in August 1980. They had worked through the various options open to livestock farmers, and Dick had been conscious that the interests of hill farmers tended to be ignored – or maybe just forgotten or marginalised – in the weight of lowland opinion. He had fought his corner tenaciously, and felt he had negotiated a reasonable compromise. They then progressed to the next session – a public relations programme for the agreed policy, and Toni Griffin from Triple A joined them. They worked through until after 6.30 pm, when the Chairman called a halt.

"I'm sorry to have kept you so late. I'd intended to be finished earlier, but we can feel happy that we've done justice to the agenda. Now unfortunately, I promised my wife that I would take her to see Frank Sinatra at the Albert Hall tonight. We were very lucky to get tickets, and I mustn't spoil the evening by being late. Toni, I think you have enough information to prepare the promotional drafts, so can we leave the next steps to you. Next meeting will be back in the normal routine. See you all then. Goodnight."

He left the meeting and, as it was the peak harvest season, the lowland farmers also departed to get back to their arable activities. Dick was staying overnight at the Club, as was his practice, and Toni Griffin was the only other member of the meeting who had not left.

"Well, that's a pleasant surprise," she said, "I'd expected we wouldn't be finished until much later. I've booked a room, but I could almost have got home tonight if I'd known."

"Do you live far away?"

"Yes, a fair distance. Staffordshire actually; I get the train from Wolverhampton – have to change at New Street which is a nuisance. Really Dick – I may call you Dick, mayn't I? – travelling by rail is such a bore."

"Yes, by all means call me Dick. I travel by train and find I can tidy up the business of a meeting before the end of the journey." He looked at her, and thought it would be sociable to have a companion for dinner. "I'm eating here at the Club if you'd like to join me."

He had not taken any particular note of Toni previously, except as a participant in committee discussion. Now he had an opportunity to make a more detailed appraisal. Her red hair attracted immediate attention. It fell almost to her shoulders, and framed a face that enjoyed liberal maintenance – powder, cream, rouge, lipstick, eye-shadow, mascara – even to his untutored eye, it was obvious that every stratagem had been employed. Her pert, upturned nose seemed almost too small for the boldness of her face. Her green eyes watched him from the frame of mascara as his gaze fell on the bright colours of her tailored jacket and dress, and continued down past her rather muscular legs – she was aware of her weak point – and came to rest on her high-heeled red shoes. As a judge of livestock Dick had learned to look past the camouflage of a trimmed fleece that disguises shape, or the polish and powder that changes colour. He could recognise the real animal underneath any degree of manicuring and beautification – he wanted to know what was really there. Toni was too overdone for his taste.

Dick enjoyed dinner, assisted by the relaxing effects of a bottle of good wine. Toni was amusing and entertaining company, and she revealed that she lived only twenty miles or so from Dick's brother. He wondered how much she knew about Harry. He tried not to dwell on thoughts of his brother, but nevertheless natural curiosity in a member of his family was aroused.

Toni looked at Dick across the table, and her predatory female instinct awoke. *H'm, not bad. Harry Bainbridge is a high-flyer, and stinking rich; reputed to have a roving eye, especially for women with a bit of class and spirit. Wouldn't mind if he looked my direction. I wonder if this brother is the same. He's a good-looking guy, and doesn't seem to be short of the ready.*

"Penny for them! You're miles away."

"Oh, I'm so sorry Dick. One or two items from the meeting still spinning round."

They went through into the lounge for coffee, and Toni asked if they could have another bottle of wine. Dick was impatient to hear more about Harry, but Toni turned the conversation to other things, and kept the exchanges light and frivolous. Having been brought up in an abstemious household, Dick did not usually take more than one glass of wine, and he was beginning to feel light-headed and flirty.

"Dick, I really would appreciate your advice on the PR for this project. If I go and get my papers, would you mind going over some points with me?"

Dick was surprised and a little disappointed by her change of tone. He had been enjoying the unusual experience of dinner with a strange woman. "I'd be delighted to help, but not in here. The Club has very strict rules about business in the Club. No phones, briefcases or papers in the public rooms."

"Too bad. Perhaps we could use one of our rooms? Mine's quite big and has a table for writing. All my papers are there. We can take the wine up with us."

❋ ❋ ❋ ❋ ❋ ❋ ❋ ❋ ❋ ❋ ❋ ❋

"Rooms in London always are so hot," said Toni, slipping off her jacket and shoes. "They must spend a fortune on central heating. How on earth do you stand it coming down from the north?" She unzipped her dress, dropped it on the floor, and put on a short dressing gown. Seeing Dick's startled gaze, she laughed. "Don't mind me. I'm just getting comfortable. Why don't you take off your jacket and tie – you'd be more comfortable too."

Toni started to take the papers from her briefcase, while Dick obediently divested himself of surplus clothing. He did find London far too hot, but he also felt strangely excited and unnerved by Toni's casual informality. Toni looked at the small table, and put the papers beside the bed.

"The table's rather small. There's more room to spread the papers out here." She sat on the bed. "But first, let's talk some more about Harry. I can see it interests you. He has quite a reputation you know! Are all you Bainbridge men like that?"

Dick knew so little about his brother that he eagerly agreed to pursue that discussion. He poured two more glasses of wine, and sat down beside her. As Toni talked, he was by turns shocked by her revelations, and then reduced to helpless mirth. He lay back on the bed laughing at a particularly amusing story, his head light from the wine, and she lay back beside him and them on him – her red hair falling over his face, the soft curves of her body pressing against him, her hand caressing him – and she kissed him. His momentary resistance dissolved and he melted into an embrace.

❁ ❁ ❁ ❁ ❁ ❁ ❁ ❁ ❁ ❁ ❁ ❁

Dick sat motionless in his own room. Confusion and shame swept over him. What had he done? He had succumbed to temptation and regretted it immediately – too late, the adulterous deed was done. He had dressed himself, returned to his own room, and slumped in a chair. Images of Judith – his darling Judith – kept flashing through his mind.

He rose early the next morning and left the Club before breakfast. The journey home was a nightmare. The rhythmic clatter of the wheels on the rails pounded remorse into his numb mind. At home he presented a cheerful face, but guilt hung on him like a leaden weight. *Should he put it out of his mind and pretend it had never happened? Could he hide it from Judith, or would she suspect something? Should he tell her the truth? How would she react? Might Toni spill the beans?* He knew that Toni had children, but had understood from conversation that she was not with her husband.

At the next NFU meeting in November, Toni presented her proposals. She conducted herself with aplomb, and interacted with Dick as if nothing had happened between them. Before she left to travel home, she asked Dick for a quick word.

"Dick, I have some news for you," she smiled at him. "I'm pregnant!"

The sudden abruptness of her announcement stopped Dick in his tracks and, before he could stop himself, he exclaimed, "But I thought you weren't with your husband."

"I'm not." A faintly amused, even disdainful, expression crossed her face. "It's yours! What do you expect when you take a woman? Is that good news or bad?"

"Mine! It can't be! You mean from that time back in the summer?"

"Yes, that's right. I'm three months gone. What are we going to do about it? Or rather, what are you going to do about it? I'm a single woman, but I suppose your situation might be more complicated."

Dick was in acute distress. Toni's pregnancy had shattered the established order of his happy world. He agonised over how, or even whether, he should tell Judith. He struggled to maintain a semblance of normality, but frequently the enormity of his crime forced itself upon him and he would don his boots and coat and walk blindly through the wintry fields, a welter of confusion and fear driving his mind to distraction. He found no comfort in familiar surroundings. The Ravock rams eyed him balefully and shepherded away their harems of serviced ewes, raddled with fertile intent. The beck hurried past oblivious to his sorrow. The wildness of the winter wind whistling through the treetops seemed to mock him. Desolation gripped his soul as he stood alone, looking without seeing, staring into the unknown.

He resolved to wait until the boys had gone back to school. He went out of his way to make it a memorable Christmas and New Year's Eve, and hid his growing fear and apprehension under a cloak of jollity and seasonal festivity, but as he made his routine daily inspections of the sheep and cattle, his thoughts ran riot. *He and Judith were soul-mates. They had been inseparable partners for more than ten years. They were a family. Oh God, what about the boys. He could not keep a secret from her. She would guess from his demeanour sooner rather than later that something was amiss. He could not bear to think of her reaction to his news; neither could he bear the thought of losing her, but he had to tell her.*

"Judith, I don't know what to say. I've been an absolute fool, but before I tell you I want you to know that you mean everything to me. We have been together through thick and thin, and we've done so much together. We..."

"Dick, please stop," she said, her brown eyes wide and frightened. "What is it? What is wrong?"

He took a deep breath, and took her hand in his. "On a trip to London with the NFU in the summer, there was a lot fooling about, and one thing led to another. I got too much alcohol down me and finished up in bed with a woman."

Judith gasped and involuntarily pulled her hand away. Tears sprang to her eyes. "Dick, how could you. How could you do such a thing? Do I mean so little to you? Who is this woman; is that the only time you've slept with her? Oh, Dick, she might be pregnant."

"That's the problem Judith. She tells me that she is." Dick dropped his gaze, and tears fell from his eyes also. "But please Judith, can we try to keep our marriage together. I love you so much – and the boys. I couldn't bear to lose the boys."

Judith's body was wracked by giant sobs. Dick moved and put his arm around her shoulders, but she shrugged him away and ran upstairs to the bedroom.

After a short while, Dick followed her. She was curled up on the bed, her anguished sobs half-stifled by the pillow, and her dark hair spread wildly across the covers. He said quietly "I know you won't want me near you. I'll move out into the small bedroom up the stone staircase. Please just give it a little time to see if the pain subsides enough for you to give me another chance."

He retired downstairs, and that night climbed the curved stone stairs to the bedroom at the far end of the house. He was beside himself with grief, and mortified by the pain he had caused Judith. He slept not a wink, and rising early went down to the kitchen to make a pot of tea. Judith was there already sitting by the table. Her eyes were red and the contours of her beautiful face haggard and sad. She turned as Dick came in, and he hesitated.

"Dick, I couldn't sleep. I've spent all night thinking. Come and sit down. We have to talk." He sat down and she continued. "You've been the only man in my life since I met you eleven years ago. You are my husband and the father of my children. Everything I do revolves around you. I could never believe that you would do anything to hurt me, but now I don't understand anything. Do you realise how desperately cruel and thoughtless you've been? Can you begin to understand the horror of knowing you've made another woman pregnant?"

"I'll do anything to make it right. Please believe me Judith, you and the boys are all I care about. I know I've made a terrible mistake. I'm so very sorry, and I'd do anything to turn the clock back. It happened only once, but I know that's no excuse." He pleaded with her. "Please don't walk away. We've done so much together – can't you forgive me just this once?"

"Dick, I can't deny that I still love you, and when I look at you I still see the man I married, but I can't live with the thought of your unfaithfulness. I've turned it over in my mind all night. I'll never forget the good times we've had, and that you've given me two wonderful sons. I do believe that you're truly sorry for what you have done, and I know I insisted you should stay overnight in London, but I can never trust you again. I'd always be afraid you'd stray again in a moment of weakness."

Dick was distraught – the lynch-pin of his life had been removed. Until that moment, he and Judith had been inseparable – perfect partners. His mind was dulled, and he worked on automatic pilot. He had sacrificed all that mattered to him in a moment of weakness. Judith, the mother of his sons, was his life.

Toni had been a casual incident – nothing more – but she was pregnant, and that made it much more. In mid-January he called her to check on her condition.

"Hello Toni, it's Dick. How are you?"

"Oh, Dick, I've been waiting for you to call. I'm not too good I'm afraid."

"What's the problem? Have you had the flu – it's been going around." He paused, before forcing himself to ask "Is the baby OK?"

"Well, that's the difficulty. I've just come out of hospital. I er... I've had an abortion. I couldn't wait any longer – it was getting too near the limit – and I didn't want to ring you at home during Christmas."

Dick's mind now was in a whirl. *She'd had an abortion! She no longer was having his baby.* He wanted to slam the phone down and rush off to find Judith. Maybe she would come back to him.

"Why did you have an abortion?" he asked.

"I was frightened. You're married; I'm 36 and already have three children. I suppose I just panicked."

Dick was in despair. He had lost Judith because Toni was pregnant. Now she was no longer pregnant – she had aborted the baby without discussing it with him. But Judith already knew – if only he had waited one or two more weeks before telling her, it might all have been so different.

Judith stayed for several months, but the situation was impossible. There still was a powerful bond between them, but she could not bring herself to risk again the full commitment they both expected from marriage. The forgiveness that was a natural part of her character, and had been reinforced by the teaching of the church, brushed aside her detestation of adultery – even her beloved husband's adultery – but it could not overwhelm the inner voice of pragmatism that insisted nothing could be built or restored without trust. In the summer she moved back to live temporarily with her parents, and with great sorrow instituted divorce proceedings to remove the temptation posed by Dick's proximity.

They kept the reason for their separation quiet for a long time, but slowly it leaked out and whole area knew about Dick's infidelity with a down-country hussy.

❋ ❋ ❋ ❋ ❋ ❋ ❋ ❋ ❋ ❋ ❋ ❋

Dick and Judith saw each other at the school sports day, and as they walked round together shouting support for Ralph and Simon, Dick said, "I went from being the happiest – and the luckiest – man alive to the most wretched when you left me."

Judith's soft expression hardened a little. "Then why do you carry on seeing that woman?" she asked looking straight ahead.

"When you left Deep Ghyll most of the meaning of my life and happiness went with you. There was nothing left. I was lonely and out of my mind. She kept ringing and saying how much she needed me, and I suppose the loneliness got to me. And then there was the guilt. I blamed myself for getting her pregnant, and therefore for the abortion. God knows, I already was sunk in overwhelming guilt about you and the boys. But when I lost you there was no incentive to do anything, or not do anything. There was an emptiness – a void – and she filled a part of it. But no one can ever take your place."

Judith softened immediately, and her heart tugged. In her own bouts of depression and loneliness, lying awake and tearful at night, she often resolved to go back to Dick, but reversed her decision in the cold light of day. Now she just wanted to throw her arms around him and tell him everything would be alright, but something held her back.

So the marital tragedy dragged on while the wheels of annulment turned inexorably to decree absolute. They were an honest and devoted couple, each with a deep love for the other. A single foolish moment of weakness had driven them apart, and now they could not find the path to bring them back together.

Dick cared nothing for his own interests in the divorce settlement – guilt hung too heavily on him. He wanted only the best for Judith and his sons. That was his priority, although it caused him financial hardship. All the funds raised from the sale of the pedigree Ravock sheep in 1981 had been placed already in the education trust policy. Dick continued as the tenant of Deep Ghyll farm, but the shop in Horsemarket passed into Judith's ownership. They both remained in the local marketing business, whereby the farm would supply the shop with home-grown produce, but they were financially separate.

❋ ❋ ❋ ❋ ❋ ❋ ❋ ❋ ❋ ❋ ❋ ❋ ❋

Dick knew that he must rouse himself from the debilitating stupor that was the sequel to his separation from Judith. The dead weight of sorrow and remorse crushed his will, and shrivelled any positive thoughts that attempted to emerge. He brooded on the tragedy of his situation. At times he reasoned that all hope had not gone until the axe actually severed the marital bond, but he knew it was a vain hope.

Finally he summoned the energy to act. During his time on the Cheldale estate and at Deep Ghyll he had amassed a vast store of knowledge on a wide range of farm and estate business. He had been in demand as a speaker at farming conferences, and his innovations at Deep Ghyll were breaking new ground. He thought maybe he could develop a consultancy service. It would enable him to exercise his mind, and would take him out of the negative influence of his present environment.

Sir Jacob Milner was delighted to receive a call from his former estate manager. Since Dick's departure from Cheldale he had learned the details of Camilla's wantonness, and felt a twinge of guilt that he had allowed a coolness to develop during the later part of Dick's tenure as manager. Sir Jacob still held him in high regard, and was enthusiastically supportive when Dick outlined his plans.

"I can assure you, Dick, that there would be considerable demand for the type of service you describe, especially if it is delivered by you. You say you intend to carry out full costing, but are you sure that your potential clients are capable of the basic record keeping that is necessary?"

"Initially there may be a problem, but it can be part of the consultancy to set up the necessary recording procedures. I think that it will have great appeal when the potential benefits of comparative costings are realised. I can publish the results for each enterprise under code to show how each farm or estate how it measures up against other units. It should be especially useful for newer break crops such as oilseed rape or linseed, or novel crops such as Christmas trees or..."

"Dick, dear chap, you don't need to convince me. Remember I saw you at work for almost ten years. I suggest you come down here and we can discuss the whole business further. I am inclined to be your first client, and I'm sure that several other estates would be interested – especially if I effect an introduction."

Sir Jacob was as good as his word. He introduced new clients to Dick and gave him personal encouragement. Most of the clients were in Lincolnshire and the East Midlands, with estates and farms of mixed livestock and arable. Dick provided advice, objective perspective, and published annual results where the performance and profitability of each enterprise was collated under code in comparative tables which allowed each client to measure his efficiency against those of other clients without loss of confidentiality.

The success of this new venture served to bring Dick back into active participation in agricultural developments, but he would have sacrificed it all if it would have enabled him to restore his life with Judith.

The finalisation of Dick's divorce from Judith in 1983 hit him hard, even though he had sought to shield himself by the intensity of his work on the farm and in consultancy. The depression of despondency returned, but he doggedly maintained his work pattern – although at times it seemed overwhelmingly irrelevant and monotonous – and his consultancy business continued to grow despite his lack of enthusiasm.

Judith remained in Teesdale, and Dick was eager to fulfil his parental duties to Ralph and Simon. Ralph endured the separation of his parents with apparent stoicism, but Simon was more sensitive and vulnerable, and his relationship with Dick more fragile. Judith settled in a new home near her parents, and Dick was the target of heavily sarcastic criticism from Nicholas. He also came under attack from the wider community, for Nicholas was highly respected. Ralph and Annie would never criticise Dick, but even they could not hide their sorrow, and retired further from the public eye.

Judith alone was vociferous in defending him. Her hopes and dreams had disappeared in the dust of Dick's folly, but she could not stand aside and see such reproach heaped on the man she loved.

Toni

Nicola Antonia Griffin, known since childhood as Toni, belonged to a Staffordshire family that affected upper-middle class pretensions. They moved in a nouveau riche elevation, suspended between the upper class, to which they aspired, and the earthy foundation of genuine working people, which they despised, but failed to connect with either. She had married David Griffin but divorced in 1973, when she went back to work in public relations. She claimed to know Dick's brother slightly, and this was a catalyst for her interest in Dick, for Harry had a reputation as a flamboyant and successful Midlands character.

Toni's mother, Margot Hope-Clavell, was a significant influence in her life, a position she cemented by liberal application of emotional blackmail. The carefully timed and unsolicited comment that all her friends seemed to be joining their children for Christmas, or the throw-away comment that she was not sure where she could go for her holidays. Since her husband had died some years earlier, and her son had removed to a safe distance, she had tied her camels firmly to Toni's caravan.

Now she evaluated the current development. Toni had told her of the pregnancy and abortion immediately the latter had been completed in January 1981. She had scolded her daughter for getting rid of the child before she had captured their quarry. She already had weighed the pros and cons of marriage to Dick Bainbridge carefully in the balance. She drew a line down the middle of a sheet of paper, heading the left-hand column 'For' and the right-hand column 'Against'. In left-hand column she listed 'rich farmer', 'rich brother', 'status (in the NFU)', 'personable', 'good-looking'. In the right-hand column she listed 'married before', 'lives in north'. There was no question – Toni must catch this one. She was aware that they could not be too choosy. Toni was not in the flush of youth, and she had three daughters in tow. Not many men would willingly take on such a responsibility.

Margot grimly counted the failures to date – too many had escaped. Toni had discarded her first serious boyfriend, Roger Smith-Blundell. He was an ineffectual fop, but he would have provided automatic entry into the upper echelons of the Conservative elite. Instead, she allowed herself as a young secretary to be impregnated by her licentious employer during the furtive drunkenness of Christmas festivities at the office. Even worse, David Griffin had been married twice before, and had children to support. Then there was the rather rakish David Court – perhaps not entirely acceptable at first sight, but he had a 40 foot yacht on the Mediterranean and she remembered the exotic summer a couple of years previously cruising round the Balearics. Yes, she could accept a life like that! But Toni had never been able to pin him down. Before that had been perhaps the most serious mistake of all – John Tate. What a miss that was! A rich Birmingham businessman who lavished attention on her, was not in good health and old enough for her to expect luxurious widowhood, and she let him fall into the clutches of a common inner-city woman. Why? Because Toni was supplementing the benefits she derived from John's wealth with the physical gratification of a furtive liaison with Garry Beavan, a ne'er-do-well who was devoid of honourable intentions. Margot almost despaired of her daughter.

Her greatest fear was that Dick would escape before he could be secured. A quick register office ceremony was called for – certainly urgency was more important than social niceties. Dick's divorce would not come through until at least mid-1983, and she fretted at the length of time he would have to be played before he could be landed. She ensured that Toni kept in regular contact by ringing Dick to emphasise how much she needed him, and implored her to be discreet in her affairs.

Margot need not have been so concerned. The failure of Dick's second marriage had left him mentally unhinged, with a deficit of rational thought. His twisted logic, tortured by his separation from Judith, considered that marriage would make partial amends to Toni and help to assuage his guilt for her pregnancy and subsequent abortion.

When she married Dick she was only two years short of 40, and she dreaded such a significant landmark. It was yet another factor that had hastened her into remarriage.

Their quiet register office ceremony changed her initials significantly. Nicola Antonia Griffin became Nicola Antonia Bainbridge. Dick's sons had noticed previously the opportunities presented by the initials of the new woman in their father's life. They saw her as the cause of their current unhappiness and the fragmentation of their family, and hated her with a deep and abiding hatred. They missed no opportunity to make reference to a nagging wife or an old horse, and wrote NAG in large black creosoted letters on the wall of the haybarn at Deep Ghyll.

After the marriage, when she became NAB, others joined the game and at least one local farmer at the weekly cattle market was heard to voice his opinion to another about both Toni and Dick..."Thou'll 'a heeard aboot yon trollop ower at Deep Ghyll. Caps all! Dick's a daft lubbart. Aye, she's nabbed 'im a' reet!"

They took their honeymoon in the west of Ireland at Ashford Castle, on the neck of land between Lough Mask and the island-strewn Lough Corrib. The grandeur of the location reassured Toni that she had made a suitable catch, although she would have wished for a more exotic and distant destination. The effect of marital intimacy on Dick was less welcome when they retired to their sumptuous bedroom at the end of the first day. Removal of layers of facial make-up and firm uplifting corsetry revealed the true pallor of Toni's complexion and the total victory of gravity over hope on every vulnerable part of her anatomy. The ravages of her dissolute lifestyle, and birth of three children, were unmistakably evident on both her face and her body. Her licentious youth was catching up with her quickly, and Dick's memories of Judith's natural beauty only served to depress him further.

Toni took little trouble to conceal the truth. She had a wedding ring on her finger, and that had been her sole objective. She almost seemed to flaunt her nakedness in front of him, and Dick could not determine whether she was taunting him or attempting to entice him. If the latter, it was a vain hope. Those female attributes that she might have expected to exert seductive sexual appeal, were repulsive to Dick in the extreme. He retreated to the protection of his pyjamas and climbed into bed. She quickly followed and, with not a hint of shame or modesty, fell on him. He winced as her breasts swung across his face and recoiled as she thrust against him. His struggles to resist served only to inflame her passion further, as she misinterpreted the signals, while he saw only Judith and his betrayal of their union. At last she felt his lack of readiness and perceived the reality of his lack of intent. She pulled back with amazed incredulity as she realised her husband would not gratify her on her wedding night.

"You bastard! Are you a man or a eunuch?" she snarled. "A guy with a two-inch tool could do better – and believe me, I know."

She slapped his face and attempted to knee him in the groin in her frustration and humiliation. Her voice and violence shocked him. He snatched a pillow and his dressing gown, and slept in the chair that would serve as his bed for every night of the honeymoon. She lay in bed filled with fury and resentment. If that was the way it was, OK. If he wouldn't satisfy her, there were others who would.

They both returned to Deep Ghyll in mental turmoil.

Dick was aware that he had failed in his expected conjugal duties and, in a sense, could understand her reaction, but he had seen new aspects of her character that filled him with foreboding. Any emotion or potential tenderness that might have been aroused, now was congealed in a mass of unresponsive despond and inertia. But he was a fair-minded man. A strong sense of justice underlay Dick's philosophy of life, and on reflection he knew that his constant thoughts of Judith were inhibiting any positive thoughts of Toni. He recognised the inherent element of discrimination, and the insecurity it engendered may have accounted for her violent outburst. He would try to be a husband to her.

Toni neither understood nor made any further attempt to discover Dick's feelings. She was resolved to satisfy her sexual urges as a matter of priority. It was of little consequence whether it was her husband, a lover, or a series of lovers, the effect would be the same. Meanwhile, she quickly decided that the farmhouse did not conform to her suburban tastes, and detailed all the changes she required. She declared that the internal décor was positively ghastly, but then Dick's previous wife would have been a local girl with little taste; and that structural changes were necessary to make the house seem more spacious.

Dick put an immediate stop to any discussion along those lines. "The house is just fine as it is. Nothing needs to be changed." Toni might wish with good reason to expunge any evidence of her predecessor, but Dick could not contemplate changing anything that reminded him of Judith.

Toni experienced a similar lack of success with Dick's family. When her daughters visited the farm for the first time, she suggested that Ralph and Simon should come over to meet them. Dick was happy to agree, but failed to anticipate the outcome. His step-daughters' preconceived notion that their step-brothers were country yokels was clearly evident from the first moment of meeting. At the same time, his sons' deep dislike for their step-mother was obvious from their unwillingness to utter more than gruff monosyllabic replies to any question. Initially, the boys were intrigued by the girls, who were a few years older, but their interest soon evaporated. The exercise was an unmitigated disaster, which Toni never attempted to repeat.

Old Ralph and Annie could not hide their sadness at the fragmentation of the family. Judith was like a daughter to them, and she had been supplanted by someone whom they instinctively disliked. Judith was an open, honest woman, always ready to help, attractive both in appearance and personality. Toni camouflaged her real thoughts and feelings from them as carefully as the mask of makeup concealed her face. Ralph was briefly curious about someone from an entirely different walk of life, but Annie immediately saw her superficiality and instinct warned her against her new daughter-in-law.

The dislike was not one-sided. Toni was not comfortable in the north. It was too dull and staid for her. And Teesdale! Well, that was the back of beyond. There were no bright lights, just dull farmers. Her husband still showed only spasmodic and lack-lustre inclination to satisfy her needs. Darlington was the nearest town with any pretensions to sophistication or excitement. Even that was hardly throbbing with life, but nevertheless she began to spend an increasing amount of time in the more fashionable stores, and in hotel bars which more affluent businessmen might frequent for lunch.

Less than four months after his marriage, Dick received a phone call from Judith. "Dick, it's Judith. I'm sorry to sound so conspiratorial, but are you alone?"

"Yes, Toni's gone to Darlington for the day. I don't expect she'll be back until late."

"Well, that's rather what I wanted to talk about. Look, it's none of my business really, and please tell me to keep quiet if you'd rather, but I can't bear to see you hurt." She stopped, not sure how to put it to him, then decided to be direct. "Your wife's been seen in Darlington on two or three occasions with a local businessman who has a fairly unsavoury reputation. Maybe I should have told you earlier, but I had nothing much to go on. Now I know they meet for more than pleasant conversation. There, I've told you. Please don't think it's sour grapes on my part; it's only because I'm thinking of you."

"I can't believe it," replied Dick. He knew that Judith would not spread rumours gratuitously, but maybe she was being over-zealous for him. "Are you sure it's not just local gossips who have their knives into her because she's not from these parts? She does spend a good deal of time in Darlington, but she misses the social life of the Midlands."

"Dick, I won't say any more." Judith felt perhaps that more discretion might have served her better, and was beginning to regret her intervention. "It was done with the best of intentions. Please take care."

Dick mulled over his conversation with Judith. He knew that she still kept a watchful protective eye on him, even though it was more than two years since they parted, but he guessed that she was over-reacting. In the back of his mind he knew that celibacy was not part of Toni's scene – and she seemed to regard anything less than daily gratification as celibacy. He could not bring himself to think about it clearly, but he wondered if the low tenor of their physical relationship might be a partial cause of her problems. He was aware that she was finding it difficult to adapt to life in Teesdale; it was very different to her lifestyle in Staffordshire. She jibbed at the restrictions of rural life, and still was envious of the reports of Harry's exploits which reached her from the Midlands.

A couple of months later, when spring had spread its freshness over the Dale and the first broods of peewit and curlew chicks had hatched, Toni made her next move. "It would be so nice to have a holiday abroad. We only went to Ireland for our honeymoon, and I really think you could have done better than that." She paused to let the words sink in. "I hear that Harry has just had a marvellous holiday in Egypt. Gossip is that he went with a black girl."

"You shouldn't listen to gossip," retorted Dick. He had little affection, and no respect for his brother, but he had no wish to hear Toni voice her opinions on the subject. He remembered bitterly that a conversation about Harry had been the prelude to his downfall at the Farmers Club. He often wondered whether his decision to marry Toni out of a sense of responsibility, with no affection, had been right. "I'm afraid foreign holidays are out of the question. Cash situation is too tight."

Toni's grimace conveyed her thoughts. *That's a dumb excuse, tell me another one; I'm damn sure he's worth a small fortune – just a tight-fisted Yorkshireman.*

Toni was content to work slowly towards her objective. She had established her position at Deep Ghyll, and reinforced her status at every opportunity despite her dislike of the place. She gradually manipulated her husband to accede to her demands. She was like glossy-leaved ivy gradually engulfing a rough-barked oak – its clasping tendrils ever circling the great tree trunk and branches until only the luxuriant ivy remained visible moulded around the shape of the oak.

❋ ❋ ❋ ❋ ❋ ❋ ❋ ❋ ❋ ❋ ❋ ❋

The greatest irritant to Toni's peace of mind was the proximity of Judith and her pervasive influence. Judith was an enigma. It seemed unnatural to Toni that her predecessor appeared so happy to remain in the area where everyone must know that Dick had cheated on her. How could she face the ignominy of such embarrassment – especially when the cause of her fall, and the usurper of her status, was in the saddle with a firm grip on the reins. Why could she not have moved away to another area? And yet, it seemed that everyone had such a high opinion of her. She had been elected to the Teesdale District Council; she was the mainspring of a voluntary group for care of the elderly, and a supporter of art and cultural exhibitions in the Witham Hall. But most galling of all, she was a youthful President of the local Business and Professional Women's Guild on the basis of her role in developing the marketing business at Deep Ghyll, and even continued to market produce from the farm through her shop. It seemed to Toni that Dick's ex-wife almost had iconic status in Teesdale.

Toni was unable to fathom the reality of the situation. She could not reconcile her expectations of her role and status with the opinions of local people. She could not understand that Judith was an integral part of the community in her own right – not as an appendage of Dick. Toni only saw what she wanted to see. She knew that Dick always seemed to be discussing his children with Judith, and deduced that Dick sought to talk with Judith, without considering that he might simply want to maintain close contact with Ralph and Simon. The resentment became a burning obsession. Judith became a figure of hate, and Toni increased the tempo of her extra-marital activities, not only to reinforce her own self-esteem, but also in some illogical way to spite Dick's ex-wife.

These thoughts jostled in her mind as she drove home from a tryst with her lover. It was early summer, and perfect conditions for absorbing the ambience of the countryside, but Toni had not noticed the warmth of the sun or the smell of new-mown hay. She had been semi-naked, committing furtive adultery in a backroom office in Darlington. Her thoughts were wandering to the possibility of new conquests. She already was growing tired of her current beau; it was time she found another who would provide a more luxurious rendezvous.

Dick was just finishing a telephone call when she arrived home.

"Who was that?" she asked.

"Just talking to the Ralph and Simon about school. They start exams next week." Why the hell did he immediately feel defensive!

"I suppose that your ex didn't miss the opportunity to have an intimate chat with you. You seem to spend your time talking to her, and going to school events with her."

"We did have a few words. I need to discuss the boys and make sure they're OK."

"I should have thought they could scarcely lack anything with all the cash you've thrown at them!"

Dick usually sought to maintain an atmosphere of calm when talking to Toni, but she had an unusual ability to irritate him, and occasionally he found himself incited to more forceful expression.

"They lack something much more important to any young child – a family unit with loving parents. I deprived them of that privilege, and I'll do whatever I think necessary to make recompense to them. I feel a deep sense of guilt for the way I treated them and Judith – but I don't suppose you understand the meaning of guilt."

❋ ❋ ❋ ❋ ❋ ❋ ❋ ❋ ❋ ❋ ❋ ❋

Toni's older daughters, Stephanie and Natasha, known as Fanny and Tash, were away at boarding school, and spent most of the holidays with their father. David Griffin looked after them well. A year after Toni married Dick, she broached the question of the education of her youngest daughter, Jeanette. She thought Polam Hall would do nicely.

"Do you think Polam Hall is good enough for Netta?" she asked Dick one evening. "She must go somewhere as good as her sisters."

"Why don't you send her to the same school?" queried Dick. "Then they all could be together."

"Oh no, she's only little, and I'd rather keep her nearer home. I'm sure we can find the funds for her fees, can't we." It was a statement, not a question.

Dick agreed that probably they could afford it, and Toni went off immediately to make contact with the school. She found it easy to take advantage of Dick's easygoing nature and push him into quick decisions. In truth, Dick would agree to her requests, sometimes even against his better judgement, rather than endure a confrontation with her sardonic barbs. Although the marriage had been founded on Dick's guilt and sense of duty and allowed little room for affection, he had tried to love the woman and do things for her, but in the final analysis he knew he could not live his life with the constant anticipation of another outburst. Walking on eggshells was not the best recipe for quality of life for either of them.

His thoughts ran on in this vein for some time, and he wondered if he was being too harsh on her. There must be some saving grace. Had she not shown genuine concern for Netta's education? Netta was a bright young twelve-year-old with a lively disposition. She was small, dark haired and brown eyed. Dick liked her, and mused over her future. She was totally unlike her sisters, who were five or six years older, tall, fair-haired and rather serious – just like their father, thought Dick. He had seen David Griffin only once rather briefly, but had not disliked the look of the man.

As he thought further, he wondered why Toni had not expected David to pay for Netta's education. As his thoughts wandered on, pieces of the jigsaw wouldn't fit together. Netta was short; Toni, David and the two older girls all were tall. Netta had dark hair and brown eyes. David, Fanny and Tash were blonde with blue eyes, while Toni was a redhead with green eyes. Dick's knowledge of genetics was good enough to tell him immediately that was not possible. Netta was not David's daughter. The whole picture was clear to him in an instant.

Dick's sensibilities were affronted. The nightmare of Camilla's revelations in his first marriage came back and overwhelmed him. Judith's warning of Toni's activities in Darlington flashed across his mind. He needed to sort this with Toni without delay.

"Who is Netta's father?" Dick's question hit Toni like a thunderbolt when she returned a couple of hours later.

"What do you mean?" she bridled, "What a stupid question to ask."

"Never mind that. Just give me the answer. I know it's not David Griffin, so who is it?"

He dragged the truth out of her piece by piece. She had given birth to Netta two years after she separated from her husband but before her divorce. She claimed she was the result of a one-night stand with a philanderer called Garry Beavan, although she was not absolutely sure. She pleaded that was the real reason for her abortion – a fear that Dick would abandon her as Garry Beavan had done after she had borne his daughter.

The stormy emotional argument exposed a host of other unwelcome secrets. As Toni revealed the culture of her social group – wife-swapping, one-night stands, cuckolded husbands – it sounded like fantasy to Dick. She attempted to excuse her conduct on the basis that she had simply copied her mother's behaviour.

But the most telling blow was her vicious jibe in the heat of the argument that Dick had not been responsible for her pregnancy five years previously. She had been sleeping around with a couple of other men at that time – the husband of one of her friends, and a virile young yachtsman – and it could have been any of them. She seemed almost boastful of her conquests – cheating on a friend and seducing an employee of a rather bohemian boat-owner, who himself was a former lover.

Dick was stunned to silence. He had lost Judith because of a monstrous and calculated lie by a congenital harlot.

The web of deceit was more than Dick could tolerate. If he had lived in the Midlands he would have known her reputation for deception, and that of her devious mother. He would have known that nobody else would even consider her as a wife!

If nobody but he and Toni had been involved, Dick would have demanded her immediate departure from the house, but why should Netta suffer for the sins of her mother? In the softness of his heart, he paid for Netta to go to Polam Hall, but his marriage to Toni was at an end.

It was unlikely that Dick would ever have been able to comprehend Toni's inner motivation. He had been brought up in a trusting, loving, God-fearing family; she had been schooled by Margot! She had grown up observing her mother's example from her earliest years – that men are there to be used. Margot's blatant consorting with Charlie Kendrick had blighted the life of her mild-mannered husband, and cuckolded him to an early grave. The significance had not impinged consciously on Toni. She was not a typical daddy's girl; she had been raised as a female predator.

In the early summer of 1986, Toni left Deep Ghyll. She gave no indication of her destination, only a note to say that Netta would be with her. Ralph and Simon said very little about it when they saw Dick, but her departure lifted a great weight off their minds, as well as fuelling a good deal of local gossip. Dick heard nothing from her for almost a year, when one morning she reappeared unannounced. Netta was not with her. Dick allowed her to stay – after all, she was still his wife – but did not bother to ask where she had been. He surmised that her bolt-hole, wherever it was, had been blocked for the time being. She offered no explanation, and Dick allowed no intimacy and continued with his life, both on and off the farm, as if she had not been there. She lived as a lodger, and it was obvious to them both that it was a temporary arrangement.

Just before Christmas in 1988 she departed for good, and immediately set in motion the legal wheels to obtain a divorce from Dick. She had spent her time during the two previous years tabulating the value of everything at Deep Ghyll, although Dick had kept his private documents and financial papers well away from her prying eyes. She and her mother expected rich pickings. She claimed half the value of the farm, expected a substantial monthly allowance from Dick, and demanded that he should pay school fees for Netta who had moved to a select school in Hertfordshire in anticipation of the outcome.

Her expectations were rudely shattered. Dick did not own Deep Ghyll. He was only the tenant of his father, and Toni's erratic behaviour had given him enough time to ensure that any assets he did possess were put carefully out of reach. She and her voracious mother left Teesdale empty-handed and with bad grace.

The clinging ivy had been stripped away, and once again the oak tree could spread its branches to the light.

Diversification

The four years from 1984 to 1988 had been Dick Bainbridge's nadir. Marriage to Toni Griffin represented the lowest ebb in his life. It may not have been the time of greatest financial deprivation, or of a debilitating illness, but his spirit was depressed to a point where he often contemplated abandoning the area that had been the home of his ancestors for generations. The uncertainties and lack of confidence that had dogged his boyhood now returned to plague him. He had been duped by a painted woman who had stripped him of his most treasured possession – a loving and devoted family.

His attention also had been distracted from his farming business, and the initiatives built so successfully with Judith began to fail. The contrast between the loving committed partner, who had given all to him, and the disinterest of his present wife was thrust forcibly into his reckoning every day. There was no opportunity to discuss a problem or share a success; Toni gave not the slightest indication of any wish to be involved. The local marketing project and the development of the Ravock sheep started to falter while Dick was hampered by the sense of isolation in his own home, and it was only Judith's insistence which forced him to maintain a supply of farm products to her shop.

A bitterness entered his soul, and he withdrew into himself.

He felt a stigma hanging over him. He imagined all the local people who sympathised with Judith – and that was most of the community – would be at odds with him. The church and chapel goers would disapprove of his repeated breaking of marriage vows, and he knew that the Dales people would be unlikely to forgive him for bringing a loose woman into their midst. Even Judith's continuing friendship, and their joint concern for their sons, could not lift his gloom.

The only saving grace was his growing interest in wildlife. In his melancholy state he would walk through his pastures observing lapwings and hares. He started to think of his wildlife conservation as a mission – a crusade that gave him a focus.

He still carried out his responsibilities with the NFU, with regular regional meetings and spasmodic visits to London, although the latter always roused unwanted memories. At a regional meeting he sat next to a follower of the local Beagles who commented innocently on the number of hares that had been caught that season. Dick said nothing but brooded on the remark. They were killing creatures that he was trying to conserve. Judith would have calmed him down, but in his isolated bitterness he called the secretaries of both the local Hunt and the Beagles to inform that they were banned from hunting over his land. It scarcely mattered to Dick that, although the Hunt country encompassed the whole of Teesdale, they rarely ventured west of Barnard Castle. It was the principle that mattered. His offensive had little impact on the Hunt, except to alienate him from yet another swath of society.

Maybe he had simply been looking for an excuse. He found hunting people offensive and arrogant. He knew that the occupiers of most small and medium-sized farms did not support hunting, but were browbeaten by landlords or Hunt officials into allowing their land to be churned up by the mounts of urban nouveaux riches, and their heavily pregnant ewes scattered by a marauding pack of hounds. If they continued to resist, they could expect their fences and land to be sabotaged by Hunt sympathisers.

He started to spend more time away from Teesdale. The consultancy business, started in the aftermath of his separation from Judith, now provided an avenue for escape from the stifling cloud of disapproval which he perceived in Teesdale. His clients in other areas were not aware of the horror of his private life.

Sir Dudley Fortescue, a baronet of ancient lineage and a long-standing friend of Sir Jacob Milner, was one of Dick's oldest clients. When Dick had taken Toni to the Royal Show in the summer before they were married, Sir Dudley had showered her with compliments, and advised Dick that the Governors' Pavilion would be the appropriate place to entertain such a charming girl. He persuaded Dick to upgrade his membership of the Royal Agricultural Society to Governor status. Toni had revelled in the attention she received from Sir Dudley, and speculated that a baronet would be a definite advance on a Yorkshire farmer. On Dick's consultancy visits, Sir Dudley never failed to enquire about her wellbeing, and upbraided Dick for keeping his wife "hidden away."

At their first meeting after his separation from Toni, Sir Dudley welcomed Dick with his usual greeting, delivered with an endearing stutter. "Dear boy, how nice to see you. I see you've deprived me yet again of the pleasure of delectable female company, but I'll forgive you. Homage to your so beautiful wife."

Dick could not help but smile. He regarded Sir Dudley as a good friend, yet they could not be more different. Sir Dudley was a stickler for correct procedure and protocol, and, despite being married, was as queer as a nine bob note.

"I'm afraid you're unlikely to see her again. She left before Christmas last year, and I haven't seen her since."

Sir Dudley exercised the control that was natural to him. Only the slightest quiver of an eyebrow betrayed his surprise. "Dear boy, you really should be more careful. Once is forgivable, but twice is careless. You're starting to make a profession of it. You've had as many wives as my wife's had husbands!"

Toni's departure in 1988 provided Dick with a window of opportunity for both moral and business regeneration. He had started to rebuild his personal life, but the finality of the decree absolute from Toni brought him to his business senses. Her attempt to strip his assets had made him look at his situation more closely and impressed on him the need to reassess his business. He realised he could not go on as he was. It was essential to get the original elements back on track.

The Ravock sheep had served a major purpose by providing funds to educate the boys at Barney school. A nucleus of the elite breeding stock had been retained and a strong export market maintained, but the sales network in Britain had crumbled. The Deep Ghyll marketing initiative was still in place, although it had not developed as far as anticipated. Dick thanked God that Judith had kept faith with him, although at times his lack of enterprise had almost driven her to find an alternative supplier for the shop. Without her insistent vigour the business probably would have failed. Now he would pull his weight, and used the slogan 'local breeds reared on native grassland' to emphasise the welfare and environmental benefits of his products, and publicised 'Teesdale Taste' to highlight food quality and local production. He drew attention to the contrast with supermarket meat products which accumulated hundreds of 'food miles' as they travelled from producer to processor to packer to distributor, each in a different region of the country.

He had never lost his interest in the peewits. He deliberately did not maintain the drainage in some areas so that the pasture became rougher, occasionally with surface water, and patches of rushes grew. It was ideal habitat for peewits – or lapwings as he had begun to call them. In March or early April each male prepared several nests, or simple scrapes on the ground, and his mate selected her preferred one and lined it with dried grasses. Dick kept a regular but non-intrusive watch on their progress as the clutches of four black-speckled olive-green eggs hatched after an incubation of about 27 days, and marvelled as the chicks were away from the nest in a few hours.

Dick worked on each aspect of his business for the next two years with considerable success, but still felt in a vacuum. He needed advice, or at least a sympathetic ear on which to bounce ideas. He was pioneering new concepts, well ahead of the field in his thinking and progress, and it was difficult to find an 'expert' who could help him. Then he saw an advertisement in the local NFU magazine:

ARM Consultants
Business Management, Diversification, Conservation
call us for a free initial consultation

The address and telephone number were in Swaledale, and he rang.

Susan Alderson came to the farm, and they sat for an exploratory discussion over a cup of tea. Despite her business suit and briefcase, she gave the immediate impression of being a homely woman, and the crisp interrogation of her client belied the evidence of the gentle humour on her face. She was attractive, but in the self-critical manner to which many women are prone, she regarded herself as remarkably plain. While that was an overly negative opinion, it was true that she would not turn heads in the street. Her features were kindly rather than beautiful; her blue eyes steady rather than exciting; her short hair somewhere between honey-blonde and light brown. She had lost the slimness of youth, although probably her figure had always been comfortable rather than willowy.

Dick asked how she had come to establish her business in Swaledale. It seemed an unlikely location for a high-powered consultant, and he needed to be sure of her credentials before they went any further.

"I grew up in Swaledale on the family farm before going to school in Richmond, and then to university at Cambridge," she explained. "I spent seven years in Canada at Guelph University, before coming back to England and joining a firm of management consultants in Wiltshire. We provided supervisory financial management and advice to many large estates in the south of England. I stayed with them for seven years, but when mother died I came home to help father on the farm. I've been there now for six or seven years, and run the Alderson Rural Management consultancy as a one-woman business alongside the farming – it helps to keep my feet on the ground. Today is a free consultation; thereafter it is £400 per day plus expenses."

Dick did a couple of quick calculations in his head. It was more than twenty years since she left university, so she must be over 40. He was impressed by her quiet efficiency – no frills, no nonsense. He felt confident and comfortable with the aura of friendly competence that she exuded. He also calculated the possible fees – say £2,500 for a one-off exercise, or maybe £5,000 plus per annum for an ongoing consultancy. He could cope with that and confirmed that he would like her engage her. She thanked him, and got down to business without delay.

Dick outlined the variety of enterprises he had established at Deep Ghyll. His new breed of Ravock sheep, direct selling of local products from all species, peewit conservation, and spasmodic consultancy. Susan listened with increasing interest. She felt the excitement of finding a real innovator – years ahead of his time – but she kept her thoughts to herself.

"The first step is to calculate the gross margin for each enterprise within the business. Do you use John Nix's Farm Pocketbook? He was a lecturer in agricultural economics at Cambridge. It's a very good guide to standard costs for any enterprise, although you have to allow for local conditions. For the time being we'll ignore fixed costs. They're not likely to be changed significantly by any immediate modifications we make, and we can analyse them at the next stage."

"You'll want to look at the account books for the last few years. I've got them here, as I reckoned you'd need them." Dick was well prepared. "I expect the overheads will be pretty low, so gross margins should give a good guide."

Although Dick used full costing in his own consultancy, he was equally comfortable with the gross margin system, but it was Susan's uncompromising and direct approach to financial management that impressed him. No shilly-shallying. Straight to the point. That's what he liked. She looked quickly through the accounts for the last three years.

"At first glance – and please remember this is just my first impression – it seems that most elements of the business are profitable, although the direct selling clearly is the major contributor. Obviously it is subsidising the wildlife conservation, and your consultancy work appears to be somewhat of a sideline." She paused, and looked at him directly. "But I really don't know why I'm advising you!" she exclaimed. "You are a consultant yourself, advising large estates in various parts of England. Why do you need advice?"

"Well, it seems to me that the client often knows more about the technical problems than the consultant. My clients could tie me in knots if we debated the relative horsepower of various tractors, or the best time to drill winter wheat. I accept what they tell me, but often they can't see the wood for the trees. My value to them is that I can stand back and evaluate the overall situation. I ask them challenging questions; I play devil's advocate. I need to know which questions to ask, and be bright enough to identify possible weaknesses, but essentially I use their technical knowledge to synthesise the most efficient system for their business."

"I'm still not clear why I should be advising you. It should be the other way round. You already have an efficient business, and you've developed new ideas that are miles ahead of anyone else I know in the farming world."

"No," replied Dick, "you've already been a great help. I may be able to help my clients, but I find it difficult to analyse my own business objectively. It grew like Topsy – just dropping one idea on top of another. It's all a bit higgledy-piggledy. You've just analysed it by a quick look at the accounts and suggested an organised framework to think about. It gives me confidence just to have the reassurance of your opinion. I'm sure you'll be able to give me advice so that I can see how to go forward on a more planned basis."

He stopped for a long moment, and then continued rather self-consciously, "The peewit project is important to me. When I stand in the pastures or on the moor and hear their wild calls, there's something almost spiritual about it. Can't explain it properly – probably something to do with growing up as a lad beside the moor and them being an accepted part of life – but I'd keep on with it even if it cost me an arm and a leg."

She softened towards this tough Dalesman, who had suddenly exposed the romantic side of his character. "I'll look forward to working with you, and I'll be interested to compare notes with you on your biodiversity projects. We're trying to re-establish the blackcock on the moorland in Swaledale, and I'm sure we'll find much in common."

A few days later a letter arrived for Dick. It was a brief note from Susan saying simply "I thought you might like this short verse by Ammon Wrigley. Seems to fit your philosophy of life," and a poem was enclosed. Dick read:

Mine is a way that is little trod,
I am bound by no sect or creed;
I say my prayers to Nature's God
In the field where the lapwings breed.

I hear the wind preach, and its Psalms are sung
In praise of the infinite free;
And ne'er a sermon from human tongue
Is half so divine to me.

Dick had never analysed his spirituality and his religion. He had been raised as an unquestioning Primitive Methodist, although parts of his family were Church of England and his sons were baptised C of E, but Susan had fathomed his motivating force, and her poem encapsulated his belief – he could identify with it, and with her. She had restored some of his faith in himself and in his fellow beings.

The conviction that life was worth living was fully restored.

6
TRY AGAIN?

Ex and Intended

The celebrations for his parents' golden wedding in 1989 had been an early step in Dick's rehabilitation. He had organised a memorable occasion for them. Ralph and Annie had lived in Teesdale all their lives – almost 80 years – and their relatives and friends were legion. Dick's greatest problem was to avoid giving offence by leaving anyone off the list of potential guests. More than 150 invitations were sent for a lunch to be held at the Morrit Arms, an old coaching house by Greta Bridge, and acceptance notes came back from almost two-thirds of the invitees. Others were too old to attend, and some were away, but all sent their good wishes, and the local florist was inundated with orders for bouquets and floral tributes.

Dick placed his two sons on either side of their grandparents at the lunch. His elder brother should have given the main speech and toast to Ralph and Annie, but once again Harry was absent. Rather than assume the duty himself, Dick determined that his young teenage sons, Ralph and Simon, should have the star billing. They both were accomplished boys, and their grandparents would be thrilled for them to take centre stage. Dick also was careful to seat Judith in a prominent position. He wanted it to be seen by everybody that she was very much part of the family.

It was six years since their divorce, and she had not yet remarried although she was approaching 40 years of age, and had begun to feel increasingly vulnerable as she approached that critical point. Dick still missed her, and often lay awake at night wondering if there was any chance of being with her again. But in his heart he knew it was a vain hope. Young Ralph and Simon were delighted to have their father and mother under the same roof again, albeit only for this special occasion, and equally delighted that the hateful Toni had gone.

Despite their tender years, Ralph and Simon did not disappoint Dick. Their speeches hit exactly the right note – better than he could have done. They sat beside him on a long settle after the lunch, while guests mingled. "I'm proud of you both, and Grand-da and Grandma are as well. Just carry on the way you are and you'll make grand men." He paused, put an arm round each of them, and continued. "Always do what you think is right, even if others try to persuade you different. You can spend your life building your dreams, and see them all knocked down by one silly mistake."

The boys looked at their father. They did not fully understand the meaning of his words, but they felt the intensity and sadness behind them, and they simultaneously gave him a hug.

Dick's obvious affection for his parents and his sons, and his solicitous care for Judith, did not go unnoticed by the assembled company. Ralph and Annie were held in huge respect in the community, and Dick benefited by association. Nor did they fail to note his self-effacing modesty in letting his sons make the speeches. They once again began to think more kindly of him. The feeling gathered pace as the baseness of Toni's behaviour became more widely understood, but the most telling factor was Judith. She made it clear to everyone that Dick had her absolute respect, and that she was proud to call him her friend. Dick was grateful to her, but her generosity of spirit made him even more desolate when he thought how he treated her and his sons, and despised himself for his treachery towards her.

He cringed with guilt, both physically and mentally, whenever he thought of it.

Dick's rehabilitation in the community was complete, but he continued to keep a low profile in his private life. He remained in regular contact with Judith, and when his divorce from Toni was finalised early in 1991 he tried to summon up courage to ask her to marry him again. He reasoned that she had not re-married, she talked to him regularly and with familiarity – maybe even affection? – and the boys were a continuing bond between them. She even continued to wear the oriental amethyst engagement ring he had given her at the River House in Lympstone, albeit on her right hand. In his heart he still longed for her; in his head he could not be sure of her response.

"Hello Judith." Dick greeted her with a kiss on the cheek. "I see you're wrapped up well." It was a school rugby match against Newcastle RGS. Ralph was captain of the 1st XV and Simon was playing for the Under-16s, and there was a keen easterly blowing.

They met regularly to support their sons, both on the sports field and in other school activities. As they walked round to the other side of the pitch furthest from the school buildings, Dick plucked up his courage.

"It's always good to see you Judith. You're looking fantastic – don't seem to get a day older."

"Don't flatter me Dick," she responded quickly. She immediately sensed the drift of Dick's remark. Her heart leapt despite herself; Dick still touched her emotions. But she also steeled herself; it was madness to harbour any romantic thoughts. "I'm a middle-aged woman, and I don't stand comparison with some of the other attractive young mothers here today."

"Judith, there's not a woman anywhere can hold a candle to you." He was past the point of no return. He could contain himself no longer, and blurted out, "Judith, I still love you. We're both free; won't you please marry me again?"

She turned her head away to hide the tears in her eyes, and her voice was choking. "Dick, don't. Please don't ask me. I might so easily give in to you, but it can't be. There's too much water under the bridge." She collected herself and turned to face him. "You are a lovely man, and I'm so fond of you, but we can't go back. We could never recapture what we had before, and it would go sour in time. Please try to put me out of your mind and find someone else."

She saw tears rolling down his cheeks, and for a moment she relented. She put a hand on his arm, but an inner voice told her that her initial reaction was the right one, and she let it fall again.

"It's been wrong of me to continue meeting you like this. It's been too easy because of the boys, and because I enjoy being with you, but now I can see it has stopped you moving on. Believe me Dick, I will always treasure the time we had together, and the wonderful memories, but there can be no going back."

At last she had drawn a firm and final line under that part of their lives. Now she thought they both were free to enter a new phase.

Almost two years later, Judith and Susan arranged to meet in Darlington. They arrived almost simultaneously at the coffee shop in Bondgate.

"Susan, I was so thrilled when you rang me last night." Judith could not wait to sit down before she started. "Are you really seeing Dick?"

"Oh, Judith, you're even more excited than me," exclaimed Susan. "I had to ring you, not just because you're an old friend, but because you're Dick's ex. I didn't know how you'd take it. But I'm not really sure we're an item at this stage. It's early days, and he's still very tender emotionally."

"I know, the poor dear," replied Judith, "I do wish he could find some happiness, and I'm sure he would with you."

Susan and Judith had known each other well since childhood when they were in the same year at the Convent school in Richmond, but they were different as chalk and cheese. Judith was beautiful by any standard, effervescent and sparky; Susan was quiet and more serious, but with welcoming smile. She had been abroad during the early years of Judith's marriage to Dick, and then in business in Wiltshire on her return to Britain. She had not returned to Swaledale until two or three years after the divorce, and then had started to pick up the threads of her old friendships and begun to piece together the events that had taken place during her absence.

"We haven't really started to date properly yet. We've met mainly on business, but he's gorgeous. So quiet and gentlemanly. I'm quite besotted with him – can you believe that at my age! But I didn't want to get in any deeper until I was absolutely sure you wouldn't mind."

"No, Susan, you need have no worries on that score. I think I was too harsh with Dick. He made a terrible mistake, and I won't deny he broke my heart because he was my whole life, but I never gave him a chance to make amends. I reacted too quickly and burnt my bridges before I'd recovered my senses." She did not mention Dick's subsequent proposal two years previously that they should re-marry. "He deserves someone who'll take care of him in every way, and it would be marvellous if you and he could make a go of it. Mind you, he wasn't so quiet when he was younger – you know he was a champion wrestler."

"Oh, thank you Judith. You've taken a weight off my mind and, yes,

I did know about the wrestling. By the way, isn't it about time you were finding someone yourself? You're far too attractive to be single." She paused with a quizzical look, then continued. "He went through the mill with his last wife. She seems to have been a complete nymphomaniac. Thank goodness his divorce is through."

"His third! Make sure there isn't a fourth!" Judith laughed. "I was talking to Ralph the other day – his father is a lovely man – and he's been very upset by the whole business. He said that Toni was 'a reet donnet'. I assume that's something very bad, but do you know what it means?"

Susan laughed in turn. "It's local dialect. It's the description of an immodest woman – no, more than that, a loose immoral woman, a whore. I think Ralph probably hit that nail on the head."

The two friends parted, one pleased that her ex-husband, for whom she still harboured deep affection, might find some happiness, and the other full of hopeful expectations. Judith had not told Susan that there was a new man in her life, but her priority was to get the boys finished at school without any disturbance. She was 41, plenty of time for a new relationship, and she had to be sure that Dick's lingering influence would not undermine her happiness. Dick's marriage to Susan would help to solve that problem.

Uncomfortable Isolation

Dick's third marriage had burnt his fingers severely. How could he have been such a fool? How could he ever have allowed Toni to separate him from Judith? But he had. The years since separation from Judith had proved what a very special woman she was, while Toni had been an even greater disaster than his first wife. He must have been mad! Here he was at 50 years of age, and three marriages already behind him. His parents must despair of him, and his grandparents would bc turning in their graves. He retired to lick his wounds. Toni had fooled him initially, but she also fooled Sir Dudley Fortescue and others. Dick was sure she soon would inveigle some other poor fool into marriage.

Young Ralph was going to college at Harper Adams in Shropshire to study for a degree in agriculture. Simon was in the midst of his 'A' level course, with the intention of going up to Newcastle University to read economics and accountancy. Old Ralph and Annie were settled comfortably in Barnard Castle. Dick went down to see them regularly and enjoyed his time with them much more since Toni's departure, but his own life had ground to a halt. He now could not fail to appreciate the dangers of marriage, but nor could he deny that he enjoyed female company. He felt utterly bereft without a woman in his life, but was very wary of anything more than casual involvement.

He also felt isolated in the wider community. Although many sympathised with him and respected his right to his opinions, there was no doubt that his opposition to the Hunt had cut him off from part of the rural community. He still attended chapel, albeit with a growing lack of enthusiasm. His marital history placed him in an unusual category that others found difficult to define. He experienced a slightly uncomfortable feeling, and imagined the eyes of those in the pews behind boring into his back as he sat through the services. The woman who came to Deep Ghyll one day each week to maintain some semblance of order and cleanliness achieved a certain status in society as the source of inside information on details of Dick's private life. The members of the congregation attended to their worship with due solemnity, but they did not neglect the opportunity to indulge in a little salacious gossip. He began to seek a seat in a back corner of the chapel, and never was quite sure what other members of the congregation were thinking.

It was in this defensive frame of mind, yet reaching out for an opportunity to reinvigorate his life in the community, that he had engaged ARM consultancy. The initial meeting with Susan Alderson had been very positive, and already they had arranged a further meeting – this time at full consultancy rates – to walk the farm and look at the situation on the ground rather than on paper. Susan declined Dick's offer to drive her around the farm – she needed to feel the earth under her feet – and they donned boots and coats in preparation for a long walk.

"I've been thinking since we last met about other organisations which might be useful. The problem is you've been so far ahead of the field that there are no good reference points." Susan had done her homework. "There's a new charity just been formed that's interested in the sort of integrated systems you've developed over the past twenty years, but I suspect they could learn more from you than vice versa. It's called LEAF – I think that stands for Linking Environment and Farming. And then, of course, there's the Rare Breeds Survival Trust. That was established about the same time as you started here at Deep Ghyll, and it's concerned with conserving our endangered native breeds of livestock."

"It's always the same," replied Dick. "You have a good idea and everybody jumps on the bandwagon. I don't know that LEAF can teach us very much – although it might be useful to keep in contact. I might be interested to have a closer look at rare breeds, but my main concern is local breeds, not necessarily rare. There's no doubt that our Northern Dairy Shorthorn cows and Dales Ponies are getting low in numbers, and maybe we should keep an eye on Teeswater sheep – they have amazing wool, those long lustrous ringlets are something special."

They walked first through the block of old rig and furrow permanent pasture, where Dick pointed out the variety of native grasses and herbs on which the Northern Dairy Shorthorn cattle were grazing; then across to the western side of the farm where the high-performance Ravock sheep were managed more intensively on meadows and pastures of good quality. They reached the river hurrying over its rocky bed and walked down until they arrived at the junction with Deep Ghyll beck. Susan had fired a stream of questions as they strode along, and they had established a lively and amusing rapport.

"It's uphill from here, I'm afraid," laughed Dick, as they turned back up the slope towards their starting point. "You're going to regret not opting for the Land Rover."

"Certainly not, my legs work perfectly well!" retorted Susan sharply. Men could be so patronising, she thought, and walked in silence for a while before continuing. "There's quite a volume of timber beside the stream. Have you thought of harvesting some of the older trees?"

"No, the trees are part of my conservation policy. This part of the farm is rougher land. The trees are allowed to fall and decay to encourage biodiversity. Then as the land rises to the highest pastures, we have the peewits and other birds. Shall we go and see them?"

Susan was aware that her touchy response had taken the laughter out of their chatter. "You mustn't mind my sharp comments," she said. "I'm rather too outspoken and direct sometimes. It's my business face,

I suppose. I'm really quite a pleasant person!"

Dick laughed. "Well, I reckon we all put on a different face for different situations. We have to act appropriately. I probably shouldn't admit to this, but when I was a junior at Barney school I once played Oberon in *A Midsummer Night's Dream*. That was a real act! Can you imagine me as King of the Fairies?"

They both relaxed again, but Susan picked up the reference to the school play. "Are you interested in the theatre? You know that Richmond has the smallest theatre in England? It only seats an audience of two hundred."

"Yes, I do – the Georgian Theatre. I remember it was reopened in the early 1960s, but I'm ashamed to admit I've never been to a performance there. It must be quite an experience. Do you go often?"

"Now and again, but not many people up the Dale have the same cultural tastes, and it isn't much fun going alone."

"Then maybe we could go together." Dick was amazed by his own boldness. It was only his second meeting with Susan, and already he had asked her out.

"That's a lovely idea. Thank you for asking. Let's do it soon."

Their visit to the Georgian Theatre was not just an evening of thespian appreciation. Susan was a cultured woman who enjoyed a wider range of activities than any of Dick's previous wives or female friends, and their discussion ranged over disparate subjects. They also discovered they had many interests in common. They exchanged stories from the times they'd spent in North America, although Dick had been there in 1961 while Susan had not arrived until nine years later – he thought it better not to mention his honeymoon there at that time. There also were many estates and farms in England that they both knew through their consultancy work, although Dick had operated mainly down the eastern side of the country while Susan had been based in Wiltshire.

But the common bond that held them together was a deeply ingrained empathy with the spirituality of the northern Yorkshire Dales.

Susan slotted easily into the Bainbridge family structure. Ralph and Annie felt comfortable with her Dales farming background; Ralph and Simon, now in their late teens, had no difficulty accepting a childhood friend of their mother. When she switched out of her consultancy mode, she was thoughtful and serious, but with an underlying desire to see everyone happy and generous to each other. She was attracted by Dick's strong sense of responsibility and the quiet kindness of his eyes.

Quality in the Pedigree

The village of Bainbridge lies in Wensleydale where the River Bain flows down from Semer Water to join the River Ure, and where the old Roman road projects its linear descent over the High Pasture to the fort adjacent to the village. Dick was proud of the history of his ancestral homeland. The Bainbridge farming family emerged from Wensleydale in the eighteenth century and spread northwards, so that by the early nineteenth century they were found mainly in Teesdale, particularly in Lunedale and around the village of Cotherstone. Dick's mother's maiden name was Metcalfe, and they also were a family from upper Wensleydale, but had remained in their old haunts. It was all part of the anecdotal tapestry his ancestors had woven and Ralph was eager to ensure that Dick's interest and imagination would be stimulated by that part of his inheritance.

Dick understood the necessity of meticulous examination of pedigree and performance when selecting breeding animals for his sheep flocks and cattle herds, and it was natural for him to trace his own ancestry as far as possible. He thought it could stand comparison with most, but when he met Susan, he found another Dales family with an even longer history.

Her earliest recorded ancestor, William Aldouesson, was born in the twelfth century, the son of Aldoue of Bolton, seven miles down the valley from Bainbridge. His son was William Alderson, and the family rapidly accumulated wealth. William's grandson, Henry, married the daughter of Robert de Sadberge, and in the mid-fourteenth century his son, Robert, married Juliana, heiress to substantial lands in Arkengarthdale and Hope. The core of the family remained in Arkengarthdale and upper Swaledale until the early twentieth century, but in the seventeenth and eighteenth centuries had begun to expand further, some spilling over the Stang past Hope into Teesdale, and others through Stonesdale into Stainmore and thence to Spital and Teesdale.

That was a real pedigree.

But Susan had no brothers. She was an only child with no children.

That branch of the Alderson family would come to an end with her. The thought that her genetics would not be passed to future generations caused Dick great mental turmoil. He had spent much of his life conserving superior genetics in his livestock, and here a long and successful line of *Homo Sapiens* was being wasted. Susan laughed at his unexpected reaction to her situation.

"You make me sound like one of your pedigree cows." Her reproof was gentle, and she snuggled closer to him as they sat at Deep Ghyll one evening. "Of course, I would have liked children, but the opportunity never arose. I've enjoyed a good life, and now it's too late to worry about something that's beyond my control."

There were examples in her female line of births in the mid-forties – her grandmother was 43, and her great-grandmother 47, when they last gave birth, and maybe it was possible the potential for persistent fertility had passed down to her through the mitochondrial DNA, but a baby was the last thing on her mind. "You're a funny old thing," she teased him, "Haven't you considered that if I had children I might pass on all my bad points – and there are plenty! I'll take you on a tour of family history, then you can piece it all together."

They chose a fine day in June to explore Susan's pedigree. Driving westwards up the A66 on the course of the old Roman road towards the Stainmore Gap through which the glacier with its load of Shap granite boulders was thrust in the last Ice Age, they came to the last house before crossing the county boundary. It was a large long house, standing at right angles to the road, and with a few wind-blasted trees for protection on the western side.

"Pull onto the verge here while I tell you the story." Susan's dialogue sometimes lapsed unwittingly into her business advisor mode. "Old Spital was an Alderson family home off and on for centuries, but it goes back much further. In the early twelfth century it was a hospital, run by Marrick Abbey and funded by Benedictine nuns. Later it offered shelter to wayfarers, and this benevolence continued until the Reformation. Then it became an inn and in 1797 was occupied by George Alderson, his wife, their son, and a maid, Bella. The animals lived on the ground floor, and the family above. At that time it was a lawless area, inhabited by bandits and other villains, waiting to prey on farmers and traders returning with the proceeds from sales and fairs over west.

"One wet stormy night a traveller knocked on the door late in the evening. It was an old woman, who declined food, drink, conversation and a bed, but sat close to the fire with her hooded cloak pulled close around her. When the family had retired, Bella was uneasy about the visitor and decided to stay up. She pretended to fall asleep on the settle in the corner, and soon the old woman rose to her feet, threw back the hood of her cloak, revealing a man's face and stature. Bella was terrified, but she continued to feign sleep, and the man took a skeleton hand from the folds of his cloak. He placed it on the table, and in the upturned palm lit a candle – it was the Hand of Glory taken from a hanged man, and the candle was fat from a hanged man." Susan paused, lowered her voice for dramatic effect, and continued.

"Then he chanted an incantation:

'Let those who sleep, more deeply sleep;
Let those who wake their vigil keep.
O Hand of Glory shed thy light,
Direct us to our spoil tonight'

"He walked to the outside door, which remember was on the first floor at the top of a flight of stone steps, stepped outside and sent a shrill whistle into the wind. Bella, who had avoided the spell, leapt to her feet, and with a sudden hefty push toppled him off the steps, then slammed and barred the door." Susan paused. "She must have been a brave girl. I'd have been paralyzed with fear. Anyway, to go on. She heard the sound of horses' hooves on the cobbles outside, and ran through to wake the family, but couldn't break their sleep. The gang was trying to break down the door, and she suddenly realised the candle was holding the spell. She tried to blow it out, but the flame wouldn't die. She threw a jug of milk over it and it extinguished. Immediately the family were awake. She told them the situation as quickly as she could. George Alderson fired his gun through a window, and there was a cry below. A voice called that they would leave peacefully if the Hand was returned, but George fired again, and there was a clatter of hooves as the band rode away. The Hand of Glory stayed in the family for many years, and now it's in a museum in Whitby."

"Good Lord," exclaimed Dick, "I didn't know you came from such a violent background! Will the whole itinerary today be as melodramatic?"

They drove on a short distance and passed a sign for Cumbria. “Bureaucratic bungling.” said Dick. “According to the signs we are crossing from Durham, the county of the Prince Bishops, into Cumbria. As far as I’m concerned we’re crossing from the North Riding into Westmorland! Why can’t they leave history alone? It’s...”

“Pull into the lay-by in the Roman camp,” Susan interrupted, “Yes, I agree with you, but here’s another example of modern vandalism. The A66 between here and Bowes is punctuated at regular intervals with examples of Roman remains – forts, fortlets and signal stations, but this is the most important, and the dual-carriageway was driven through the middle of a historic site.” As they sat there, it was easy to imagine the Roman legions. The walls of the camp were still defined clearly two thousand years after it was abandoned, and it was steeped in historic atmosphere. “They also removed Rey Cross – or Roi Cross as it should be known. The cross of the kings was erected by King Edmund of Northumbria in the tenth century to mark his boundary with the British kingdom of Strathclyde; all this lost for the sake of two strips of tarmac!”

As they resumed their journey, they soon came over the summit of the pass, and the road started to descend. They turned left onto a small lane, which after two or three miles emerged on the brow of a hill with the view of Stainmore immediately before them and the Eden Valley beyond with a hazy backdrop of the Lakeland mountains. Dick smiled wryly to himself as he looked out over the glorious vista and his thoughts went back to Grasmere and the missed opportunities of his sporting youth. Then they made another left turn, climbing up again into the high Pennines, and after a few miles came upon a house standing in splendid isolation at a junction of the unfenced roads in that vast expanse of space where the moors of Stonesdale, Arkengarthdale and Sleightholme meet. Its bright whitewashed walls were incongruous in the sober brown landscape.

“Well, here we are,” announced Susan, “Tan Hill, the highest pub in England – 1,732 feet above sea level. More to the point, it always had a reputation for being open 24 hours a day, even when there were strict opening hours. You could see the police coming when they still were miles away, and escape in another direction.”

They entered through the porch and found themselves transported back into another world. The walls were heavy with photographs of bearded Dalesmen from earlier decades proudly holding prize-winning tups from the Tan Hill Show; polished brass hung from the beams and surrounded the fireplace; and a grandfather clock measured time in a space from the past.

"If you look across there," Susan continued when they emerged again into the sunlight, pointing to the south-west, "that hill – Alderson's Seat – was given its name because the Aldersons were the predominant clan in mediaeval upper Swaledale, when the area belonged to Rievaulx Abbey. Some of us still keep the name alive in our native haunts."

They stopped for a picnic a couple of miles past Tan Hill, after the open moorland road climbed up from Mirk Fell Gill to a high point. The empty undulations of Stainmore Forest stretched out before them. The forest was long gone, and now it was heather moor mixed with coarse nardus and molinia grass and white swaying cotton grass in boggy patches. Later in the summer it would be a transformed into a sea of purple as the heather came into flower, and the moor would be alive with the staccato call of grouse alerted by the shooting parties. In spring the plaintive calls of the curlew and peewit, and the drumming of the snipe, would provide background music, but now as Dick and Susan lay and looked over the view, it seemed to be populated only by the local black-faced Swaledale sheep. They ate their sandwiches in therapeutic silence.

"It looks so peaceful," mused Susan, "and we have it all to ourselves. It must have been more active in times gone by. They still hold Tan Hill Show, but the lead mines closed more than a hundred years ago, and the coal mine too. Did you know that coal mined here was an important part of the local economy?"

"You forget I'm a native too," replied Dick, with a smile, "You've dropped into tour guide mode again! But seriously, the more we talk, the more amazed I am by our common interests. I suppose we shouldn't be surprised when you think that our families have followed the same path over the centuries." He paused and looked across at her. "You've travelled widely in the last twenty years, and business has brought you into contact with all sorts of people. It must have been an exciting life; very different from farming life in the Dales. Doesn't it worry you that your horizons have changed? Don't you miss it?"

"No. I came back from down south seven years ago to help Dad on the farm after Mum died, and I continued with my consultancy business. As time went on I realised that I felt less comfortable with business, and more involved at home on the farm. I became choosy about my clients, and the whole emphasis of life changed because I wanted it to."

"Then I must have been very lucky to be one of your chosen clients!"

"Not lucky," she replied softly, "just yourself."

They drove on into Swaledale past names redolent in Alderson history – Thwaite, Keld and Muker – before turning left into Arkengarthdale and up the narrow steep road towards the Stang, then down past Hope on the road to Barnard Castle to rejoin the A66.

"Well, we're back in time for tea," said Susan. "Thank you for a lovely day. Now you know a bit more of my background, you can work out whether it's to your liking!"

"It's not your background that I'm marrying, it's you."

Susan blushed. "Is that a proposal?" She did not wait for an answer. "If so, the answer's 'Yes' and I'm very happy."

She kissed him on the cheek. They would link the two old families of Bainbridge and Alderson and complete a circle of history.

Susan

Susan brought Dick face to face with the marriage vows for the fourth time in his life in February 1994, and this time she determined he would abide by them. She had not pried too deeply into the nature of his previous marriages, but he had understood her need to have some explanation of his rather dubious record. She accepted without any question that his marriage to her old friend Judith had been based on pure and unconditional young love, but the first and third marriages were a mystery to her.

Dick answered all her questions honestly and frankly, and concluded "So you see, I'm not by any means a saint. My first marriage took place because of lack of thought on my part in the weeks ahead, and lack of courage in the church. My third marriage was a disastrous amalgam of guilt and confusion – maybe also pity, though it wasn't deserved, and now I can see I was taken for a fool. I can bring no strong references from my past; you'll have to take me on trust."

Susan was more than happy to take him as he was. She was confident that their mature, solid love would stand the test of time.

The wedding was a quiet ceremony, followed by a small reception. Young Ralph, in his 21st year, was best man, and Susan was given away by her father. Her matron-of-honour was Judith, herself starting to entertain thoughts of remarriage. Only family were invited to the reception, although that included several cousins, aunts and uncles. Harry was not invited. It was reported that he had married for a second time the previous year – to an Irish woman this time – but there had been no word from him, and Dick felt no duty to invite him.

Ever since his contact with Jan Bonsma, Dick had felt an urge to visit South Africa. It was a time of great change with the first fully democratic elections about to take place, and Susan agreed it would be special go there for their honeymoon. They were advised it might be dangerous because of the political situation, but Dick's contacts reassured them and promised them a marvellous time. They flew to Cape Town and explored the vineyards of Stellenbosch and the botanical gardens at Kirstenbosch, before taking the Blue Train to Johannesburg. There they embarked on a circular tour on which they found an ANC rally in the midst of Kwa Zulu in Natal, giraffe and impala in the Mkuze National Park, the obstructiveness of officialdom at the frontier with Swaziland, and finally the beautiful jacaranda avenues of Pretoria, and the delights of the Gerard Moerdyk restaurant.

It was impossible to keep Dick away from farm livestock, and in Swaziland they stayed at the Mkhaya Game Reserve. Dick also had a personal reason for including Swaziland in the itinerary, for it was there that his mother's cousin had been a missionary and had brought back as a present for Annie a wooden stool, carved from one piece of wood, and christened the Idi Amin chair.

Ted Reilly maintained the largest herd of Nguni cattle at Mkhaya, alongside a wildlife conservation park. The Nguni were an endangered native breed, currently enjoying a resurgence of popularity on the strength of their finely-tuned adaptation to the climatic extremes and parasitic problems of southern Africa. Ted was a feisty, no-nonsense conservationist, his weather-beaten face peering out under a battered brown hat that almost matched the colour of his permanently exposed arms and legs. As they sat in the shade of acacia trees on the first evening, sipping gin and tonic and surrounded by the hard-baked brown earth, Ted regaled them with stories of wart hog and zebra, leopard and hyena, ostrich and elephant. His accounts of the enormity of the poaching problem were reinforced by tiered rows of yellowing rhinoceros skulls – 34 in total, each minus its horn – which he had collected from carcases of rare black rhino killed by poachers on his property – and had arranged near his house for maximum effect.

That night, as Dick and Susan lay under mosquito nets in the hut in the park allocated to special guests, they could hear the sounds of wildlife all around them. The thatched hut had no external walls. Four stone pillars supported the roof, and an internal wall separated the bathroom from the living area. When Susan had taken a bath, one side of the bathroom opened directly into the bush. During the night a leopard made a kill only 50 yards from the hut. It was hair-raisingly unforgettable, and they lay thrilled with excitement until the tea boy stood on the open threshhold in the morning and announced his presence by calling "knock, knock."

On their return to Pretoria, they visited the Willem Prinsloo Museum, where old breeds of livestock were kept. Two elderly red Afrikaner trek oxen, with horns as long as a man's arm, were a sharp reminder of nineteenth century Boer history, while the Nooitgedacht (literally translated as 'never thought of') ponies were an example of a modern development within South Africa – almost contemporaneous with Bonsmara cattle. The day at the Museum concluded with the inevitable braai, at which all their friends, old and new, assembled to share an evening with them.

Dick and Susan returned from the veld and the braais to the more serene and cultivated landscape of England and barbeques in the garden. South Africa, especially at such a momentous point in history, had been an uplifting experience, but it also held many valuable lessons. It confirmed the conviction held by Dick and Susan that native adapted livestock were the key to sustainable livestock systems, and it demonstrated that genetic conservation is a universal movement. The evolution of the Nguni and the Bonsmara in South Africa was governed by same principles as those applied to the Northern Dairy Shorthorn and the Swaledale in Teesdale.

Young Ralph had discussed his future plans with Dick, and they had agreed that he should come home the following year when he had completed his agricultural degree course. The fallout from 'Black Wednesday' in September 1992, and the fall in the value of the pound, may have been embarrassing for the Government and the Chancellor, but had given farmers higher prices and higher subsidies, and there was an air of agricultural optimism. Dick was trying to run both Deep Ghyll and the farm in Swaledale. It was proving an onerous workload, and he would be glad to have Ralph alongside him.

Ralph had become engaged to Jennifer Simmons, a dark-haired, brown-eyed girl he had met at college. She came from a prominent Gloucestershire family who farmed on the western edge of the Forest of Dean near Lydney, and they planned to marry in 1996. She was a smiling extrovert, strong in mind and body – more than capable of matching Ralph in force of personality and in intellect, and not afraid to carry her share of responsibility on the farm.

In preparation for the new arrangements, Dick and Susan had built a new house – Ghyll Cottage – in the paddock 50 yards west of Deep Ghyll during 1995, so that Ralph and his new bride were able to move into the farmhouse immediately after their marriage. As soon as they were organised, Jennifer invited her parents-in-law for a small family house-warming party. She also invited Simon, who was in his final year at university, and his girlfriend, Angela Grant.

Dick had already divined Jennifer's ready sense of humour, and sought to draw her closely into the family without delay. "Jennifer, I hear from Ralph that he's a couple of months younger than you. You should know there's a history of toy boys in this family! My father, grandfather, and my grandmother's father, Joseph Alderson, all were younger than their wives."

"Well, I'm all for maintaining tradition," replied Jennifer, smiling at her father-in-law. Then she turned to Susan. "The Alderson name seems to crop up now and then. Ralph tells me it was your maiden name, Susan, so are you the same family?" she asked. "Are you related to Joseph Alderson?"

"More than likely," replied Susan, "but it's a common name up here, and I may be from a different branch. Still, it's good to know that

Alderson blood runs in the Bainbridge veins!"

The blood soon ran through the veins of the next generation. On 24 August 1997, Ralph and Jennifer gave Dick a grandson, Richard, a healthy 3.9 kg of robust lung-power. Dick converted his weight to 8lb 9oz, and wondered why couldn't they be satisfied with the old measures, but he was elated by his new status.

"Maybe you're starting to establish another Bainbridge tradition." Dick laughed as he turned to Jennifer. "You managed to give birth to this grand young fellow on a Sunday. Well, I was born on a Sunday, and so was Ralph – how does that rhyme go? The child that was born on the Sabbath..."

"Yes," replied Jennifer joining in the laughter, "You men seem to have all that sewn up very nicely. I was born on a Saturday – 'work hard for a living' is my lot!"

"Ditto," exclaimed Susan. "That must be why you and I seem to do all the work round here, Jennifer."

Richard interrupted the noisy hilarity with his demands for attention, and Jennifer picked him up and rocked him back to sleep.

There were more celebrations in 1999 when Dick again prepared a party for old Ralph and Annie's diamond wedding, but on a more modest scale than ten years previously. This time it was mainly for family, and everybody was there, except Harry who continued to have other matters on his mind.

There were four blue-eyed Bainbridge generations in direct male line, old Ralph, Dick, young Ralph and Richard, and the flashing cameras ensured that the group were recorded for posterity.

7
SNAKES AND LADDERS

Mass Hysteria

Susan's father retired when she married. He did not enjoy good health, and Dick took over the management of the Swaledale farm on an extensive environmental system. Both Susan and Dick continued with their consultancy work, but agreed that it should be amalgamated under ARM with Susan as the senior partner.

Young Ralph assumed primary responsibility for Deep Ghyll. When Dick had been at college, the total emphasis of his course had been focused on maximum production – Britain still was living in the legacy of the post-War philosophy of self-sufficiency in food. When young Ralph arrived at college 30 years later, he had experienced an entirely different approach. He had been exposed to a wider concept of farming that embraced conservation, biodiversity and quality of products. Ralph's education and the evolution of a radically novel system at Deep Ghyll based on Dick's personal convictions were entirely sympathetic, and they had little difficulty agreeing on policy for the farm.

Their priority was to build on the enterprises that Dick had established, but extend the underlying concept by re-establishing breeding units of native breeds of livestock to exploit the traditional systems already in place. They would keep Northern Dairy Shorthorn cattle and Ravock sheep at Deep Ghyll, and Blue-grey cattle and Swaledale sheep in Swaledale. The low-input systems and high quality premium products, would dovetail neatly into the business of local marketing which Dick and Judith had created in the 1970s. Naturally, there were one or two Dales Ponies in addition to poultry, including geese. They could never understand why anyone would choose to eat turkey once they had tasted goose.

The first cloud on the horizon appeared in mid-March 1996 with an announcement in the House of Commons by the Health Secretary.

Ralph and Dick were sitting in the kitchen at Deep Ghyll after tea, while Susan was outside shutting up the hens and geese safe from the foxes. Ralph put down the 29 March issue of *Farmers Weekly,* open at a report about a disease of cattle called Bovine Spongiform Encephalopathy.

"That announcement to Parliament seems to have caused a bit of a stir. They're saying that BSE in cattle could be dangerous to humans."

"Yes, I've been hearing some disturbing claims," replied Dick thoughtfully. "If they start making links between all the transmissible spongiform encephalopathies – BSE in cattle, scrapie in sheep, CJD in humans – we could be in deep trouble. Some Government scientists are claiming already that CJD in humans can be caused by eating BSE-infected beef – and they'll probably extend that theory to scrapie before too long."

BSE had emerged from intensive systems of dairy production, where cheap feed based on waste animal products was part of the search to maximise profit by paring costs to the minimum. The philosophy was completely alien to the concepts applied at Deep Ghyll and Swaledale, but nevertheless the greatest damage would be suffered in beef herds. The disease was of some concern to livestock owners, but its critical impact was the implications for human health. Dick's prediction proved unnervingly accurate. Governmental agencies did associate BSE with a new variant of human CJD. There were no hard facts, only circumstantial evidence, but it was enough to cause mild mass hysteria among the general public and send the consumption of beef tumbling by 70 per cent in the space of a few months.

Initially, Dick and Ralph did not anticipate that they would be affected to any significant degree, but as the panic spread they began to assess the potential effect on their business. Consumers did not know the provenance of beef bought from supermarkets, and lack of trust inhibited sales. Prices for beef cattle plummeted. Whereas the price in October 1995 before the BSE announcement had been 134.5 pence per kilogram, by 1998 it had fallen to 101.5 pence and by 2001 fell further to 82.7 pence per kilogram. Mainstream lowland beef and sheep farming was in crisis. It had not generated a healthy profit for many years – even in 1995 the profit averaged less than £10,000 per farm. Since 1997 it had been nil, and farmers survived only by plundering their meagre savings.

The policies established at Deep Ghyll during the previous decade, and extended to the farm in Swaledale, now showed their benefits. Products sold under the 'Deep Ghyll' brand were different. Consumers knew the provenance – they trusted it, they appreciated the quality, and they responded to the personal service. While mainstream beef was in decline, demand increased for Deep Ghyll products, and they were able to hold their prices. The value of their beef animals sold to the shop was more than £150 higher than the average market price, and Judith still was able to make a healthy profit at the shop.

It was too good to last. The quango which advised Government insisted that an age limit of 30 months should be imposed on beef animals. This was incompatible with 'grass-fed Deep Ghyll beef' so much in demand by Bainbridge customers. The imposition of this illogical restriction not only undermined the profits of the business, it also denied consumers in Teesdale a product of high quality. But the quango went further and required a programme to control scrapie, which had a further detrimental effect on the business. British agriculture had been driven by politics and greed down the path of intensive production. The warnings had not been heeded by the mainstream industry, and now the bitter harvest was being reaped. Once again, the innocent suffered with the guilty, and Dick and Ralph watched helplessly as the ability to operate their business was systematically and clinically taken out of their hands.

A Council of War

Dick, Susan and young Ralph called a council of war. In general their eclectic business was thriving, and profits had been high. They had moulded the best elements of traditional farming, conservation, diversification and business management into a radical and cohesive framework. They had identified and evaluated the main problems, such as the 30-month age limit on cattle and the restrictions of the scrapie control programme, and their strategy encompassed the solution to these difficulties.

Other problems were more complex. Intervention by Government seemed likely to be an integral part of farming in the twenty-first century, and that complicated forward planning. How could they plan to anticipate the changes ahead when they could not determine the major influencing factors? How could they make a prognosis for the future of their eccentric system of farming when the implications of Common Agricultural Policy reform were not understood even for conventional farming?

They also needed to consider tax implications for a profitable business, and the threat of inheritance tax. Old Ralph had gifted Deep Ghyll to Dick in 1994 when he married Susan, and all tax liability on that front would be removed on the completion of the seven-year period in a few months, but Dick himself was now in his sixtieth year and needed to be making some provision. The Swaledale farm remained in the ownership of Susan's father, and he was not in good health. That posed a difficult problem.

Extra advice was essential, but they agreed that the necessary expertise existed already within the family. Simon had joined his grandfather's accountancy firm when he left university, and the name was changed to Parkin & Bainbridge when he became a partner shortly thereafter. They need look no further.

Simon and his brother were close friends, but very different personalities. Simon had been much more deeply traumatised than Ralph by his parents' divorce, and the deep-seated memories of that time had never left him. He inherited his brown eyes and sensitive nature from his mother, and still lived at home with her in his mid-twenties. He had met Angela, a beautiful, tall, slim girl of youthful innocence, in his last year at university. She was devoted to him, and had moved in with Simon and Judith two years previously, but he could not bring himself to ask her to marry him. He knew he risked losing her, but each time his thoughts turned to marriage the spectres of his mother weeping flashed before him – times when he had entered a room and found her crying quietly, or as he lay in bed hearing her lonely sobs in the night. Old Ralph and Annie understood. They had seen Simon's unhappiness during his vulnerable years, and Annie had gently encouraged him to talk to them. He had not found it easy to forgive his father, but now there was an opportunity to work together

Simon had been tutored by Nicholas with systematic intensity, and was erudite and precisely logical. The whole family, with the exception of old Ralph and Annie and the children, gathered for a meeting. Jennifer and Angela were included. Simon recommended that the ownership of all property should remain in private hands, but that the necessary action should be taken to avoid inheritance tax. All other elements of the business, with the exception of the consultancy, should be incorporated. The exclusion of the consultancy led to heated discussion, as Dick felt that limited liability would be protection against claims for professional negligence. Simon disagreed, and felt that the consultancy should stand alone. His advice was clinically sound, and finally Dick agreed there was merit in separating the two wings of the business.

There was general agreement that a company structure was desirable for other parts of the business, and that the shareholding should extend to the wider family. Limited liability was an obvious advantage, but also it conferred the advantage of total family involvement. That might not be considered an advantage in some families, but Dick welcomed and endorsed a development that encapsulated his concepts of Bainbridge heritage and tradition. Dick would be Chairman and young Ralph would be MD.

Simon had two further proposals, which he presented in tandem. He suggested that Susan should discuss with her father the possibility of including the Swaledale farm in order to prevent possible fragmentation of the business, and he recommended that Judith's shop should be integrated fully in the business. He had taken care to obtain the agreement of both Susan and Judith beforehand, and had found no opposition. He had been determined to bring his mother back into the family circle, although he was aware of the risk of offending Susan. The new company would be the tenant of Dick at Deep Ghyll, of Susan's father in Swaledale, and of Judith at 'Deep Ghyll Farm Produce'.

Their inspiration lost its impetus when the discussion moved to a name for the company. Eventually, the simplicity of Bainbridge Enterprises Ltd was agreed.

Simon laughed. "That's a good acronym – BEL. Did you know that Bel in Babylonian mythology was the god of the earth – seems very appropriate to me!"

They all joined in the laughter. "That's what you get from a university education!" said Dick. "Anyway, it seems a good enough association of ideas for me, although I'd not want to be in that area at present – they say the remains of ancient Babylon went under concrete."

They toasted their agreement with a fresh pot of tea, and as an added bonus for Simon, Dick and Susan asked him to become a partner in the ARM consultancy. Now, maybe with his involvement in all the businesses, which included both his father and mother, he might be able to purge his sadness, and move forward with Angela.

The Public Good

Moorland is a special environment, and the rolling expanse of heather-clad peat bog between Tan Hill and Cauldron Snout has a unique quality. The vast openness of the hills on which the Swaledale breed of sheep first emerged strikes a chord of emotional harmony with those who have been imbued with the essence of its tranquillity. In the early evening Dick and Susan had driven up the valley and through Lunedale to a vantage point at the watershed where they turned and sat in easy silence. They looked back across the virgin landscape towards Grains o' Beck and Wemmergill Hall. In the distance, the tree-crowned landmark of the Bronze Age fort at Kirkcarrion stood guard where the Lune emptied into the Tees and the bustle of human endeavour increased, but peace surrounded Dick and Susan as they absorbed the spiritual quality of nature. A suspicious grouse stood on a grassy hillock 30 yards away, and two inquisitive sheep ambled over in hopeful anticipation, but nothing else moved. The scene evoked memories of Dick's Ellerbeck childhood – an uncluttered space unspoilt by wires or poles or pylons, distant from the roar of traffic, and where the stars at night were bright.

Many times, as he travelled to London, his natural curiosity feeding on the changing landscape as the new high-speed train hurtled to the metropolis, Dick had been astounded by the plethora of pylons, poles and masts and the network of electricity and telephone wires they supported poised as if to slice the earth like a giant cheese. When he stayed in London, he closed the windows to shut out the constant traffic noise, and if he took a short walk at night before retiring, he could see no stars. The constellations were blotted out by urban lighting – he knew that Orion with his three-starred belt was facing the red-eyed bull, and that the Plough would direct him to the North Pole Star, but he could see them only in his mind's eye.

He mused on the negative effects of progress and modern facilities. Even at Deep Ghyll, where the concessions to modernity were minimal, wires stretched across the fields from the road; they had become part of the scenery and almost past unnoticed – but not entirely. He again thought back to Ellerbeck – no phone, no electricity, but an abundance of peace and close communion with nature. Which was the better balance? In his mind there was no doubt. He determined that the unspoilt quality of his native Pennine hills must be preserved – they were a national asset that must not be squandered on the pretext of supposed benefits of advanced civilisation.

"It's a grand sight, Susan," he said quietly. "I could sit up here till dark just looking. It's good for the soul, but you know there aren't many parts of the country where it's like this, and it'll change here if we aren't careful."

"The price of progress," replied Susan, "although I'm not sure progress is the right word. It's changed already. What about the roar of traffic down the A66, the telephone masts for the mobile phone culture? And you can hardly move in town on a busy day."

Dick pondered for a while, then suddenly looked at Susan with a sparkle in his eyes. "What would you say if we were to turn over both farms entirely to conservation; run them as near as we can to the old traditional systems, and try to keep the special character of Dales farming as it used to be 50 years ago. The policy at Deep Ghyll for the past twenty years has kept much of the old system in place, and we've taken the process even further in the last year or two. We're a long way down the road already, and it's much the same in Swaledale. What do you think?"

Dick's earlier quiet reflection had suddenly been transformed into enthusiastic excitement. "Oh, Dick," exclaimed Susan, "you are lovely. You're as excited as a schoolboy when something catches your imagination. I'm entirely in sympathy with you, as long as you don't expect me to go into the hayfield with a pitchfork or get up at five o'clock in the morning to hand-milk cows!"

Some of the old meadows and pastures on the farms had never been cultivated, and their pristine conservation was a priority for Dick and Susan. They profited from the earlier work initiated by Dick and Judith in the 1970s, and other fields were restored to the state of natural Pennine meadows. They were herb-rich with deep-rooting, drought-resistant yarrow and plantain that drew up health-giving minerals. The greedy modern ryegrass gave way to quaking grass and meadow grasses that filled the fields and haybarns with the aphrodisiac aroma of coumarin. One or two fields were devoted to wild flower seed production, and quickly the idealistic vision that Dick and Susan had seen on the moorland drive became a business as the demand for their products grew.

The policy also provided an opportunity to re-establish the niche markets for Deep Ghyll products with the benefit of premium prices. The products for both farms were devoted to the business, and once again there was a happy coincidence of their chosen policies and the growing political opinion throughout Europe that farming must be diversified and more in sympathy with the environment. Other farmers followed their lead, and were contracted to supply quality-assured products for them. In 1998 they formalised the arrangements in a co-operative with the creation of Richmond Diversification Developments and Dick was appointed as the first Chairman.

Richmond Diversification Developments rationalised the farming policy, but both Dick and Susan also had a deep interest in wildlife, and felt they could extend their conservation concept to moorland birds by involving others in their programmes.

❋ ❋ ❋ ❋ ❋ ❋ ❋ ❋ ❋ ❋ ❋ ❋

It was a spring morning, fine and dry and waiting for the sun to show his face above the horizon. Dick and Susan had risen early and were parked above Langdon Beck on the St John's Chapel road. Across the moor was the sight which had drawn them from their bed – an area of open ground known as a lek, the courting arena of black grouse.

"Aren't they magnificent," said Susan. "They're big birds, and those cocks do think they're splendid fellows. Mind you, I have to agree, just look at the purple gloss on those black feathers, and the flashy white bars under their wings."

"It's their vivid red eyebrows that appeal to me," rejoined Dick, "It gives them a permanent air of surprise. And what about those lyre-shaped tails – they're like a troupe of dancing girls from the Moulin Rouge when they display; lifting their skirts and showing a lot of fluffy underwear!"

"Trust you to make such a comparison. I just feel sorry for the dowdy little hens. They have to run the gauntlet of all the inferior specimens to get to their chosen cock."

They watched as the mating ritual continued, each polygamous cock attempting to out-display his rivals and attract the hens to maximise the spread of his genes.

"Yes, female birds are dull in many species – although not humans!" added Dick quickly, as Susan was about to dig her elbow in his ribs. "It's always seemed a very poor arrangement for the dominant cocks to choose to occupy the centre of the lek. Any female who wants a superior mate runs the risk of being caught by an undesirable fellow on her way past."

"I don't think black grouse are blessed with much intelligence," said Susan. "Remember how many used to commit suicide by flying into fences? They just assumed they weren't there, unless they were made painfully obvious by hanging strips of foil from the wire."

Dick and Susan withdrew slowly and quietly in order not to disturb the birds, but they were too engrossed in their mating priorities. It had been an early start, but well worthwhile.

The peewits were much easier to observe. They usually were the first of the waders to return to the moorland in the spring, sometimes in February but more often in March. They also suffered high mortality, but in their case mainly from predation of chicks. Crows, gulls and stoats all took a share, but Dick admired the courage of the parent birds as they dive-bombed marauding crows, oblivious in their protective aggression to the enormous disparity in size. He had a soft spot for peewits, but he also was fascinated by other long-established residents – curlew and snipe, and also by the red-billed oyster-catcher, which had arrived more recently in the early 1970s driven inland by lack of forage on seashore.

Following the positive experience of co-operation on the farming projects, Dick began to involve neighbouring farmers and persuaded them to co-operate in both the black grouse and peewit projects. A group of farmers in Swaledale and Teesdale formed the Ridings Conservation Trust. Five Trustees were appointed, and Dick was elected Chairman. However, the financial situation was not as easy as it had been with Richmond Diversification Developments. There was no saleable product from wildlife to meet the costs, and Dick found it necessary to cultivate the interest of English Nature to generate funds. The

RSPB was beginning to develop the concept of Operation Lapwing, and was perhaps a little miffed to find that a group of farmers had beaten them to the idea and stolen their thunder, but they also agreed to provide support.

❀ ❀ ❀ ❀ ❀ ❀ ❀ ❀ ❀ ❀ ❀ ❀

Dick had been involved from time to time with a few fund-raising projects, and in 1999 he was invited to be Chairman of a Fund-raising Committee established by the local Methodist circuit. An ominous crack had appeared in the north wall of the local chapel, and a survey had revealed the need for major structural strengthening. It was thought an opportune moment to undertake some internal refurbishment of the chapel, and the total cost would be in excess of £85,000. Dick was obviously the man for the job.

He now had a fund of goodwill in the community, partly inherited from the high respect in which Ralph and Annie were held and partly from his own recent record of public service, but he felt that it would be a wise move to involve Lord Liffey. Dick did not regard him as a close friend, but their acquaintance was sufficiently developed for them to be on Christian name terms. Ivor Liffey not only owned the Scargill estate, where he had extensive plantations for the Christmas tree market, but also a foundry business in town. In addition, he was proprietor of the Ridings Journal and the Teesdale Times, and Dick could see many advantages if his support could be realised.

He telephoned Scargill Grange around 10.00am, and a secretary answered his call. "Good morning. I wonder if I could speak to Lord Liffey if it's a convenient time."

The secretary enquired about the nature of his call, and asked him to hold. After a while, she came back on line and advised that she would "put his call through to Lord Liffey."

"Good morning. What can I do for you?"

"Good morning Ivor. I hope you and Lady Liffey are both well."

"Yes, thank you. Now what's the problem?"

Liffey was brusque and direct. He did not wish to waste time on the niceties of social conversation with local people, and was effortlessly condescending. He suspected that Dick Bainbridge wanted something from him, and he wished to keep the exchange as brief as possible, but

Dick Bainbridge was too important a figure in the community for even Liffey to offend.

"I've been invited to be Chairman of a Fund-raising Committee for the local Methodist chapel. I've accepted and I'm very happy to do my bit for the community. They need substantial funds, and I'm sure we need as much help as we can get. You're a major figure in the district and the town, and I hoped that I might be able to count on your support and advice."

Ivor Liffey had no committed interest to the area. It was simply a source of income, and his estate offered an opportunity to invite friends for the grouse-shooting season. As a member of the Church of England – although scarcely a regular attendee – he had no sympathy for Methodism, and he was not sure whether Dick was looking for funds or for his name as a figurehead.

"I really make a point of not getting involved in fund-raising unless I am absolutely confident of the management of the project. Obviously, I know you as Chairman, but who is your Treasurer? I would want to see the financial details and cash flow projections. How much do you estimate the total cost will be?"

Dick bit his lip. He found Liffey's tone offensive and sensed his lack of interest. "It will be in the region of 85 thousand pounds," he said, "but I can see it probably lies outside your sphere of interest. I'm sorry to have troubled you with my problems. Don't concern yourself any further."

Liffey was caught off-guard by the dismissive note in Dick's words – he was not accustomed to responses of that nature. At the same time, £85,000 was a modest sum to him, and he realised that he could deal with the situation and prevent Dick feeling aggrieved. His response was immediate. "No, Dick, that's no problem at all. I'm willing to underwrite the sum of £85,000 to ensure your project can go ahead. I'll make up any shortfall to that figure."

"Thank you Ivor," replied Dick in measured tones, "your generosity is much appreciated. I'll report to the Committee immediately, and the Treasurer will write to you to confirm the arrangement." Dick was not taken in by the change in Liffey's position. He could see through the veneer of supercilious civility that masked layers of self-interest. It mattered not one jot. The chapel had its funds.

Dick's selfless efforts on behalf of the chapel did not pass unnoticed. The good opinion of him was reinforced further when he organised a bonfire party and fireworks display at Deep Ghyll on the eve of the new Millennium for youngsters from the Dale. As the party got under way and flames from the bonfire leapt into the sky, Judith and Susan were in deep conversation.

"It's only right that something should be done," said Judith. "The fund-raising effort for the chapel was fantastic, but what about all the other things he's achieved?"

"Yes, I agree. There's no doubt that the whole community in the Dale has benefited – and I'm sure not many people realise how much he is ahead of his time. His conservation and wildlife projects set new benchmarks and probably embarrassed Government departments into more positive attitudes."

"Wouldn't it be marvellous if we could get him an award in the Honours – you know, the New Year and Queen's Birthday. D'you know how to go about it?"

"No, but I can soon find out," replied Susan with enthusiasm. "What a wonderful idea Judith."

The two friends were set on their mission. Their conspiracy involved careful planning and secrecy. They speculated about OBEs and knighthoods, and Judith teased Susan that she wouldn't want to socialise with the 'common people' when she was Lady Bainbridge. In the months ahead, they contacted all the figures of influence who had worked with Dick to obtain letters of commendation. Sir Jacob Milner and Sir Dudley Fortescue, although both of advanced years and retired from active business, were very pleased to support the application. The President of the NFU, himself an ex-Barney boy, and Lord Gotherington, a noted ornithologist, willingly agreed to add their names to the list. Judith and Susan persuaded Lord Gotherington to act as the main sponsor; they felt his name would carry more weight. The application was duly submitted to the Cabinet Office in the summer of 2000, while Dick remained in blissful ignorance of their intrigue.

Mixed Emotions 2000

Annie reached the milestone of 90 years in 2000, two years before her husband. Invariably someone remarked on their age difference, and old

Ralph in the seniority of 88 years was growing rather tired of toyboy jokes. It was a year ripe for great celebration. It had started with the millennium bonfire and fireworks display at Deep Ghyll, but Annie's 90th birthday on the 19 October was an event of much greater significance for the Bainbridge family. It almost coincided with Simon's 25th on the 10 October, Susan's 50th on the 23 September and Sarah's birth on the 18 September, and they would share in Annie's celebrations. Despite lack of any response to earlier invitations, Dick had written a personal appeal to Harry to attend, but again there had been no reply. The wider Bainbridge family was joined by four of Ralph and Annie's old friends, a few of Susan's family and friends, although her elderly father was too ill to travel, one or two of Jennifer's friends, Nicholas and Evelyn and Judith. All the arrangements had been made by Dick and Susan. Each guest had a souvenir menu – with a photograph of Annie and Ralph on the front and a guest list on the back – and a large cake stood on the table in front of Annie with nine candles.

The party was held upstairs at Beatties. The guests gathered at twelve noon in the front room which looked out at the Market Cross where Annie had sold homemade butter and cheese 70 years ago. Ginger wine was served in the established practice of the Methodist Bainbridge tradition, but with the option of champagne as a concession for the younger guests. At 12.30 Dick announced that lunch was ready in the big room at the back of the building overlooking the castle ruins. Lunch had been set out on a long table, with thirteen seats down each side, with two at each end. Annie had pride of place in the centre of one side, flanked by Ralph and the others of her generation. Great-grandson Richard was opposite Annie, with his parents and Simon and Angela near him. Dick and Susan were on the end furthest from the entrance, and Judith was facing them next to one of Jennifer's friends at the other end.

Judith couldn't quite explain her emotions. She felt a little put-out; she was such a caring, understanding person, that it was an unusual feeling for her. Was it that Susan was now at the focal point of the family – organising Annie's party? She felt at a loss and somehow superfluous. Was it because she remained unmarried, when Susan and Dick were obviously so close? Every time she saw Dick in an intimate moment with Susan, there was an unmistakable pang of regret. She tried to fight it, but she knew it was there. Now it hit her harder.

She had looked in the mirror that morning as she prepared for the party – not the small mirror on the wall, but the long mirror in the wardrobe door. She stood and looked at herself full length and naked. Her black hair was shorter than formerly, but still thick and lustrous, her eyes still held their brown intensity. But she saw only a turkey neck, crows feet, sagging breasts, and pounds of sugar hips. She grimaced at the signs of age on her knees and elbows. It was of no consequence that others regarded her as a beautiful woman, with smiling eyes and waving hair, with an amazing figure and shapely legs. She felt alone and neglected. She was 49, and the prospect of the big 5-0 next June filled her with alarm – even fear – that she was alone. She had forgotten what it was like to be cuddled in bed. Her mind went back to that night in March 1973 – the night Ralph was conceived – and Dick's words "you're the most cuddlesome girl I know." She had never forgotten that night. How she wanted Dick – how she wished she had not let him go!

As lunch drew to a close and the speeches were about to begin, she felt tears welling up, excused herself, and went outside quickly to conceal her emotions from the other guests.

Jennifer and Angela missed Judith. She seemed to have disappeared from the party, and they went to look for her. They discovered her in the front room gazing out into the street. They saw she had been crying, but she brushed their concerns aside. She knew they were not totally happy, as both had confided their problems to her, and she would not burden them with her troubles. Jennifer was suffering a bout of post-natal depression, and Angela was in a state of uncertainty, wondering if Simon's intentions were serious, as they had been going out for more than four years but he had shown no signs of wanting to make her his wife. Neither of them had seen Judith upset before. Usually she was so much in control and, despite their own unhappiness, they insisted she tell them what was the matter.

She knew that she would not be able to contain her emotions once she had started to talk, but she began nevertheless. She had to talk to someone. "I'm old and alone," she began hesitantly. Jennifer and Angela rushed to reassure her that she was both attractive and loved, but she pressed on.

"I hear what you say, and I know that I have you, but it's how I feel.

I'm nearly 50, and there isn't a man in my life." She paused, and dabbed a tear from her cheek. "I miss Dick. I miss him so much. I almost married again about five years ago to a very nice man – you probably don't remember – but in the end I couldn't because I hadn't managed to leave Dick behind. I threw myself into all sorts of activities to try and forget him, but he was always in the back of my mind. After we separated he wanted us to try again, and even asked me to marry him again after that terrible Toni woman left, but I refused. My silly, silly logic got in the way; I thought I was being strong – my stupid principles! And so I lost him. He was the love of my life."

She stopped and tears poured down her face. Jennifer hugged her, and Angela held her hand. "If I've learned anything it is that perfection isn't realistic. Everyone makes mistakes, and it's not wrong to make some compromise of priorities and principles to forgive them. Don't risk finishing up like me. Don't lose something precious because of stubbornness. No matter how awful it may seem at the time, never let a good man go!"

They were lost for words. They had not had the slightest suspicion that Judith still held such powerful feelings for Dick. But they both heard her final advice, and understood the relative triviality of their own problems.

"Go back into the party, my dears," said Judith, still tearful, "everyone will wonder where you are. I just need a little more time by myself."

Jennifer and Angela left her reluctantly, and went back to the jollifications. Dick was holding centre stage with a moving eulogy to Annie. He looked a man comfortable in his skin, a man at peace with himself. He felt no inhibitions in expressing forthright opinions, or taking unpopular action – a man in control. The impression he gave was true to a large extent, but not totally. He had come to terms with some of his deeper problems. Harry's lingering effect rarely troubled him. Even his guilt for the hurt to Judith and his sons was mostly contained, although there remained a deep pain festering inside him whenever he allowed himself to dwell on that episode of his life. He deliberately kept it firmly battened down, otherwise he knew the mental anguish could destroy him. Jennifer and Angela saw only his confident exterior, and thought of the weeping woman outside.

They also saw Susan organising the large bouquet which young

Richard would present to his great-grandmother. As Dick's wife, she looked so calm and untroubled, filling the shoes that Judith could have been wearing. But even Susan harboured hidden sorrow, and it was sharpened by the presence of baby Sarah – Dick's grand-daughter. As she quietly and efficiently orchestrated the proceedings, her thoughts grappled with her regrets. *Why had she not tried to give Dick another son – it would have been a son – obviously he was a 'tup-getter', as the old Dales farmers described androgenous men. Then they really would have blended the Bainbridge and Alderson blood, and she would have had her place in the family tree.*

Beneath her calm exterior, Susan was highly aware of her own mortality. The illness which prevented her father attending Annie's celebration, forcibly reminded her that her mother had died in her late fifties. She feared that she would not make old bones. She looked at Annie, revelling in the party atmosphere on her ninetieth birthday; and Ralph, perhaps a little frail and with silver-white hair, but still mentally active in his late eighties. Judith's parents, Nicholas and Evelyn, also were at the party – the former rather gaunt and serious, and the latter a little forgetful, but both in good health. Longevity genes seemed well assured for both Dick and Judith, and Susan had a sudden brief premonition of them together after she had gone.

Repeat Prescription

Dick and Ralph were philosophical about the vicissitudes of agriculture. They considered they were fortunate to have survived the BSE crisis without critical damage to their business, and they were confident that they could deal with the problems posed by scrapie. The Ravock sheep had a high level of scrapie-resistance and presented no problem. The genetic makeup of the Swaledales rendered them more susceptible, but the foresight of the Breed Society had prompted a long-standing programme of selection more than twenty years previously, and the breed had sufficient strength in numbers to overcome the threat. The greatest concern was caused once again by the over-reaction of the Government, which seemed incapable of applying remedies proportionate to the risks. The caucus of Government continued to give the impression that it neither placed any value or significance on the interests of farmers, nor set store by agriculture in Britain.

Those perceptions were tested to the extreme in 2001. From February to September a massive foot-and-mouth disease epidemic raged across Britain. No one could be sure of its origin. Apparently, it began in Northumberland, sweeping across to Cumbria, down to south-west England in one vast leap, before surging back northwards to Durham and Yorkshire. More than ten million farm animals were slaughtered, not because they had caught the disease, but mostly because the mathematical model commissioned by an incompetent Government suggested that they might catch it.

The rampage of the disease brought it in the summer to Middleton-in-Teesdale and to the Eden valley above Kirkby Stephen – a pincer movement, with both jaws desperately close to the Bainbridge properties, and they waited for the inevitable.

The last case was reported on the last day of September, and gradually both Dick and young Ralph began to breath more easily – had they been spared? Maybe, once again they had escaped the worst effects of a national farming tragedy.

If Dick and Ralph were grateful that the disease had not delivered the *coup de grace* to their animals, they now discovered that the cure could be worse than the disease. The Bainbridge flocks and herds had escaped the slaughter, although it came alarmingly close, but the control measures decreed that the farms should be closed, permitting neither ingress or egress of animals. The closure of the farms under the notorious Form D movement restrictions meant that they must continue to feed their livestock, and manage the farms, but could derive no income from livestock sales. Nor could they supply the customers of either their local marketing business or their consultancy service.

Dick was reading the *Sunday Telegraph*, and perused an article on the foot-and-mouth epidemic. He noted one paragraph in particular:

> 'The government has imposed a series of animal-movement restrictions which are paralysing the industry. At this time of year hill farmers have to sell their current crop of lambs and calves because, once the first frosts have felled the grass, there is nothing for them to eat. This year, hundreds of thousands of healthy animals, including both valuable breeding stock and much of next year's prime stock (e.g. meat supplies) will have to be killed and thrown away, at vast expense, because the

> Department of Environment, Food and Rural Affairs refuses to introduce logic and common sense into its rules.'

"This chap Christopher Booker has hit the nail on the head," he announced to no one in particular, and everyone in general. "It's a pity that our cynical vote-grabbing Prime Minister doesn't take more notice of those who know what's going on, and pay less attention to his spin doctors or scientists and mathematicians that never set foot outside a city office."

During the next desperate months their funds drained away. They calculated they could ride out the storm if the restrictions were short-term, but in the end they remained in force through most of the year. They suffered substantial financial loss, and simple survival became a priority. Each month Ralph sifted through the accounts and prioritised them for payment. The debit column in the cash book grew steadily longer, while the credit column was empty. Cattle and sheep that should have gone for sale, grew bigger and thinner in the fields and barns as they devoured the dwindling resources. Cattle passed the critical age limit imposed under the BSE controls, but could not be moved because the rendering plants were overflowing with 300,000 animals awaiting destruction under the mandatory slaughter regulations, and the Government's forlorn plan to kill two million lambs on welfare grounds would leave thousands of farmers bankrupt. It was an object lesson in a tragedy of human misery and animal cruelty.

❋ ❋ ❋ ❋ ❋ ❋ ❋ ❋ ❋ ❋ ❋ ❋

Dick and Susan had been unable to conduct their normal consultancy business while the FMD epidemic raged, and in any case the growing crisis at Deep Ghyll was sufficient to demand all their attention. As the full horror of the national situation unfolded, Dick realised that the severity of their suffering, great as it was, did not compare with the enormity of the damage being inflicted on many other farmers. He determined, despite his own distress, that he would devote time to help others and provide them with support and advice. He let it be known through all the networks and media available that he was available at any time to give assistance.

He could not have anticipated the response. The telephone at Deep

Ghyll rang with depressing frequency from early in the morning to eleven o'clock at night, and occasionally during the night. Dick advised on the rights of livestock owners, he referred urgent cases to specialist solicitors in Bristol and Exeter, he prepared valuations of condemned animals, he provided expert witness in arbitrations, but mostly he simply gave comfort by lending a sympathetic and understanding ear. The sound of strong stolid farmers weeping unashamedly, or women pleading for help, tore at his heartstrings. He could recount the harrowing experience of Wendy Shore, a defenceless lady farmer living on her own, who had been handed a notice by a MAFF official at her front door to inform that her animals would be culled and, when inquiring when it was intended to carry out the cull, was told that they were already being shot in the fields behind the farm buildings.

During a period of three months Dick took more than one thousand calls, and he could not rid his mind of the desperation of the callers. One was burned in his memory. The call came at 10.30 in the evening.

"Mr Bainbridge, my name's Peter Williams and I've been advised to call you." The well-spoken voice was hesitant and hoarse.

"Hello, Peter. What's the problem? How can I help?"

"They're coming to kill my cattle tomorrow – they won't listen to anything I say. I've spent my life building up this herd – it's all I have – and now..." He stopped, and Dick heard the sobbing break in his voice. "Now – now they're going to do it."

"Peter, I'm so very sorry. I understand what you're going through, and I'll do anything I can to help. Can you tell me who came to see you and what they said?"

There was no answer for a while. Dick waited, and he knew that Peter Williams was in tears. "Take your time," he said. "I've got all the time you need."

Eventually he learned the whole story. Peter Williams' herd did not have FMD but nevertheless had been condemned under the 'contiguous premises' regulations. It was a herd of special pedigree animals handed down by his father, and they were like his family to him. He had put strict procedures in place to protect against infection as soon as the epidemic began, but these had been brushed aside by the Government veterinarians. He had been subjected to threats and ominous warnings of the consequences of non-compliance, and had capitulated in the face of bureaucratic bludgeons – a farmer in isolation faced by a battery of officialdom. He had been forced to accept Ministry valuations, and he was on the verge of zero hour for the slaughter of his beloved cattle.

Peter Williams broke down several times while he recounted incoherently the horrors of the previous 24 hours, and Dick gently eased him through to the end.

"Peter, please listen carefully, because I don't think yours is a lost cause. First, lock your gates, put some barricades across your entrance, and don't admit anyone. Second, I will call the solicitor in Exeter now – I have her hotline at any hour, and she will put in an injunction first thing in the morning. Third, use your mobile phone, because I will give the solicitor your landline number and you need to keep it free for her. Are you sure you've got that?"

"Yes, yes. How can I thank you, Mr Bainbridge? I've been stranded at my farm with no one to turn to, and you've given me hope. Thank you, thank you."

"I'll be praying for you, and God willing it will turn out right."

Next evening the phone rang for the twenty-second time that day. Dick answered.

"Mr Bainbridge," The voice on the other end was empty, devoid of any expression or emotion. "They came today and shot them all. One by one. The cows and calves calling for each other, and they shot them. They chased them round the field and shot them and left them lying in the field – dead. There's nothing left; I might as well shoot myself."

Dick had no time to dwell on the financial loss suffered by Peter Williams, or the remorse that he had failed him. It was too late for the cattle, but now he had to get help for Peter Williams himself without any delay.

Peter Williams survived, but he was a broken man and gave up his farm. The nightmare of his tragedy and the injustice of authoritarian decree broke Dick's sleep for many weeks as the epidemic steamrollered to its conclusion.

C*alling their Bluff*

Dick and Ralph were sitting in the kitchen finishing their mugs of tea. Susan and Jennifer had gone outside to shut up the hens and geese for the night. A fierce wind was rushing down the Dale heralding a turn in the weather.

"This situation is beyond any reason," exclaimed Ralph, throwing a tax reminder on the table. "How can we be expected to pay tax when we've no income? By my calculations we'll exceed our overdraft limit in about two working weeks. None of the Directors have drawn any salary since April, and we've been surviving only by drawing on private investments."

"I suppose we're luckier than some," replied Dick. "There are plenty of farmers – especially those with only small businesses – who have no investments. Many of them have gone to the wall already. We'll just have to tighten our belts. The problem is that even when the restrictions are lifted and we're free to trade again, it'll be like starting from scratch. We'll have to re-build our client base, and hope our customers still have confidence in Deep Ghyll products."

"You know, Dad, it's the injustice that riles me as much as anything. We were running a very efficient business, we were conserving the countryside, our animals didn't have foot-and-mouth – we were innocent on all counts. Yet we find ourselves paying for the sins of the guilty – only in this case, the Government is the guilty party."

"It's hard to figure out sometimes," agreed Dick. "In black moments I sometimes almost wish we'd caught the disease; then at least we'd have been eligible for compensation. But then I think of Peter Williams, and that helps to put things in perspective. As it is, we're suffering a desperate financial penalty, and won't receive a penny of compensation. Blasted Government!"

Ralph and Dick finished tea, put on their boots and caps, and were just leaving the house when the telephone rang. Ralph pulled off his boots, cursing under his breath – Dick did not like too much cursing – and ran to lift the receiver before it stopped ringing.

"Hello, Deep Ghyll farm."

"Ah, hello Mr Bainbridge. Pleased to have caught you. It's James Thomson from the bank. Do you have a moment?"

Ralph sensed crisis. He signalled to Dick who closed the door and came back into the house. "Well, we were just on our way out, but I've got a minute or two."

"You've advised us previously that you avoid coming into town while foot-and-mouth disease remains a problem, and therefore I thought it prudent to give you a call. You may be aware that borrowing on your company account is very close to its limit, and we wish to know what steps you are taking to contain it."

Ralph took a deep breath, smothered the sharp report that sprang to his lips, and replied in measured tones. "I'm sure you're aware that we aren't in a position to take any steps at present. We are locked in by Government restrictions."

"I understand your problem," said Mr Thomson primly, "but there are standard procedures which dictate the appropriate action. The current overdraft limit for Bainbridge Enterprises Ltd was agreed on the basis of normal trading. It's clear that you are unlikely to achieve normal trading for some time. In those circumstances you will need to provide extra collateral to cover the anticipated increased borrowing. May I suggest that you consider personal guarantees?"

"I'm disappointed that our bank – and we've been with you for four generations – should take such a hard and unreasonable attitude. We would have expected some sympathetic understanding from a rural branch in a time of farming crisis."

"I'm afraid the matter is out of my hands – I really don't have any flexibility. May I repeat my suggestion regarding personal guarantees?"

"Perhaps you'd like to have the livestock as collateral. It would save us the cost of feeding them." Ralph's voice took a sharp edge, and Dick held up his hand to calm him down. "The assets of BEL are almost totally livestock – we have no other assets to offer, and we certainly have no intention of binding ourselves to personal security. Why do you think we have limited liability?"

"I regret that you find it necessary to take that tone." Mr Thomson voice became even more nasal and clipped. "I'm sure you appreciate that my next step will be to call in your loan. Perhaps you would care to consider your options, and I'll call you again in two or three days."

Ralph put down the receiver, and looked at Dick. "Well, you heard that little exchange. I suspect they'll try to close us down, but they won't get far. They wouldn't risk taking on the tenancies, would they?"

At that moment the door opened, and the wind blew in as Susan and Jennifer sought the sanctuary of the house, relieved that they finally had persuaded the unruly and unco-operative hens that it was warmer and safer in their hut. They immediately saw something was wrong, and when Ralph explained, they all sat down with another pot of tea.

Ralph was fuming with anger and frustration, and Dick was volubly uncomplimentary of all officialdom. It was left to Susan and Jennifer to calm down their troubled menfolk, and bring the discussion back to a rational consideration of action.

"If the rumours are right, and the movement restrictions will not be lifted until next year, then we can calculate the likely cost." Susan reverted to her pragmatic consultancy mode, and made some scribbled notes. "On the other side we now can calculate the possible income from the cull – say ten pounds per lamb and £350 per beast. From a current starting point of nil funds, we might expect income from the cull, when the Government allows us to move any animals, to be no more than say five per cent of our normal income from both farms and the shop. On the other side, basic costs in the next six months – rents, wages, rates, tax, overheads, etc – will continue as usual plus, of course, the living costs for two families totalling maybe 50 thousand pounds.' She passed her calculations to Dick and Ralph.

"So, if you're right – and I can't disagree with your figures," replied Dick, "we will have a shortfall of more than 70 thousand pounds in the next six months, in addition to our current borrowing of twenty thousand. That doesn't include our living expenses – we'll have to raid savings for those."

"Thank goodness Simon got the company up and running. At least we have limited liability." Jennifer's equilibrium had not been disturbed. "I propose that we give the bank the bald facts, and request a re-negotiation of the overdraft facility to give us an 80,000 facility through next year. If they don't like it, then they must present a better option. They can declare us bankrupt, but it won't do them much good, either in recovering funds or in their reputation in the Dale."

The bank did not accept their proposal. They demanded that the borrowing should be reduced by £,3000 per month and eliminated in the seventh month. If the company failed to meet that requirement, full and immediate repayment of the loan would be demanded. The outcome for the Bainbridge family could only be the collapse and winding up of their total farming business. They still would have the property, and the consultancy business when it could begin to operate again, but they saw generations of family endeavour being stuffed down the gullet of an insatiable finance house by the reckless actions of a feckless Government.

It was the end of the road. They had given it their best shot and failed.

✽ ✽ ✽ ✽ ✽ ✽ ✽ ✽ ✽ ✽ ✽ ✽

Simon was about the close the office. It was fine sunny day, and he thought perhaps he would take Angela for a drive onto the Yorkshire Moors. Business for 'Parkin & Bainbridge' was good, although it was not easy to feel positive when the tragedy of the foot-and-mouth epidemic left such a sour taste in his mouth. As he tidied his papers, the telephone rang.

"Hello Simon." It was Ralph's voice – not his usual strong, devil-may-care voice, but rather with a weary, care-worn note. "Glad I caught you. Thought I should bring you up to scratch on recent developments, especially as you're Company Secretary. Fact is, the bank's going to call in its loan and we're going belly up in the water."

He described the situation in detail, while Simon listened carefully without interruption. When he had finished, Simon thought for a moment before he replied.

"They're bluffing – or maybe not bluffing, they just haven't thought through the consequences of their demand. Whatever, call their bluff. As things stand, the assets of the company are worthless. If they carry out their threat, they'll get nothing except a very angry ex-customer and a bad reputation. If they help us to ride out the storm, they could have a grateful and profitable business remaining on their books. In any case, they will have to refer the decision to the regional office before any action is taken, and my guess is that when a more senior executive gets sight of it someone's head will roll for putting them in an untenable position."

Ralph took Simon's advice. He made no attempt to meet the borrowing restrictions. The overdraft increased, and the bank sent periodic warning letters, each creating less impact than its predecessor. Finally, early the following year, restrictions were lifted and the prospect of a return to normality began to be perceived. Letters from the bank ceased to arrive, and Ralph was invited to discuss the company's requirements for the year ahead. Bainbridge Enterprises Ltd had survived.

Dick ruminated over the previous few months. It had been a precarious and nerve-wracking time, but it had not been without value. He nodded to himself with quiet satisfaction at the united family effort. Susan's sound grasp of essential details, Simon's valuable advice, and Jennifer – she had been a real revelation – calm, resolute and clear-thinking. Ralph had made an inspired choice when he took her as his wife.

As they emerged from the crisis, financially battered and emotionally bruised, Dick and Ralph were appalled by the tragedies of BSE and FMD. They attempted to learn from their experiences, and they invariably reached one over-riding conclusion. If political incompetence was ignored for the time being, most of the problems facing British agriculture and food could be laid at the door of intensive farming. It was easy to draw that conclusion from the arable monoculture of eastern England, where the earth was no more than a sterile base for the transfer of fertiliser and chemicals to plants, but it applied also to livestock enterprises. Animals had been systematically detached from their natural behaviour and environs, forced to ever higher levels of performance by unnatural high-energy feed and antibiotics, and crammed densely into the minimum space possible.

That philosophy of farming was alien to Dick. He saw the value of natural systems. He wanted quality of life for farmers and animals, and that demanded non-intensive agriculture. Old native breeds had been reintroduced when Ralph came home. They produced less than the mainstream modern breeds, but they were healthier, more efficient, and enjoyed a good quality of life. They were adapted to an outdoor environment.

Now Dick reasoned it was time to rediscover alternative health therapies. He unearthed the old homeopathic books, and researched current practice. He discovered that many of George Bainbridge's medicines had been accepted and applied in modern veterinary practice, but it had taken the acute dangers of bacterial resistance to antibiotics to bring both the agricultural and medical industries to their senses, and make them realise that there was a place for traditional remedies. Maybe one positive outcome of the disease epidemics of the last ten years would be a genuine evaluation of homeopathic medicine. His grandfather would have been proud to know that he was determined to keep the family heritage alive.

During the three years after the FMD crisis, Bainbridge Enterprises Ltd restored the various segments of its business. The recovery was built on the basis of total family commitment and endeavour. The younger members of the family came to terms with the experience and psychologically moved on, but Dick was never the same. His selfless support for those in need during the crisis left him mentally scarred. He could not erase the memories of the fear of vulnerable women and of strong men weeping in the face of bureaucratic bullying. A hardness and cynicism had entered his soul, and a deep distrust of all the trappings of Government and officialdom.

Dick's personality had always embraced powerful sentiments of egalitarianism. He admired those who progressed through their own endeavours, and respected both ambition and success, but he believed powerfully that everyone should have the same chance to achieve success. If he had been asked the question, he would admitted this quality with fervour, but almost surreptitiously a different motivation had begun to drive his philosophy. He had learned hard lessons at various times in his life; the innocence of his youth was buried by the corruption of sophistication to which he had been subjected.

The folly of his initial natural trust of his fellow human beings had been exposed first by the amorality of his brother Harry, and then by his marriages to Camilla and Toni. Following his separation from Judith he had seen the hypocrisy of many who profess religious conviction even in his own community. He had bitter memories of the immorality and incompetence of Government in several spheres. A catalogue of unwelcome experiences that had changed him irrevocably. His faith in human nature was qualified by many reservations, and his natural espousal of the principle of equality, now was overshadowed by an abhorrence of officialdom, abuse of power and bureaucracy.

When notification arrived in 2004 advising of the intention to propose him for an award in the Queen's Birthday Honours, his immediate response was not one of joy or pleasure, or even satisfied acceptance. In fact, he was shocked by his own reaction. His thoughts were uncompromising. *These are the same bastards that destroyed Peter*

Williams, that abused Wendy Shore, and would have let us sink without trace if we had given in. Sod them! How can I accept anything from hands that are covered in blood?

Primogeniture

After the CBE Investiture in London, the family stayed overnight at the Farmers Club just along the Mall in Whitehall Court, before travelling back by train to Darlington the following morning. Jennifer and the children were there to meet them with the Range Rover, and Angela arrived separately to collect Simon. They said goodbye to Simon and Angela who were going direct to Wycliffe.

The trip to London had been a breakthrough for Simon. He had been in continuous contact with Dick for a longer period than at any time since his childhood, and it had helped to lay old demons to rest. He thought back to Dick's words at the golden wedding, and then to Angela who had waited for him for more than eight years. He looked across from the advantage of the passenger seat as she drove him home. He saw anew the perfect profile that was the outer expression of her inner sweetness; he saw similarities to his mother in the dark-haired girl – Girl! No, she had been a girl when they met, but now she was a beautiful assured young woman, and he was running the risk of losing her by his dithering inaction. He remembered his father's exact words..."You can spend your life building your dreams, and see them all knocked down by one silly mistake". Well, he would take those words to heart, very late perhaps, but not too late. He determined he would ask Angela to marry him that evening. He was a fortunate man that the option remained open for him, and again he owed thanks to his mother. It was her words at Annie's 90th birthday party..."never let a good man go!" – that had persuaded Angela to be patient.

The rest of the family made their way towards Barnard Castle. Ralph was driving with Dick in the passenger seat beside him, and they listened to Susan giving Jennifer a non-stop blow-by-blow account of the ceremony. They called for old Ralph and Annie, and all returned to Deep Ghyll for a family celebration. The Bainbridge family had secured its status in the local community over the past few generations, and now felt confident in its position. The CBE had put the seal on recognition at a national level.

It was mid-afternoon when they reached the farm. Annie settled in the rocking-chair and swayed gently to and fro, gazing through the window. In her 95th year she retained her tranquillity and ever-pleasant disposition, but her memory had begun to fail. Susan and Jennifer busied themselves in the kitchen, and the children started to take toys from the cupboard. Dick sat with his father, old Ralph, and his son, young Ralph. On the table beside them was an open leather box displaying the 22-carat gold CBE Insignia. The striking blue of the cross surrounded the red circle in which the words 'FOR GOD AND THE EMPIRE' were picked out in gold. The whole was suspended from a red ribbon. His expression was serious as he gazed at the Insignia.

"For God and the Empire!" said Dick with emphasis. "Well, I'm a religious man – or at least a spiritual man – but I've never held any great affection for the Empire. Think back over history, and what has religion or the empire done?" He paused and looked around at the others. "Religion has caused endless wars and been an excuse for persecution throughout history. The Empire drew straight lines across continents – no thought for tribal homelands, and what do we have? A legacy of genocide and revenge. Then put religion and empire together, and they eliminated local culture and customs wherever they went – I'm ashamed sometimes of our supposed civilisation."

The family were dumfounded by Dick's outburst. He was accustomed to making forthright statements, but not with such vehemence.

He looked at them and continued. "I can see you're a bit taken aback – maybe you haven't thought about it yourselves – but you can't do without a sound set of values. I believe we can only be true to ourselves, if we can be tolerant towards others. You see this stool – we call it the Idi Amin chair – our second cousin brought it back from Swaziland where she was a missionary. I'm sure she was sincere in her work, but what right did she have to impose her beliefs on Africa? I'm not proud that anyone in my family had the arrogance to assume they could dictate to people with different opinions and habits."

Dick reached across and closed the box.

"No point in leaving it open. It'll just encourage more pride and conceit. We'll put it away in a safe place if you've all seen enough of it. It's more about what it stands for – I'd like to think our work up here in Teesdale has been genuinely beneficial – it's a medal for conserving our Dales rather than for Dick Bainbridge."

Dick's words put the gathering in sombre mood, but Susan was determined it should be a celebration.

"Dick, why don't you pop across to the Cottage and see what the postman has brought while we've been away? Jennifer and I have one or two things to get ready for tea."

Dick went across to collect the morning post, and brought it back to Deep Ghyll. Among the usual assortment of bills and junk mail there was a large brown envelope for Susan. It was the quarterly magazine from the Alderson Family History Society, and the editor had inserted a copy of an old letter sent by an American member that he thought would interest Susan.

It was written on 10 September 1801 by Henry Alderson, of Cane Run in Lafayette County in Kentucky, and addressed to 'Mr Thomas Alderson, Briscoe, Barnard Castle, North of England'. It gave a revealing glimpse of Kentucky life 200 years previously, but there was one passage in particular which caught the attention of both Susan and Dick. It read as follows:

> *No right of primo geniture in Kentucky. The land descends to the younger Sons and Daughters equally with the oldest. One of my Nephews must come to Heir my Plantation. It will be worth his while.*

It had been very different in England. Much of the history of the Alderson and Bainbridge families had been governed by primogeniture, but in the ensuing discussion both Dick and Susan questioned the wisdom of the practices in both Britain and America, and everyone agreed they were outdated. Should not the basic principle be the choice of the best person for the job? As it happened, young Ralph had wanted to continue Dick's work at Deep Ghyll, while Simon's interests lay with his maternal grandfather's accountancy business, but Dick would have been equally happy if it had been the other way round. They all understood, without any need to articulate the thought, that the family would have been in a quandary if primogeniture had been applied in his generation with Harry as an absentee head of family.

Old Ralph's thoughtful silence indicated that this blemish still worried at the edges of his happiness, and Susan began to despair of creating a joyful atmosphere.

"The same rules apply to a Coat of Arms. It can be passed down only in a direct male line of descent." Dick had been reading the brochure which had arrived when the award of his CBE had been first announced in May. "The whole system is as archaic and obsolete as the monarchy – it's all part of the same set-up anyway. Why shouldn't it go down the female line as well? Young Sarah should have as much right as anyone else."

He picked up his pretty four-year-old granddaughter, and put her on his knee. The injustice of the rules annoyed him. A letter from the Garter King of Arms had arrived in June advising him of his rights and privileges, couched in the obtuse language to which he was becoming accustomed:

> 'As Commander of the Most Excellent Order of the British Empire you are eligible to Petition for a Grant of Armorial Bearings. Such Grants have been made since the fifteenth century by Letters Patent of the English Kings of Arms under powers delegated by The Sovereign. These Grants have been recorded at the College of Arms since its incorporation in 1484 and the right to any Arms granted to you would pass to all your descendants in the male line.'

Dick had not been interested to pursue this opportunity, but Susan had persuaded him. The Alderson family had a Coat of Arms in at least two branches, but she could not use either of them because she was a woman. She felt this lack of privilege keenly, and encouraged Dick to think of future generations. He may not put any value on a Coat of Arms, but he should not deny opportunity of the privilege to his descendants. Susan's arguments carried the day, and Dick was mollified to some degree with the arrival of the next letter in response to his request for information. In particular, he noted:

> '...an heraldic Badge if such is required. The latter is particularly useful as it has wider limitations than Arms and Crest and can be used by other persons or bodies associated with the grantee and his male line descendants. For example it can be used by non-armigerous sons-in-law and grandchildren in the female line.

It was far from ideal, but it was enough to satisfy him for the time being, and the serious business of deciding what should be included in the Armorial Bearings began. Susan had been looking at the College of Arms newsletter and had acquainted herself with the official terminology.

"Arms refers to the shield which is the basis of the design, Supporters are the figures at the side of the Arms, and the Motto goes at the bottom," she declared with a smile.

Some elements excited no debate – all the family were agreed that the Supporters should be a lapwing and a black grouse to record the major role that Dick had played in their conservation – the lapwing with cotton grass in its beak, and the black cock with a sprig of purple heather. There were suggestions for the inclusion of elements to signify his achievements in wrestling, fund-raising for the local community, NFU committee work and marketing, but simplicity appealed to Dick.

A ram's head on the Arms seemed appropriate, but should it be a Ravock or a Swaledale? The creation of a new breed was an accomplishment that few men could boast, and the Ravock had been exported to several countries, but Dick felt that the Swaledale was a better historic representation of the area where he had fought to conserve both traditional native breeds and the local environment. An oak tree, firmly planted above the Arms, reinforced the wider environmental benefits which had sprung from his early initiatives with ancient rig and furrow pastures at Deep Ghyll 30 years previously.

Susan made a rough sketch, which received general approval, although old Ralph joked that the tree seemed to be growing out of the ram's head. Susan was grateful for a sign of humour, however small, and she left it on the table in front of Dick. When they had reached a decision, it would be sent to the Garter King of Arms for preparation of the Letters Patent on vellum, with Dick's Armorial Bearings hand-painted in the top left hand.

Simon had drawn up a family tree going back in direct male line to his great-grandfather, John Tallen Bainbridge, born in 1833, and showing how three old families of the Dales – Bainbridge, Alderson and Metcalfe – were blended together. Jennifer brought it out and unrolled it on the table.

BAINBRIDGE FAMILY TREE

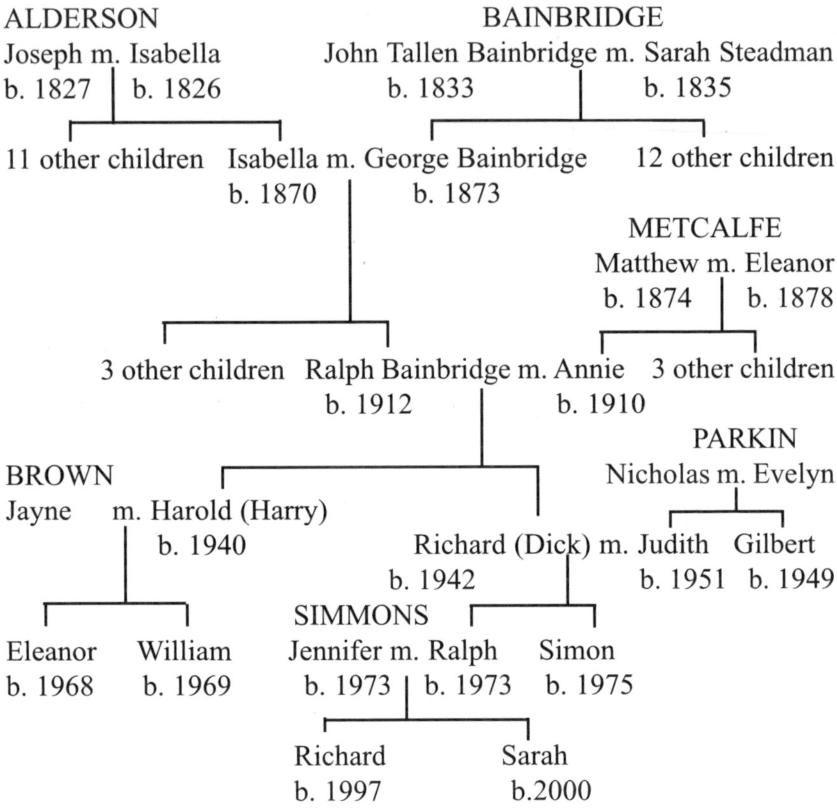

"There you are," said Dick, "six generations tabulated. Jennifer, you were asking Susan about my great-grandfather, Joseph Alderson. Well, there he is at the top on the left – born in 1827. There's one or two dates missing, but Simon's done a grand job putting it together – look at that fancy script."

In previous discussions with Dick, Susan had soothed his concerns on her behalf that a branch of the Alderson family would end with her, but when she saw the Bainbridge family tree, a renewed wave of regret swept over her. Too late to worry about it now at the age of 54, but maybe ten years ago she could have given Dick another son and taken her place on the family tree.

She and Jennifer had excelled themselves with a special afternoon tea in the Dales style – a traditional repast of ham, salad with a sweet mustard dressing prepared to Annie's own recipe, buttered scones and jam, apple pie and cheese, and the *piéce de résistance* – Teesdale trifle with a generous layer of thick yellow custard. That restored a spirit of happiness and soon the gastronomic delight had absorbed everyone's attention.

"Now have you men finally made up your minds? Designing a coat of arms is a rather serious matter." Susan asked brightly, and could not resist adding, "Mind you, it's time we had the American system and allowed it pass down the female line as well! What do you think Jennifer?"

Jennifer nodded her agreement, but made no reply. Her name was in the family tree.

Susan knew how much family heritage meant to the Dick and his father, and added quietly. "It will be a permanent legacy for future generations of Bainbridges."

Old Ralph glanced across at his great-grandchildren, Richard and Sarah, playing near Annie, and smiled. "Aye, Susan, likely thoo's reet, bud we can nobbut plan seea far aheead."

The smile broadened across his wrinkled cheeks as he contemplated the two youngsters, and then was overtaken by sadness as he thought of the grandchildren – Harry's children – that he had never seen.

Dick saw the abrupt change of expression on his face. He went across and put his arm around his father's shoulders. "Let's be happy. The Bainbridge dynasty is safe for a long time to come." Ralph's hand tightened on Dick's, and the smile flitted briefly again across his weather-beaten face, but he knew his dearest wish to have all his family around him would not be realised. The disappointment that gnawed continually at the corners of his mind could not be ignored. It chilled the warmth of his daytime joys, and caused sleepless nights. Even after all the years, the absence of his elder son left sorrow in his heart and a withering drain on his happiness.

Part II

THE GOLDEN BOY

REFUGE IN PINEAU

The peace of the autumn afternoon was broken by the tearing screech of rubber on tarmac as a powerful green sports car with British number plates came to a juddering halt. The street was deserted except for a dark-haired woman – her face obscured by the collar of her coat turned up against the cold – who spun round with a start at the sudden noise before continuing on her way. The driver wrenched at the wheel, cursing the narrowness of the street, performed an erratic three-point turn and accelerated back up the road. Drawing alongside the woman, her startled expression, full of indignant apprehension, was enough to tell him that it was not the woman he had expected. He had been so sure, so confident she would arrive soon, but it had been hope built on wishful thinking.

"Madame, pardon!" She scarcely heard his apology as she hurriedly continued on her way. The surge of heart-thumping expectancy that had filled him was swept away in an undertow of crushing disappointment. He turned again and resumed his original route as the chill of the declining day settled on the coast of the Charente Maritime. A fresh breeze ruffled the treetops still moving gently in the leafy canopy, and a few wispy clouds scudded across the sky. The sports car cruised slowly between the vineyards near St Thomas de Conac on the road from Mirambeau, the driver lost in confused thought following his earlier encounter.

He scarcely noticed the teams of pickers gathering the ripe bunches of grapes along the rows of vines, urgently filling their baskets with the last of the harvest. Merlot grapes predominated, with a sprinkling of Cabernet Franc and Cabernet Sauvignon. The vines had completed yet another cycle – the spring freshness of their leaves drained by the demanding harvest to a dull green tinged with yellow. Some workers were bent low, swiftly and expertly snipping off the hand-size bunches of rich-hued fruit – blue, purple and even black; others carried full baskets to waiting trailers on which large vats were already almost filled. Further up the valley a tractor was hauling a laden trailer to the winery. The local farmers had told him it would be a great vintage.

His dark curly hair reflected strong tints of copper in the declining sunlight, but also showed distinct flecks of grey at the temples. He was dressed casually and his light attire betrayed that he was accustomed to a colder climate. Harry Bainbridge had spent the day with Claude, a local agent, assessing the property market in the area around Saintes. Two thousand years ago, Saintes had been a town of great importance, and the Roman amphitheatre still stood in ancient splendour. Harry had been absorbed and elated by the potential for property investment among its architectural variety. Now his excitement had been deflated by his encounter with the dark-haired woman, and all he wanted was a relaxing drink to revive his spirits.

His mood had lightened by the time he reached Resteulet. He pulled in through the wrought iron gates, and parked on the gravel in front of its imposing façade. He had moved in only a couple of weeks earlier, and the novelty had not yet worn off. He still was surprised that a native Yorkshireman could settle so easily into life in a foreign place, but already he felt himself a part of Resteulet, as if it always had been his destiny. It was a property of rare quality; a *maison de maitre*, facing a little east of south, constructed in typical Charentaise style, but untypically situated in an elevated position, and with a few hectares of land. The broad front door was slightly recessed, but the balcony above projected beyond the plane of the symmetrical wings of the house. Tall windows completed the symmetry, two above and two below in each wing; all under the security of a double layer of red roof tiles. The windows were closed behind light blue shutters to keep out the sun, although the front of the house now was almost in shadow.

Harry ascended the three stone steps to the front entrance, which opened into an airy high-ceilinged hall. He went through into the salon, picking up a bundle of letters that had arrived earlier, and poured himself a glass of pineau. Pineau des Charentes, the fortified variant of the local wine, was a tradition of the region that he had embraced with enthusiasm. Leaving his notebook and letters on the bureau, he climbed the broad curving stairs from the hall to a large landing. It had a wooden floor with a richly-patterned oriental carpet in the centre. Several doors led off to the right, left and rear. The wall on the right was covered from floor to ceiling by custom-built oak shelves and packed to overflowing with an impressive library of books – some modern volumes, but many betraying evidence of historical importance. An antique Chippendale mahogany desk was placed diagonally in the front left-hand corner. On it stood a magnificent bronze statue of a bull with the signature 'Tom Nichols, Finnbennach 1998'.

The vigour of Harry's step, and the alertness of his demeanour, could not hide an expression of sadness on his face, but a light came into his blue eyes when he turned and looked out at the rolling countryside through the tall double windows leading onto the balcony. He stepped out and relaxed with his drink. The land on the left-hand side was undulating with areas of woodland. The land on the right-hand side sloped down steeply to the flats and to the Gironde estuary beyond. The sun, sinking in the western sky, sparkled on the water as the mingled currents of the Garonne and Dordogne rivers drifted to their destiny in the Atlantic Ocean. Yes, he thought, a view like that is worth a fortune.

Turning away reluctantly, he returned downstairs. On the wall facing him at the turn in the stairs was a painting – a large equine study in oils. Harry stopped in front of it, as he always did. Eight muscular, neck-arched, high-stepping horses pranced and reared and paraded in a pattern of grooms and riders. In some parts the colours were strong, in other parts bright flashes of colour – reds and blues – projected from a sombre backcloth. Two greys trotted to the right, and a group of bays gathered towards the left, but it was the centre group that always caught his eye – a rearing white stallion with his wild gaze fixed on the black filly alongside him.

"You could tell a story," he said aloud. "You've shaped my life for the past three years, and maybe you hold the key to my future. I've brought you back to the land of your creator, but I'm sure Rosa Bonheur didn't know what human drama would be played out around you when she stroked her brush across your canvas 150 years ago." He paused, and gazed wistfully on the picture for some time before continuing down the stairs.

Back in the salon, he opened his notebook and glanced through the scribbled jottings he had made. He needed to analyse his notes while they were fresh in his mind. The volume of houses coming onto the market was growing by the day, but the number of Britishers wishing to buy was increasing even faster. Good for his business, but probably not good for quality of life in the region in the long-term. The choicest properties were selling quickly, and he had been lucky to find his maison de maitre in such a superb location. He had been accustomed to life in a manor house in England, but this was far superior. Resteulet was spacious and elegant, with a garden front and rear, and those fabulous views. Perhaps he did rattle around in a five-bedroom mansion, but he liked space and vista.

He completed his notes, and picked up the bundle of mail. Two letters caught his eye; one a thick brown envelope with a typed address and an Oxford postmark, and the other a tinted pale-blue envelope addressed in a hand he recognised instantly. His heart leapt. It was from Ami. His mistaken identity of the dark-haired woman in the village had simply been a premonition. The letter must presage Ami's imminent arrival. He began to open the letter, then hesitated – an inexplicable doubt flickering across his mind – and put it aside.

Instead, he opened the large envelope to find a note from Antonia Mountjoy. 'Dearest Harry, Miles has gone away to a conference, but he asked me to send the enclosed. He is not sure whether you are able – or wish – to keep in touch with developments at PFA. Hope to see you soon. Love. Antonia.' The October 2002 issue of a company newsletter was enclosed, and Miles had marked two items in red.

On the back page in Stop Press: 'CONGRATULATIONS to Pamela and Duncan Croft on the birth of a son, Duncan Harry Croft, on Sunday 6 October 2002. Both mother and son are doing well. Pamela first joined the staff of Portway Fine Arts in 1993. She left in 2001 but rejoined this year.' He was delighted for Pamela. She had almost given up hope of children, and she would be a wonderful mother. He noted the baby's name with a mixture of emotions, and mused on its significance. He wondered if it would be known as Duncan or Harry, and what part – if any – Duncan had played in the choice of names.

The other item was inside on page 2:

> 'NEW TEAM AT OXFORD. Portway Fine Arts showed its true cosmopolitan character last month with the announcement of senior staff appointments in the United Kingdom. The new Chair of the British subsidiary will be Irish-born Ms Theresa Murphy.

> She will be assisted by MD Miss Ami Kotze, who was born in South Africa, and Mrs Pamela Croft who will be her personal assistant. Following the temporary difficulties experienced last year, and the transfer of the headquarters of the company to Australia with offices in Melbourne, the Chair of the company, Rebecca Payne, paid a lengthy visit to England to review the future direction of the British office. It will remain at its existing premises in Oxford, and Mrs Payne held a press conference there on Wednesday 18 September to announce the key arrangements. Mrs Payne expressed her confidence in the ability of the new team to take the company forward to a successful future. Theresa Murphy said that the prospects were encouraging, despite the current downturn in the global stock market, and she anticipated a rapid return to a profitable position...'

Harry did not read any further. He put the paper down, and the other letters fell from his hand onto the floor. The sadness that before had flickered across his face now was replaced by a mixture of shock and incredulity. He could not believe what he had read. It was only two-and-a-half years since he had stepped down as Managing Director of Portway Fine Arts, and he could not have imagined the speed or direction of change in that time.

A triumvirate of women in control of the company! He knew them all. Each was a beautiful, desirable woman as an individual – but in a business team together! Soon they would be fighting like ferrets in a sack. Theresa in the Chair – Good God! Was everything being turned upside down? She had even reverted to her maiden name. But Ami in his old position – how could that be? It was the ultimate betrayal. His mind struggled to comprehend the implications. It seemed to answer the question that had been troubling him, and the obvious interpretation stopped his breath like a double blow to the solar plexus. He desperately grasped at other explanations. Maybe Ami was an innocent party in a charade orchestrated by Rebecca Payne. Maybe – but then, maybe not.

Only a feminist like Rebecca could have been motivated to exclude men entirely from her senior management team, especially those with expertise and knowledge of the company. He had worked with her for several years, and had been left in no doubt of her views, but he had not been aware they were so extreme. He had been part of a five-man Board of Directors, and had seen the unacceptable side of masculine authority. He would not wish that brand of chauvinism on anyone, and yet such a sudden and complete gender reversal was incredible. What subterfuge or conspiracy had been afoot, he wondered. Maybe women were as susceptible as men to the temptations of power.

He held Ami's letter in his hand. He had been waiting for its arrival for eight days, but the newsletter announcement raised such torment in his mind that he no longer had the courage to open it. He put it aside again, and poured himself another glass of pineau.

The chain of events that had started on Friday 25 February 2000 had caught a group of people in its coils – mere mortals unaware of the unpredictable forces that shaped their destiny. He had been one of those mortals, and maybe it was best he had not been able to see the future on that day.

1
LAST DAY AT THE OFFICE

It was Friday lunchtime when Harry Bainbridge emerged from his office. He was a tall, distinguished figure, exuding the calm assurance and easy authority of the Managing Director of a thriving international company. He was confident in the trust and respect of his staff, and they were gathered in the main office waiting for him with expectant anticipation. He had given clear signals that they should not arrange anything special for the occasion of his retirement at the end of the week, but they felt justified in ignoring his wishes. They were not prepared to let him go without a chance to show their true feelings. They had established an easy relationship with Harry, which had earned him their total loyalty, and which ensured a spirit of friendly efficiency and effective teamwork.

Despite his protestations and his genuine dislike of emotional public declarations, Harry was flattered by the demonstration of affection by his staff, and – if he was honest – he had expected it. However, he was surprised to see that his four fellow Directors had joined the party. He had known Walter King since university days; Miles Mountjoy, the Chairman, was a close friend; Jack Maladonis was a long-standing member of the Board, although still somewhat of an unknown quantity to Harry; Peter Loder was a quiet self-contained man of few words.

He welcomed them all with warm greetings, but it was Terry Williams his Finance Officer who took charge of the proceedings. His accolade on behalf of the staff was followed by another on behalf of the Directors from Miles Mountjoy who presented him with a set of engraved Dartington crystal glasses and decanters. There were more personal words – fortunately not too personal – from Harry's PA, Pamela Croft, who in turn presented him with a silver galleried tray inscribed 'Harry Bainbridge, founder, partner and Managing Director of Portway Fine Arts: 1970–2000: from his grateful colleagues'.

Harry's response was brief, but direct and poignant. They understood how much he appreciated them as colleagues, and valued their commitment to the company. The occasion reached a proper and appropriate climax, and Harry relaxed with obvious satisfaction.

"If I might be permitted to say a few words." Jack Maladonis moved to the centre of the room. He was short, dark and saturnine, with heavy black eyebrows and stubby hands. "We will be very sorry to see you go. You've made a notable contribution to the company, and you have been a valuable member of the team. We must admire your sense of responsibility to our future wellbeing in deciding to step aside early." He paused to ensure the full effect of his words, delivered in a deliberate and measured monotone. There was a sudden silence, and perplexed apprehension at the unplanned and now slightly sinister intervention. "You have appreciated that no one is irreplaceable, even someone with your long record of service, and your absence will permit the company to move forward in new and profitable ways. We thank you most sincerely for your wisdom and understanding in placing the company's interests before your own."

Harry smiled coldly. He thanked the speaker for his kind words, and observed to himself that there must be a snake in the grass and master of double-speak in every company – but not always in the same person. Why had he not detected it previously? He had sat on the PFA Board with the Jack Maladonis for sixteen years, and had not found him an admirable person, but this was a new and undesirable dimension of character. Maybe his imminent departure had emboldened Jack to shed a skin of caution. He caught Walter King's eye and saw that he also had taken offence at the back-handed compliments.

"What an obnoxious little turd," said Walter, *sotto voce*, "how can you be so polite to him?"

"Best to ignore him," replied Harry.

Most of the others quickly put the exchange behind them, and directed their attention to the party drinks. Their high spirits gradually restored Harry's bonhomie. He relegated the unpleasant words to the back of his mind and relaxed again.

He looked around with a sense of pride; pride in his staff, pride in his business, and also – more carefully concealed and only covertly admitted – pride in himself. Here he was, an international businessman, who had risen from humble beginnings, enjoying an exotic lifestyle. He had not forgotten his roots, but showed no evidence of them. He had been born in the dark days at the start of World War Two in a remote rural area of northern England, part of a family with few resources and little incentive to look further ahead than the next farming season. There was no comparison between that life and his present situation.

His progress through life had not been smooth. It had been the fluctuating, heady roller-coaster of a restless, rootless itinerant. He had never remained in a house long enough to call it home; he had negotiated two marriages, one divorce and several intense relationships; he had climbed the social ladder from working class origins to the upper echelons of the meritocracy. For many generations his family had endured the deprived sameness of Pennine isolation, but his life had been punctuated by change – change of home, change of social class, change of partner. Enough change to account for the dysfunction that was Harry, but of which he was unaware and never had felt impelled to explore. Self-analysis was a dangerous indulgence that might force recognition of undesirable truths. The veneer of self-assurance that was his trademark masked an inner turmoil of spirit and lack of security. Where did he belong? A raw working class lad camouflaged in layers of modern sophistication.

Harry had no sense of belonging, no focal point around which he revolved. Now he was about to embark on the biggest change of all, and the barb of Jack Maladonis' words had disturbed his equanimity. Was he really not irreplaceable? Briefly, a hint of vulnerability hung about him. Would retirement be a new challenge to test and prove again his undoubted talents, or would it be the last straw that breaks the fragile structure of a flawed personality?

The party atmosphere persisted throughout the afternoon. Harry returned to his office, but productivity was not a priority on his last day. He was standing by his desk when Pamela slipped quietly through the door. Without saying a word, she ran over to him, kissed him and held him in a tight embrace. He was very fond of her. At first sight she appeared a pretty flirtatious young thing – pert face, short blonde hair, short skirts and fabulous legs – but she was the epitome of efficiency, and had been his impeccable personal assistant for three years. Harry felt the fullness of her breasts against him, and the pressure of her thighs. “I think maybe another time and place would be better,” he whispered; “I’ll succumb very quickly if you hold me like this.”

“Working for you has been a dream come true for me,” she replied; “but this is the first time I have been able to hold you. Always close to you, but never close enough. You’ve no idea how often I have dreamed of giving myself to you, and now you’re leaving and I’ll never have the chance.”

There was a movement outside the door, and they drew apart abruptly. No one knocked, but the moment had gone. She kissed him again quickly, wiped her eyes, and left the office. Harry regretted that they had not been able to take it further, but was relieved that it had not come to the surface sooner as it would surely have ruined their working relationship.

He sat and mused over what might have been.

The regular chime of the security alarm at the front entrance betrayed the prompt departure of staff at five o’clock. He glanced out of the window. It was getting dusk. His office door opened far enough for Terry’s balding head to appear horizontally. “Goodnight, have a good weekend”. Terry was his right-hand man. Very correct, procedurally inscrutable, and true to his civil service background. His strict observance of rules and regulations contrasted with Harry’s more flamboyant and instinctively unorthodox business style. Together they made a good team. Terry had joined Portway Fine Arts at a time of rapidly expanding business in the 1980s, and had seen the company diversify from a successful local enterprise into a high-flying international leader on a range of creative arts. He was a sound administrator but, like the other staff, his commitment was strictly nine-to-five and no more.

It was different for Harry. He always was in the office an hour before any of his staff, and was the last to leave in the evening. Work had become a way of life. His protective paternalism towards the company was natural – after all, he was the founder – and his reputation as the MD of an international company with offices in Europe, Africa and Australia opened doors around the world. It was a heady cocktail of glamour, power and influence, and long hours were no hardship.

This week was different. It was his last week – his last day – as MD. He had taken the decision that 30 years was long enough and that both he and the company would benefit from a change. He was stepping aside and a new MD had been appointed. He had declined the offer to remain as a Director, and preferred instead to be retained as a consultant for the value of his accumulated experience and expertise. He felt it would be the best arrangement for everyone.

Louise Crossman had been a business manager with a large firm of accountants. She was a not particularly attractive spinster, but she knew how to present herself to best advantage. Her sturdy legs and the stoutness of her hips were concealed under long skirts, and a voluminous blouse disguised the absence of womanly contours. She had avoided power-dressing during the process of selection for the position of MD, in order not alarm any elderly Directors who might interview her. Her smile was carefully constructed to disguise crooked teeth, and highlighted bouffon hair belied her 51 years, and gave no indication of her deep-seated frustration that she remained a virgin in her sixth decade.

Harry had questioned whether her background indicated a lack of creativity and artistic flair, but she had impressed the interviewing panel. Her earnest declaration of a deep interest in photography was convincing. Her strong attitude to staff management and productivity targets would bring a new strand of expertise to the company. Harry also had questioned her age. He knew the company would have benefited from an injection of more youthful vigour, and had favoured the application from Ami Kotze, a vibrantly exciting artist from South Africa. His fellow Director on the interviewing panel, Jack Maladonis, and Robert Gator, who was the third member, placed more weight on the experience of age, and in any case they suspected that Harry's support for the attractive and vivacious Ami might be motivated by more than a professional interest.

Harry had put his reservations to one side and looked forward to a new phase of development for the company, and for himself an opportunity to return to the practical and recreational aspects of art which had been denied to him in recent years by the demands of business management.

2
A NEW BUSINESS

Harry Bainbridge 1940-1970

Harry had started Portway Fine Arts working from an office in the garage at his home. At the time he had been approaching his thirtieth birthday, and already could look back on a meteoric early career having amassed considerable assets within a few years of leaving university, before discovering that fortunes can disappear even more rapidly than they accumulate. He was not insolvent, but he was short of funds and prepared to take a few risks to revitalise his career. He was a committed risk-taker – an instinctive gambler, whose optimism sustained him through even the deepest crises. It was not clear whether this was an inherited trait, or a product of his upbringing in a remote rural area of Yorkshire. His father had not been afraid to launch new ventures in unknown territory, and Harry could recognise elements of his father's response to a situation of risk in his own behaviour, but he inclined to the belief that he had been shaped by the experiences of his youth, rather than his genetics.

Harry could not claim to have had a deprived upbringing. He and his younger brother, Dick, had sufficient food, adequate clothes and open countryside around them. Their loving parents, Ralph and Annie, were hard-working, but that was a necessity forced upon them by the need to extract even a basic living from the limited acres of damp pasture and barren expanse of rough moorland of a hill farm. No doubt they would have preferred to spend more time with their curly-haired sons, but the harsh reality of life dictated that animals and crops had precedence during a working day that started before dawn and ended after sunset for most of the year.

Hardship was an accepted feature of life for hill farmers. The monotony of routine drudgery was broken only by market day on Wednesday and chapel on Sunday, apart from the occasional christening, wedding or funeral. Life always had been hard, although maybe it was less difficult now than it had been previously. When Annie was young she had walked to school. In the period between the two World Wars she travelled to town by pony and trap on market day with her basket of wares to sell in the Market Cross – pats of rich yellow home-made butter and delicious Cotherstone cheeses. Later Ralph had purchased a car from a friend who was going to the War – a little Morris 8 that seemed like a Rolls Royce to Annie. They no longer were exposed to the vagaries of the climate, and the car was a definite symbol of status.

Sundays were focused round the simple Methodist chapel up the valley – a single-room stone building with a black metal stove in the centre for warmth, and a few pews facing a raised varnished wooden pulpit. John Wesley had made a powerful impact in the Yorkshire Dales, and the continuing fervour of the Primitive Methodists two hundred years after his evangelistic visits bore testament to the imprint of his message. Sunday school, not football, was the rule for children. The Bible and prayer, not work, for adults on the Sabbath. The wrath of Wesley, albeit at a distance of many generations, deterred even the laxest adherent from gathering in sweet ready-made hay on a Sunday; no matter that the expected rain on Monday would ruin it completely.

It was not surprising that in such austere circumstances Harry often found refuge and comfort in his doting grandparents, especially after the birth of his sibling. He resented the proportion of her limited spare time that Annie devoted to Dick. His paternal grandparents, George and Isabella, lived in the white-washed cottage only 50 yards across a small field, and even as a toddler he could cover those yards fast enough to escape any impending reprimand from his parents – his curly golden head bobbing along the path with focused intent. His reward invariably was a slice of gingerbread. Grandfather George credited him with qualities far beyond the capabilities of any small boy, and subconsciously boosted his self-regard even at that early age. His maternal grandparents, Matthew and Eleanor, lived further down the valley, and he visited them every Wednesday while his parents were at market. Grandfather Matt was more stern, but even so Harry could do no wrong.

Looking back with perspective wisdom, Harry had to admit that the conflicting messages – lack of parental contact and indulgent grandparents – probably were the key factors in determining his character. His assumption, fostered by his grandparents, that he could have whatever he wanted, and his determination to get it, could be traced to those early years. But there was another factor. He became aware at a very young age that other children from the more prosperous area on the other side of the village lower down the valley had possessions which he lacked. This sense of deprivation reinforced his aggrieved feeling of perceived parental neglect, and created a deep well of insecurity and inherent shyness, but also motivated a resentment which grew into the driving ambition that was to colour much of his life. Maybe genetics did make some contribution to this development in his character. Other children and adults in his community seemed happy to accept their lot, resigned to the same style of life as their parents and grandparents that was modified only slightly by the march of technological progress. He was not prepared to settle for that.

Things are not always what they seem. Harry was reared in a strict puritanical code which inhibited sexuality, and thereby made the forbidden fruit of conquest an ingrained ambition in later years. The repressive religious zeal that permeated most parts of the upland rural community, concealed relic activities reminiscent of pre-Wesley days and at the same time spawned the very activities that it wished to conceal. In his later life, maybe in the alcohol-hazed bravado of the rugby clubhouse, Harry may have mentioned a former class-mate at the village school who was not sure whether to ascribe the cause of her early-teenage pregnancy to the headmaster or a fellow pupil. He may have recounted with apparent censure the story he had heard of another naive young girl who had fallen pregnant to her reclusive uncle on a neighbouring farm. But never, even in his most unguarded moment, would he have hinted that there were two gaping holes in his own pedigree. His unmarried great-great-grandmother produced two sons to the same married man, and his great-grandmother on the other side of his pedigree fell unwilling prey to the forcible attentions of an aristocratic member of a grouse-shooting party. Sexual predation was not unusual in the late nineteenth and early twentieth century when cohorts of deerstalker hats and plus-four trousers paraded the moors, and Harry knew of several residents in the dale who owed their parentage to visiting royal personages. What innocent and lowly country girl would dare to refuse when commanded to submit by the heir to the throne!

Nevertheless, life in the dale continued in a timeless way, uninterrupted by these minor deviations. Family feuds persisted through generations. Harry's own great-grandfather had been the victim of the legacy of local feuding when he was convicted of sheep-stealing on the malicious evidence of a vindictive neighbour. He had been imprisoned, and the shame was so great that he could not face his family on his release, and fled abroad. His wife, an extraordinary woman of great beauty, single-handedly brought up her six children to be respected members of the community.

With such a confused genetic and environmental background was it any wonder that Harry, even in adulthood, remained an unfathomable character and a man of many paradoxes? His years at public school and university had laid a veneer of polite pronunciation over his broad Yorkshire vowels, and his association with upper class friends distanced him increasingly from his family and the working class friends of his childhood. It may or may not have been a deliberate decision, but his negligence of filial duty led in a short space of time to almost complete loss of contact with his Pennine roots.

In idle moments, Harry occasionally reflected on what might have been. He could have been a hill farmer in the true tradition of his male line, following in the footsteps of his father, grandfather and great-grandfather. He might have been happier pursuing quiet communion with nature, walking the purple-clad heather hills, with larks and curlews above, and the river bubbling over its pebbly bed below. It was easy to look back at the romantic qualities of rural life, but he knew the realities. The beauty of the dales is easy to appreciate by fresh eyes, but it is invisible to those who toil in the midst of it. Would he have wished to drag his weary body out of bed at five o'clock on a freezing winter morning to hand-milk twenty cows before breakfast? Would he have had the will to recover after losing more than half his sheep in the blizzards of the great storms of 1947? Did the back-breaking toil of cleaning out cow sheds and spreading manure really appeal to him? He may have suffered from the stresses of business life and the untrustworthiness of business colleagues, but he was not sorry that he had chosen to follow a path away from the hardship of farming in the Pennine hills.

Jayne Leighton-Brown, 1967-1970

The path away from farming on the northern hills first took Harry through public school, by virtue of a scholarship and great personal sacrifice by his parents. Despite his natural idleness and continual search for the easiest route round any problem, he excelled on the sports field, and achieved respectable – but not notable – examination grades. It was his skill on the rugby pitch, rather than his 'A' level grades, that ensured his place at Cambridge University. There he fell in with a free-wheeling group of undergraduates, whose interest was focused essentially on the intoxicating social attractions of university life. Most of his friends were from well-heeled families, and some were indecently wealthy. James Farndale, a fellow Yorkshireman, would inherit the title of Lord Banthorpe a few years later. Julian Duffell, whose father had been killed in the Second World War, already owned a large estate in East Anglia and would take possession on his 21st birthday. Walter King's family had owned a successful manufacturing company for three generations, and Walter was expected to follow the family tradition. Harry could not claim such advantages, and his credibility rested on his sporting ability, but at Cambridge that carried more kudos than mere material possessions.

The friends and contacts he made at Cambridge were a mixed blessing. They opened up new horizons for Harry's opportunistic tendencies, but they also reinforced his social ambitions and his expectations that success could be achieved without undue effort. The gulf between the values of his family and the temptations of his new life was a barrier that he allowed to become a formidable obstacle, and that he had no inclination to cross. His early career did nothing to dispel his illusions, or offer hopes of reconnection with his family. The exceptional returns achieved by his initial speculative investments did not ring a cautionary bell. He had no fund of family experience to enable him to recognise the extraordinary character of his success. He continued to speculate, and his fortune followed.

It was rather more than four years after coming down from Cambridge that an invitation to Julian Duffell's wedding arrived at Harry's Worcestershire home, some miles north of the county town. Julian now was firmly established in the higher echelons of the social pecking order in East Anglia, and had met a delightful girl of appropriate standing from a Hampshire family of comparable wealth. The ceremony took place in 1967 on a mild sunny day in early April, and the lavish reception could not have disappointed even the most demanding guest. There were several old acquaintances from Cambridge that Harry was pleased to see again, particularly Walter King who remained a close friend. But Harry's attention had been focused on the chief bridesmaid from the moment she had walked down the aisle behind the bride, and he lost no time in making her acquaintance at the reception.

Jayne Leighton-Brown was an effervescent girl, whose sparkling eyes and lively smile revealed an impatience to escape from the limitations of her rural conventions and enjoy the pleasures of the wider world. She was twenty years old, and felt restricted by the pattern of girls' boarding school and country pursuits that was the accepted lot of her class. It was a feeling that struck an immediate chord and empathy with Harry. He saw the look of disappointment when she failed to catch the bride's bouquet, and determined that he could realise her ambitions. It proved easier than he expected. It was clear from her eager response to his initial overtures that she had been made aware already of the glamour of his Cambridge status, and readily accepted his invitation for dinner the following evening.

The Leighton-Browns were overtly conscious of their status. Their estate on the borders of Wiltshire and Dorset enabled them to rub shoulders with the high and mighty. They favoured the local village of Leighton with their presence for a brief and perfunctory inspection of the annual fete, and entertained friends with an ostentatious picnic at the local point-to-point. They allowed the local group of carol singers to enter the hall of their country house at Christmas and rewarded them with mince pies. Simon Leighton-Brown regarded himself as the squire of Leighton, and the deferential tugging of forelocks by his wary tenants confirmed his opinion. He had plans for his daughter, and they did not include a northern opportunist who lived by his wits. No, his daughter was intended for someone of substance and property – more in the mould of Julian Duffell. Julian's best man suited his plans admirably, but unfortunately in Jayne's eyes the best man seemed very staid and proper in comparison with the dangerous excitement and promise of novelty which Harry generated.

Jayne's stubbornness was more than a match for her father's

domineering determination to force her into conformity. She continued to see Harry despite her father's threats. Harry introduced her to delights of which she had been only vaguely aware – cheering the May Bumps from the Plough at Fen Ditton, and a May Ball at Magdalen College. Cambridge was a new world to her and a thrill of adventure. Instead of joining the ranks of the establishment for the Derby at Epsom, and the ritualised parade of hats and female flesh at Royal Ascot in mid-June, they absconded to Westmorland and mingled for several days with the gypsies and horseflesh at the Brough Hill Fair at Appleby. The colourful assembly of horse-drawn Romany caravans had been replaced to some degree by opulent motorised homes, but still the traditional ambience of the Fair prevailed. Harry and Jayne strolled over the bridge that stretched its warm sandstone across the River Eden, and watched the gypsies washing their horses and ponies in the clear water. From a respectful distance they gleaned the rudiments of the art of horse-trading, sealed with the slap of spat-on palms, and ventured into the fortune-tellers lair. Life was a hedonistic whirl throughout the spring and summer.

It was in August, after a day sailing off the coast of North Wales at Abersoch and a picnic on the deserted island of St Tudwal's in the company of only a few primitive Soay sheep, that Jayne turned to Harry with a serious expression. "Harry, I must talk to you. There's a complication that will change things between us."

Harry knew that he was *persona non grata* with her family, and was fully aware of the pressure exerted by her father. He put his arm around her. "Don't worry. Your father will calm down when he realises how happy we are together. It's only a matter of time."

"No, Harry, it's more than that. I'm pregnant. I've missed three monthlies, and have been so scared. At last, I had a test and it was positive." She stopped and looked at him, searching his face for his reaction.

Harry was nonplussed. Pregnancy was not a thought that had crossed his mind. Had Jayne not been on the pill? He had not bothered to ask. The implications were endless. Abortion? No, that would not be an option that found favour with the Leighton-Browns. Even a ne'er-do-well husband would be preferable to an abortion. Marriage? His heart sank at the thought. His present style of life was too good and carefree to lose in the responsibilities of wife and children.

Illegitimacy? Even he would not do that to the girl who had been such a delightful companion.

She read his expression immediately and accurately, and burst into tears. “What will I do?” she sobbed, “Daddy will disown me, and you don’t want me.”

Harry had many shortcomings, but he had a soft centre and he could not bear to see Jayne so distressed. “Jayne, my darling, I do want you. You mustn’t take my silence as rejection. Your news came as such a shock, that I couldn’t gather my wits.” His arm was still around her, and he pulled her close. “We’re so good together, and life has been charmed since I met you. It’ll be even better when there are three of us.”

The characteristic smile returned to Jayne’s tearful face. “Oh, Harry, I’m so happy. What a relief – I thought you might walk away. I love you so much, and couldn’t bear the thought that I might lose you. You’ve brought so many new joys to me since we met.” She paused, and a pensive frown crossed her brow. “Daddy will be furious. He’ll be incandescent. Please can we tell him together!”

Simon Leighton-Brown was incandescent. The purple veins stood proud on his flushed features. He shouted, he blustered, he blasphemed, but in the end there was little he could do. His daughter – his only child – was pregnant and she must be married. The tall young man standing in front of him beside his daughter was not only of inferior breeding, but also possessed an unconventional disregard for the social customs and proprieties so dear to the establishment that it boded ill for future familial harmony. No matter; the young man held all the trump cards, and would play them. The pregnancy was advanced to a point that either indecent haste to arrange the sumptuous wedding that Simon Leighton-Brown had always envisaged would broadcast the obvious reason; or it could be held in a more proper timeframe, but with a growing bump under her wedding gown; or it could be held quietly in a register office.

Secretly, Harry hoped for some miracle that might enable him to evade marriage, and he prolonged the negotiations with his potential in-laws on the pretext of seeking to accommodate their wishes as far as possible. As summer passed into autumn it dawned on Harry that a miracle would not be his salvation, and that he must reconcile himself to a new phase of life. A quiet ceremony in the local register office on a damp day in late October terminated his batchelorhood. The Leighton-Browns did not press Harry to issue invitations to his relatives, and Harry was happy to comply and keep his lowly origins at a distance. After a Caribbean honeymoon, he faced the realities and responsibilities of married life. His cottage in Worcestershire was not large, but it would suffice for the time being. Jayne was not accustomed to living in a small house, and occasionally chafed at the lack of space she always had taken for granted, but she still was in that first flush of romantic bliss which glosses over a multitude of problems. She was happy to remain at home while Harry was away on business, and she was grateful to him for spending winter evenings with her in the cosiness of the cottage, instead of going down to the local hostelry. That was not a hardship for Harry; he took little pleasure in exchanging gossip over a pint of bitter, and was more interested to discuss names for the baby. They decided that they held the names of their grandparents in special affection, and chose George William for a boy, and Eleanor Rachel for a girl.

Eleanor Rachel was born on Harry's birthday – 1st March 1968. His transformation from reluctant husband to doting father was cemented by that coincidence of birth. He was present throughout the long labour and parturition, and thenceforth Ella became the centre of his attention. Jayne relaxed in the comfort of his support to her and devotion to his daughter. Sleepless nights and lack of a lavish lifestyle were a small price to pay for the security of a happy family. Even her father relented, and brought her mother to visit on several occasions. Soon after Ella's birth an invitation arrived to his brother Dick's wedding, but it lay unanswered. Harry was too absorbed in his new daughter, and any lingering interest he may have felt for his Teesdale roots were conveniently submerged in his new obsession.

A second pregnancy arrived a little earlier than prudence would dictate. In the context of their active sex life, perhaps it was inevitable, but pregnancy combined with the demands of caring for a young baby took their toll on Jayne. Suddenly the lack of sleep and limitations of the Worcestershire cottage assumed greater proportions, and the thought of dirty nappies stretching into the foreseeable future caused an upsurge of apprehension. She was still young – a mere 21 years of age. Her first pregnancy, and the precedence of marriage arrangements, had deprived her of a 21st birthday party, and now all the excitement of their earlier social life seemed to be submerged in domestic duties. Bill emerged into the world on Midsummer Day with an urgency and lack of warning that precluded preparation or planning. Harry literally was left holding the baby.

Harry was totally absorbed with his children, and shared parental duties with eagerness. He thrived in the novelty of his new station in life. Meanwhile, Jayne declined. She no longer counted the benefits of having an attentive husband, but rather railed that she was being neglected. She began to bewail the loss of her freedom and absence of her friends. Harry redoubled his efforts to reassure and comfort her, but it was not enough.

Harry's business depended on entrepreneurial flair, accurate evaluation, rapid decisions and a large slice of luck. He seemed to have them all and, with a growing family to provide for, they were essential. Details of property for sale formed a large proportion of his mail. Most were discarded immediately; a few were put aside for more detailed evaluation. A brochure had arrived some while ago with particulars of The Lovett, a large piece of land in Scotland with some semi-derelict houses on the fringe of an expanding town. His initial evaluation had been that it was a substantial investment – bigger than any of his previous ventures – and its potential value for development marked it out as a priority. He calculated that it would be worth a small fortune with planning permission. The sealed bid system practised in Scotland did not sit easily with his style of bargain-hunting; it gave no opportunity for negotiation and allowed only one bite at the cherry. He should have researched the property in detail, but his focus on family problems had distracted him from responding and the closing date for sealed bids was close. However, he swiftly calculated its worth, completed his bid, and caught the afternoon post. He felt a glow of satisfaction. It was an opportunity that would enable him, if his bid was successful, to appease Jayne's perceived deprivation.

His elation when his bid was accepted was in absolute contrast to his usual laid-back reaction to successful business transactions. This time it had so much more meaning, with its contribution to family life. The profit margin would be substantial, but there would be a serious short-term cashflow problem, and therefore he urgently needed to obtain planning permission to resell the property for development. His call to the planning department yielded all the necessary information – but not the information he sought. He had made a monstrous investment blunder. He had failed to research and evaluate all the details. There would be no planning permission for The Lovett. His bid had been two or three times the real value of the property, and depleted his financial reserves to a point that prohibited other investments. It was a disaster that ended his career in the property market.

Entrepreneur Reborn

Now Harry found himself in the converted garage of his Worcestershire home pondering how to make a new fortune as an art dealer and photographer. It might have seemed an unusual career move, but he had shown an early interest in photography with his mother's old Brownie. Of more significance, one of his Cambridge friends, James Farndale, had taken his degree in Fine Arts and subsequently joined Sothebys. Harry had never pursued the creative arts as more than an enjoyable hobby, but he had watched James's progress with interest, and to his opportunistic eye it offered a promising next move at that uncertain stage of his career.

Simon Leighton-Brown took a different view. It confirmed his earlier opinion of the unsuitability of his son-in-law, and he wondered if the marriage would founder. Maybe he hoped that it would. His daughter deserved better than a trader in pictures, and he could see that she was not happy.

Initial costs for photography were low. Harry had a couple of good quality Canon cameras, and the incentive to succeed. The time would come when medium-format cameras, enlargers and other expensive equipment would be necessary, but he would accumulate some capital first with routine work. However, it was the excitement of being an art dealer that really caught his imagination. He knew there were valuable paintings in many houses, sometimes languishing unseen in a dark attic, sometimes hanging unrecognised and unappreciated. He was sure that was where the greatest potential lay, and he applied his energies and ability with ruthless single-mindedness. Old friendships were exploited, and no inhibitions prevented him drawing regularly on James Farndale's expertise. He used every stratagem at his disposal to build a network of contacts and local introductions that slowly spread from his Worcestershire base into surrounding areas.

He was disappointed that Jayne showed no interest in the business, and gave him no support. She spent more time visiting her parents, but he made no complaint and presented an optimistic and smiling face to his family and the world.

His old friend, Walter King, who lived in the Home Counties, had rung to say he was passing through, and Harry arranged to have a drink and lunch with him at the Talbot Inn in the village. The village in which Harry lived was well endowed with three hostelries, but lacked a church, in contrast to the three neighbouring villages of more ancient foundation, each of which had a church and no pub. The Talbot was noted for the quality of its food, and Harry knew they would find a wide choice on the bar menu.

Walter had been an outstanding scrum-half in the college team when Harry was the other part of the half-back pairing. They played regularly for the LX Club, and occasionally for the university, but not in the Varsity Match. A rugby Blue had been a heady target for both of them, but the Cambridge selectors had ensured that their berths were securely occupied by international players and that was an end to their ambition in that direction. Nevertheless, both were outstanding sportsmen and earned their Blues, and election to the Hawks' Club, by alternative routes – Harry for athletics, and Walter for cricket. Walter was small and lithe, with sharp features and a ready smile; straight, neatly-combed, dark hair, and a firm handshake. His dark suit was tailored, and the shine on his black shoes was a mirror. His walk and demeanour denoted a man of action.

They had a couple of drinks before lunch – Harry's tipple was a glass of Burgundy but Walter still retained the 'pint of best bitter' habit from college. The merest wisps of white cloud still hung in the blue backdrop of a summer sky, and they sought refuge from the strength of the sun at a garden table in the shadow of a large sycamore tree. Birds had been silenced by the midday heat, and the landlord's black Labrador was stretched out nearby.

As they settled down with their drinks, Harry learned that Walter still had made no progress in the direction of marriage, but his business acumen had been well rewarded. His advertising agency had exploited a glaring gap in the market and was thriving. He also had a lucrative private property business as a sideline. He hadn't changed, Harry thought, and life seemed to be treating him well. Fashionable clothes, big Mercedes – good for him.

Walter also was interested to catch up with news. He saw that Harry still retained his natural informality – open-necked shirt, casual trousers, and soft brown shoes. "What about you; what mischief are you getting up to these days, you old rogue?" he asked as lunch arrived. "You always seemed to be chasing three girls at the same time." Harry laughed. They had not seen each other for more than five years, and yet they dropped straight back into an easy routine. It was as if they were transported back to The Plough at Fen Ditton – their regular haunt for the May bumps a decade earlier.

"You're talking to a respectable married man. Tied the knot almost five years ago – rather urgently in fact. I've got a beautiful four-year-old daughter and a three-year-old son and heir. It shows how long it is since we have seen each other – I guess it was at Julian's wedding. I would have invited you up for lunch to meet them, but Jayne's away visiting her parents in Wiltshire. D'you remember Jayne? She was a bridesmaid at the wedding." He would have liked Jayne to meet Walter. He was a friend he valued.

"No, I can't place her – I'd probably had too much to drink to remember anything – but I'll look forward to meeting her and the children. And what about business? Wouldn't be surprised if you'd made enough to retire already. You were splashing the cash around the last time we were in London." It had been a Hawks' Club dinner, and both of them had been spectacularly unsuccessful at the poker table afterwards.

Harry hesitated. Walter always had been a good sounding-board and had a keen business brain, but Harry was not sure that their first meeting in five years was the right time to become involved in an analysis of his current situation. Walter noted his hesitation – it was not like Harry to be lost for a reply. "What's the problem? You're not bankrupt?"

"No, no, nothing like that." Harry smiled. "There have been some pretty crazy ups and downs since we left Cambridge – mainly ups, but I had a big down recently. Paid a heavy price for flamboyant investment in a rash speculation – took a risk on planning permission for a development and didn't get it. Needed the cash, and had to sell at an unmentionable loss just before property prices took off. Far from bankrupt, but sufficiently short of cash to take a more serious view of the world as a married man."

"So, where d'you go from here?"

"Well, I started a small art business about a year ago – always been interested in it. Working from home, and it's going well, but a bit steady and slow."

Harry paused, and Walter cut in. "Can't really see you in a steady business. You always did best in a crisis with a challenge right in front of you. That's why you were such a bloody good fly-half running rings around those hulking wing-forwards."

Harry recognised immediately that Walter had gone straight to the kernel. He was very happy to be a family man, and adored his children, but he needed action. The business must grow – and fast. "You're right," he said; "I hadn't realised there was a problem, but it does lack the excitement that comes with growth and change. The potential in this business is huge, but capital is the limiting factor at present. I'm following two or three different lines. I buy quality paintings wherever I find them – probate, provincial auctions, and it's surprising how many are still hanging unrecognised in ordinary homes around the country. I'm also looking to contract young artists and build up their portfolios for future promotion. The bread and butter work is in photography, mostly portraits, but occasionally with a touch of glamour. Takes a while to get if off the ground. I guess it'll come in time, but that will depend on cash flow."

"What sort of cash are you looking for?" Walter's question came out of the blue. "We always got along pretty well, and I know your entrepreneurial streak. I wouldn't mind having a stake in your business as long as you go easy on risks!"

Harry hesitated. He knew very well the dangers of going into business with friends and family, but he trusted Walter and immediate capital was a very attractive proposition. "To set up a professional photography studio with the necessary extra equipment and working capital to provide steady business, we would be looking at something in the region of twenty grand. The opportunities for big money are in the art dealing and contract, and that needs ready cash for investment; say a minimum of 30 grand. Altogether maybe 50 grand, plus whatever was considered a reasonable return to me for managing it. I wouldn't want to start anything that might put a strain on our friendship, and we would need to make sure every detail was on paper to prevent any misunderstandings."

"Well, what if I put in 50 grand and you put in two years for no salary. Then you draw a salary thereafter and we split the profits fifty-fifty."

"Who calls the shots if we disagree?"

"You do, but the initial capital is the total of my commitment. It's up to you to make a go of it, and I'll be happy with my share of the profits."

Harry leaned back in his chair and looked up into the blue sky. There was now not a cloud to be seen. This was a development he had not expected, but he knew the rough and tumble of business, and the need to make rapid assessment. Walter's response had been unhesitating and unequivocal. He must be doing well if he could risk that sort of money. It was a good offer, even though the valuation of two year's salary at 50 grand was a bit of a slap in the face. Still, it gave the opportunity for rapid expansion of the business, and the profits would compensate. "Let's shake on it," he said. "Good to have you in the firm – partnership to be correct." They shook hands, and Walter ordered another round.

"This is on me. Incidentally, does the business have a name?"

"Portway Fine Arts. Always did believe in choosing a name that's bigger than the business. Gives incentive to grow into it."

Partnership 1970-1984

The cash injection from Walter gave the stimulus necessary for PFA to change up a gear. Harry now had the margin for error that successful gamblers need, and the astute acquisition and resale of paintings generated sufficient capital for more speculative opportunities. Initially, he particularly sought out works by minor artists painted in the style of one of the great masters, as he had discovered that usually he was able to pass these on at remarkably inflated prices. Some even carried the master's signature, maybe added by the artist or an unscrupulous dealer. No doubt some collectors mistook such paintings for preparatory works of a later masterpiece, and Harry was not inclined to inform them that he believed such preparatory work most likely would be done only in pencil or charcoal, if at all. He started to accumulate specific collections, and he had a particular interest in the nineteenth century works of the Bonheur family and those of George French Angas.

He continued to be amazed how many people had masterpieces hanging under their noses in their home, or stored away in a dark cupboard, in total ignorance of their value. Introductions by mutual friends gave him immediate personal contact and a credibility which he was not slow to exploit. Often the works could be obtained at knockdown prices and he was careful to convey the impression that he was only a casual amateur collector. He lived in hope of happening upon a masterpiece of sufficient value to keep him in comfort and enjoyment for the rest of his life, but meanwhile lesser works served his purpose well.

Walter left Harry to conduct the business in his own way. They were in regular contact, but only to discuss the generalities of business. Harry jealously guarded his freedom of action. He now had sufficient capital in PFA to follow his whims, and the trials of the wider world had little impact on the increasing success of PFA.

Harry had always had the flair necessary to succeed, but the financial crises of his early career had given him a hard edge, and now he also was a ruthlessly efficient businessman. The complexities and contradictions of his character were a reserve on which he could draw subconsciously and selectively as circumstances demanded. By nature he was a generous man, open and trusting, easygoing and with a natural aptitude for risk. But the hard lessons of life had superimposed other qualities. The flamboyant largesse that typified his early career, now was balanced by the emergence of a tight fist inherited from his Yorkshire ancestry. The philosophy of "if thou ever does 'owt for n'owt, div it fer thisen" was more prominent. The laidback idleness of youth now was masked totally by a work ethic, driven by ambition, that gave him a remarkable resilience and fighting spirit. He had a conscience, but it was selective. He was a soft touch for friends, but ruthless in business affairs.

PFA prospered, and the partners became relatively wealthy men. Some of the business was transacted in cash, and it gave them acute satisfaction to evade the predations of the taxman. In pursuit of the same objective, but with the added bonus of legality, they both established private offshore accounts.

In 1976, on the basis of Walter's expertise in the property market, they decided to invest in real estate in Florida. The Sunshine State was becoming the destination of vacationers from the northern states, and the permanent home of wealthy retired businessmen. Capital was not an absolute pre-requisite. Borrowing in the United States could be obtained to cover almost the full value of property. They identified Fort Myers Beach on the Gulf coast as the ideal location, found a local agent, and invested in an 80-acre plot of virgin woodland, Cedarwalk, which they were assured would soon be ripe for exploitation. If Harry had any lurking memories of The Lovett, he did not allow them to inhibit his present action. It was unlikely to show any return for three or four years, but the additional purchase of Spanish Lakes, a nearby Recreational Vehicle park on a spit of land between two small lakes with fishing, would provide immediate rental income.

Private Indulgence 1976-1977

Once bitten by the investment bug, Harry could not resist a house on exclusive Useppa Island, and purchased it privately although it was alarmingly expensive. Jayne adjusted immediately to the new lifestyle around the islands during their regular visits. It was a return to the standard of living of her youth, and which she accepted as her right, especially in view of the privations inflicted on her by Harry's earlier irrational property deals. Meanwhile the children splashed and swam in the warm waters of the Gulf of Mexico during their holidays, and Harry took them to collect shells from the soft silky sand of neighbouring Captiva Island.

Harry was in spending mode, and the following year he moved his family from Worcestershire to the manor house in a secluded Shropshire village between Ludlow and Shrewsbury. Manor Farmhouse represented a significant step up in value compared with their previous home, but Harry reasoned that it had paddocks for ponies, and the open country was an ideal environment for nine-year-old Ella and young Bill.

The same year he loosed his purse strings yet again. The Highcrags Estate in Northumberland caught his eye. Maybe it aroused an inner need to return to his roots in the northern Pennine hills, or maybe he simply recognised a bargain. He bought it for little more than a quarter of a million pounds through his private offshore account. Compared with either Florida or Manor Farmhouse, it was a give-away. It was a 1,500-acre oval hollow in the hills, a green strip of fields with brown pastures rising on each side. A small circular lake at the eastern end, frequented by moorland birds, fed a stream which flowed into a large long lake, and onwards through its outlet at the western boundary. There was a farmstead at each end of the estate, and 30 acres of ornamental woodland with a proliferation of rhododendron among native rowan and silver birch, all dominated by a tall Monkey Puzzle tree. An austere grey 24-room centrepiece, with coach house and stables, stood on a small bluff at the edge of the woodland overlooking the large lake. Its severe lines and unadorned hand-cut stone were not immediately welcoming, but it blended with the rocky crags that surrounded it, and with the drystone walls that divided the fields. Bellridge Hall was an integral part of the landscape, and Harry felt at peace when he was there.

To add to Harry's vanity, the Lordship of the Manor of Broomgrafton was tied to the property, and he toyed with the thought of business cards and headed paper for 'Lord Broomgrafton'. Miles and Antonia Mountjoy sometimes visited. Miles had an ambition to bag one of the reputed monster pike from the lakes, and Antonia revelled in the luxurious ambience of the oak-panelled reception rooms and the magnificent four-poster in the guest bedroom. Walter King had an open invitation and a few other friends were occasional guests. Harry had an army of close acquaintances, but he could count his real friends on the fingers of one hand.

He established a herd of the ancient White Park breed soon after he bought the estate, and the cattle usually grazed a large pasture which sloped down gently to the larger lake, in full view from Harry's bedroom window. They were an inspiring sight, their porcelain white coats patterned by the black points of their nose, eyes and ears, set against a backdrop of green and brown pasture and the blue lake. He derived enormous pleasure from watching them, or from going down to the pasture and standing quietly with them. Harry's earlier interest in bloodstock now served him in good stead, and he applied the same principles of animal breeding to his cattle to ensure he obtained the best results. He resented any suggestion that it was only a hobby, and eventually it became the premier herd in the breed, led by the elite bull Finnbennach. The cows always came up to greet him, especially the old favourites, with a lick of their rasping tongues on his outstretched hand. He was in no danger from their long, curved horns, although they could have inflicted fatal injury if they had wished. Even watchful Finnbennach accepted his presence with calm indifference.

Jayne did not enjoy the bleak isolation of Highcrags and, after an initial visit, avoided it completely. Occasionally, Ella and Bill accompanied him, and they revelled in the wide open spaces, but Jayne did not encourage their forays to the north and her lack of enthusiasm dampened their spirits.

A Risk too Far 1979

Seven years after Walter had invested in PFA, he was visiting Harry at Bellridge Hall and they were basking in their continuing success. "It was *bon chance* that you called to see me at Worcestershire in 1972," said Harry, "Otherwise I might still be sitting in my garage earning peanuts."

"I doubt it. You'd have been bankrupt or a millionaire, one way or the other. By the way, if you carry on spending as you have during the past couple of years, you probably will be bankrupt."

"You're becoming a pessimist! I suppose Florida is a risk, and for sure the Useppa Island house is a bit of a luxury, but come on, business is flying," Harry replied flippantly, "I have no doubt Highcrags will be a drain on the exchequer, but it is my battery charger. Why worry? Incidentally, talking of risk, what do you think of the idea of joining Lloyd's? Julian did mention some risk, but he painted a very rosy picture. A ten per cent return on uncommitted investment sounds to me like money for old rope, especially when you can continue to use the funds elsewhere." Julian Duffell had been a Name in Lloyd's of London for some years. He avowed full confidence in the insurance market, and pitched a strong line at Harry and Walter to become Names and take advantage of easy money.

"I'm game if you are. It sounded a very attractive proposition to me. I worry sometimes that Britain seems to be on an uneven keel, but we never seem to feel adverse effects, and fortune smiles on those who help themselves."

"Excellent. I'll give Julian the good news. You know, it's an interesting phenomenon, but we seem to be most successful at times of national crisis. Maybe it's something to do with works of art offering a safe haven in times of uncertainty. Look at the artists we've contracted. In the Bear Market of 1973 the value of shares dropped by more than 30 per cent, and we contracted Grant Donaldson. His paintings of the native peoples of East Africa are already valued higher than those of Joy Adamson. In 1974 there were the Birmingham Pub bombings, and yet we contracted Carolyn Overend from the Jewellery Quarter. I'm willing to bet that her jewellery will command huge prices in the near future. It is so individual and distinctive. Then this year there was the Winter of Discontent with piles of refuse in the streets, and we found that gorgeous little South African girl, Ami Kotze. She's a cracker."

Ami had evoked immediate memories for Harry of Elizabeth, the exquisite Ugandan princess who had visited Cambridge as a shy young girl, and first kindled his undergraduate affections during a memorable party on Huntingdon Road. When she later became the first black model to grace the covers of glossy international magazines, and even many years after, his pulse still rose with a nostalgic beat when he thought of her. Ami – another vision of beauty from Africa – had the same effect, and Harry had been unable to take his eyes from her when they first met.

Walter smiled. "And I thought you said you were a respectable married man! I hope you contracted her for the quality of her work, and not for your own nefarious designs. Anyway, you forgot Tom Nichols and his amazing bronze sculptures. You found him in 1976, and the only unusual occurrence that year was a summer drought. As a matter of interest, how do you persuade such outstanding artists to sign a contract with PFA?"

"The secret is finding artists who are superb craftsmen, but penniless. Not a difficult task as most artists are too busy concentrating on creativity to worry about money. I offer them security and marketing opportunities to allow them to concentrate on producing works of art. They're bound into tight contracts which commit them to sell to PFA at a fixed price, with a let-out clause for us to reject sub-standard work."

"Where does restriction of trade fit into that arrangement!" exclaimed Walter, "not that I'm objecting: I've been more than happy to benefit from the profits."

"We have competition from the London galleries, but I think we've got their measure. We've much lower overheads, we're more astute in recognising raw talent at an early stage, and remember the big galleries will charge artists 60 per cent or more commission. In any case, their real interest lies in poaching established artists."

"I've never properly understood how you worked – maybe I should after seven years. Tell me how our contract applies to an artist. What about Grant Donaldson, for example?"

"Yes, a typical case," reflected Harry. "He was hawking his pictures around company offices, and putting them in local exhibitions in municipal halls. He was getting maybe two hundred per painting if he was lucky. A financial cul de sac, and he was on his uppers. But there was real quality shining through. We put him on contract and paid him five hundred per painting plus 45 per cent of any extra over that figure realised on sale. With a planned programme of judicious exposure and promotion, his work is now commanding more than ten thousand pounds per painting. He gets around five thousand, and we keep five thousand. His work might well command maybe 40,000 at some stage, and we would retain almost 22,000 from that."

"It sounds a good arrangement from our point of view. But is it ethical – are we taking advantage of them?"

"No, not at all, and anyway, since when did you become so holier than thou! The contracts work in their favour in the short term, and in our favour in the long-term. *Quid pro quo*."

❋ ❋ ❋ ❋ ❋ ❋ ❋ ❋ ❋ ❋ ❋ ❋

Early in 1983 a letter arrived from the First Credit Bank in Florida. First Credit had been ready to provide loans with the least questions asked when Harry and Walter had required funding for their American investments. They had borrowed heavily for both Cedarwalk and Spanish Lakes in 1976, and subsequently had taken out an additional Letter of Credit. Harry had borrowed even further for his house on Useppa Island.

There had been little to disturb the calm progress and enjoyment of the Florida projects, and Harry opened the letter, interested to have an update on the financial situation. His casual interest rapidly transformed to astonished disbelief. The bank was calling in not only its loan, but also the Letter of Credit. In total more than one million US dollars. It had been unnerved by an adverse business assessment and reports of an impending downturn in the property market in Lee County where the properties were located, and lost no time in covering its position.

Harry and Walter held an emergency meeting. They had very little time to find an answer.

"There's no point in beating about the bush," Harry stated firmly. "If we deplete our liquid assets here in UK, our business goes face up in the water. Our only other assets are in Florida."

"I agree," replied Walter, "but we'll have to sell immediately on a soft market, and we're likely to take a heavy loss." Walter was the property expert, and he feared the loss might not cover the borrowings.

"We've no option. I have a suspicion that our agent may have been playing with the bank behind our backs, but there's not much we can do about it now. Will you contact the agent and First Credit? I have the unenviable task of breaking the news to Jayne. You should thank your lucky stars you're not married."

He did not relish the task. Jayne had accustomed herself with practised ease to each step back up the ladder of affluence. She was a slave to designer labels, and had not been reticent in her demands on Carolyn Overend for jewellery commissions. But Useppa Island had become the epitome of luxury for her. It provided the elegance and sophistication that she craved, within a private and select community, which exceeded even the indulgent pleasures of her youth. She regarded it as her second home.

Harry chose his time carefully. One evening, after a delight of cuisine at their favourite restaurant, and a Remy Martin at home, he felt the moment opportune.

"The markets have been pretty bloody recently..." he began.

"Oh, Harry, do we have to talk about such mundane matters on a lovely evening. You know I'm not interested in them, much less understand them."

"Our standard of living, including the childrens' education, does depend on business success."

"Yes, I know," she snapped at him, "but do you have to harp on about it. Things are fine as they are. Let's just leave it at that."

As he expected, this was going to be hard work. "I'm afraid things are not as fine as we would like. The situation in Florida is looking decidedly fragile, and I..."

Jayne's attention now was focused. "What do you mean? I hope you're not building up to some suggestion that we should sell the house on Useppa."

Harry took the bull by the horns. "More than that. We're selling all the Florida property to keep the bank happy. It may even mean some cutbacks here in our British business, and possibly some reduction in our standard of living." Best to get it all out at once, Harry thought.

He was not prepared for Jayne's reaction. "How dare you sell my favourite house without consulting me? It may be just a property to you; to me it is the centre of my life. I'm happier there than anywhere. And then you tell me that I must lower my standard of living as well. You can think again. What is there to stay with you for? You moved us here only a few years ago, and now even this is under threat. You wasted your money on that ridiculous farm in Northumberland, and you expect me to sit around while you try to patch things back together?"

"Calm down, please," he begged her. "I'm sure we can sort it out without drastic measures. I'm afraid Florida will have to go – the bank has given us no option. Beyond that, I think that if we tighten our belts for six months or a year, we'll get through. I don't want to economise on the children's education. They are both coming up to important exams, and it would be wrong to disturb them. So, we just need to exercise some discretion in the use of plastic for the time being."

Jayne was far from mollified, but she declined to discuss the matter further, and stalked out with a sullen expression. Her marriage to Harry had never recovered its initial joy after the birth of Bill, and the financial restrictions caused by the disaster of The Lovett. It was almost as if she had been keeping Harry under permanent scrutiny, in case he committed another blunder.

Harry contacted Barclaycard and American Express and halved the limits on all the private credit cards, but noted with grim foreboding that Jayne's spending continued as normal. He was unable to clear the account on her cards at the end of the first month, and in the next month she returned home from a shopping expedition in a furious temper.

"I've never been so humiliated and embarrassed in my whole life. To be told in front of strangers and, even worse, people I know, that I'm not creditworthy. How dare you do that to me! Standing looking like an idiot, with my purchases piled on the counter, and both my cards rejected. Over their limit! How can they be over the limit? I've not been doing anything different." She stopped, exhausted by her own fury.

Harry was genuinely sorry that she had been publicly exposed to ridicule. "I'm sorry you were embarrassed, but we agreed that we would have to restrict our spending..."

"We agreed! You mean you decided. I never agreed, and I see no reason why I should. My father never was penny-pinching with my mother. We always were able to have what any self-respecting woman should expect. I ignored them when they warned me not to marry a northern nobody from an impecunious background. I should have taken their advice. I probably would have done if you hadn't already got me pregnant."

"Jayne, please, you're over-reacting..." It was a forlorn plea.

"Let me tell you something," she resumed. "You may think that you can spread your largesse around, and play the big businessman, but I am not going to scrimp and save and suffer for your stupid mistakes." She would not lose an opportunity for yet another reference to Harry's investment blunder that caused such problems in Worcestershire. Then she returned to the attack. "Why don't you sell Highcrags?"

There she hit Harry's non-negotiation zone. "Not a chance," he replied, "that's the best investment I ever made."

"In that case, you can enjoy it on your own."

Jayne was as good as her word. She packed her belongings and returned with her children to the bosom of her affluent family in Wiltshire. Harry without his wealth did not provide the incentive she needed to stay in Shropshire, and his upbringing in a stable rural family had not prepared him to deal with a matrimonial crisis. Suddenly he was out of his depth – thrashing about desperately in an emotional storm. Events had moved with such suddenness that he was taken totally unawares and swamped. He seemed powerless to stem the tide as the focus of his life flowed away from him. Ella and Bill were his raison d'etre and he could not contemplate life without them. His love for Jayne had persisted despite the increasing evidence of her superficiality, and he had watched with dismay how she wallowed in the pleasures of opulence. Now his love eroded rapidly as she revealed the emotional hardness of her social class.

Harry's desperate sadness at the departure of his children, and the disruption of their education at such a vulnerable time, was matched only by his bitterness that his wife should run for cover the first time her support was needed. It was a time of great upset for Ella and Bill, both in their mid-teens, but it became an acute trauma for Harry when Jayne moved with indecent haste to live with Heinrich Lusser, a humourless but wealthy Swiss, on an estate near Zurich and married him as soon as she was free. She used distance as an opportunity to restrict Harry's access to Ella and Bill, and the telephone proved an unsatisfactory substitute for direct parental contact. It sowed in his previously trusting nature the seeds of a deep mistrust of women that was to haunt him and influence his actions for many years.

Harry sold the Shropshire manor house and moved back to Worcestershire to Blake Hill, a smaller house covered in Virginia creeper. It stood at the end of a tree-lined drive, off-set to the left so that it was not visible from the roadway. He was not particularly attracted by its old-fashioned architecture or the varying levels and passageways of the interior, but it took him away from the emotional memories of Manor Farmhouse.

Incorporation 1984

Harry and Walter considered their options with PFA. "We could walk away from it," mused Harry. "It's given us a damn good living for eleven years."

"That might not be a problem for me," replied Walter, "I have other businesses to keep me in wine and women, but PFA is your entire livelihood. And you're getting too old to keep starting from scratch again."

"That was below the belt, but probably there's an element of truth. If we look at the situation clinically, the underlying business still is viable. Our problem is capital. We could find financial backers, but they would want a piece of the action and some say in the direction of policy." Harry understood the implications of his suggestion. He would no longer have a totally free hand, but he was prepared to risk that limitation. Risk was his métier. Get the funds first, and then think about ways to overcome the problems.

Walter guessed that Harry's reaction to the trauma of Jayne's departure would be to bury himself in his work. That perhaps was no bad thing, but Walter thought that he should keep an eye on his old friend. "I don't see that as a problem, but you have been the active partner and you'll need to decide whether you can live with it."

"OK, let's give it a whirl."

Harry had done his homework. He knew of a company that might serve their purpose. Hayfell Industrial Holdings specialised in taking a stake in small businesses that had a surfeit of technical excellence and a lack of liquidity. Harry had met the Chairman, Vernon Sowerby, at a fund-raising function in Oxford. Walter was happy to leave the matter in Harry's hands, and he opened negotiations. It did not take long to reach agreement, but there were three conditions – HIH required that PFA would be incorporated, that one of HIH's two appointees to the Board would become Chairman, and that the main office and gallery would be located in Oxford. HIH would take a 40 per cent shareholding, leaving Harry and Walter 30 per cent each, and would make a loan to PFA of £500,000 interest-free for five years, and thereafter at two per cent over base rate.

Harry and Walter had no difficulty with the first two conditions. Incorporation made sense. The business was growing and more susceptible to claims for damages or professional negligence. As HIH was taking the largest stake, it also was reasonable that one of its appointees should be Chairman. There would be five Directors on the Board; two HIH appointees, Harry and Walter as the existing PFA partners, and a fifth new recruit from the City. Harry would become Managing Director. The third condition was not a real problem, although Harry would have to contend with a one-and-a-half hour commute at each end of the day, but it seriously dented the pride of two fervent Cambridge men to be based in Oxford. The advantageous terms for the substantial loan enabled them to swallow their pride.

The two HIH appointees were Jack Maladonis and Miles Mountjoy, both relatively new members of the HIH Board, and the latter was nominated as Chairman. Three years later there was a shake-up on the Board of HIH when it was discovered that Vernon Sowerby had been dispensing substantial favours to his mistress at the expense of the company. Neither his wife nor his fellow Directors were forgiving, and he was forced to resign. Miles Mountjoy was appointed as Chairman in his place. Jack Maladonis assumed that Miles in his new position would not wish to continue with PFA, and that he would become Chairman. However, Miles had developed a personal interest in PFA and declared his intention to continue as Chairman, much to Jack's chagrin and scarcely-concealed annoyance.

Miles Mountjoy came from the legal profession. Despite many years of residence in England, his accent still betrayed his Canadian origins. Although domiciled in UK, he owned property in North America and elsewhere, and was an itinerant for part of the year. He brought valuable expertise to the company, but more important he and Harry discovered a compatibility of spirit that expanded beyond PFA into social life. Miles had an amazing capacity to absorb and analyse information. He quizzed Harry relentlessly regarding all aspects of the business, and soon had an encyclopaedic grasp of the subject. Harry's accumulated experience and knowledge contrasted with Miles' analytical intensity, but they were complementary qualities which gave PFA a powerful drive and cemented the friendship of the two men.

First impressions did not convey anything special about Miles Mountjoy. He was medium height, medium build and medium fitness. The roundness of his rather pudgy cheeks was accentuated by the flatness of his well-groomed hair. But his tanned face had a smile, his brown eyes had a sparkle, and his seeming self-effacing manner hid a steely resolve. He was courteous and understanding in both private and business life, until he encountered deceit or incompetence. Then he was ruthless. He was a man to have on your side.

An International Business

Harry Bainbridge had retained one passion from his youth in the Pennines and the nearby Lake District. He was an ardent hill-climber. The exhilaration of reaching the first summit on an ascent, only to find another beyond, and then yet another and another, did not diminish his enthusiasm; the attainment of each horizon simply fuelled further determination and ambition. It was the same in his business life. Accumulated family wisdom of the structure of corporate Britain had not been handed down to him. Each step was a new experience, which opened up yet another opportunity, and each opportunity was seized with increasing confidence and vigour. It was a voyage of discovery, and he was driven by a combination of risk and ambition that was ingrained on his template of motivation.

With Harry Bainbridge at the helm, Miles Mountjoy giving full support and Walter King guaranteeing a majority vote on the Board, PFA enjoyed another period of remarkable success and high profits. They built on those programmes which had already had demonstrated their value, but expanded the 'backroom' activities of cleaning and restoration. Restoration of great paintings yielded handsome profits, but removal of accumulated grime on a lesser work often gave greater satisfaction by revealing a beautiful painting of special sentimental value to the owner.

Profits increasingly depended on the American market, where Miles' contacts were invaluable, and the growing strength of the dollar gave American clients the will and the opportunity to collect British works of art. The gallery provided the major income, especially through the judicious acquisition of work by rising stars in the art world. There was less opportunity to find valuable paintings at auction or in private houses, but Harry had a network of contacts that enabled him to maintain a steady flow of merchandise. The portfolios of contracted artists were also accumulating rapidly, and soon would enable a planned policy of promotion. One or two contracts were terminated, but many more were agreed.

Walter frequently enlivened Board meetings with his humorous interjections. "Mr Chairman, I wonder if PFA might benefit from having a marketing arrangement with the Erotic Print Society. It might be an opportunity to widen our constituency." He sat back and looked innocently at his colleagues.

Jack Maladonis was devoid of a sense of humour. "I can not believe Mr King would seriously make such a suggestion. I am deeply shocked," he spluttered. Peter Loder was about to follow with a similar sentiment when he saw the twinkle in Walter's eye.

"Do we really wish to be known as Stuckists?" continued Walter.

"In the definition of Tracey Emin, we are stuck in a time warp!"

"You've had your bit of fun, Walter," Miles said laughing, "but I suspect you prefer traditional art as much as the rest of us. I'm afraid I have no empathy for the conceptualists; pickled cows and soiled beds have no place in the Portway Gallery. Now can we get back to serious business."

They decided that their business as art dealers and restorers must have priority, and that the photography department must be curtailed. It added an extra dimension to the business, but it had not shown the level of profits necessary to justify further investment of funds or time. Association with royalty gave Lichfield and Snowdon a head start in that field. In future PFA would focus on summer workshops, using facilities at major public schools, under the guidance of Les Bracken, a disciple of Ansel Adams and noted exponent of the zone system.

New areas of business were developed selectively. Miles had a particular interest in majolica, and was a regular visitor to the Minton Museum. A fascination with the Renaissance, when the glazed pottery originally was imported into Italy from Majorca, fuelled his interest. Rare pieces occasionally came on the market, and Miles invariably was forewarned. The Directors also were eager to expand the international activities of MFA beyond North America. They made exploratory ventures to evaluate the potential of African, Australian and Chinese indigenous art. Encouraged by their initial findings, they identified local artists and craftsmen and established lines of supply.

Sitting in Harry's office, Miles was admiring the profusion of mismatched artefacts on shelves, cabinets, desk and any other spare surface. "This is a beautiful piece," he said, picking up a model of a woman in tribal costume. "Give me the background to your collection."

Harry was accustomed to Miles' detailed interest in anything to do with the company. "Yes, it is superb. I found it in Pretoria, and haven't yet been able to track down the artist. It's a Ndebele tribeswoman and her bangles and head-dress are genuine silver. My interest in African tribal costume started with paintings by Joy Adamson, and now of course we have Grant Donaldson under contract with his magnificent portfolio in the same vein. And look at these for lighter amusement," he reached and picked up two ostrich eggs, "Zulu and Xhosa women in costume, hand-painted on eggs by Carol Smit-Eggart."

"That etching would seem to fit the same theme." Miles pointed to a picture on the wall behind Harry. It was a litho print of a native tribe with cattle and sheep.

"That is an Angas. Amazing fellow. Born in my part of the world in County Durham in 1822. Took off for the Antipodes at a very young age and made an invaluable record of Maori costume, and Aboriginal to a lesser extent. But he also visited Africa and produced a large folio *The Kaffirs Illustrated* which was published in 1849. That picture is a study of a Zulu kraal. I'm particularly fond of it because, as you see, the native Nguni cattle are the same colour pattern as my White Parks at Highcrags."

"You've an incredible range of knowledge," said Miles with genuine admiration, "and much of our display in the gallery is based on the experience gained from your private collection. Not just the African items; I'm thinking also of those exquisite silk wall-hangings from the Chinese hinterland – individually hand-embroidered with gold and silver thread. We've done extremely well with those."

Demand for some items had multiplied rapidly. They had particular success with African art and Chinese silk, and the rapid growth of these new ventures required better local management. Initially PFA appointed managers to offices in South Africa and Australia, but as business continued to expand a more permanent solution was necessary. In 1991 they established subsidiary companies in both countries with local Directors. PFA retained a 30 per cent shareholding and the appointment of at least a third of the Directors for each company. The local Directors had incentive to make the business successful, and PFA retained the ability to monitor progress without imposing on indigenous enthusiasm.

Harry's glow of self-satisfaction in his ascending status received an occasional reality check. A letter from Dick urging him to attend his parents' golden wedding anniversary may temporarily have touched a sensitive nerve, but it was quickly ignored and forgotten in his focus on matters of greater importance. Teesdale seemed a long distant memory. Nor was it entirely a period of unbroken business success, but ladders of opportunity were only slightly inconvenienced by snakes of risk. In October 1987 Black Monday threatened, but capital was not a limiting factor for PFA at that time. The entry and exit from the Exchange Rate

Mechanism at the beginning of the 1990s scarcely caused a ripple in the smooth progress of the company.

Privately, both Harry and Walter were temporarily embarrassed. After they had become Names in Lloyd's of London in the late 1970s, they discovered it was difficult to obtain information about the inner workings of the Lloyd's syndicates. This was a cause of slight concern, but their worries receded as profits flowed into their accounts for no apparent outlay.

"I would like to know how it works," said Walter one day during a break in a Board meeting. "It sometimes seems too good to be true."

"It's served us very well so far," replied Harry, but Walter's words sat on the fringe of his thoughts. His principle regarding investments had been to cash them when they seemed to be too good to be true. Was not that what Walter had said? The more he pondered the situation, the more sure he became. Their lack of understanding of the market only confirmed his opinion. As they left the meeting he said to Walter. "I think I'll resign from Lloyd's. I feel uneasy."

"That's a remarkably swift change of mind. Do you think we should be working harder for it?" He joked, but guessed there was a reason for Harry's unease.

"There's too much uncertainty in too many places. Black Monday caused us no embarrassment, but it was a symptom of a volatile market. And then the recent storms in Sussex will produce a flood of claims from owners of expensive property. I am not frightened of risk, but there comes a point beyond which gambling must be curbed by sensible judgement."

"Coming from an inveterate risk-taker like you, that is a significant statement." Miles had overheard their conversation. "I've never understood why two sensible men would risk everything in a venture of such mystery and complexity."

"You've a good point, Miles," replied Harry. "It's not so much the unlimited liability that worries me, as the fact that I still have not been able to discover how the Lloyd's market works ten years after I became a Name. I can't tolerate secrecy in a business arrangement, and that is why I'll resign."

Harry and Walter resigned as Names from Lloyd's with effect from 31 December 1988. They each had underwritten £600,000 worth of insurance and their 25 per cent deposits – £150,000 for each of them – would remain in place while there were open syndicates. That was a severe, if temporary, inconvenience. Nevertheless, in 1989 Harry bought a splendid residence eight miles west of Worcester. The soaring inflation in house prices in the years after 1983 collapsed in 1988, and values had fallen by more than a quarter before he purchased Whitstone Court the following year for not far short of three hundred thousand pounds. It was as distant from Oxford as Blake Hill, but it was in his style. Despite his current single state, he felt relaxed and free in a spacious house.

He was comfortable in his lifestyle, and it was not until 1991 that he realised both how fortunate he and Walter had been, but also how vulnerable they were. Corruption had already eaten out much of the heart of Lloyd's. Some brokers repeatedly reinsured business through spirals of their own syndicates, taking commission at each step; other brokers spirited away vast sums – almost 50 million pounds in one case – to their off-shore accounts; and others covered up excessive risk with creative accounting. Lloyd's losses escalated through the early 1990s. In the end Harry and Walter were relieved to escape with the loss of only their deposits. They had enjoyed several years of easy profits, and they were not to know that the storms of 1987 in southern England were a foreboding of disaster that would engulf the ancient tradition of Lloyd's Names. They lost their deposits as the result of one bad year, but many friends who had continued to underwrite insurance into the 1990s faced total ruin – Lloyd's of London, after all, was unlimited liability!

Despite these setbacks, prosperity had been the keynote during the sixteen years since the directors of HIH had taken a stake in the business. It had been a profitable decision for them, and a happy development for Walter and Harry. Walter continued to preserve his single state, but Harry, after a series of entertaining entanglements, had indulged in matrimony for the second time in 1993 and now had been married to Theresa for seven years.

Harry had met Theresa Murphy after she had forsaken a successful business career in London for a more relaxed life in the country. Her flaming beauty and volatile temperament had attracted the attention of many a metropolitan Lothario, and had perhaps an even greater effect in rural Herefordshire. The legacy of her Irish Catholic upbringing had thwarted their desires for the most part, but she had succumbed to Harry's charm offensive and now was mistress of Whitstone Court.

It was 30 years since Harry had established PFA as a one-man business. Now it had an annual turnover in excess of four million pounds, but he was still standing tall and active, with a full head of curly hair, and of ideas; still enthused and inspired by his commitment to his original business objectives. Portway Fine Arts had filled him with excitement from the moment he scribbled the name on a scrap of paper. It was a very different business now, but it still had the power to raise his adrenaline levels. Now, in his last day in office he could look forward to a new situation.

3
A NEW SITUATION

Destiny in the Diary 2000

Harry reached for his notebook and switched to appointments for the following week – his first week as a free agent. 'Monday 28 February: 10.30am, meeting of YPF.' The Young Photographers Foundation had been created by PFA in 1990 as a charitable organisation to aid promising young photographers from disadvantaged backgrounds. There were three Trustees and he was one of two appointees by PFA. It was a worthy cause and the meetings were enjoyable and constructive, except for the frequent interventions of the third Trustee – Robert Gator – whose self-interest often seemed to take precedence over his support for the Foundation.

'Tuesday 29 February: 9.00am, meeting of Fiveways at Peterborough.' That would mean an early start, probably 6.00 am at the latest if he was to avoid the worst traffic, but it promised to be an interesting meeting with representatives of a property business and the possibility of developing links outside the art world. It was a contact that had been suggested by Miles Mountjoy, and he appreciated the concern that Miles had shown for his step into the unknown of retirement.

'Wednesday 1 March: 12.30pm, lunch at Bath & West Showground.' This was one of the perks of his job. It was a special event organised by English Nature, a government agency, to launch its pet environmental project for which his assistance had been sought. There would be copious alcohol, and he made a note to remind himself that he would need to arrange a chauffeur to drive him home.

'Thursday 2 March: Foremans exhibition of black-and-white photography at Leamington Spa.' No time was noted, but he knew the normal arrangements would apply – arrive around 10.30am for a glass of champagne, mingle with distinguished guests, address a few choice words and pithy quotes to the assembled press, and leave around midday unless he chose to stay for lunch. This was a commitment arranged some time previously, and it had been agreed that he should attend although it was post-retirement. He would need to be careful not to tread on Louise's toes, as the exhibition was a high-profile event that she might regard now as her rightful territory.

'Friday 3 March: 10.00am, meeting at IOD in London.' He flinched as he contemplated a 5.30am start – damn the rail service. He could not risk the inevitable train delays and cancellations, and would need to drive to the meeting. He disliked driving into London, he disliked even more driving out of London, especially on a Friday evening, and he was not looking forward to a dull and dreary meeting with legal experts and civil servants to discuss IPR and copyright issues. Despite the excellent facilities and ambience at the Institute of Directors, he could have wished for a better end to the week.

He switched off the notebook, put it in his briefcase, and tidied the papers that covered most of the surface of his desk into separate piles, one for each current item of work. He worked comfortably and efficiently with bundles of documents around him. Evidence of ongoing projects relaxed him, and a clear desk made him uneasy. As he arranged the papers his thoughts moved back to the week ahead, and he realised with a start that he would no longer be MD. He would be retired. And yet the programme for the week seemed remarkably familiar. Had he really thought life would be easier when he retired! Well, he would soon discover. At least he was going to continue to use his office for a while, as Louise was moving into a new office further removed from other staff, and his desk could remain cluttered for the time being. Now he was going home. Theresa would be expecting him. He gathered up his briefcase and car keys, went downstairs, keyed in the security code, locked the front door behind him and left the office for the last time as MD.

Theresa 1948-1992

The weekend was a disturbing mixture of excited anticipation and unexplained apprehension. Theresa outwardly was full of the joys of having Harry at home, of him not having to commute to the office, of doing things together; but inwardly she had a gnawing fear that his retirement would disturb the settled pattern of life to which they both had become accustomed. For several years they had both had time-consuming interests. He had been committed to developing his business, with frequent trips away. She had plenty of time for amateur dramatics and charitable work, especially Riding for the Disabled. Now it would be different. She wondered how he would cope with separation from his life's work. She wondered how she would cope with his presence around the house. She had lived alone until she married Harry, and thereafter had still enjoyed a great deal of personal space for most of the time. She now was moving into unknown territory.

Theresa was a complex character. Born in north-west Ireland not far from Galway, she alone among her siblings – one sister and two brothers – had felt the need to escape. She made the move to England in her late teens in the mid-1960s, determined to discover what opportunities there might be further from home. Her undoubted talents, projected on a gregarious Celtic sociability, soon ensured promotion from temporary secretary to research assistant. She continued up the promotion ladder and finally in 1978 at the age of 30 years she was appointed personal assistant to the Managing Director of an export company in London. She was given her own business card, and attended meetings of the Board where her direct opinions were valued highly.

Inevitably, her beauty and mercurial temperament made her the target of several ambitious suitors, but they were disappointed. A deep distrust of men and their motives was an integral part of her Irish Catholicism. For several years after her arrival in England she found comfort in the safety of group outings or parties, and avoided as far as possible any one-to-one situations. She dismissed the loud brashness of most of her male colleagues and found them childish and irresponsible. She expected it might be different when she became PA, but she was disappointed. Only one colleague was different. Tony Devonshire was Marketing Director, and had opportunity to be pompous and overbearing if he was so inclined, but he had a serious, gentle demeanour – courteous and unassuming. He was attractive in a quiet way, and showed no sign of arrogance or conceit. He made no advances to her, and she did not expect any, but gradually she found herself drawn to him. It was more than two years after she joined the company before he asked if she would have dinner with him, and she accepted without hesitation.

Tony Devonshire was married. Theresa did not learn this until they had spent several fulfilling but harmless evenings together.

Immediately her defences were raised, as the warnings instilled during her youth sprang to her mind. Tony soothed her alarm. He was separated from his wife, and they had not lived together for some time. He hoped that they would divorce before too long, and then he would be free to marry again. This did not entirely dispel the teachings of her Catholic faith, but she already had grown very fond of him, and put her doubts to one side, albeit with severe misgivings. He was a marvellous companion and a gentleman. She told herself that it would be alright when he was divorced, although she still had to face the possible hurdle of marriage to a divorced man. Nevertheless, she allowed their relationship to continue and strengthen. It moved from intellectual to emotional and finally to physical intimacy.

As time went by her love for him deepened, and he professed his love for her. They were regular patrons of the theatre and opera, and included Paris and Milan in their cultural itinerary. Their lives settled into an established pattern of semi-domesticity, without the tedium of a formal relationship.

Over time, a feeling of unease slowly and inexorably enveloped Theresa. Her professional life was fulfilling. She was a valued member of a dynamic business group, and she relished the challenges that the demands for success placed upon her. Her private life gave access to cultural variety that she had not dreamed of in her youth, but she knew there should be more. She was conscious from time to time that there was no evidence of any move on Tony's part to divorce his estranged wife, but there never seemed to be the right opportunity to discuss it with him. Her younger sister in Ireland already was happily married with two children, and a recent letter announced the expectation of a third.

Theresa called to congratulate her. "Brigid, your letter just arrived. What marvellous news. Of course, I'd be delighted to be a godmother, especially as she – he – is due so near my birthday."

"Hello, Theresa. It's grand to hear from you," Brigid's Irish lilt came back down the line, "I hope it's a girl this time. We didn't plan deliberately for a February baby, it just happened. You know the Irish propensity for large families."

That hit a raw nerve. Yes, Theresa thought bitterly, she did know. "I'm very pleased that you are keeping up the tradition, because I'm not making any contribution. Maybe I forfeited that privilege when I opted to chase a career in England."

"Oh, no, I'm sure that's not right," replied Brigid quickly, realising she had unwittingly exposed a sensitive subject. "There will be a Mr. Right out there for you somewhere, but you always were difficult to please. Is there nobody in the frame at present? What about Tony?"

Theresa had mentioned Tony to Brigid occasionally, but never indicated the seriousness of the relationship. She had always been restrained; now emotions overcame restraint. "Do you realise, Brigid, that I'll be 40 next birthday? I was 32 when I first went out with Tony, and I'm still unmarried and childless. I began to have doubts about four years ago, and he proposed to me when I questioned his intentions. I suppose I assumed that it would progress from there, but nothing has changed. He still is married, my body clock is ticking past child-bearing, and I don't know what to do." Her voice was breaking with emotion.

Brigid had never heard her sister so upset, and she had not known the full story before. She was furious on her behalf. "Theresa, it may not be my place to give you advice. I'm seven years younger than you, and I haven't moved far from County Galway, but I know that man is no good for you. He's a charlatan and a scoundrel. He's stringing you along, and has no intention of marrying you. Get rid of him."

"But he's had the best years of my life. I can't just throw it away..."

Brigid cut in. "Yes you can. You're still young and attractive. Plenty of men would give their eye-teeth to marry you, and you're far too good for Mr Tony Devonshire. He will have a piece of my mind if I ever see him."

Brigid's sisterly advice brought Theresa to her senses. An article in a women's magazine that she would not have noticed before, now immediately caught her attention. She was dismayed by an American survey which showed that among female executives only two per cent got married after the age of 40, and only one per cent had a child after the age of 40. A feeling of panic welled up inside her. *"What have I done?"* she thought. *"I never intended not to have a family, but I became too absorbed in my career. I've gained admittance to the boardroom, but have lost my chance to have children. I've been overtaken by time."*

Desperation born of panic propelled her to precipitate action. She decided there were other areas of life to explore beyond a London business office, and she wanted to be free of Tony Devonshire. She gave notice of her intention to resign. The Directors were horrified, and exerted every stratagem and argument at their command to persuade her to change her mind. But her decision had been made, and was not to be changed, and she noted grimly that Tony made no attempt to stop her. She worked through her notice with diligent conscientiousness, was genuinely surprised and delighted to receive a leaving gift of an antique writing desk at a lavish party, sold her apartment, and moved to a picturesque cottage in the peaceful beauty of the Welsh Marches near Hereford.

Some may have ascribed her success to her arresting Irish beauty. Tall, slim, long-legged and green-eyed, she was the archetypal girl from the Emerald Isle that English men find irresistible. As she entered her fifth decade, she still retained her youthful figure and fresh beauty, together with her irrepressible enthusiasm for new experiences and her thirst for knowledge. But it was rather the other qualities of her personality that had laid the foundation of her status in the business world. Her open honesty and her reliability, evident from the moment she arrived on English shores, were characteristics which took her unaccustomed colleagues and competitors by surprise.

Why had such a strong-willed and able woman allowed herself to trust a devious man for so long, and so unquestioningly? Maybe the answer lay in her childhood. The combined coercive collusion of church, school and parents in Ireland had left her with a strong sense of duty and an overpowering sense of guilt. Her Irishness encapsulated the mass of contradictions that is the product of her national birthright. Theresa never tired of telling Harry they'd had the Book of Kells when the British still were savages, and yet in the twentieth century many of their women remained second-class citizens. They boasted a pantheon of poets and musicians, and yet they could easily be capable of electing a foreigner as President simply on the strength of having coached the Irish soccer team to a successful World Cup campaign. In the Ireland of Theresa's youth, the strongly paternalistic culture did not encourage or reward girls, and it punished pride in achievement. How could any girl cope with such an avalanche of mixed messages? Despite her considerable talents, Theresa was left with a deep-seated lack of confidence and an unwillingness to actively project and promote her own qualities and abilities.

Now that she had broken free from her emotional and professional shackles, she determined to be her own woman in future. She would give rein to other interests, and particularly indulge her passion for the theatre. Her great regret – apart from her single status and lack of children – was that she had never had time to pursue her childhood dream of the stage. Now maybe she could remedy that deficiency. She had no great thespian ambition, but the thought lurked at the back of her mind that Margaret Rutherford had been much older before she decided to tread the boards. She had exhibited considerable acting ability as a girl, and she had a remarkable soprano voice. She joined the local dramatic society and auditioned for the next production.

Her arrival in Herefordshire generated a great deal of interest. A single woman – and an attractive one into the bargain – was good cause for excitement and gossip in pubs and clubs. There were several eligible bachelors who were confident they could exercise their charm to good effect. They all were politely dismissed. Tony Devonshire was still a raw memory. She intended to involve herself gently and cautiously in the local community, testing the temperature slowly and pleasurably, before risking total immersion. She became a recognised, if slightly distant, part of the community, known for her impeccable dress sense and her willingness to help good causes. They were unprepared for another side of her character which emerged during the general election in 1992.

Transport was being arranged to ensure that those who had indicated their intention to vote Conservative, but were without a car, could get to the village hall. Theresa offered to help although she was not an active member of any political party, and cheerfully set about ferrying all and sundry to the polling booth to vote. She quickly discovered that was not the intention! Assisting voters of other parties was not on the organisers' agenda, but her priority was to help those who needed help. Her qualities of innocence and strong sense of fair play were completely incomprehensible to the members of the local Conservative Party.

Lady Jane Smith-Blundell, the local party chairman, stared in disbelief as Theresa helped three elderly local residents from her estate car. "We only ferry our own," she intoned imperiously. She was a statuesque figure, attired appropriately in a blue suit, who was accustomed to issuing reprimands.

"I'll provide transport to those who need it, in whatever way I see fit. Their political allegiance is no concern of mine." Theresa's response was immediate and crushing.

Harry also gave a helping hand at election time, and this was the first time that he had seen Theresa. Her disregard for the establishment and her unambiguous declaration of her belief captivated him. He watched fascinated as she dismissed the pettiness of local officialdom. Here was a woman of character. She had thick rich auburn hair and a striding haughty elegance – both matched perfectly by Boru, the Irish Setter that was constantly at her side. Her long coat, unbuttoned and flowing, swirled as she turned away, and the fine features on her up-tilted face held an expression of utter disdain.

Although their homes were only a few miles apart, Harry did not see her again for four months. Then they found themselves invited by a mutual friend as the single man/single woman combination in a dinner party of married couples. His initial impression of her was confirmed. Superficially she was haughty – almost supercilious – but Harry guessed it was part of her protective shell. She also was independent. Her successful business career in London gave her an air of authority, and a clear signal of indifference to attention from the opposite sex.

Until now the bitter experience of his first marriage had prevented Harry from allowing himself commitment to another binding relationship, despite the attractive women who had fallen across his path. But that inhibition began to disappear as he talked to Theresa. He did not have to evade her attentions – even if he had wished to. She did not wish anything from him. He was intrigued by a woman who showed no interest. He tried to rationalise his thoughts. *How could a woman have such an immediate impact on him! Was he really prepared to enter another permanent relationship? How was she different from other women he had known, and especially from Eva Garcia?* He could not provide any sensible answers, but if fate had determined that this woman's path should cross his, then he was happy that it should be so.

Eva 1992

It was only five months since he had parted from Eva Garcia, and Harry's mind slipped back over their brief encounter.

Business had been booming in the late 1980s, and it continued in a similar vein into the 1990s. Harry proposed that PFA should take all the Directors and staff, together with their partners, for four days in Andalusia for the festivals, including the World Expo '92 on La Cartuja, and the quincentennial celebrations of Columbus' first voyage to the Americas. Two days in Seville and two in Cordoba. The summer schedule of events for PFA determined that the visit would be in April, and it suited British visitors better than the heat of the summer. Local Spanish agents made all the arrangements, and the party was met at the airport by Eva who was to act as their guide and interpreter. She attracted the immediate attention of all the men. She was dark, vital and irresistibly alluring, and wives and girlfriends involuntarily moved protectively closer to their partners. They need not have worried. Eva Garcia Munoz was a very professional guide and an excellent interpreter. She had a great sense of fun, but she kept her distance.

Seville symbolised the character of Andalusia, with its imposing architecture among a maze of narrow streets. It was the inspiration for Carmen, Don Juan and Figaro. Eva took them to the picturesque Barrio de Santa Cruz area, the immense gothic cathedral and the delicately-patterned Moorish Giralda Tower, and they marvelled at the birdlife in the swamps of the Parque Nacional de Donana. Harry was well pleased. It was proving to be an excellent piece of employee relations. The party then moved up the Guadalquivir valley to Cordoba, an even more ancient city that traces its history to Phoenician merchant sailors, and was the political centre during the Moorish era in Spain.

On the coach journey to Cordoba, Eva took Harry and Miles aside. "Tonight we have a banquet at the hacienda of El Cordobes, the famous matador." She spoke with a slight lisp and an intriguing Geordie accent acquired on exchange visits to Newcastle-upon-Tyne. "There is a bull-ring beside the hacienda, and it is our custom that the leader of our guests must fight the bull." Harry and Miles looked at each other and smiled. Eva had already shown plenty of evidence of a quirky sense of humour. "I see you do not believe me. Perhaps you will believe me when the bull is looking at you. Which of you will have the honour?"

"PFA is your company, Harry," Miles jumped in quickly. "Even if Eva is serious, I wouldn't dream of depriving you of your rightful perks."

"Good," replied Eva, "I am glad you are so enthusiastic Harry.

When we arrive at our hotel I'll tell you what you must do."

Cordoba was reached in the late afternoon, and as they left the reception desk Eva came over to Harry. "I will come to see you in one hour to prepare you for the bullfight!" She smiled at him mischievously.

Harry had unpacked, taken a shower and was relaxing in casual clothes when Eva knocked at his door. She came in, and Harry was lost for words. She was wearing a long, low-fronted, frilled and flounced red gown, closely fitted to her body down to her hips, but ruffled, full and swirling below. Her curly hair was gathered high with a peineta – the traditional patterned comb head-dress – and she was wearing loose bracelets on both wrists. She took his breath away.

"You do not like?" she asked. The disappointment at his silence clearly evident in her face. "Is it too much?"

"Oh no," Harry came to his senses. "You're absolutely stunning. I was temporarily overcome. You are a most beautiful woman." He could not take his eyes from her. "Come and have a drink."

"No thank you," she replied, "I must teach you about the bullfight." She came over to him. "I am dressed for the flamenco. In the dance the man is the matador and the woman is his cape. It is symbolic of the fight – and the matador always wins! This is how it is done." And she taught him the steps of the dance, her red dress swirling around them, and their arms intertwining. She was not tall and willowy in the accepted style of the flamenco, but as she fell under the spell of the dance her sensuous rhythm created a tempo of fiery elegance underlain with mystery and sadness. It bore little resemblance to the clatter of heels and castanets that Harry had always associated with flamenco.

This was the first time that Harry had been so close to her. Her exciting beauty, exotic dress and heady perfume were an intoxicating mixture.

"I would be happy to do this with you all night," he said at last, "but should you not be teaching me about the bull?"

She stopped and looked at him, sad that he had broken the spell. "Yes. I would prefer to dance with you, but we must prepare for the bull."

✽ ✽ ✽ ✽ ✽ ✽ ✽ ✽ ✽ ✽ ✽ ✽

Harry stood in the centre of the bullring at El Cordobés hacienda in the impending dusk of early evening not knowing what to expect. He was dressed in his white linen suit, with a red cape draped over a real sword as he had been instructed. Large doors opened at one side of the ring and a black beast charged out. It stopped a little distance from him. It was not full-grown – in reality little more than a bovine adolescent, but it was black, big enough, and it looked ferocious.

He heard Walter's voice from the gallery. "Play him like you did the wing-forwards at college. Plenty of body swerve."

Harry did not have a witty response, nor did he have time. The beast was charging at him, head down. He held the cape extended on the sword on his right-hand side, and he felt the surge of bovine aggression as it charged straight through. They both turned, repeated the movement in a series of passes as if it was choreographed, and continued for some minutes. Harry felt a thrill of excitement. Fear had turned to challenge. He did not approve of bullfighting, but he began to sense the same feeling of poetry in motion that he had experienced when dancing with Eva. He began to enjoy himself, and was disappointed when the assistants came and lured the beast away. He returned to the side of the ring to loud applause.

"That was brilliant." Eva's eyes were flashing with pride for him. "Maybe it was only a baby, but you were very brave. As a reward you will dance the flamenco with me after the banquet."

Later that evening, when they were sitting close together on the terrace recovering their breath under a dark velvet Mediterranean sky, Eva looked at him. "All the others in your group are with their husbands and wives, but you and Mr King are alone?"

"Walter – Mr King – is a confirmed bachelor. He's never been married, and probably never will. I have been married, but I was divorced several years ago."

"Ah! You will marry again?" Her voice was quiet and hesitant.

He looked at her. In the short time since they had met, he had developed a special feeling for this young woman. He was attracted to her, but he was not without a vestige of reason. She was beautiful, young and Spanish, and a Catholic to boot; he was much older, not particularly religious, and divorced. Not a propitious foundation for a successful relationship. He did not answer, but put his arm around her and pulled her close to him.

"Tomorrow night I will show you Cordoba," she whispered.

Next day, after they returned from the day's excursion, Harry and Eva slipped away into the city. She showed him the magnificent Mezquita – a mosque large enough to house a cathedral inside it – with its fortress-like exterior but a stunning interior of double-tier, two-tone arches in red and gold. They wandered hand in hand through the narrow lanes of the old mysterious Jewish quarter, and Harry bought a pair of delicate filigree silver ear-rings for her. They ate in Bodegas Campos, an old wine factory converted into an exclusive restaurant. Eva introduced him to the local specialities of *choco* – the delicate small cuttlefish, *jamon serrano* – a thinly-sliced mountain-cured ham from the village of Jabugo, which derives its special flavour from the acorns that are the staple diet of the native black Iberic pigs, and *yema* – candied egg yolks with exotic Moorish flavours. Harry had his name chalked in large letters on the barrel of wine that he purchased. Afterwards, they walked back slowly to the hotel together, arms linked, oblivious to all around them. It was late when they arrived.

"You are leaving tomorrow, Harry," she began, "when will I see you again?"

"Tomorrow is a long time away. Come to my room, and let us dance the flamenco once more." He kissed her gently on her cheek "I want to remember the magic of holding you in my arms."

They went upstairs together, but at his door she stopped. "No, Harry, we must not. If I dance with you again it will go too far, and it is too soon for me. I need to know you more before I lose myself completely." He did not argue, but held her close. There were tears in her eyes. Passion was roused in both of them, and she broke free and ran from him without another word.

Harry's first urge was to follow her, but he resisted the temptation. He thought back over the past two days. *He had been a fool for breaking the magic spell when they had been dancing in his room before the banquet, and maybe he should have been more insistent tonight when they returned to the hotel.* But there was a special quality about Eva that made him feel perversely happy that she retained her chaste purity.

Early next morning the PFA party travelled to Madrid by the new AVE fast train developed for the World Expo, and then onwards by air to London. Harry and Eva exchanged letters for a while, but he never saw her again. He was left with memories of a prize that had hung briefly and tantalisingly almost within his reach. And within a month Theresa had come into his view.

Courtship 1992–1993

Harry wasted no time in pursuing Theresa's acquaintance after the dinner party. He finally had put the painful memories of Jayne firmly behind him, and Eva had played a significant role in that process. Theresa also was overcoming the disappointment of Tony Devonshire four years previously, although she retained the doubts that face most Catholic women in a relationship with a divorced man.

They had a brief and joyous courtship – full of laughter and spontaneous excitement. An Irish Catholic and a Yorkshire Primitive Methodist – at least by upbringing – would scarcely seem an ideal match, but they discovered and explored an accumulating pattern of unexpected common interests and shared values.

Harry rarely discussed his upbringing in any detail, but he felt able to confide in Theresa. "You'll probably find it difficult to understand the poverty that existed in the remote areas of the Yorkshire Dales. No electricity, no telephone, no bathroom and a loo across the farmyard. It probably was the driving force that allowed Primitive Methodism to become established."

"I can understand, believe me," she replied. "It could have been no worse than the poverty in the western areas of Ireland. What's worse is that poor Catholics, with scarcely any possessions to their name, are required to donate regularly to fund the extravagant excesses of the Vatican. Have you ever seen the obscene and ostentatious wealth in the Vatican? How I wish Pope John XXIII was alive. He was a Primate who understood the needs of the poor."

"Yes, I've been to the Vatican and, like you, was appalled by the gold and marble and precious works of art, but I think it's the same everywhere. The establishment feathers its nest at the expense of the poor." Harry could see that Theresa's philosophy coincided closely with his own. "Historically, the British aristocracy has manipulated the political and business hierarchy to ensure that its privileges and wealth remain intact. And the monarchy! That is something else. I'll never understand how a supposedly free and independent-minded British citizen is prepared to consider himself the subject of anyone, let alone a family of German-Greek descent."

"That's something the Irish find almost impossible to comprehend. We consider everyone equal. Putting someone on a pinnacle – a throne – because of an accident of birth is an insult to any self-respecting citizen. It's totally contrary to the ethic of reward for effort and achievement, which is so precious especially to those who come from an unprivileged background."

They both nurtured a deep dislike of insincerity. Their friends were open genuine people, whose word was their bond. They found joy and freedom of spirit especially in the open countryside, and they bonded most closely during long walks on the Malvern Hills with Boru bounding beside them.

As their relationship deepened, thoughts of marriage began to cross Harry's mind, and with them the inevitable doubts. *Was Theresa the right woman? Was this just the chance of time? Did being in the right place at the right time, make her the right person? She was independent, and could be haughty and remote. Should he not stop and think! Impetuous man. If he had laid the ghosts of the past earlier, might he not have established a permanent relationship with Ami Kotze? In fact, why was he not now with Ami? She was a total contrast to Theresa – soft and tender, and she relied on him.*

Ami 1960–1993

Ami Kotze had been born in South Africa 33 years earlier. Her family lived in Mitchell's Plain, a suburb of Cape Town, and she was classified as coloured in her native country. Despite the disadvantage of her social status, the gods had smiled upon her; she was spared any physical hazards which might have afflicted racial mixture, and instead was blessed with remarkable beauty.

She was a true daughter of African soil. The graceful litheness of the pastoral Simba was evident in all her movements. The more ancient San heritage was imprinted in her broad forehead, wide-set eyes, high cheekbones, delicate pointed chin, and small finely-shaped hands. The Simba and their cattle had been part of the great Bantu southward migration which came to a halt about one thousand years ago in northwestern Namibia where their nomadic culture became unsustainable, and the San have been almost totally dispersed from their specialised adaptation to their native homelands, but they lived on in Ami. The honey-gold skin tones of the San were overlaid and darkened by the same raiding Arab influence that is evident in female beauty in eastern Africa from Eritrea to the Cape, and the later European invasion pressed its stamp on a virginal Simba mould. Ami had inherited these native and exotic blends, and her genetics encapsulated the history of southern Africa. An impartial observer would have been spellbound by her beauty and grace, but the ethnicity of her native country branded her a crossbred – a coloured – barred from recognition by any unalloyed ancestral culture. She possessed the finest attributes of all the elements of her ancestry, but had the privileges and recognition of none.

She had always been attractive. Her light-coffee complexion framed in black, wavy hair, that hung down below her shoulders, was accentuated by deep-brown almond eyes. Her slender hands and long sensitive fingers, smoothly-athletic legs, and a slim but decidedly feminine figure, flowed together into a presence that lit up a room when she entered. She was a girl of contrasts. In quiet moods, her eyes were soft and demure, and a shy, wistful half-smile played on her face. She appealed with the sensitive vulnerability of a delicate fragile flower. But when her emotions were roused, she was like a wild gypsy – an unbroken mountain filly. Her white teeth shone through a broad smile, her dark eyes flashed; she embodied rebellion and spontaneity which excited the natural emotions of any man she encountered, yet sent a subliminal warning to ardent admirers.

Deprived of love from an early age, she longed for it desperately. The frequent absences of her disinterested father left a void that she ached to fill, yet the legacy of his occasionally violent presence was an ingrained fear and automatic acquiescence to male authority. Her whole being cried out to be loved, and she absconded from an unhappy home and an unhappy country at the age of seventeen. She had shown great artistic talent in an environment which did not encourage it. She knew she must seek fulfilment elsewhere.

When Harry Bainbridge first met Ami, at the house of an artist friend two years later, she was dressed in the style of a gypsy girl. Her long black hair was interwoven with a red patterned scarf of the same material as her colourful, flowing, calf-length dress. The blue top was cut low on her full breasts, and tied behind at the waist. Her ear-rings, bracelets and rings were bold. The whole ensemble was a dramatic – even blatant – announcement of her presence, but quite contradicted by her quiet retiring demeanour. Harry was entranced by her.

"Let me guess," he said, a playful smile on his lips, "I think you are a princess from Ethiopia, a descendent of the Queen of Sheba. Such beauty can only come out of the Horn of Africa".

Harry's compliments received a muted response, and he wondered why such an apparently extrovert girl could be so withdrawn. However, he had seen Ami's work and recognised her great talent. He did not allow his emotional speculation to over-rule his business instincts, and contracted her to MFA in 1979. She was very grateful to him for his interest and support. She was virtually penniless and the security of a contract with PFA, with the promise of regular income, was a welcome luxury for her.

✿ ✿ ✿ ✿ ✿ ✿ ✿ ✿ ✿ ✿ ✿ ✿

Her prolific talent proved a profitable asset for PFA, and for some years she was happy to express her personality through her creativity and experiment with a variety of art forms.

As her confidence was restored she began to assess her situation, and her ambition quickened. She began to question the PFA contract, and suspected that it might not be in her best interests. The rebellious spark that had lain dormant for a long while began to re-emerge. By 1983 she reached the conclusion that she should become independent, and requested a meeting with Harry to discuss her contract.

She could not decide how to present herself to best advantage. She laid out her limited wardrobe. *Would he be more impressed by a sober, serious appearance, or would a little feminine allure be a profitable distraction?* In the end she compromised. She thought that a dark green suit would convey the seriousness of her intent, and her hair was tied back severely. But her sheer stockings, the shortness of her skirt, and two escaping wisps of hair that hung cheekily over her left eye, betrayed her real intent.

"Ami, do come in." Harry noted her attire with amusement, and his eyes went immediately to her elevated hemline. With a mischievous grin, he indicated a low easy chair in his office. "Have a seat. Coffee or tea?"

"Thank you. Coffee, please, Mr Bainbridge." Ami was feeling

distinctly apprehensive. She was on a delicate mission, about to enter negotiations with an accomplished businessman, and his cheeky smile and quick downward glance had both encouraged and unnerved her.

"Let's not be too formal. Please call me Harry." He asked his secretary for two coffees, and sat down opposite Ami. "Now, I'm intrigued by your request for a meeting. Have you some exciting new ideas – ." He paused as she crossed her legs and exposed a delicious sliver of smooth flesh above her stockings.

Ami sensed her advantage. She gathered her thoughts and her courage. "I've been with PFA for four years," she began tentatively, "and I'm grateful for all the help you have given me. I hope that I have worked hard to repay your faith in me. Now I think that I would like to work as a freelance artist, and take the risks of success or failure myself." She stopped, not sure how much to say. She had said enough to cause Harry's gaze to swivel from her legs to her face.

He looked at her intently. His bold blue eyes held her soft brown ones for a few seconds before she looked away. Ami was the brightest star in his growing galaxy of contracted artists, and he did not want to lose her. "Ami," he said deliberately, "it's a big, bad world out there. We – PFA and myself – are here to protect you. We have invested a great deal in you, and we wouldn't want to see your talent torn apart by the sharks of the art world. I think it would be best if you continued in your contract."

Ami was deflated. Despite her apprehension, she had assumed in her youthful naivety that Harry would agree to her request. She tried again. "I would like to take the chance. I can be strong when I want to be."

The disappointment on her face was obvious. Harry relented a little, but not very much. "This is a major decision in your life, Ami." His voice was soft and reassuring, and he smiled. "Let us give it much deeper thought and consideration. You work extremely hard, and you should take a break. Visit Paris or Rome; see the Musee d'Orsay or the Cistine Chapel. You can relax and widen your artistic repertoire at the same time. I am going on a visit to Egypt early next year for the same reason. Let us talk again about your ideas when I return."

Ami left the office in a daze. She had not contemplated rejection, and she was embarrassed. She was sure Harry had understood the reason for her choice of clothes, and he probably now was laughing at her.

As she gathered her scattered wits, her determination returned. Tears of frustration welled in her eyes. She *would* be free from her contract. She thought back over the conversation. He had said they would talk again, and that gave her some hope. Maybe his visit to Egypt would make him more sympathetic to her plea. Maybe – and an idea began to form in her mind. After four years in England she was fully aware of her effect on the opposite sex, and she felt sure that in the right environment she could exercise enough seductive charm to persuade Harry to agree to release her. She had deduced that men are pathetically easy to flatter and, knowing that Harry had been separated from his wife recently, guessed he might be emotionally vulnerable.

Ami was friendly with Harry's PA, and they often chatted idle girlie gossip. It was not difficult in casual conversation to discover the details of Harry's Egyptian visit. He was travelling alone with Kuoni, leaving Heathrow on 28 February. That was enough for Ami. Next day her booking on the same tour was confirmed.

❊ ❊ ❊ ❊ ❊ ❊ ❊ ❊ ❊ ❊ ❊ ❊

Harry was surprised to see Ami in Terminal 3 at Heathrow airport as he headed towards the departure gate to catch his Egyptair MS778 flight. "Ami, this is a coincidence. Which exciting resort are you heading for?"

"I'm travelling with Kuoni on an Egyptian tour. I've never been to North Africa before."

"Good lord," he exclaimed, "I'm on the same tour. That is unbelievable!"

Ami smiled to herself. They boarded the plane together, and arrived in Cairo late that evening. The group had been booked into the airport hotel in readiness for an early start next morning. They checked in sleepily at 4.30am and were airborne on a small plane by five o'clock. Harry suggested to Ami that seats on the left-hand side would be a good idea, and she realised why when the sun came up over the eastern desert. As the blood red orb rose like a bubble from the flat brown horizon, before slowly detaching itself, she clutched at Harry's arm and pointed excitedly at the sunrise. Harry was charmed by her childish amazement.

"It is an awesome sight," he said. "Fix it in your memory, and you'll recall it when you need inspiration in the future. Look down below. See there's the Nile flowing like a narrow ribbon, edged with a hem of green cultivated fields, and squeezed between vast expanses of burning desert."

She leaned across him for a better view. "Oh, Harry, isn't it wonderful." She was holding his hand in a tight grip, and he did not mind.

They sat in this manner in silence for a little while until Ami glanced at him and, still holding his hand, said, "Would you have enjoyed travelling alone? It seems too good not to be shared."

"I separated from my wife last year – you probably know about that – and I thought this would be a good opportunity to forget all about it."

"Maybe you should have planned more carefully," she replied, a teasing smile on her tempting lips, "have you forgotten it's a Leap Year. I can propose to you today."

"Now that *is* something for me to look forward to." They both laughed, and Harry continued, "It's also my birthday tomorrow, and I'm glad you're here to celebrate it with me."

They reached Aswan before 6.30am, and continued on to Abu Simbel, the great temple rescued from its original site in the 1960s to prevent inundation in the waters of Lake Nasser when the Great Dam was built. Galleries inside the artificial mountain took them behind the massive statues, and added to the sense of awe and wonder.

That night they stayed at the Aswan Oberoi Hotel on Elephantine Island in the middle of the Nile.

"Happy birthday, Harry." Ami greeted him with a kiss and a hug as he came down to breakfast the following morning. She was wearing only a white T-shirt with a single red flower motif, and pink shorts. She had a small cluster of bougainvillaea gathered from shrubs around the hotel. "Put these in your hair, and pretend it's your hippy days again."

He enjoyed the attention that Ami was lavishing on him. After breakfast the whole group embarked for the eastern bank on graceful, narrow feluccas – the triangular-sailed boats of the Nile. Most of the group went off to visit the Aga Khan Mausoleum, but Harry and Ami opted instead for a camel ride into the desert. They soon adjusted to the easy rocking gait of their mounts, and as they left the river behind Ami's gentle softness was abandoned. Her *joie de vivre* was infectious and, as they turned for home, their camels broke into a gallop and the full force of Ami's rebellious hedonism emerged in shrieks of laughter. Harry fixed in his mind the picture of this dark, crazily beautiful girl urging her mount to even greater speed, her T-shirt blown back against the thrust of her breasts, and her long hair flowing in the wind.

They returned on the feluccas to Elephantine Island for lunch in the Nubian restaurant, and there was no organised itinerary for the rest of the day. After lunch, Ami sat beside Harry with a long, cool gin and tonic. "As it's your birthday, will you let me organise it as a surprise for you? Only you must not ask what is planned, and you must be a good sport and do as I ask. Promise."

Harry laughed again at her infectious enthusiasm and enjoyment. "I promise. I love surprises."

"I'm sure you'll love my surprises." She flung her arms around his neck and kissed him with passion. Then equally abruptly, she jumped to her feet. "Come on, let's go for a walk." Harry was still reeling from the suddenness of her movements. She took his arm and went out into the gardens. The hotel grounds were full of bougainvillaea with beautiful red-purple blossom. They meandered slowly through the shrubs down to the edge of the river where they could see local women with their washing on the far bank, and sat on the rocks to watch the graceful feluccas gliding past. After a while, Ami took his hand and, without a word, led him back to the hotel and up to her room.

She stood beside the bed, facing him. "Please Harry, undress me."

Harry had been celibate for more than a year. The later stages of his marriage to Jayne had been devoid of sexual pleasures, and he had not been tempted since they had been separated. But he would have been happy to be celibate for many years even if the reward had been only a fraction of the intense, ecstatic sensations that swept over him that afternoon with Ami. Neither of them was aware that it was a long time since the other had made love, nor what a contrast it was to their previous experience. But they both knew they had just experienced something very special.

They lay in bed until it was time for dinner. "Harry, your birthday doesn't finish until midnight, but now I release you from your promise. My bed is yours tonight, but only if you want it."

"I want every night on this holiday with you."

It may have crossed Harry's mind that he was swimming in dangerous waters with an employee. Ami may have felt her stratagem had been even more successful than she could have hoped, but already pangs of guilt were cutting across the glow of success as she felt herself drawn closer to him. Already they were being carried along together in a current of emotion over which they had no control.

The next four nights and days on the cruise boat, *Osiris*, passed in a haze of unforgettable experiences. They visited an amazing series of temples at Edfu, Esna, Luxor, Dendera and Karnak. They walked through the Valley of the Kings and the tomb of Ramses II; they passed the Colossi of Memnon, and explored the long, low Temple of Hatshepsut set into the rocky hillside. Harry and Ami floated through them all cocooned in their own world.

Lying in her cabin on *Osiris*, Harry held her close. "I know nothing about you. Tell me about your life before I knew you."

"It may not be a story you want to hear. I'm not proud of it." She hesitated, but Harry nodded and waited. "I wasn't happy at home in South Africa. You can have no idea how difficult it is for coloureds. I think I had artistic talent, but I was a rebel. I was always in trouble at school, and at home my mother had to manage with very little, and my father was very cruel to all of us when he was there. I was still only a girl of sixteen or seventeen when I met Federico. He was an Italian artist who was visiting South Africa. I was so excited to know a real artist – a famous artist. He made me many promises – that he would take care of me and show me many exciting places – and I ran away with him. He took me to Italy, but when he had control of me in his own country, he broke his promises and treated me very badly." She stopped. Tears welled up in her eyes, and she started to sob.

"Don't tell me if it's painful, Ami," Harry said softly, "Please don't upset yourself."

"No, I want to tell you. It's important to me that you should know. But it will not be easy, and you must be patient." Her head was resting on his chest, and her voice was low and faltering. "I was a virgin, but he took that away, and I still remember the pain he caused me." Her fist clenched and her knees drew up involuntarily at the memory of the pain on that first night as he forced himself on her. "I screamed with the pain and the sheer terror, but he didn't stop. He was brutal. They say you never forget the first time. I never will, but I wish I could. I've tried to forget, and after a long time put it to the back of my mind, but it will always be there." Her body shuddered and tears fell on Harry's chest.

"I became his slave. He controlled me entirely, and there was no one else to turn to. I cooked and cleaned, and he took me whenever he wanted. I tried to shut off my mind, and then he beat me because I showed no reaction or pleasure. Pleasure!" She gave a short bitter laugh. "He beat me worse than my father had done. It was torture. The physical pain was bad, but the mental agony was worse. After several months I could stand it no longer. I think I would have killed myself, but I managed to escape while he was away one day and I came to England. I would have gone anywhere to escape from him, but it happened to be England. By then I knew I was pregnant and I had an abortion. That was terrible, and painful again. But it was his seed, his child, and I felt contaminated. I knew it was wrong, but I couldn't bear the thought that my body should nourish his evil." She stopped again. She closed her eyes and tried to blot out the memory. She expected a reaction from Harry, but there was none.

"Do you hate me for that? I was on my own and it wasn't easy, but I was determined to make a new life for myself. I still wake up at night with agonising feelings of guilt. I often think it all must have been my fault. But you, Harry, have been so gentle and loving. I know now what a joyful experience it can be. There has been no one else since I escaped from Italy. I wish you had been the first, then I would have wanted to remember for ever. Please don't hate me because of what I was or what I did."

"Of course I don't hate you. How could I ever hate you?" exclaimed Harry. The picture of the brutal Italian forcing himself on lovely, gentle Ami had filled him with rage and he could scarcely contain himself. He understood now the reason for her aloofness when they first met, and why she had kept all men at arm's length. "I admire you for your courage to cope on your own." He wanted to tell her that he wished he had been the first for her, but that would be no help now. It was too late. He gently kissed the top of her head, and held her closer.

She was quiet for a short while, then resumed. "When I was in Italy, that man – Federico – introduced me to Capodimonte porcelain. Oh, it is exquisite, Harry. Such amazing detail," Ami smiled at the memory. "There was one piece which I thought was so beautiful; it was called

'Gypsy Girl and Guitar,' and I modelled myself on it. Such delicate shades of red and blue. I was wearing that costume the first time you saw me."

"How could I forget it," replied Harry. "You were a picture then, and you are now. Many people talk of the beauty of Egyptian queens such as Nerfertiti and Nefertari. But I think they were not half as beautiful as you."

She lifted her head and kissed him. "You don't know what a weight has been lifted from me. I thought that you might think me a slut or a whore. I was frightened that you would reject me, but I could not go on under false pretences. Now you know, and yet you are still holding me close. Oh, Harry, I love you."

The Kuoni group was a cosmopolitan assemblage. All intent on soaking up the history and atmosphere of the ancient world. A Japanese goldsmith and his bride were honeymooning; a Texas oilman had brought his young Peruvian village wife on her first visit outside America; a New York stockbroker was trying to impress his air stewardess fiancée; and a handsome Cuban exile had a rich Californian socialite in tow. Ami outshone them all, and Harry was proud to be with her.

At the end of the cruise they stayed for four more days in Cairo at the Mena House Hotel, where the golden aura of the spacious chandeliered foyer was an ongoing sumptuous legacy of colonial grandeur. The great pyramid – the towering memorial to Cheops – was in direct view from their rooms. On their last night, Ami snuggled close to Harry. "I've never been so happy. To be in such a place with the most wonderful man is more than I deserve."

"You're an amazing girl. I was entranced by your beauty from the first moment I saw you, but now I know the even greater beauty of your spirit – I've looked into your soul. I'll never forget this time with you. Fate was kind to put us both in the same place at the same time." She stiffened slightly, guilt playing across her mind, but Harry did not notice. He stroked her cheek. "Tell me, which of the sights we have seen are strongest in your memory?"

"Oh, there are so many, but the most important memory is the first time we made love, and just being with you. That will be etched in my mind for ever. Which places? I think the sun rising over the desert on that first morning, climbing up through the tunnel to the chamber in the centre of the Great Pyramid, and the Serapeum – those echoes in the labyrinth tomb of the sacred Apis bulls at Saqqara. But there are so many more."

The Serapeum also had been significant to Harry. Only bulls with special colour markings were buried there, and it reminded him of his own herd in Northumberland. "Yes, I agree with you. You must have bewitched me. We even think the same thoughts. There is another place that had a powerful effect on me – the Temple of Hatshepsut. Do you remember the long approach as we walked across the desert, with the wide arms of the temple seeming to draw us into its heart in the hill-side? It's hard to imagine how Hatshepsut could have achieved her position in a male-dominated culture. She must have been a formidable woman, and a great pharaoh. She was determined not to be deprived of her inheritance, and fought for it – quite remarkable."

A flicker of association clicked in Ami's mind. She had been lost in the emotional delights of her deepening passion for Harry, and had almost forgotten the original purpose of her presence in Egypt. The urgings of ambition prompted her again. "She sounds like a real model for a modern woman. She must have taken enormous satisfaction from her achievement against such odds. I admire her for that. Maybe I should take a leaf out of her book." She paused. "Harry, it's nothing against you, because you know how I feel about you now, but it would mean so much to me to be my own person. D'you think it would be possible to release me from my contract with PFA?"

How could he refuse her? At this moment he would do anything for her. "I'll see what can be done as soon as we get back to England."

❋ ❋ ❋ ❋ ❋ ❋ ❋ ❋ ❋ ❋ ❋ ❋

They arrived in Heathrow the next morning. It was Saturday, and Harry took Ami to the small shared flat she rented in Kentish Town, before travelling home.

There was a meeting of the Board of PFA the following week at which Harry was due to review the progress of contracted artists. He showed graphs of items produced by each artist, the cost per item, total cost, items sold, total income, cumulative surplus and items in stock. He produced comparative tables which highlighted the priority for contracted artists, such as Grant Donaldson, Tom Nichols and Carolyn Overend, and he confirmed the ongoing security of their contracts. He was a master of information manipulation and he also was able to identify trends which indicated that Ami Kotze was a declining asset. He recommended that her contract should be terminated, and that she should be given the opportunity to buy her accumulated portfolio at a discount rate. After some discussion, the other Directors were prepared to defer to his expert analysis, and the Board accepted his recommendations. He felt some sense of guilt that he had not acted in the best interests of the company, but it was submerged in his infatuation for Ami.

Harry knew that Ami did not have the business skills or the interest in management to succeed on her own. Nor did she have any capital. He made her a loan to enable her to buy her portfolio, and he took the lease on an old warehouse in Narrow Street. It was a typical brick four-storied building, with redundant winches and pulleys still in place. Harry intended to renovate the ground and first floors as apartments for rent. The second floor would be Ami's studio, and the top floor would be living quarters.

Ami congratulated herself. In negotiation with an astute businessman, she had won her freedom from the formal contract with PFA, without losing Harry's support, and he had become her lover. Harry congratulated himself. He no longer had the potential complication of a contractual arrangement between his company and his lover, but she remained dependent on him. She had a free hand with her studio and apartment. She converted the top floor into one large open-plan area. It was an expression of her free spirit. The furniture was low and soft with bold-coloured printed fabric. The kitchen was in one corner, and an old Victorian bath in another. The greenery of large potted plants – a jardiniere of palms, *Ficus, Philodendron* and Monstera deliciosa – served to break up the space, and in the sleeping quarter a large mattress on the floor, with sheets and a profusion of pillows and cushions in pastel shades, was an inviting finale for the evenings that Harry and Ami spent together.

The distance between their homes was an inconvenience. The lines of transport to London from Harry's home in Worcestershire were not efficient, and he did not enjoy driving into London, but he often came down to spend time with Ami after meetings in Oxford. During the next seven years they spent many happy times together, sometimes at the warehouse, sometimes at Highcrags, and often on visits to Paris. Ami was conscious that twenty years separated them in age, but it was of no consequence to her. Harry was a man with whom she could spend the rest of her life.

The bitterness of his divorce from Jayne still rankled in Harry's mind. He had lost something of himself and still was bruised and sore. It had brought to the surface long-hidden insecurities of his youth, and the deprivations of his upbringing in a rural backwater. Self-preservation built a protective shell, and blocked his attempts to make the moves he knew Ami expected. In the final analysis, he could not again bring himself to trust a woman totally – he was unable to surrender control, even to a woman he loved. He was torn between an urgent desire to lose himself entirely in union with the woman who filled his thoughts, and the fear of a repetition of the emotional trauma he had experienced. If he was honest with himself, he also knew that he need not marry Ami in order to keep her. She would stay with him married or unmarried.

Ami experienced an undercurrent of unhappiness. She knew that complete happiness lay within her reach, but had not the courage to grasp it. She dare not express her fears to Harry, and instead sought out the friend who had first introduced her to him.

"Can you believe I've been with Harry for seven years. It's twelve years since I first met him here. Do you remember?"

"How could I forget. I never realised then that you would capture the heart of the great Harry Bainbridge, although it was obvious that he was bowled over by you."

"We fell in love on a cruise on the Nile three or four years later, and we have been almost inseparable since then. I was in heaven. It was ecstatic at first, and then settled down a little, and I thought that I would spend the rest of my life with him." She stopped, and looked away.

"And... ?"

"I don't know. He had a very acrimonious divorce from his wife, and I sensed hurt and bitterness in him. I knew I mustn't push him, and I was careful to back off, and let him recover in his own time. But it's so long. We're still good friends, and he's still there whenever I need help. But the passion has gone. In the last few months we've scarcely ever made love. It almost seems now that he takes me for granted, and he doesn't need to make me feel special."

"You say there has been a change recently. Did anything happen to cause it? Anything unusual before he changed?"

"Nothing particular that I can recall. He did go to a conference in Hungary in the summer, and didn't call me for quite a while after he returned. Apparently, there was a serious problem at the office. Actually, it has never recovered properly since then. We rarely make love these days, and it used to be so good. I miss it and him so much, but I daren't say anything in case I frighten him away for good."

"I can't tell you what to do, Ami. You must follow your heart. But I can give you some advice, if you'll allow me?" Ami nodded. "First, you've been with him for seven years, and it's time he put his divorce behind him. He can't keep you waiting for ever. Second, I don't like the sound of the Hungarian episode. I don't buy excuses like 'problem at the office'. There's usually more to it than that, and I think you should ask him for a straight answer. Third, if you want him, Ami, go for it. If he really loves you, you won't frighten him away. Tell him you want to make love. Tell him you want to marry him – but be sure that you *do* want to before you say anything." She paused, and saw Ami in the grip of indecision. She needed to provide an alternative. "Remember there are plenty of men who would be bowled over by your beauty. You could be another Iman or Waris. You don't need Harry, but you do need to believe in yourself."

Ami listened, but the words spun aimlessly past her comprehension, and Harry's face blotted out all other images.

The intense initial heat of their relationship had subsided. Such intensity could not have been maintained, but as it cooled it would have been natural for the emotional bonds that had been forged between them to have linked into a chain that unified their lives. There was a flaw. Harry was the weakest link, and Ami allowed that weakness to determine their future. She could not find the courage to follow her friend's advice. It was almost as if she preferred the certainty of Harry at a low intensity, than the possibility of not having him at all. It was a decision she would live to regret. They still enjoyed some time together, and Harry continued to help to sell her paintings, but the moment had passed – the urgent desire had gone. They became close friends rather than lovers, kindred free spirits with a common interest in art.

Marriage 1993–1997

Harry had wrestled with his doubts. He had spent many hours reminiscing of his times with Ami and Eva, smiling at their adventures, recalling his mistakes, and he had determined that this time he would not let the prize slip from his grasp. Theresa also finally had put the damage of Tony Devonshire behind her, and was ready to embark on a new phase of life. They were married the following year on her birthday – 14 February 1993. They had allowed little time to discover each other before marriage. During those few brief months they only scratched the surface. Now they were taking the risky voyage of discovery after the knot had been tied. They must reveal their greater depths – if they existed – in reciprocal trust and love and in the solemn context of marriage.

Whitstone Court was beginning to feel like home. Harry had lived there alone since he bought the property four years previously, and Theresa was comfortable that she did not have to fit into another woman's space. They took supper on the patio whenever the weather permitted, and watched clouds of dancing insects spiral in the evening sunbeams. House martins swooped past, swallows chirped as they sat on the electricity wires, and a few black scimitar-winged swifts soared high above. A thrush serenaded from its favourite ash tree at the bottom of the garden, and the staccato tattoo of the woodpecker echoed across the paddock. In the dusk of warm summer evenings Harry held lengthy dialogues with the owl that perched on the post across the drive.

The marriage began as their courtship had ended. In the first flush of emotion and enthusiasm, they talked through the evenings and loved long into the nights.

Harry was eager to enthuse Theresa's interest in Highcrags. "It's such a pleasure to sit here and watch the birds in the evening," he said as they finished supper alfresco, "but the birds at Highcrags are incomparable. Just to hear the long drawn-out melancholy bubbling trill of the curlew gliding down to its nest, or the musical throbbing of the lapwings' broad rounded wings as they wheel and tumble above the rough pasture – they're experiences that can never be forgotten. They're a wild yet soothing influence away from the urgency of modern life. I derive such an emotional uplift from the barren isolated beauty of Highcrags. You must visit it with me soon."

Theresa loved the soft romantic side of Harry's character, but she was not sure that the wild desolation of Highcrags held much appeal for her – she was much more likely to find uplifting inspiration in the opera and ballet of London's cultural life – but she did not voice her opinion at that point, and Harry continued. "I have a herd of special cattle at Highcrags. The breed originated in Ireland more than two thousand years ago, and I've been to the area around Galway several times to see if any remnants of the old breed remain."

Theresa was thrilled to know of Harry's interest in Ireland. She told him more of her early life and they discovered that Ireland was a focus of common interest. She had not lived there since the mid-1960s but it still was her home, and they determined that they would visit Ireland every year, and escape into the wild beauty of Connemara, the Burren and the Dingle Peninsular.

National problems passed over their heads and made no impact on their joyous progress. Harry's cup was full and running over, and Theresa felt that she had at last found true happiness after the disappointment of her previous foray into a serious relationship. Harry described his various business projects, and Theresa was able to interject many ideas and opinions from the experience of her time in London. She also encouraged him to indulge in metropolitan culture, and he was persuaded – albeit reluctantly – to experience opera on two visits to Covent Garden. He went to please Theresa, but his reluctance also may have owed a little to an underlying feeling of guilt because Ami was in London.

Even when Theresa could no longer inveigle him to London, she found alternatives closer to home.

"Harry, I know you find journeys to London tiresome, but there's so much that we miss by refraining from the effort. Maybe, we can find an easier alternative. Will you indulge me?"

Harry knew that she missed the cultural richness of the metropolis, and did not wish to deny her enjoyment. "Of course," he replied, "what have you in mind?"

"I was looking through the programme for the Symphony Hall in Birmingham and I see there is a recital next month by the stunning new mezzo-soprano, Cecilia Bartoli," she said with obvious excitement. "It would be a wonderful treat if you could bear to take me."

Harry was not a Philistine, but his tastes were attuned more to traditional jazz and intellectual Ingmar Bergman films. Nevertheless, he was true to his word and accompanied Theresa to the recital. A Simon Rattle performance of the Mozart opera, *Cosi fan Tutte*, followed later in the year, and Yehudi Menuhin's eightieth birthday concert the following year. Theresa was in her element, but Harry was increasingly discomfited by the tedium of entertainment that was unrewarding for him.

Both Harry and Theresa were uninhibitedly outspoken. It was a characteristic they both admired, although one that had the potential to make more enemies than friends. At first it was refreshing and stimulating, contrasting with the obfuscating deviousness they encountered elsewhere. Gradually they came to value it less, and eventually to be wary of it. Harry in particular had always been an individualist who did things his own way, and subconsciously began to see Theresa's pertinent observations as implied criticism of his work. A gradual feeling of resentment grew. The initial excitement of marriage cooled, and small problems assumed significant proportions before they accepted the need to deal with them. The good times were becoming rarer, the magic was disappearing, and problems were filling the growing gaps.

Theresa was disappointed by Harry's reluctance to appreciate opera, ballet and other refined arts. She missed Covent Garden and Glyndebourne. She was prone to excessive refinement and fastidiousness. She began to be irritated by his informality, his casual dress, and his gradual regression to rural interests. She increasingly came to regard them as 'unsavoury habits'.

Theresa's disillusionment expressed itself in doubts about her appearance. She had always been susceptible to the female obsession with her own faults – real and imaginary – but now when she looked in the mirror every flaw was magnified. Her neck and the skin of her upper arms received detailed scrutiny. Her smile-lines became evidence of age rather than happiness. The merest suggestion of a wrinkle produced bottles of potion and tubes of cream. The discovery of a couple of grey hairs sent her hurrying to her hair stylist, and she emerged as a honey-blonde.

Harry's reaction had been to throw himself more intensely into his work. Three years into the marriage he had moved into a separate bedroom. He reasoned that he did not wish to disturb Theresa when leaving for work very early each morning. He arrived home later, and tired.

Now there was less communication between them, and he rarely discussed business matters with her. His thoughts turned more frequently to Ami's easy companionship and her hedonistic lifestyle in the warehouse apartment.

Ami Continued 1993–1997

Ami had been working for some while on a new silk-screening technique, and called the PFA office in February 1993 to discuss the marketing opportunities with Harry. She asked to speak to Mr Bainbridge.

"Good morning, Miss Kotze. I'm afraid that Mr Bainbridge is away from the office at present." It was a voice she did not recognise.

"I don't think we've met," she said, "have you joined PFA recently?"

"Yes, my name is Pamela and I've only been here for three weeks."

"I hope you enjoy it. When will Mr Bainbridge be back in the office?"

"Just let me check the diary," said Pamela. "He will be back on Monday 1st March. He was married on St. Valentine's Day and he's away on his honeymoon. Terribly romantic isn't it?"

Ami froze. She could not answer Pamela's innocent comment. Momentarily her mind was numb, and the phone dropped from her hand. She sat immobile for a few seconds and then her thoughts returned in a mad frenzy of questions. *Harry married – and without a word to her. She, who was so special to him. How could he do this to her – how could he betray her so utterly? She knew he had kicked over the traces after his divorce – she knew he had to get Jayne out of his system, and she had been prepared to wait, but she always knew he would come back to her. He had mentioned his casual relationships, but she contained her jealousy because she knew she was his real love. She never doubted it. He was her rock. She depended on him. Now he was married!*

Her secret dreams, her expectations, were tatters in the wind. It had taken Ami several years to overcome the emotional damage inflicted on her by Federico in Italy. During her time in England she had grown in confidence, bolstered by Harry's presence and support, and had begun to build a degree of self-esteem, but it was a fragile foundation. She was 33 years of age, but still a vulnerable girl, and Harry's rejection – as she saw it – left her without hope or inspiration.

She did not know which way to turn, and spent much time in isolation in her apartment at the warehouse. She cut her long tresses to a short elfin style, which accentuated her high cheekbones and delicately pointed chin, and decided to replace the furniture to try to remove memories of Harry. At an antiques shop she met Quentin – charming, handsome and debonair – a superficial product of the public school system. He used his privileged background to move easily in many layers of society, but lacked the application to be successful at anything except perhaps emotional parasitism. In his mid-50s, he had progressed no further than dealing in antique furniture of doubtful authenticity, but his application of seduction was as smooth as the polished veneer on his questionable antiques. He had a knack of being on hand at opportune moments, and Ami – even at 33 years of age – was vulnerable. The impact of her abusive father's cruelty had not ended when she left home. His lasting influence was to pitch her headlong into the arms of any substitute father figure. Quentin capitalised on her fragile state of mind. Her quest to fight clear of memories of Harry delivered her defenceless into his snare, and he manipulated her into a state of dependence.

He used the warehouse apartment when it suited him, but continued to spread his favours elsewhere when he chose. He expected Ami to acquiesce immediately to his demands, even when he had just returned after indulging his appetite elsewhere. Ami's mental pain of knowing where he had been, was compounded by his physical abuse and rough uncaring gratification of his urges. He separated her from her old friends and contacts, and she fell back almost as if in a trance into a passive acceptance of abuse from her male partner – it was a replay of her time with Federico. She became isolated and unsure of herself. Her creative talent was stifled, and gradually she became little more than a domestic chattel of her dominating lover. She was unhappy, but she could not break free.

She maintained only infrequent and indirect contact with Harry through PFA, but in early September 1997 she answered the telephone.

"Ami, have you been hiding? It's ages since I heard from you." Harry's distinctive deep voice came down the line. She swallowed hard, and tears pricked her eyes. Yes, she probably had been hiding in a sense, and it was too long since she had seen him. "There's a Charity

Gala Dinner and private preview of an exhibition of wildlife art at the Halcyon Gallery in Birmingham on the 20th of this month. It's a Saturday. Oils, acrylics, watercolours, sculptures, the lot – all the leading artists are represented. Are you going by any chance?"

"Oh Harry, how good to hear from you. I *have* missed seeing you. I am rather out of touch and haven't heard of the exhibition, but it sounds very interesting. Will you be there? How can I get a ticket?"

"Don't worry about that. I'll get one for you. Will you be alone or will your friend, Quentin, be with you?" He forced the name out with clipped tones. He was aware of Ami's unsatisfactory domestic arrangements, but he was guiltily conscious that he was the cause. He had not met Quentin, but enough adverse reports had reached him through the grapevine to make him hope for his absence, and he resented Ami's relationship with him.

Ami did not answer immediately. She knew Quentin would expect to be asked, but why should she? A sudden resolve entered her soul. The gypsy rebellion flared up. Why should she allow the sham to continue, now Harry was there again? "I'll be alone," she replied.

The exhibition was a great success, showing the work of many of the leading contemporary artists. Theresa was with Harry, and he introduced her to Ami. He hoped they would establish a friendly relationship, and noted with relief that they seemed to be chatting very amiably. He and Ami also spent a long time bringing each other up to date, and they soon had each other in fits of laughter. After his initial surprise, he thought her short tousled hair brought out her real character, and complimented her on her elfin look. She complimented him on his beautiful wife. She heard that he was working too hard; he heard that she had seen the light with Quentin; and Theresa heard voices in her head telling her that her husband liked this woman too much.

The close contact between Harry and Ami was restored. She again more regularly sought his advice on marketing her work, and he sought her advice on the evaluation of paintings. Quentin received his marching orders.

Marriage Continued 1997–2000

At their first meeting time at the Birmingham exhibition, Theresa and Ami had talked politely with apparent ease, but mentally they sparred

– each on her guard, and both disturbed by the beauty of the other. One tall, fair-skinned, blonde and haughty; the other slight, dark and alluring. Theresa had been aware of Ami since Harry had talked of his past in the first outpouring of their early conversations. Her name had cropped up subsequently from time to time, and she had guessed that she was an attractive woman, but this was the first time she had been able to face the reality.

As she watched Harry and Ami talking and laughing so easily and animatedly at the exhibition, she thought bitterly of her own lack of communication with Harry. She had realised for some time that this was a low point in their relationship, but the evening brought it home with full force.

As they drove home, she asked him "How long is it since we slept together?"

"Good Lord," exclaimed Harry, "what a question out of the blue. I really can't say off the cuff."

"Then it must be a long time," she retorted. "It is a long time; I can remember. They say the libido of men by the age of 50 is so low that they might as well be impotent, and in your case it seems to be true."

Harry bridled at the implication. "I don't think it's a matter of libido *per se*," he replied grimly, "there just seem to be less opportunities, and too many arguments maybe. We both are busy people, and you often are not feeling well..."

"Yes, I thought in the end it would be sure to be my fault. Silly me. Of course, you're not to blame at all."

"That's not what I said or meant. You are twisting my words and the argument..."

"Oh, so it's an argument," she exclaimed, "I thought husbands and wives were supposed to be able to have discussions. You seem able to have pleasant discussions with other women, and I'll bet your libido would soon return if Miss Ami Kotze was available."

"Don't be ridiculous." They lapsed into a bristling silence which persisted long after they reached home.

❋ ❋ ❋ ❋ ❋ ❋ ❋ ❋ ❋ ❋ ❋ ❋

All the volunteers at RDA were women. They exercised their philanthropy while they exercised the ponies and their disabled riders.

They returned to society some of the value that their husbands extracted from it. Theresa did not fit the usual mould. Her husband was a successful businessman, living off the fat of a thriving enterprise, but she had carved out her own niche of success earlier in life. She had both time and ability to devote to the charity, and soon became Chair of the management committee.

The stables were part of an extensive range of farm buildings owned by Steve Kent, a pleasant jovial man in his mid-30s. He made the premises and horses available at an affordable rate to a charitable organisation. He lived alone in the traditional farmhouse adjacent to the buildings, and often came across to see the RDA in action, and stayed to talk in the tea room afterwards. He was an easy conversationalist, and Theresa was delighted to find someone who enjoyed conversation as much as she did. She and Harry had talked endlessly when they were first married, but now there never seemed to be the time or the mood to indulge in conversation for its own sake. It was always mundane, routine matters of living, if it occurred at all. Steve was attracted by the beautiful woman who seemed very willing to spend time with him.

"Your husband is a very lucky man to have such a beautiful and intelligent wife," Steve interjected one day after a particularly stimulating discussion. "You must be a great help to him."

"Oh no, I have no particular skills that apply to my husband's business," she replied smiling. She was caught unawares by his directness, but flattered by his words. "Even if I had, he rarely discusses his business at home."

Steve sensed a whiff of wistfulness, almost of sadness, and his nose for opportunity twitched. "Well, I think if I was your husband, I'd be very glad of your support. I take all the decisions here, and it can be a lonely job. You always make astute comments whatever we discuss, and I'd be grateful for your advice." He was ready to supply this lady's needs if her husband was failing in his duty.

"You're very kind. I doubt that I can be of much use, but I'm very happy to discuss any problems if you need a second opinion."

Steve proceeded to cultivate Theresa's friendship. He involved her in decisions – business at first, but then with personal overtones. He gradually encouraged her to take him into her confidence. He was drawing her slowly into a web of commitment that he hoped would end in his bed. Theresa's native naivety obscured Steve's sexual motivation, and she saw him only as a friend who needed help and as an outlet for her need for discussion and human interaction. Maybe subconsciously Theresa did detect a sexual context, and maybe it played a subliminal role in drawing her to him. These days she and Harry rarely made love – one or the other usually was in a bad mood, or she was feeling unwell. They both retained the desire, and sometimes advanced towards it, but then a mood or dispute would break the spell.

In 1998 Harry organised a 50th birthday party, cum fifth wedding anniversary, for Theresa at Towron Castle. More than 50 guests assembled and showered her with compliments and presents. She was full of vibrant energy, and circulated through the guests with growing jubilation and excitement. That night she and Harry made love as if it was the first time. It seemed to restore a high point in their relationship that lasted for some months – and yet, it was not the same as it had been in the beginning. Theresa still continued her intimate discussions with Steve, and Harry remained in regular contact with Ami.

In the early autumn an invitation arrived. Theresa opened the envelope and took out the crested card. She turned to Harry, and excitedly exclaimed, "Look, an invitation to a party at Buckingham Palace." She passed the card to him, and his face immediately conveyed the utter distaste and contempt he felt as he read the tortured language. How he despised the self-indulgent congratulation of privilege embodied in every phrase. They even sent personal invitations by proxy!

The Master of the Household
has received Her Majesty's command to invite
Mr and Mrs Harold Bainbridge
to a Reception to be given at Buckingham Palace by
The Queen and The Duke of Edinburgh
on Friday 13th November at 6.00pm
to celebrate the public work of
His Royal Highness The Prince of Wales
on the occasion of His Royal Highness's 50th birthday

RSVP
The Reception Office
Office of H.R.H. The Prince of Wales
St. James's Palace, SW1A 1BS

Dress: Lounge Suit/Jacket
Uniform optional

Theresa's lack of sympathy for royalty evaporated in the face of such a social opportunity. "Oh, Harry, how fantastic! What a coup! Aren't you excited?" she exclaimed, noting his unenthusiastic expression. "I don't expect any of our friends will have an invitation. Prince Charles's 50th – that is a really special occasion."

Harry may have been a sharp operator in business, but some of his principles were immovable. "I wouldn't be seen dead at such an event, even if the Queen had the decency to invite me herself. Who the hell do these people think they are? I might have been tempted if they were throwing a party to confess their public parasitism, but non-existent public work is an excuse too lame to contemplate." It was a sharp reversal of roles. For once Harry was standing on his principles, while Theresa abandoned hers.

"But there'll never be another event like this," she pleaded. "Please let us go to it. It would mean so much to me."

"Why on earth should we get an invitation anyway?" Harry mused. "Maybe it's because of my charity work with YPF or the English Nature project, or maybe yours with Riding for the Disabled. Whatever, I'm not interested."

Theresa raged relentless arguments for a couple of weeks until Harry grudgingly conceded apparent defeat, and a letter of acceptance was dispatched. In the end, Friday the 13th lived up to its reputation when Harry drove Theresa to London, then refused to accompany her to the Palace and offered her dinner at Le Manoir as an alternative. She was furious, but – stranded at the entrance gates – her options were limited. She could either miss the party, or attend alone. She chose the latter course, but bore a festering abscess of resentment towards Harry from that point on.

They both had become increasingly aware of some fundamental differences in their ethical approach to life, and usually it was Theresa who took the moral high ground. Harry did not even tell her that he had received, and ignored, an invitation to attend his parents' diamond wedding anniversary. She already was mystified and disturbed by his unusual relationship with his family in the north, and would have been appalled by his discourteous dismissal of the invitation. She became increasingly critical, and they reached a crisis point on their annual visit to Ireland the following year.

They had broken their return journey at a nondescript hotel in a small town in Roscommon. The foyer was deserted, but eventually they raised a member of staff, distinguished mainly by his obvious disinterest in guests who had disturbed his routine of inactivity. Harry ordered two coffees and then, anticipating a lengthy delay, wandered around looking at any picture and objet d'art that he could find. Theresa was relaxing with a local newspaper.

He entered a dimly lit room opening off the lounge. It was no wonder that the clientele of such establishments was dreary. The small windows diminished still further the grey light of a damp Irish morning, and the décor was appropriately faded and sombre. One or two pictures were hung awkwardly with no particular sense of presentation. He looked at them with a jaundiced eye. The picture in the dark corner was hanging with a drunken tilt, and the canvas was damaged by an object protruding from the wall behind it.

Harry was intrigued. He had not expected to find an oil painting here. It was a substantial equine study that was in need of cleaning. The faded colours and the dim light made it difficult to pick out detail, but something in the style of the grey horses on the right caught his attention. He peered closer and recognition hit him like an electric shock. It was a Rosa Bonheur, he was sure. He looked closer and, yes, he thought he could make out her signature. It was not unlike a smaller version of her major work, the Horse Fair. What a find! He had several works by the Bonheur family in the studio – one by Rosa of sheep being transported on an open boat in the Hebrides, named appropriately 'Changing Pastures', was a particular favourite – and now maybe he could add to the collection. Nobody had observed his close interest in the painting, and he quietly withdrew to the lounge.

"Just having a look around," he said to Theresa as he walked past without stopping.

"Seen anything interesting?" She knew his inability to resist searching in even the most unlikely places.

"Not very likely in a backwater like this, but you never know".

He was aware that Theresa would have different ethical views on his proposed purchase, and he needed to buy a little time before broaching the subject with her. He went through into the back of the hotel, found the surly waiter and asked to see the manager. He was away.

Harry was disappointed – he had hoped to act immediately and make a quick deal – but he took details of the manager's name and noted the address and telephone number of the hotel.

Their coffee finally arrived. It was not the best, but the break had refreshed them. As they continued their journey on the main Dublin road, Harry hesitatingly opened the discussion.

"It's surprising what lurks in the corners of unlikely rooms," he offered nonchalantly. "You'd never think there would be anything of interest in a dingy place like that."

Theresa immediately sensed a confession, "I thought you said there was nothing there."

"Well, there was a painting that could be interesting. Probably not worth much, but I may make an offer for it just in case."

"Fascinating," she replied quizzically, "and how much are you going to offer?"

Harry hesitated. Already he was on the back foot in this exchange. "I thought maybe £1,500 or so."

She let him thrash around mentally in deep water for a while. "Why would you want to bother with such a cheap painting? Not in your usual price bracket. How much is it worth?"

"Any item of art is worth as much as the owner values it..." he began.

"What balderdash!" she exclaimed. "You mean you're hoping to obtain a valuable piece for a song because the owner doesn't know its true worth. You will make a fat profit at the expense of some poor Irishman. Typical English!"

Harry sought to extricate himself. "Any business deal can be concluded only if both parties agree. Morality doesn't enter into it. It's a fair negotiation between buyer and seller. If I can buy it at a lower price, it's a just reward for the expertise that I have accumulated over the years at great expense."

Theresa was not to be diverted. "It's a dishonest deal, done between an unscrupulous Englishman and an innocent Irishman."

There was little use in explaining that he had not yet even talked to the owner. The owner may even know its true value, although Harry was confident he would obtain it for much less than its proper value. He would talk to Ami on his return. Between them they would ease it out of Irish ownership, and so he held his peace. In any case, Theresa was no longer receptive to argument on the matter. She had ascertained his intention, and in her eyes that was sufficient condemnation.

The incident was symptomatic of the current state of their relationship. They had perfected the art of transforming trivial incidents into matters of principle and destructive confrontation. He felt deprived by the lack of relaxed intimate interaction. She still had great admiration for his achievements in the business world, but was losing respect for him because of the disparity of their ethical standards.

Karen 1991-1992

Harry slowly began to understand that Theresa's high ethical standards might be a major obstacle. It was a new experience. In the past it had been the questionable ethical standards of women that had worried him. Jayne had departed without a backward glance when financial security appeared to be disintegrating. And Karen Richmond – how could Harry ever forget the amazing transformation of Karen Richmond? She also gave wealth a higher priority than personal relationships.

Karen had been invited as a key speaker in a technical programme at a conference in Hungary at the University of Technology in 1991. On the platform she was an accomplished performer, articulate and composed, totally in control of her audience. Her hair, swept up in a tightly symmetrical coil, reinforced the clinical efficiency of her analysis of motivation as a tool of man management. She was a professional operator.

Harry and Karen bumped into each other on the first evening of the conference at the Gellért, a unique blue-domed establishment in old Buda on the banks of the Danube, where both were staying. They fell into conversation and Harry suggested that they should dine on the marble terrace of the hotel's famed Duna restaurant. During dinner Harry sensed that Karen's platform persona concealed a very different character. Her hair now fell in blonde tresses to her shoulders. Her blue eyes, sparkling with excitement, matched the metallic sheen of her low-cut dress, and her conservation was animated. A group of three gypsy violinists, moving slowly from table to table, added to the exotic aura, and if thoughts of Ami crossed Harry's mind, they failed to deter him.

A mutual sense of urgency dictated their actions and they headed to

Karen's room. Harry was in a mood to let things flow, but he was totally unprepared for the woman that burst from her shell when they reached her room. She was out of control; she abandoned all inhibitions, and every touch sent her into spasms of ecstasy. The straight-laced lecturer of the day, who had become the glamorous evening companion, was now a rampant sensual partner. The transformation was complete, and repeated the next day.

On the third day of the conference Harry presented a paper on business management. He found some difficulty keeping his mind on the subject – his imagination already was in Karen's warm embrace. He was a popular speaker, usually noted for the power and spontaneity of his delivery, spiced with humour that verged on the risqué. On this occasion, he was grateful he had prepared a PowerPoint presentation to keep him on track. That night they crossed over the Danube into Pest and ate at one of the little cafes in Vaci street – a perfect place for people-watchers, as it seemed all the population of Hungary's capital city meandered slowly by. But Harry and Karen noticed little of the human throng. Their thoughts were for each other and the rest of the night. Harry paid the bill and they walked arm in arm over the Szabadság Bridge and into the Gellért.

Harry went to collect the keys, and the porter handed him a message from the pigeon-hole. It was from Walter King via the PFA office, and read: "Serious problem with YPF. RMG confrontation with Charity Commission. Your intervention essential. Walter." Damn! He did not want a problem right now. It must be serious or Walter would have dealt with it, and he knew Robert Gator was capable of causing trouble both accidentally and deliberately. But he did not want to spoil the evening.

"Nothing serious," he said to Karen. "I just need to send a message in reply. Be ready for me upstairs. I'll be with you in two seconds."

He saw Karen into the lift, then went into the executive business office adjoining the foyer. First he asked the girl to book the first flight possible to London the next day, and then he sent an email message to Walter: "Returning soonest tomorrow. Will advise exact time from airport. Please meet me and we can discuss on way to office. Best regards. Harry." He then firmly put it out of his mind and moved with the speed of a man half his age to the lift and Karen's room.

He did not tell her of his new arrangements that evening. He was awake early next morning, and she was still half-asleep when he was ready to leave. "I have to go," he said quietly, "there's a crisis back in the office that needs me there."

"You're leaving now?" She stretched out her hand and caught his. "But what will I do without you? We're having such fun."

"I know, and we will often. Call me as soon as you get back to England, and we'll set the nights on fire again." He kissed her swiftly, and left before either of them had time to prevaricate further.

Karen's husband was an affluent but disinterested man. An estate in Derbyshire, a grouse syndicate on the North Yorkshire moors, a pink hunting jacket, and an attractive wife on his arm at Ascot, were the symbols of status that underpinned his raison d'être. His wife's intellectual reputation gave an unusual and added piquancy to his status. He had not the slightest idea of the vital woman that surged beneath her cool exterior. Karen had soon tired of him, but was canny enough not to risk disenfranchising herself from the considerable benefits of his wealth. Her affair with Harry gave her all the sexual and mental stimulation she lacked at home, and gave Harry the joys of being with an attractive woman whose married status removed the dangers posed by Ami as a single women. They met at irregular intervals, usually at his home, but occasionally finding an opportunity to take a weekend away together. Karen gradually she began to recognise the dangers of falling in love with Harry and losing control totally. She was happy to be out of control in the security of the bedroom, but not elsewhere.

In 1992 Harry invited Karen to go with him on visit to Seville. It was an impetuously rash suggestion. He had not invited Ami, and it did not occur to him to pause to consider the effect if might have. Nor would there be any way to explain the visit in innocent terms to Karen's husband, and thus it was elevated to the status of a point of no return. Karen gave the offer some thought and declined. She weighed the physical pleasure and emotional excitement that Harry provided against the wealth of her husband. It was no contest. She opted for the security of tangible assets, and ended her affair with Harry to find another lover in a lower key.

Harry, by default, had escaped a potentially embarrassing situation. In his experience power and wealth seemed to be the primary aphrodisiacs for the fairer sex. The long-forgotten, painful memories of Jayne had been forced back to the forefront of his mind – the treachery and untrustworthiness of women confirmed for him again.

Whatever problems there were in his marriage, thought Harry, *no one could accuse Theresa of accepting anything but the highest standards of ethical conduct. She could be trusted totally. On that score he could feel confident.*

Harry's party: February 2000

Theresa determined that Harry's retirement was an opportunity – maybe the final opportunity – to inject new life and vigour into their declining relationship. Her unscrupulous honesty set standards that others found difficult to attain, and grated on Harry's free-wheeling philosophy. She was disturbed by Harry's willingness to let the search for success take priority over ethical conduct. Also, her Irish sociability longed to run at a furious pace, and she was unable to come to terms with his ability to retreat into himself. On the other hand, they shared a passionate love for Ireland, and a healthy disrespect for the establishment. She told herself that his lack of attention in recent years was simply due to the pressure of work, and she tried to convince herself that there was nothing significant in his relationship with Ami Kotze. She found her own arguments unconvincing, and an inner voice told her it was a lost cause, but her strong moral sense would not let her give up without making every effort to save her marriage.

Without Harry's knowledge, she had arranged a select Sunday lunch party at Tornow Castle to celebrate his 60th birthday-cum-retirement on 27 February. She had booked the Cedar dining room and invited a small group of their friends and Harry's close business associates. Patrick and Christine Giles and Martin and Rose Lancaster lived a few miles away near Bridgnorth and Welshpool respectively, but Michael and Norma Evans were driving up from Hampshire. Theresa was not sure which of Harry's business associates were close to him, and she knew she was taking a risk that she might invite someone that was not acceptable. In the end she limited the invitations to Miles and Antonia Mountjoy, Johan and Sabine Barck, Walter King and Ami Kotze.

She deliberated for many days before she sent an invitation to Ami, and had done so eventually only with many misgivings, prompted partly by her innate perverse sense of fairness that would not allow her rival to be disadvantaged. She had been alarmed by Ami's beauty when she met her two or three years previously at the exhibition in Birmingham, but knew that she had been involved in business with Harry for many years and it might seem odd if she was not invited. She also needed a female guest to balance the sex ratio as Walter King was a bachelor, but she still had recurrent suspicions that Ami might still be more than a just a friend to her husband.

Harry was conscious that their marriage had not maintained its early enthusiasm and idealism – in fact it was in danger of foundering fatally. Maybe now that he would be at home more frequently it would be possible to restore the intimacy and closeness they had enjoyed previously. He would be able to organise his activities at a more leisurely pace, and he would not be exposed to the constant and flattering attention of attractive young women. He felt in his heart that it could be good with Theresa. If only the dynamics of their contrasting personalities would release the positive energy of combined vigour: instead, like nuclear fission, they seemed to press the self-destruct button. It must not be allowed to disintegrate without one last effort. He wrote a card for her birthday, but decided he would send a separate card for Valentine's Day – an old-fashioned thought perhaps, but appropriate.

It was a personal card, designed and prepared by Harry on his PC. On the front was a picture of a framed heart with the words 'Happy Valentine's Day to a very special lady from a not so secret admirer.' Inside was his message.

> *Forgive the unusual style of this Valentine's Day card but, as it may be the last one I will send, some unorthodoxy may be understandable. I love you very much, but it is clear that you no longer feel the same way. I am aware that there is a widening gap that soon will be too great to bridge. I know that there are issues that should be discussed. I know because you have told me so, but I do not know what they are – only that there never seems to be a right time to discuss them. Mornings are not right, nor are evenings. I am not even sure that you wish to discuss them. Life has become an Aunt Sally – something to be knocked down just when it is getting to its feet. Maybe I should be more aware.*

> *From time to time you have hinted at major matters that disturb you, and I find it hard to come to terms with the possibility that we could have gone through all the memorable times we had together while you kept matters of such apparent importance under wraps. I do not know what to make of it. You hold the keys, and you must decide whether or not to unlock the closet and get all the problems out into the open and hopefully into the waste-bin. Life is on hold and happiness is elusive while we remain the way we are. No plans are laid, no decisions can be made. Life is too short to sit in neutral; it must be put in gear. Love, Harry.*

Theresa's response was positive. Perhaps a little more muted than he hoped, but positive nevertheless. When she suggested lunch at Tornow Castle a fortnight later for his birthday, he was delighted. They had held their wedding reception there, and it was a special place for them. He looked forward to it with eager anticipation. The sudden appearance of a group of his close friends as he entered the castle was a genuine and delightful surprise.

Theresa had arranged the seating plan with care. The large oval dining table allowed ample opportunity to sandwich Ami between Johan Barck and Michael Evans at a good distance from Harry, who was placed safely in the mature company of Antonia Mountjoy and Sabine Barck. Theresa was directly opposite, flanked by Patrick Giles and Miles Mountjoy, and she engaged them in animated conversation. The conviviality of the occasion, the frequent toasts, and her natural excitability, all contributed to Theresa's vitality and she became the focal point of the conversation. Harry was in deep conversation with Sabine, but at intervals Theresa's voice penetrated their private discourse. She was in mid-flow, describing a walk she had taken in the Yorkshire Dales. "...the path to High Force on the Yorkshire bank meanders through meadows of mountain flora that surpass the most fertile imagination. We traversed rough and treacherous terrain before our travail culminated in a sudden view of Britain's mightiest waterfall. The impact bore comparison with my first foray to Haworth Moor when I experienced the full range of seasons within the confines of one day; the weather was most inclement. But the tourists! One must lament the intrusion of the general populace..." Harry smiled. He loved to hear her vivid use of language when she was in full voice, borne along on the sheer exuberance of her recollections of the wild splendour of the countryside.

She was, after all, imbued with the Celtic joy in flamboyant phraseology. She was a linguistic sponge that absorbed local and national dialects so instantaneously and accurately that new acquaintances often wondered if she was poking fun at them. Theresa was an avid reader of novels by the Brontë sisters, although perhaps her conversational language bore more evidence of the influence of Jane Austen, and sometimes it was almost possible to imagine Theresa as an Austen character. Her speech could have been lifted from *Pride and Prejudice*. Harry often teased her that she regarded him as a mixture of Heathcliff and Rochester, and joked that he should distance himself from the style of D'Arcy who she described as an 'insufferable prig.'

After lunch they retired to the drawing room, and the party continued in full swing until early evening. Michael and Norma were staying overnight at Tornow, but the party began to disperse when the Mountjoys, Walter and Ami left. The others, although more local, also took their departure. It had been a long day. Theresa had been a marvellous hostess, vivacious and attentive. Harry noted that she had been especially welcoming to Ami – perhaps too much? He was pleased but surprised. She maintained the tempo until the last guest had departed, and then sank exhausted into an easy chair in front of the welcoming log fire in the hotel. She did not feel the warm glow that follows a successful party. Perhaps she had enjoyed her wine too much and been over-indulgent, but that was normal. No, the problem had been Ami whose dark beauty weighed on her mind.

4
THE NEW REGIME 2000

Monday 28 February

The next morning Harry awoke as usual at 5.30am. He had no need of an alarm no matter how exhausted he might have been the night before. His body clock had long since adjusted its daily routine to an early start. He eased slowly out of bed and wandered over to the window stretching his sleepy muscles. The first suggestion of dawn was just breaking on the horizon. He could see the silhouette of the old oak at the end of the paddock, and the early dawn chorus was getting in tune.

It was not until he was in the shower that he realised he need not be in the office at his usual hour. Unless he had a meeting elsewhere, his morning routine always followed a precise pattern which brought him to his desk at 8.00 o'clock sharp. But today his meeting started at half past ten, and he need arrive only half an hour or so in advance. He wondered what time Louise would reach the office. It would be better if he did not arrive too early, and give her a chance to adjust to her new surroundings.

He stepped out of the shower and, reaching for a towel, saw himself in the full-length mirror. He decided he was in pretty good shape for a 60-year-old; no sign of the pot-bellied decadence sported by so many of his contemporaries who retained little evidence of their youthful fitness, honed on the rugby field and dissipated at the bar. He had looked after himself, and it showed. Some of the youngsters at the office might take a leaf out of his book.

Ah yes, the office. No need to hurry, and the lack of urgency irked him. The novelty of time on his hands was an ambivalent experience, and he would have to learn to come to terms with it. He decided to take Theresa a cup of tea. Normally he never disturbed her in the morning; she was not an early riser.

Theresa had not been in a good mood when she went to bed. The party had exhausted her physically and mentally. She had been keyed up throughout the evening by the presence of Ami Kotze and the need to appear especially welcoming to her. She had lain awake for much of the night with a feeling of resentment towards both Harry and Ami, and slept only fitfully, but she had fallen asleep when Harry went up just before eight o'clock. He took in the tray and placed it on the empty side of the bed. Theresa awoke with a start; her initial startled stare translating quickly into an angry frown.

"What are you doing?" she demanded. "I've not slept well, and I'd rather not be disturbed just when I'd gone to sleep. I'm very tired."

He apologised quietly, indicated the tray, and left the room. What was that about! His good intentions seemed to have misfired. It was beyond his comprehension, and it disturbed him because he did not understand. He had not noticed her concern while he was talking to Ami at the party, nor was he fully aware of the depth of her unhappiness with their marriage. He picked up his briefcase and car keys, and left for the office in an unsettled frame of mind.

He arrived in good time. It was an unusual experience to walk into an active office. Normally he unlocked the door, keyed in the security number, and settled down for an hour of uninterrupted work before the staff arrived. This morning everything was up and running. He looked into Terry's office to say good morning, and they joked about the joys of retirement. He then looked into Louise's office, but she was engrossed in paperwork and did not seem inclined to converse. After a brief word he collected some papers from his own office and went into the Board room where the meeting of YPF would be held. His fellow Trustees, Robert M Gator – he liked the inclusion of the initial for his middle name of Milland – and Walter King were already there and he joined them with a cup of coffee.

Half of Harry's mind was still at home, trying to unravel the difficulties that the morning's unusual routine had caused. After the usual pleasantries and inconsequential chatter, he brought the meeting to order, and went through the first items on the agenda on automatic pilot. Correspondence from the Charity Commission was noted, new guidelines for presentation of accounts for charities was discussed, and a report from the recipient of a sponsorship the previous year was noted and approved.

The next item on the agenda was an application for sponsorship by a young photographer from Uganda. His name was Joseph, aged 23 years, from the south-western corner of the country in the region that reached up to the Mountains of the Moon. He had shown commendable initiative already in working to buy his own equipment and in seeking out subjects in his native country, and the prints which he sent showed a good eye for composition. True, the geography and wildlife of Uganda, and the social deprivations and divisions created during the Idi Amin era, provided an enviable photographic palette, but it was well presented and Harry was pleased that the Foundation was attracting applications from candidates of this calibre. His landscape and wildlife studies were vibrant with colour and it was almost possible to smell the humid heat of the forests. But it was the monochrome studies of the native people that magnetised attention. They captured the wrinkled texture of age and the rounded contours of youth in exquisite tonal subtleties of skin colour. Most of all, they encapsulated both the hope and the despair of his fellow countrymen and women. The portfolio was a magnificent collection. Joseph was seeking sponsorship to visit England for the express purpose of making a photographic record of the Queen's Jubilee in 2002. He requested funds for travel from Uganda, for accommodation in London, and for access to darkroom facilities. He did not ask for introductions or help with access to prime positions on procession routes or at any of the events that were being planned.

Robert Gator was the first to speak. He was a large untidy man – large hands with blunt fingers, large head with a receding hairline on a receding brow, and a prominent proboscial nose. He was the second son in a long-established East Anglian farming family, and was resentful that his elder brother enjoyed all the privileges of a landed country squire. His sullen air of resentment had first exhibited itself in response to a series of cruel nicknames, such as Milly, Alli and Croc, to which public schoolboys are prone. Robert had sought to retain some status and contact with rural affairs by joining a firm of estate agents in Suffolk. His conversation was deliberate and heavy, as if he felt the weight of his words was sufficient without the superfluity of content, and that meaning was incidental and unimportant, provided the gravity of his delivery was sufficient to impress his interlocutors.

"We have here," he began, "an application which we cannot refuse. It is an unprecedented opportunity to elevate the profile of the Foundation by association with royalty. The Jubilee provides a stage on which we can show our loyal devotion as subjects of her gracious Majesty, and be seen to do so, as well as help this young fellow. I am sure I can arrange some helpful introductions."

Walter King, trim and active in contrast, cut in sharply, "Mr Chairman, I think Mr Gator would do well to confine his observations to the objectives of the Foundation."

Harry knew instantly that he should have anticipated this situation, and if he had been more alert he would have avoided the exchange between his fellow Trustees. Robert Gator was an unquestioning, unyielding royalist, who had his mind set firmly on mention in the birthday honours. Walter King was a committed intellectual republican, and there was always a simmering antipathy between them.

"We cannot afford to act contrary to the mood of the country," continued Robert, as if Walter had not spoken. "We are all aware that Her Majesty has devoted 50 years of her life in selfless devotion to her country and her subjects. The British royal family is an example to us all and to other nations. Look at the Princess Royal's days of duty, and the courage of the Queen Mother – determined to stay in London in the war during the blitz, and adamant that she would appear for the public at race meetings to see her horses run, even when not in good health..."

"I really must protest, Mr Chairman." interjected Walter. He pointedly did not address Robert Gator directly. "You'd think we were attending a royalist rally rather than a meeting of the Foundation. The royals are an accomplished family of parasites who have accumulated vast wealth at the expense of the ordinary British citizen. No businessman or genuine worker would class their activities as work, and I'm sure the treatment lavished on the Queen Mother would be better divided among the many nonagenarian ladies who are lying on trolleys in hospital corridors, or being turned out of nursing homes that are closing for lack of funds."

Robert rose to his feet. His dull stubbornness evaporated, and his face assumed a reddish-purple hue. Harry had never seen him so agitated. Fishing usually was the only occupation that excited his passion, although it was difficult to associate Robert Gator with passion. Much of his life was spent standing up to his thighs in cold water, and his ungainly style of walking as he paced across the room suggested that he had forgotten to remove his waders.

"Gentlemen, please," Harry was aware that he was losing control of the meeting. Effective chairmanship was a quality for which he was noted, and normally he kept a tight rein on the conduct of a meeting. On this occasion his attention had not been focused and he had let them hijack the discussion. He would have difficulty bringing them back to order. "Can we attend to the item on the agenda?"

He knew that both of them wished to draw him into the argument. Both suspected that they could count on his support, although neither was sure, and he always had been sufficiently astute not to show his hand. He knew that the monarchy was an anachronism in the twenty-first century, and a contradiction in a democracy. The extravagance and arrogance of the extended royal family would not be tolerated in any other situation. But he also knew that they gave some British people, oppressed by political correctness, an opportunity to wave their national flag and remember their history. He found it more difficult to understand the perversity of the wider general public, especially those who struggled with poverty and hardship, that drove them to worship a privileged figurehead. Maybe the explanation could be found in the superficial spin and sound-bytes of New Labour which had given enough warning that the glib verbiage and glad-handing of the Prime Minster might be a presidential model the British would prefer to avoid. On balance, despite all its deficiencies and scandals, the monarchy still represented a safer bet than presidential sleaze.

"Robert is correct," Harry attempted to bring his most difficult colleague on side. Robert turned, decided to give the benefit of the doubt, and returned to his seat glaring at Walter. "It is an excellent application," Harry continued. "It meets all our criteria, although we will need more detailed and precise costings. I propose that it is approved. However, I believe that we must keep strictly to our terms of reference. The Jubilee is simply a subject for a photographic project for our applicant. We can not complicate our objectives with obtrusive motivation. Walter, do we have your agreement on acceptance of the application?"

Walter nodded his approval, but Harry sensed at the same time that he had alienated Robert again – not because he had obtained Walter's support, but because he had dismissed the potential monarchical connection for the project. He guessed he was now marked down firmly in Robert's black book as a republican and a traitor. Well, that was too bad. It had been inevitable that at some stage his position on the subject would emerge, but he would prefer not to have been forced into revealing it by his own shortcomings. He must expect future meetings of the Foundation to be fraught with tension, and he would need all his skills of management to steer clear of confrontation.

As there were no further items on the agenda, they consulted their diaries, chose a date for the next meeting, and Harry declared the meeting closed.

Tuesday 29 February

Harry conceived that he would need to fit into a pattern of life at home that did not cause friction, or even tension. The meeting of YPF Trustees had been a disaster, and he could not afford to let the focus of his attention at meetings be distracted by domestic problems. He determined that henceforth he would adopt an easy and attentive manner that would not give Theresa any cause for concern.

On Tuesday morning he left home before six o'clock for a meeting in Peterborough at nine with two brothers who were partners of Fiveways, a firm which specialised in locating residential property abroad for British clients. The partners were friends of Miles Mountjoy, and he advised Harry that it was a rising market.

Harry listened with interest to the statistics showing that Spain and Italy were still the main destinations for Britons moving abroad, but that France was the most rapidly growing market. He queried whether the increasing demand would not drive up prices, and asked how many buyers changed their mind within the first five years. The answers were smooth and practised, but lacked the rigour of precise detail that he required.

"It varies from area to area," said Mike Loxton the senior partner. "For example, in the Lot department in central France prices have risen by maybe only twenty per cent in the last two years, but in the Albi-Carmaux-Cordes triangle in Tarn, which has been made fashionable by the London set, prices have risen by more than 60 per cent."

"And what is your prognosis over the next five years?" asked Harry.

"That's anybody's guess," The answer did not impress him.

He left after lunch, and on the long drive home – mercifully eased by the new A14 leading onto the M6 and M5 motorway network – mused that if amateurs such as the Loxton brothers could make a living from it, there might be good opportunities for an efficient operator in the foreign property business. He noted it for future reference, but decided not to take any further action at present.

Wednesday 1 March

His appointment on Wednesday held much more interest for him. He had persuaded Theresa that she would find many trade stands at the Bath & West Agricultural Show of considerable interest, and she had agreed to drive him there. He expected to imbibe a significant amount of alcohol which was an adequate excuse for not driving. The morning post brought some birthday cards, and Theresa gave him a bronze sculpture. It was a study by Tom Nichols of Richard I, mounted on his charger, wielding a sword, and it was an admirable piece of work. Harry expressed great delight, but silently wondered if it might not have been more appropriate for a monarchist or even his brother Dick. After a leisurely breakfast they departed in Theresa's snappy little red MG sports car, and reached the Showground at Shepton Mallet in Somerset in good time for the 12.30 appointment.

"I expect I'll be finished by mid-afternoon," said Harry. "Shall we meet at the car, or maybe at the Members' Pavilion?"

"You may have succeeded in being driven here, but your chauffeuse has no intention of kicking her heels for three hours, even on your birthday. I'll be joining you at the lunch."

Harry had not mentioned a lunch, but Theresa's professional career had not left her without some understanding of the likely programme of the day. In any case, she had not yet seen Harry in action in a business context, and she was curious to discover how he performed. They went over to the English Nature marquee, and were directed to a group of officials on the left. A tall, slim man, with a narrow smiling face, turned to greet them.

"Harry, so delighted you're able to be here for the launch." The greeting by Mark Hopkins was effusive and genuine. "It's been a long time reaching fruition, but I think we have something special."

"I wouldn't have missed it on any account." replied Harry. "Darling, can I introduce Mark Hopkins, who has masterminded the whole project? Mark, my wife, Theresa, who'd like to join us for lunch if that's OK."

"Oh, absolutely. We need charming ladies to lighten up our stuffy business gatherings."

"I know very little about your project, Mr Hopkins," said Theresa. "I'd be very interested to hear more."

"That would be my pleasure. We're making a pictorial record of the English countryside to encapsulate its character at the start of the third millennium – a modern visual edition of the Domesday Book. We've commissioned artists and photographers, and Harry is acting as our technical adviser. I'm surprised he has not discussed it with you. Let's get a drink, and I'll show you the progress to date." Theresa shot Harry an accusing glance as she and Mark moved to the far side of the marquee where a demonstration of the project had been laid out, and Harry turned to engage in conversation with other guests. He noted with approval that more than 50 were present.

Lunch was served with full silver service at seven circular tables, each seating eight guests. Harry was placed next to the Regional Director of English Nature, while Theresa was at another table beside Mark. Harry was accustomed to high standards of corporate hospitality, and the meal did not disappoint him. Four courses, all based on British produce, were each accompanied by a different wine. A terrine of game pate, traditional Devon beef, old-fashioned fruit pie with native apple varieties conserved at Brogdale, and a selection of sheep's milk cheeses. "Who needs Roquefort when we have these?" he asked. He indulged himself but, with the knowledge that he might be expected to contribute to the discussion afterwards, he was not over-indulgent. When coffee was served, the Regional Director offered a brief welcome and then handed over to Mark.

"Ladies and gentlemen, welcome. I'm delighted that so many of you have been able to join us today. It is a very special event, because it marks the end of the first phase of a major millennium project for English Nature. But before I tell you more of the results, I must say a very special word of thanks to Harry Bainbridge." He walked over to Harry. "You've been a key player in the success of this project, Harry;

you've given your interest and your expertise willingly and readily, and you've done it all voluntarily. It is not often that men of your status are prepared to devote their time so freely, and I wish to thank you publicly for your support and interest."

There was a ripple of applause from the guests. Harry acknowledged Mark's kind words, and Mark went on to describe the project in more detail. Harry glanced over and saw Theresa looking in his direction. There was a glow of pride and approval on her face, and Harry felt a surge of pleasure and surprise that she should react in that way.

On the drive home she glanced across at him. "I'm very glad I came with you today. I had no idea how highly other people regard you. You must be very proud."

"I appreciated Mark's words of thanks very much, but I'm not comfortable with such public declarations. If something is worthwhile I'm prepared to put a great deal of effort into it because I believe in it."

Theresa considered his reply. She could see how he applied that principle to most of his business activities, but she wondered if it applied equally to his personal affairs.

"I'm surprised you hadn't mentioned the project to me. Do you deliberately keep your business life and private life in separate compartments?" Harry would have laughed it off, but her tone was too serious. The truth was that her outspoken directness, which had first attracted him to her, had proved less comfortable when it was directed at him. He had found it easier to avoid discussion, even though he was aware that her opinions often were pertinent and useful.

"I must make sure to keep you informed in future," he replied, and they drove home in silence, both aware that once again a promising opportunity for communication had taken a wrong turn.

Thursday 2 March

Harry lay in bed on Thursday morning reflecting happily on the success of yesterday's events, with just the faintest feeling of unease at Theresa's complaint. He already was starting to adjust to the possibility of not rising at half past five every morning, and he expected the meeting today would match yesterday's in relaxed enjoyment. Maybe retirement had its advantages after all.

He needed to be at the Pump Rooms in Leamington Spa by 10.30

for a photographic exhibition organised by PFA with sponsorship from Foremans, an oil fuel distribution company. Foremans cultivated an association with cultural and conservation organisations to counterbalance the negative publicity generated by the pollution of oil spills such as the Exxon Valdez environmental disaster in Alaska and the Braer wreck in the Shetland Islands. Johan Barck, MD of Foremans, was a good friend who had worked with Harry on several projects. They shared an interest in colour photography, primarily of animal life and landscape, but this exhibition featured Robert Capa, who as a war correspondent produced an outstanding portfolio of monochrome studies.

Harry left home at nine o'clock and, missing the worst of the traffic on the M42, arrived promptly at the Pump Rooms at 10.30. He was performing a dual role at the exhibition. Primarily he was there as the representative of PFA to host a bevy of distinguished guests, but he also had been requested to prepare a report on the event in his new capacity as consultant to PFA. That would need to be carefully edited. It would be submitted to Louise Crossman who, even though she was only four days into her new position, probably would be somewhat resentful that she was not representing PFA at such an august gathering.

He accepted a glass of champagne as he entered the impressive foyer. Pamela had organised the event, and came over immediately. Her pale-cream suit, with touches of blue on the pockets and lapels, was cut modestly at the neckline and as high above the knee as decency would allow.

"Hello, young lady, you're looking beautiful as usual," said Harry as he gave her a kiss and a quick squeeze. "Any problems?"

She smiled at him with affection. "You're looking pretty good yourself. Retirement must be suiting you. Everything is in order. Champagne and canapés are ready, the main guests and the press are expected before eleven o'clock, you'll say a few words followed by a short tour of the exhibition, lunch will be at 12.30, and the doors will open to the general public at two o'clock – by which time you'll have left."

Marvellous girl. He knew he could relax, confident that she had everything under control. "And how are things at the office?" A slight frown crossed her face. "Probably too early to tell," she replied, "but for sure it'll not be the same as when you were there."

Harry assumed she was making an oblique reference to the sexual *frisson* that existed between them, but Pamela continued, "You always were open and friendly with everyone, no stuffiness and a minimum of formality. Ms Crossman's first edicts have been that no one enters her office without a specific invitation – or should I say instruction – and that male members of staff must wear jacket and tie, and trousers and short skirts are banned for female staff."

Harry could see that Pamela was genuinely concerned. "They seem very trivial items for the initial focus of priority." He attempted to lighten the mood. "Maybe she feels jealous of your gorgeous legs, whereas I couldn't see enough of them." He was aware of the dangers of being drawn into a personal disagreement between his successor and his former PA, but it troubled him to see Pamela upset. The first guests were arriving, and he took the easy way out. "Give me a ring and we can talk about it further."

Harry had seen Johan Barck approaching, and turned to greet him. Johan was a slight man, five or six inches shorter than Harry, with a receding hairline. But he kept himself in good shape; he carried no surplus weight and his face showed no sign of wear. They had co-operated through the work of their respective organisations for many years, and they also met socially as they lived only a few miles apart. They discussed the programme for the day, identified a few guests who should be given priority treatment, and arranged to talk after lunch as there were one or two items that Johan had in mind.

At eleven o'clock exactly Pamela asked for silence, and Harry climbed onto the platform.

"Distinguished guests, ladies and gentlemen, I am delighted to welcome you to an event which marks a further stage in Portway Fine Arts' policy of bringing art of special quality to the attention of a wider public. We again are most grateful to Johan Barck of Foremans for sponsoring the event, and I am delighted that Johan is present with us today. This exhibition features the work of the charismatic Hungarian exile, Robert Capa – born Endre Friedman in 1913, a friend of Ernest Hemingway and Pablo Picasso, and probably the finest war correspondent and photojournalist there has ever been. His pictures speak volumes. You may find some disturbing, but Capa was intent on the portrayal of truth, even when the truth was brutal. He founded Magnum

Studios, of which he became President, and was killed by a landmine in 1954. A book of his work was published in 1996. This is our first excursion into monochrome photography, but it will not be our last. I am sure that I speak for Johan when I say that both of us feel very privileged to be able to present a Robert Capa exhibition. I hope you will take time to look around, and then join us for lunch at 12.30. Thank you."

While he was speaking, Harry had noticed Ami Kotze among the guests. He had sent her an invitation, and was pleased to see that she was there. He went over to her and they exchanged a kiss. She was a study in casual elegance; the sensuality of her dark complexion intensified by her bright red halter top and denim trousers. "Ami. Great to see you again. You look fabulous. More seductive every time I set eyes on you."

She blushed. She had known Harry for more than twenty years, but he still made her pulse race. "Thank you, kind sir," she murmured. "How could I refuse your summons to attend? It looks an amazing exhibition. What about the Bonheur in Ireland – have you made any progress?"

"Yes, I think we'll get it, but I'm playing a waiting game. Probably I'll pay another visit soon to clinch a deal, and I may need your help." Harry had asked Ami's advice about the picture after his visit last year. "But come with me. I want to introduce you."

He led her across to Johan Barck. "Johan, I'm sure you remember Ami Kotze from my birthday party. She's an old friend of mine and a superb practitioner of exotic art."

"Delighted to see you again Ami, and maybe very opportune. Any friend of Harry's is a friend of mine." Johan turned to Harry. "I wanted to talk to you about future exhibitions. I favour the idea on concentrating on unusual subjects or presentations, and the timing of your introduction seems like the intervention of fate. Maybe we should look at your work, Ami." He addressed the final remark to her, and Ami was visibly excited. She started to describe her work to Johan and soon they were engrossed in discussion.

Pamela was at Harry's elbow. She had noted with a twinge of jealousy his intimate exchange with Ami. "Harry, you won't forget that you need to prepare a report, will you? I could rough it out for you if you wish."

"No, thanks for the offer Pamela, but it won't take me long. You have done a superb job here today." Her flushed face had not escaped his notice. "Are you OK?"

"Yes, fine," she replied, and walked away, her short blonde hair bobbing, and her shapely *derriere* swaying with each emphatic stride.

Harry was sufficiently responsive to women to know that something was wrong, but not understanding enough to know what it was. His mind did not dwell on it; he already was thinking about the report, and that he should include a recommendation to PFA to request sponsorship from Foremans for an exhibition of Ami's work. On second thoughts, he wondered if it would be better for him to go direct to Foremans for sponsorship. He knew that Johan's reply would be positive. He could not guarantee that Louise Crossman would accept his recommendation, but nevertheless he decided to follow the proper procedure and make the recommendation to PFA.

He left after lunch in an excellent frame of mind. The meal had been good, the guests had been complimentary, and he hoped for many column inches of favourable comment from the press. He enjoyed working with Foremans, and Johan's continuing interest was encouraging. But none of that could account entirely for his good humour. He came to the conclusion that Ami's presence was the cause, and he felt a twinge of nostalgia as he drove home.

Friday 3 March

Harry toyed with the idea of catching the train on Friday morning. He would undergo a great deal of inconvenience to avoid driving into London. His meeting was at ten o'clock which would bring him into the peak traffic congestion and the subsequent problems of parking. The rail station at Worcester was only a few miles from his home, but the thought of the wearisome meander along the myriad of small stops on the Paddington line through Oxford and Reading, and the knowledge that the train almost certainly would be late, made up his mind. In the end, he rose early and left home at six o'clock in the hope of missing the morning rush. The meeting had been moved from the Institute of Directors – pity, he found the facilities there to his liking – to the Farmers' Club in Whitehall. A peculiar choice, he mused, maybe something to do with intellectual property rights for native crops from the developing world. How would works of art and Andean potatoes fit cheek by jowl in the same discussion? It was an intriguing thought, and it kept his mind occupied as he continued the journey.

He left his car in the park just off Trafalgar Square and walked down Horse Guards Parade past Scotland Yard, before turning left into Whitehall. The Farmers Club obviously was one of the less fashionable London Clubs. It occupied part of 3 Whitehall Court – close to the Ministry of Defence – and it was necessary to ascend to the upper ground floor to reach the reception desk. He was directed to the Eastwood Room, along a narrow corridor. As he emerged from the corridor into the lounge, a painting caught his eye. It was a white bull by Norton dated 1876 and titled the Killhow Bull, and around the corner was a sculpture of a group of three Suffolk horses. Maybe he should have a look around after the meeting.

There were already about dozen people in the Eastwood Room when he arrived. He was surprised by the size of the room. They could not be expecting an attendance of more than 40 or 50. Further delegates drifted in, and the meeting began on time with a rather sparse group. There was a series of short presentations, ranging across the full variety of intellectual property rights. Harry's interest was focused mainly on a speaker from the British Association of Picture Libraries and Agencies who dealt with the protection of copyright under both civil and criminal law. He had not appreciated how much it applied to PFA, and he was appalled to learn that more than ten billion pounds are lost each year in copyright theft. Although the major part of PFA business rested on original works of high value, the trade in reproductions was increasing, and this was a vulnerable area. Electronic communications had not only opened up great opportunities to transmit millions of images, but also placed temptation more easily within reach of those who wished to circumvent the law.

Harry was thoughtful as he drove home. He had run into copyright problems before, with the first painting he'd ever commissioned. He had assumed in his youthful ignorance that the act of commissioning acquired the copyright. He rapidly discovered his mistake when the wife of the artist prohibited the sale of postcard reproductions he had printed. It was not an expensive lesson, but it was well learned. Maybe it would be prudent to establish a system for PFA to monitor the use of its images.

5
CONFLICT

Whose photos? May 2000

Harry had not been overly impressed by the Loxton brothers in Peterborough, but in retrospect he realised there might be greater potential in their business than he had appreciated during their brief meeting a couple of months ago in March. He mulled it over one weekend while he enjoyed a good bottle of wine on the terrace watching the swallows and house martins inspecting potential nesting sites, and thought he should do a little homework. There was an extensive catalogued photo library at PFA, mostly consisting of his own colour transparencies, and he surmised that the foreign section probably contained material relevant to the property business.

He picked up the phone on Monday morning, rang the PFA office and asked to speak to Louise. After a lengthy interval, she answered. "Good morning, Harry, what can I do for you?" That was rather brusque. He would have to find a diplomatic way of telling her how to be a little more customer friendly and improve her telephone manner.

"Hello, Louise. Haven't seen you for a while. I hope everything is going well," he began. "I was intending to call in the office on Thursday to have a look through the photo library, and hoped to use the film scanner if no one else has need of it. Would that be OK?"

There was a pause. "I'm not sure who will be needing the facilities on Thursday. It would be helpful if you could write to ask formally, then it can go into the system."

It was Harry's turn to pause. Had he heard correctly? "Are you suggesting that I should write to request the use of the scanner?" he asked.

"No, I am requiring that you should write. There are now proper procedures for the use of all equipment and facilities, including books and photographs, and I am afraid everyone must follow them."

Harry's hackles began to rise. "You will be aware that most of the transparencies in the library belong to me," he was going to continue, but he thought better of it. He sensed the conversation was heading towards a dead end.

"As far as I am aware, all items in the office belong to PFA," she responded sharply. "I'll expect to have a letter from you if you wish to come in on Thursday."

Harry was not amused. It was less than three months since he'd retired, and already he was required to request permission in writing to use facilities at the premises of the business he had founded. His first reaction was to ring Miles, but superficially it was too trivial a matter to invoke the Chairman's authority. He would follow an easier and more direct route. Pamela would send him a full list of photos and a copy of all documents in the office relating to the library and copyright. He rang her and she agreed to his request without question. The information arrived in the post next morning. He then looked through the notes he had made on IPR at the London meeting in March, and composed a letter to Louise.

The core content of the letter read:

> 'Thank you for advising me of the new procedures being applied in the office. I will not require to use the facilities on Thursday. Please let me know which day next week would be convenient for me to call and collect the transparencies which are my property, and meanwhile you should note that use of those transparencies is not permitted without my authority.'

He drove down to the post office in the village in good time to catch the afternoon post. Harry's telephone rang late on Wednesday morning. It was Jack Maladonis.

"Harry, old chap, how *are* you? Far too long since we saw you. I hope you're finding plenty to do." Harry winced at the glaring insincerity, and Jack continued. "Louise tells me she's had a letter from you. Rang me this morning, and seemed rather upset. Something to do with photographs. She's doing a marvellous job in the office you know, really pulling things together. It will take time, and it's up to us old-stagers to give her all the support we can. The elder statesman act you know, old chap."

"Hello, Jack," Harry replied in measured tones. "Yes, I did find it necessary to write to Louise. I hope she's brought herself up to date, and the matter can be resolved."

"I think it would be terribly useful if you were able to take a lower profile for a while. Everyone in the business knows you, and you have such a reputation that you're bound to attract the attention when you are present. We need to let Louise into the limelight..."

Harry cut in. Jack was about to launch on one of his lengthy soliloquies, and Harry was not inclined to listen. "Have no worry, Jack. I'm now a consultant. I act when consulted, and have no wish to take the limelight from Louise. At the same time, please remember that she has taken the position of MD, and she is expected to be competent to fill it."

Harry had a keen nose for conspiracy, and he smelled a big one now. His letter had caused Louise a problem, but she had not gone to the Chairman, Miles Mountjoy. Instead, she immediately had contacted Jack Maladonis, and he had rung Harry with no delay. The Board of PFA was too small to allow for an internal cabal, and intrigue between Louise and Jack had serious implications.

Jack Maladonis was not a popular man. His father was a Greek immigrant and his parents, who called him Andreas, were kept far distant from contact with his business acquaintances. Jack was an adopted name that he felt endowed him with Britishness. His black hair and sallow skin betrayed his mixed ancestry and further fuelled his insecurity. His domineering rudeness to weaker and more sensitive colleagues, especially women, was matched only by his ingratiating slyness in the company of persons of title and blatant fawning to those of robust personality. He was not a big man in any sense, but he compensated with an overabundance of pomposity. Short in stature, but long in opinion, he had built his reputation round elaborate turns of phrase and the ability to contort simple statements into a complexity of name-dropping repetitiveness which few others could achieve. He practised a verbal version of the Chinese water torture technique, and by its persistent use he eventually had worn down his opponents and insinuated himself to the core of the Board of HIH and from thence to the Board of PFA. It had done very little for his popularity, but it had served its purpose.

Colleagues who held strong convictions, especially if founded on genuine motivation, were seen as obstacles. He sought, by devious and subversive methods, to undermine and outmanoeuvre them. Some were easy prey. Their trust that others shared their values of openness and sincerity, failed to understand the web of self-interest and personal aggrandisement that spun Jack Maladonis ever closer to the centre of power. Others understood his purpose and methods with greater transparency, and on occasion he was put firmly in his place, but if his ego was bruised it was difficult to detect, and he continued as before. He could with justification boast a thick skin.

Off with the Old: June 2000

Louise Crossman and Robert Gator were closeted in her office one morning in early June. The door was closed firmly, and she had forbidden any further interruption after Kate, the plump ginger-haired girl from the back office, had brought them coffee. It was a month since her altercation with Harry regarding the transparencies, and she still was smouldering inwardly.

"This place is claustrophobic," she was saying. "It is impossible to escape from Harry Bainbridge. Everything that happens seems to trace back to him, and everybody I meet asks about him. I wish he would vanish off the planet."

"He has been in the business for a long time," replied Robert carefully, "and will not be moved easily." He also retained dark thoughts of Harry from the last meeting of YPF trustees. "I have no direct involvement with PFA, but I do have the dubious pleasure of working with him on YPF."

"That's really why I asked you to come here today." Louise's face assumed an expression of serious intensity. "I understand that YPF was founded by PFA, and in the new circumstances there is only one PFA-appointed trustee. That can not be right. Do you not think that I should replace Mr Bainbridge as a trustee." It was a statement, not a question.

"Of course I would prefer that you replaced him. When we worked together on the accounts of that difficult client of mine in Essex last year, I think you and I reached a mutual understanding and you will remember we succeeded in ending that matter as we wished."

"And we will in this matter too," she added with finality. "The Board of PFA will decide who will represent them on YPF. Peter Loder is the floating vote among the Directors, and we need him on side.

Maybe you could lean on him. You are the independent trustee, and he would take note of your opinion."

"I would be pleased to do that. It would certainly make life more comfortable if Bainbridge was out of the way."

They both leaned back in their chairs with grim satisfied smiles.

❋ ❋ ❋ ❋ ❋ ❋ ❋ ❋ ❋ ❋ ❋ ❋

Harry opened the franked letter from PFA. Inside was a scribbled note and a photocopied memorandum. The note read 'Thought you should see this. Love. Pamela.' The memorandum was short and sharp. It was from Louise Crossman to Robert Gator, and was dated 8th June 2000. 'Positive results from your contact with Peter Loder. He has indicated to me that he supports my appointment as trustee of YPF. Jack will support it, and he will propose it at the next meeting of the Board. A majority vote is assured. Will confirm soonest.'

The situation became much clearer to Harry. He had harboured suspicions, but now they were confirmed. He had the option of direct confrontation, but it seemed that Louise preferred to play behind his back. Well, if that was the way she wanted it, so be it. He called Walter. "I'm not as closely in touch as I used to be. Anything exciting happening that I should know about?"

"Between you and me, PFA has not been running smoothly since you retired. We expected some changes and fine-tuning with a new MD, but we are becoming a little uneasy. I can see no justification for the significant changes that have been made. Did you know that Terry Williams has gone? That was madness, and I opposed it, but I was out-voted. PFA was on a roll at the beginning of the year – and I know you were happy to go out on a high note – but now it seems almost as if Louise wishes to expunge from the record anything associated with you."

"That sounds ominous. And what about YPF? There should be a meeting next month."

"Yes. Have you prepared the agenda?"

"It doesn't look as though I will need to. I hear that there are moves behind the scenes at PFA for Louise to replace me as trustee. You hadn't heard?"

There was a short silence at the other end of the line. "Not a word, but I'm not surprised. They will need the support of Peter Loder to push it through, but on present form they probably will get it. Miles and I are keen to keep you as involved as possible, but Louise and Jack Maladonis would be happy to see the back of you"

"That's the ways things go," said Harry philosophically. "How are things otherwise with the company?"

"Well, normally I would be more circumspect, but after your news I have no inclination for soft-pedalling. My assessment after more than three months of the new regime is that Louise has an acute lack of knowledge of our business, and as a result suffers from lack of confidence. She seems scared to have you around. I suspect it is because you know too much and make her look small by comparison. She has an unhealthily close relationship with Maladonis and Gator, and I think they both share her paranoia."

Harry had to take Walter's comments regarding Jack and Robert with a pinch of salt – he had a deep dislike for both – but there was no reason to doubt his comments regarding Louise, and there was no stopping him now. "I get the impression she is driven by self-interest. She seems to have no commitment to the company for its own sake. She came up with a proposal the other day to sack most of the staff, and pack the office with fresh-out-of-college young girls. Makes one suspicious doesn't it? The other Directors are a little apprehensive, but she bulldozes through objections, and Maladonis backs her on every item."

The Rift Deepens: July 2000

Following his exchange with Louise on the telephone in May, Harry had been in no hurry to call at the office for his transparencies. However, there was no point in further delay, and in July he called unannounced. Louise observed his arrival and remained in her office with the door firmly closed. Harry collected the boxes of magazines in which the transparencies were stored, and carried them to his car in three journeys – more than 30 magazines, each containing 160 transparencies.

Before leaving with the last load, Harry slipped into Pamela's office. "Hope I haven't caused any trouble for you, but I've just rescued my pics from the photo library. How are you?"

"Better for seeing you," she said, "but it's going from bad to worse here."

"What's the problem?"

"Most of your old staff have been given their notice. Terry has left because he couldn't stand Ms Crossman any longer. She informed him that she wasn't interested whether or not he respected her, and that it was up to him to earn her respect. Seems like she makes the rules for her own benefit." Pamela was into her stride. "Her temperament is precariously unbalanced. The slightest hint of disagreement with her and she throws a wobbly. Her eyes bulge, she shouts and yells. Once she couldn't find something in a file and she threw it across the office, with paper flying everywhere. When she doesn't understand something she blames the old system – it's always your fault. She says she can't comprehend how the business ran at all under your control. She's mad."

Harry thought it prudent to halt the conversation at that point. If Pamela was overheard, it might have serious consequences, but she had confirmed the fears that Walter had voiced the previous month.

Harry now was fully aware of the dangers, but he was reluctant to enter into open dispute. It was not his style, and he felt that any intervention he might make would compromise Miles Mountjoy. But he was becoming increasingly agitated by the policies adopted by Louise, and concerned for the long-term wellbeing of the company – his company! In his heart it was difficult not to feel for the company in a possessive manner, even though he knew it was no longer his. He had hidden his thoughts and fears to this point, but how much further? He was conscious that criticism of Louise coming from him might well be seen in the same light as Edward Heath's carping attacks on Margaret Thatcher: a disillusioned, discarded leader sniping at his successor; and think of the damage that feud had done to the Tories. He had no wish to be seen as a sour old man, with bitterness gnawing at the threads of reason. He must weigh carefully the damage that Louise was doing to the company, against the damage he would do if he openly declared his position.

❊ ❊ ❊ ❊ ❊ ❊ ❊ ❊ ❊ ❊ ❊ ❊

Louise Crossman had every intention of squeezing Harry out of the company. She had little knowledge of any aspect of art, and was not prepared to spend time acquiring it. She was uninterested in the values and purpose of the company, but saw Portway Fine Arts as a vehicle to achieve her personal ambitions. She was well versed in the mechanisms of deviousness, and camouflaged her unpleasantness when appropriate with ingratiating flattery, and she used her new position as MD of PFA to full advantage. In contrast to Harry, she only made a move when she was very sure of the outcome. As a result she made few mistakes in business, but missed many opportunities.

She was assisted by the alliance with Jack Maladonis. They both were outsiders, both naturally devious. Jack was the ultimate sycophant. His hand-wringing obsequiousness lulled many unsuspecting colleagues into decisions which assisted his upward climb. Louise could contrive a helpless female act that had the same effect. This unholy pairing schemed to take control of PFA. Individually they were of little consequence; in tandem they were a different proposition. They both lacked knowledge; they both lacked confidence, but their alliance of convenience spelt trouble – serious trouble.

Jack was a frequent visitor to the PFA offices, and spent long hours with Louise. His ambition to be Chairman of PFA was undiminished, and he saw Louise as his chief ally. Miles Mountjoy and Walter King stood in his way, but Harry Bainbridge still was the main obstacle although he was no longer a Director.

"Greetings, Louise." Jack was the only person who entered her office without being announced. "What news this morning?"

Louise was basking in her appointment as trustee of YPF, agreed at the recent meeting of the Board. "We are making progress, and thank you Jack for your support at the meeting. Trusteeship of YPF was the first step, but it is frustrating not to be able to move faster."

"Then we must prepare our plans carefully." Jack felt in his element as a modern businessman Napoleon. He strutted around the office. "Harry Bainbridge is an off-the-cuff operator. He has pleased some people, but he has made enemies. I am sure we can find enough of those to make life very uncomfortable for him. When he is gone, Mountjoy and King will be easy to remove."

"He marched into the office the other day, large as life, and collected several boxes of transparencies without permission from anyone. It would be heaven to be rid of him. Have you any ideas?" Louise was an able executioner, but she had little capacity for strategic thought.

"We must build on the success of your appointment to YPF. Now, where else has Bainbridge retained a toe-hold?" He paused, but Louise was waiting for his pronouncement. "There are two that come to mind – Foremans and English Nature. If we can ease him out of those, and slot you in, we will be on much stronger ground."

"Does he have enemies in either organisation?"

"No, none that I can identify immediately, but we can make discrete inquiries. From the rumours that I hear, our best chance may lie in another direction. I understand that he was a rather reckless womaniser." Jack cocked an eyebrow at Louise. "Maybe you should flutter your eyelashes, and see if you can compromise him!"

It was rare for Jack to attempt a joke, and even rarer for Louise to recognise one. "Heaven forbid!" she exclaimed.

On with the New? August 2000

Louise considered the report that Harry had submitted following the Capa exhibition in mid-March. She deliberately had not responded to it, partly to demonstrate that she controlled the timetable of events, and partly because she needed time to exploit any weaknesses that she could discover. The report in general was innocuous, apart from one item – a recommendation that PFA should request sponsorship from Foremans for an exhibition of Ami Kotze's work. Louise noted that Harry expressly hoped this would be agreed. She remembered Jack's words during their conversation the previous day. Maybe this was Harry Bainbridge's weak link.

"Good morning Jack. It's Louise." She called him early from the office. "I hope I'm not disturbing you, but I think I may have something of interest. I've been thinking about the advice you offered yesterday." She told him of the report and suggested that it should be an early item on the agenda of the forthcoming meeting of the PFA Board. "The others may be interested to hear of Harry Bainbridge's interest in Ms Kotze," she concluded.

"If I may offer some advice, it might be prudent not to present his report to the Board." Jack was an old hand at this game. "It might have greater effect if you made a summary which minimised the positive items and emphasised his support for the girl. It would give you opportunity to question his judgement and cast doubt on his motivation."

Louise and Jack devised a presentation that she would initiate, and he would support. It would seek to drive a wedge between Harry and the Directors of PFA, and enable Louise to capture the sponsors for her own purposes.

The Board meeting took place two weeks later. The Directors were pleased by the positive tone of her report, and eager to continue their association with Foremans. They were disturbed by Louise's concern that Harry may be allowing his personal affairs to colour his judgement. Miles and Walter had often felt that Ami might be Harry's Achilles heel, and they remembered that he had released her from the PFA contract many years before. Louise put sufficient doubt about Harry in their minds to obtain a carte blanche to pursue her own negotiations with Foremans. She was fired with exultation.

"We have won the war," she exclaimed to Jack after the meeting, almost bounding into her office.

"My dear girl, I think we have won a skirmish," replied Jack suavely, following more sedately. "We must not count the chickens before they are hatched. You now must be absolutely sure that your proposal is watertight."

It was the wrong advice to the wrong person. Louise's progress at the best of times was deliberate and painstaking, but now she checked all possible routes for danger, and valuable time slipped by while she struggled to finalise her plans. Time was vital. Harry was temporarily distracted and psychologically off balance. His relationship with Theresa was deteriorating, while a letter from his brother Dick, couched in uncompromising language, reminded him forcibly of his neglect of his parents and demanded his presence at Annie's 90th birthday party in October. Harry was unnerved by the authoritative tone adopted by Dick to such an extent that he began to consider the possibility of responding positively to his brother's request. He took his eye off the PFA ball, and gave Louise an invaluable window of opportunity.

❋ ❋ ❋ ❋ ❋ ❋ ❋ ❋ ❋ ❋ ❋ ❋

It did not take Harry long to revert to character. Dick's letter was consigned to the waste paper basket without reply, and Teesdale once again dismissed from his mind. He failed to recognise the irony of his own disgust that after almost five months he had not had a reply, or even an acknowledgement, from Louise about his report on the Capa exhibition. He was aware that it presented an excellent opportunity for

Ami, and had hoped to pursue it with some urgency. He spoke to Johan Barck fairly regularly, and during their next conversation he mentioned Ami. Johan immediately picked up on their discussion at the Leamington Spa exhibition. "I expected to hear about that some while ago, either from you or PFA," he said, "but not a word. I had a long talk with Ami at the exhibition and was very impressed with her. I would be interested to progress the idea of sponsorship."

"I'm sorry about that, Johan. Leave it with me, and I'll come back to you within the next few days." Harry regretted now that he had included the proposal in his report to Louise, but he would put that right without delay.

He rang Pamela. "Hello, Pamela Croft at the PFA office. Can I help you?"

"Pamela, it's me. What on earth are you talking about!" There was no answer. "Pamela, are you there?"

"Sorry, Harry. Madam was standing just outside my door and we now have very strict instructions about how to answer the telephone."

"Sounds more like a madhouse every day. Look my lovely, you remember the report that I sent in after the Leamington Spa exhibition in March. Has anything happened as a result?"

"Yes, *she* presented a précis of the report to the Board, and suggested that your proposal to sponsor Ms Kotze was based on personal motives." There was a slight edge to Pamela's voice. "Maybe she was right! In any case, the proposal was turned down, and she is now looking at an alternative scheme to obtain more sponsorship from Foremans."

"Thanks for letting me know. Would you give me a call if anything further transpires?"

"Harry," There was different, half-plaintive note to her voice. "I'm not sure how much longer I can carry on here. I think I'm going to resign."

Harry thought quickly. He needed Pamela in the office. She was an invaluable source of inside knowledge, and it was imperative that she remained there as long as possible. "I can understand how you feel. I wish I could do more to help. But you know, you hold the key to putting PFA back on the right track. The company means a lot to me, and I do rely on you. Together we stand a chance of solving the problems and restoring some sense to the situation. Please think carefully before you jump to a decision." He knew while he was doing it that he was a bastard for putting emotional blackmail on someone of whom he was sincerely fond. He almost felt guilty.

For Pamela, the possibilities engendered by the word 'together' were enough.

He called Johan immediately after talking to Pamela. "Johan, I've checked out the situation as I promised, and it seems that PFA have decided not to proceed with an exhibition of Ami's work. It's a pity, as I know how keen you are to sponsor her, and I suggest we should go ahead anyway. We have ample time if we plan for the event next March, and I am sure that Pamela would be happy to organise it for us in a private capacity."

Johan needed no further persuasion, and willingly gave Harry authority to make arrangements with Pamela and Ami. He had worked closely and successfully with Harry and Pamela for several years, and he had decided that he wished to sponsor Ami. Harry was satisfied with his day's work.

Tables Turned: December 2000

Harry and Mark Hopkins arranged to meet at the English Nature offices in mid-September. Mark had organised a meeting for early December to detail progress made on the Domesday project. The initial notice had gone out to interested organisations, and he wished to bring Harry up to date.

"The Government has become very interested in the project," he told Harry. "They can see that it has potential for good publicity. A record of Britain at the start of the new millennium is also a record of New Labour."

"In that case we must hope that there are no disasters to record in the next year or two. From all points of view, we can do without bad news."

"I agree," replied Mark, "and in that context, what is the problem with this woman Louise Crossman who took your place at PFA? She called me the other day and virtually demanded that I send her an invitation to the meeting. She implied that you were no longer an active player, and that she was replacing you on all committees and consultative bodies of any significance. When I gave a non-committal answer, she was rather offensively aggressive, to put it mildly."

"She is a peculiar person. Maybe your best answer is to send an invitation to her and then you can see for yourself at first hand."

"I'm happy to invite her if you don't mind, but let's be clear Harry, it's you we want on this project. The original invitation to be involved was made to you on the basis of your expertise, not because you were MD of PFA."

The meeting in early December was held in Bristol. Representatives of the Farming and Rural Conservancy Agency were present to discuss governmental policy for the environment. Several large landowners and local dignitaries had been invited. Mark and Harry had both prepared presentations on progress of the project. They were surprised when Robert Gator arrived to represent PFA, but he announced that he was attending at the request of Louise Crossman.

The presentations in the morning session were well received, and during the lunch break conversation centred around the economy. A relaxed informal atmosphere far away from London offices, reinforced by a liberal flow of wine, usually lifts the stereotypical inhibitions of civil servants, and encourages them to step outside their normal non-committal responses. Wastage of funds at both local and national level soon entered the conversation.

"What are they going to do with the Dome? Leave it as a monument to Blair?" asked a suave young Somerset landowner.

"You have to hand it to Blair. How many other politicians could get away with blowing eight hundred million quid on a white elephant that stays open for one year while the health service, the railways, and most other things we value are grinding to a standstill..."

"...and his closest Cabinet colleagues are sinking in sleaze," added a florid-faced gentleman. "Mendelson a kept man, Byers a compulsive liar, Cook divorced at an airport? How much worse can it get?"

Another guest chipped in. "Blair is all promises and no delivery. All froth and no substance. How long can he get away with it?"

"Well, he's fooled the majority of the voting public so far," replied one of the civil servants. "His formula seems to work. People talk of other politicians who they say have intelligence, who understand the economy and principles of management, who talk sense and have some sense of decency. How far do they get? Hague doesn't stand a chance in the election, simply because he looks like a garden gnome and talks like a nasal northerner. Brown was conned out of leadership of the Labour Party, and yet it's his stealth taxes and manipulation of the economy that keep Blair in power. Tells you something about public opinion doesn't it?"

"Tells you something about Labour MPs as well," snorted a local Conservative councillor.

"His relationship with Brown is the key," interposed another civil servant. "Blair's vanity, his compulsion to always be in the centre of attention, and his inability ever to admit his mistakes, is all down to fear of Gordon Brown – the bear in the background – and his influence and identification with old Labour principles."

"Blair learned his lessons at the feet of Clinton. Same strategy, same smile, same phrases. Clinton bluffed his way through, and I guess that Blair thinks he can do the same. I suspect he will." The young landowner shrugged with resignation.

It was clear that the Prime Minister was not held in high regard by either city or country denizens. As the light-hearted banter continued, Mark drew Harry to one side. "When I open the session this afternoon," he said quietly, "I will make the point specifically, for the benefit of both civil servants and Mr Gator, that you are a fixture in the project."

Robert Gator did not participate in the general conversation. He felt totally out of place, and said nothing as he stood dourly at one side. Whatever his thoughts, he was not risking any chance that they might escape and jeopardise his chances in the birthday honours. It was an ambition that devoured him. An OBE would be some compensation for disadvantage by the laws of primogeniture, or maybe even a knighthood which would elevate his status well beyond that of a country squire. He knew how the system worked. It was necessary to have the endorsement of the Cabinet Office, the Lord Lieutenant, and other well-connected persons. He was paranoid that he might say anything indiscreet, and that anyone – civil servants in particular – might misinterpret his words and report them. When in doubt he played safe and kept quiet. It was enough that he had been seen. He hoped his face and name would stick.

Harry guessed there had been an ulterior motive when Gator had been nominated to represent PFA, and also he had no illusions that Louise would have a full report of the meeting. It would be interesting to watch their next move, but he had no worries on that score. The deal with the English Nature was wrapped up securely. As they re-convened for the afternoon session, Mark Hopkins gave a brief outline of the programme for the next two years. He made specific mention that "Harry Bainbridge will continue to be our official consultant on all artistic aspects of the project."

Harry smiled in acknowledgement. Robert Gator frowned. Louise Crossman and her allies had won the early rounds on points, but Harry now was piling on the pressure as the confrontation moved closer to the final bell.

Separation 2000

Harry was on an incline of success. If he had applied his normal principles of business management he would have known that excessive success always precedes an equally dramatic fall. But Harry, for all his business acumen, still had not realised that business principles may apply also to personal matters. Even if he had realised, he would have argued that personal happiness can not be linked in that way to business success. Murphy's Law has little regard for such theoretical niceties – and he was married to an Irish woman!

The visit to Ireland in 1999 had been a defining moment for Harry and Theresa. They had enjoyed brief moments of happiness. Sitting together on the summit of the Hill of Doon above Oughterard, looking down on the scatter of islands across Lough Corrib, with the misty mauve backdrop of the Maumturk Mountains to the north, they shared a sense of peace and contemplative calm. A lark was singing overhead, and the brown hillside below was patterned with purple heather on the slopes and white cottongrass in the damp hollows. There were derelict old crofts, and abandoned fields, from which man had retreated and nature resumed control. It was far from the brash newness of EU-funded projects that spread their tentacles through much of the Emerald Isle.

But such interludes were brief, and frequently the visit had exposed the raw wounds of their marriage. As they moved further west through Connemara on the road to Clifden, Harry saw a sign ahead. "There's a craft shop. Shall we call and see if they have anything interesting?"

"Well, maybe..." Theresa was non-committal.

"Yes or no; we're almost past," said Harry urgently.

"I'm not that fond of crafts..."

"I'll take that as a negative. I should know better by now than to expect a straight answer from a Celt," Harry exclaimed with annoyance as the craft shop fell behind.

"You should indeed. The Irish answer in their own way. We won't be stampeded into a reply, and I've no intention or wish to change my ways now."

The visit had been punctuated by similar exchanges, and culminated in their major confrontation over the Bonheur painting.

Theresa was very downcast after their return, and the acid argument with Harry about the purchase of the Bonheur hung heavily on her mind. She went to RDA the following week, although she felt little enthusiasm, and fell into a long conversation with Steve. After the others had gone, Steve asked her to go over to the farmhouse to discuss a problem. He usually was able to find a problem every time Theresa was at RDA.

"There is a difficulty which is causing some changes here," he began. "It may affect the arrangements for RDA, and I thought that it would be useful for us to discuss it first. As you are Chairman of the Management Committee, I am sure the others will follow your lead." He paused. He could see that she was in low spirits as she sat on the sofa, and he offered her a drink. She usually had one drink, but tonight she emptied her glass several times as she conversed abstractedly. Steve had bided his time, but tonight she was in a different mood and he decided the moment had come to press his advances to a closer communion.

"Theresa, you seem unhappy today," he ventured. "Is anything wrong? You've been listening to my problems, but is there anything you need to talk about?"

She did need to talk – she had a desperate need to let out her feelings. She could not talk to Harry without falling into an argument, and she felt comfortable talking to Steve. "I am a little upset," she began tentatively. "I've just been to Ireland, and it was not as enjoyable as I expected. We – I – seemed to do nothing but argue. I do enjoy talking so much – you know I do – but I have lost the ability to do it in my marriage. Sometimes I wonder where all the joy has gone..." Her voice trailed away as a sob rose in her throat. The alcohol had intensified her sadness. She put her head in her hands and began to cry.

Steve moved over and sat beside her. He put his arms around her and she responded as she buried her face in his neck. She was sobbing as she held him, and Steve gently pushed her backwards. "There," he said softly, "let it all out." He felt the contours of her body as he leaned against her, and slowly moved one hand up towards her breast.

The reaction was instantaneous. Theresa pushed him away. "No, no, no!" she shouted, "get your hands off me. I thought you were a friend, but you are only interested in sex. You are as filthy as all other men." She leapt to her feet, grabbed her coat, and rushed out of the house.

She felt betrayed, insulted and violated. Tony Devonshire, Steve Kent, Harry Bainbridge – they were all the same. Uncaring, self-centred, disgusting men! She began to see some sense in the advice her mother had given her almost 40 years ago: "Stay away from men, keep your skirt down and your knees together." In the innocence of a juvenile Catholic girl she had not understood her mother's meaning, and the lack of explanation had served only to heighten her apprehension of the consequences – and her curiosity – if she deviated from the advice. In the end, she had learned the hard way that, in matters of the heart, experience is difficult to pass on to the next generation – each generation is intent on re-learning old lessons.

She had hoped that Harry's retirement party might renew the spirit of marriage, but it caused her more pain than pleasure. Ami Kotze always seemed to be there as a fly in the ointment – a very colourful, and far too attractive fly! Or maybe she was the spider spinning Harry into her web. Far from being a launch pad for future happiness, Harry's retirement had imposed further stresses and strains on their relationship. A secure marriage might have resisted the negative pressures, but in their case the cracks opened still further.

Even on the infrequent occasions when they succeeded in maintaining a dialogue, it often descended into personal criticism. In the early stages of their marriage, Theresa had vigorously defended his position in any business dispute; now she took a more acerbic line. She threw back at him his confessions of the women he had known – Ami, Karen and Eva. "You use people. You don't know the meaning of love. You are shallow – no depth. If you can't rise to my level, I certainly am not going to fall to yours. Business is the only passion of your life. Women are simply a quick fix – a convenience."

She did not entirely ignore his virtues, but they were dismissed in the overall condemnation of his character. "You're a weak impulsive man, always with an eye for easy opportunity. Your strengths are your weaknesses. You have a heart of gold and your generosity is amazing, but you're easily tempted. I think you're addicted to risk and gambling in any form, whether it with women or in business. You're adored by those who see you from a distance, but those who really know you have seen a different man. You'll live to regret that you've wasted those things that really matter."

Harry had no answer to such stinging rebukes. He held his peace, but he despaired of their future together. His silence served at least to remove opportunities for further dispute.

Through the late summer and autumn they seemed to reach a temporary truce. Harry's mood improved as he gradually became more confident that the problems at PFA might be solved, and he speculated that Theresa also was making an effort. He even wondered if the invitation from Dick for Annie's 90th birthday party in October might not offer an opportunity to further restore relations with Theresa. In the end, the potential embarrassment dissuaded him, but it suggested that seeds of family reconciliation might yet germinate. His mindset showed signs of amelioration.

It was early December – a crisp winter morning at Whitstone Court, and the pale rays of the sun filtered down through the leafless branches and sparkled off the lingering frost on the lane. At the meeting with English Nature the previous day, Mark Hopkins had confirmed his ongoing contract, and he thought maybe he would take Theresa away for Christmas – skiing in Andorra, or a villa on the Costa del Sol – to try and mollify her obvious bitterness. He was in buoyant spirits. He was down at the village shop buying some supplies for Boru, whose rich red colour now was tinged with grey, when Theresa answered the telephone in his study at the house.

An Irish female voice responded. "Ah, Miss Kotze, I'm glad I caught you. I'm ringing to let you know that the painting for Mr Bainbridge has been dispatched to Bellridge Hall as you instructed."

"This is Mrs Bainbridge. To whom am I speaking?"

There was a pause at the other end of the line. "I'm very sorry to trouble you, I must have the numbers mixed. I'm Mr Joyce's personal assistant from the Clonfert Cross Hotel. I thought I was ringing Miss Kotze's number, but if it is Mrs Bainbridge's perhaps you would let him about know the painting."

"You can be sure I will," said Theresa with feeling.

Her face was impassively serious when Harry returned, singing quietly to himself after the brisk walk. "There was a call for you while you were out." He found her steady gaze distinctly unnerving, and stopped singing. "It seems that someone expected to contact Ami Kotze here. Why would that be?"

His mind was whirring. "That seems most peculiar. In what context..."

"You know damn well in what context," she screamed at him. All the frustration and anger came pouring out. "You've been scheming with that hussy behind my back. You've bought the painting in Ireland, and goodness knows what else you've done together. No wonder you haven't wanted to sleep with me. How long has she been lying on her back for you? The pair of you have been doing it in front of my face and laughing at me. Don't think I didn't see you whispering together in Birmingham at the exhibition, and at your retirement party. You disgusting, revolting man – how could you go to bed with another woman? Oh, I hate you, I hate you..."

"I haven't..."

"You are despicable. I never want you near me again. I'll go and stay with my sister, and I hope you will have the decency to be gone before I get back."

She burst into tears, ran upstairs to her room and locked the door. He knocked and asked her to let him in, but she shouted at him to go away. He tried to reason through the door and explain that nothing had happened with Ami, that he would return the painting, and that everything would be fine. Her mind had passed the point of rational discussion on the matter, and eventually he retired downstairs.

The next day Theresa went to Kenmare and stayed until the beginning of January. Harry moved out of Whitstone Court immediately. He rented a cottage on the edge of Chipping Campden. It had a neat manicured thatch above mellow Cotswold stone, but Harry did not notice its attractive features and took no joy in it. He was distraught. In the immediate aftermath of Theresa's departure, Harry's deep-seated insecurities came to the surface again. What would he do without Theresa? Why did it have to happen, just when it seemed they might be overcoming their problems? When he thought about it, he realised that in the past two or three years an argument had always wrecked any possible rapprochement. They argued a great deal, and maybe their separation had been inevitable. The accumulated tension of the last couple of years, and the memory of some of his more bitter verbal exchanges with Theresa, convinced him that their marriage was beyond redemption.

Ami 2000–2001

Whenever Harry was emotionally bruised, he retired to his Northumberland estate. It was like returning to the womb – a feeling of safety, cocooned away from the realities of the world. In the trauma of Theresa's departure Harry retreated again to the upland fastness at Highcrags. He had kept the estate through all the troubled times. Its glorious isolation and open spaces rejuvenated him, with only wild pastures, upland lakes and mountain crags visible from the balcony of his bedroom. He walked the length and breadth of the estate to ease his anger, frustration and confusion. In quieter moments he wandered among the herd and allowed the calming presence of the cattle to soothe his raw nerves.

His few close friends telephoned with sympathetic words. He talked at length to Walter, who tried to rouse his spirits with reminiscences of old times. Johan Barck called to see him and Harry was touched by his concern.

Ami packed her case as soon as she heard the news and arrived unannounced. She spent Christmas 2000 and New Year with him at Bellridge Hall, boosting his flagging morale, and was a source of immense reassurance and comfort. They sat close together in the snug on New Year's Eve – the real end of the old millennium, he told her – with mince pies and mulled wine. On the wall opposite hung the Bonheur painting – it symbolised their current position. It had been obtained by their joint efforts, and it had triggered Harry's separation from Theresa. Ami put one hand on his knee, and with the other indicated the painting.

"That gorgeous white stallion has designs on the little black filly, and she seems quite attracted by the idea." She smiled at him roguishly. "I seem to remember you once called me your little filly."

Later, lying in front of the fire, as he held her in his arms after making love, Harry mused, "You are a wicked woman. I'll never be able to look at that painting now without feeling randy. My black filly! I've known you for 23 years. You have been closer to me longer than anyone else other than my children. Do you remember that amazing holiday in Egypt, when we saw the sun come up over the desert? That was almost twenty years ago – fabulous memories."

How could Ami forget it? There had been so many memorable and life-defining moments with Harry – his faith in her as a young unknown artist, standing in the central chamber of the Great Pyramid, buying the Bonheur – that was why she always was there when he wanted her. Yet she was aware of an undercurrent of resentment which she had never before been prepared to admit. Was it because she felt under an obligation to him? Was it because she was still single? She was not sure.

"Yes," she replied, "my life is bound up in memories of my time with you." She paused. "But I think you take me for granted – I'm your refuge when you're in trouble. Our first time together was after your divorce, and now your second wife has gone and you need me again."

"No, it's not like that, " he said quietly. "We have always helped each other, ever since I released you from your PFA contract. You understand how I feel. With you there's no need to explain – you accept me as I am."

"Maybe I should have been more demanding. Then I might not be here now – 42 years old and childless, lying in the arms of a married man who will never make an honest woman of me. Do you not understand how much I have longed to be the mother of your baby; to feel part of you growing inside me?" She had never pressured him before. Many times it had been only her pride which prevented her from forcing the issue. Now, not even her pride would stop her. "The trouble is, I love you. Even when I was in the thrall of that beast Quentin, I loved you. In truth, I have never loved another man. You are imprinted on my mind, and my body longs for you. I resent you for it, but I want you. I want you so much."

"I want you too. Let's go to bed."

She went with him willingly, but her heart sank – disappointed that again he had so disarmingly side-stepped her plea. However compelling their relationship might be, vital parts of the jig-saw still were missing. Her thoughts were confused. *Did he really want her? Was it fate that one of them always felt too vulnerable for commitment at critical points in their relationship? She wanted Harry desperately.*

They stayed at Bellridge Hall until they returned home in mid January – Harry to Chipping Campden and Ami to London. During the following weeks they saw each other regularly. The March exhibition of Ami's work sponsored by Foremans was a huge success. Pamela again had excelled in her organisational skill, although her ongoing job with PFA prevented her attendance. They went to David Shepherd's seventieth birthday party at the British Museum of Natural History in April, and to the Fine Arts and Antique Fair at Olympia in mid-June.

They valued this time together, for thereafter other pressures encroached on their lives. Through the summer Harry's attention had been increasingly distracted. He was irrevocably locked into the battle within PFA. The advantage was moving away rapidly from Louise Crossman and her allies, and Harry did not want to relax the pressure on them. Meanwhile, Ami was on the verge of an exciting new development. The major project she had been negotiating had reached a critical phase. However, the overriding factor was Highcrags. Harry was deeply worried by the continuing threat of the foot-and-mouth disease outbreak which had occurred in February in Northumberland. He feared for the safety of his herd of White Park cattle, and after Olympia he moved back to Highcrags and was thankful for the technology of telephone, fax and email to keep him in contact with the outside world.

Ami flew to South Africa in late July, and expected to be away for several months. She sat on the plane trying to read a novel. She had selected *A Sense of Belonging* because it had a black heroine, and had reached the chapter where she marries her white lover after innumerable obstacles and difficulties. She lowered the book onto her lap. She could not concentrate. She was miserable and confused. *She wanted Harry so much; she had wanted him for so long. Why was he so flippant? Was he frightened of commitment? Then why had he married again? Did he not mean to be flippant? Then should she have been more forceful? Had she missed her chances? Did he really want her? Did she really want him if he was not prepared to pursue her? Was it fate that pulled them apart whenever they seemed to have a chance of happiness? Or were they at fault for once again allowing the demands of their business lives to overtake their personal priorities? Time is running out. Why did I not ask him to marry me on the plane in Egypt while we watched the sunrise? Why did I not ask him a hundred times?*

Why did he not ask me?

Her heart felt like lead, and tears fell onto the pages of her book.

6
THE PRICE OF VICTORY

Finnbennach's Battle 2000

Finnbennach represented a pinnacle of achievement for Harry's breeding programme with White Park cattle. He was named after the great white bull of the Connacht herds in Ireland during the reign of Queen Medb, who had died in battle with Donn Cuailnge, the brown bull of Ulster, 2,000 years ago. Literally translated his name is 'Fair-haired Horned', a true description of his powerful curved horns, and his white coat set off by the black points of his feet, muzzle, ears, horns tips, and eye rims – a colour pattern revered in ancient Irish and Welsh history. Finnbennach, Finn for short, weighed almost a ton in working trim. He was not a bloated, overweight animal fitted for the showring. His territory was the rugged mountain pasture. Highcrags Estate was his kingdom.

Most bulls would have been content with a herd of more than 40 cows, but Finn had heard the urgent lowing of other cows on the neighbouring estate owned by Colonel Blackett on the opposite shore of the big lake. The estate was home to a pedigree Limousin herd, led by a massive brown French bull. Finn stepped into the lake, waded out a few yards and then swam boldly across, driven by the urgency of testosterone. As he climbed up the slope from the lake he uttered a menacing bellow to announce his presence. The great brown bull heard the challenging call, and advanced majestically with arrogance born of mature strength and territorial advantage. His answering bellow rang through the still evening air with the authority of dominance and possession.

They were separated by 50 yards of grassland, and their rapid approach slowed as they drew close. They both roared breathily in low guttural warning threats, and the muscles of their shoulders bulged and rippled as they pawed the earth and flung divots over their withers and back. They circled warily in a side-stepping ritual, heads lowered, waiting for an opportunity – a fractional opening or loss of guard. The brown bull was heavier by a quarter of a ton, and taller by a good hands-span, but at the fury of Finn's first onslaught his eyes rolled in fear. He fought in desperation, his earlier arrogance evaporated, using his huge bulk in a vain attempt to stem the agile aggression of the smaller bull. Finn's horns raked his sides, their dark tips smeared with blood. The brown bull was driven backwards and, as he turned to flee, Finn impaled him broadside, flexed the massive muscles of his neck, and hurled him bodily down the slope into the lake. He did not know he had avenged the death of his names-sake two millennia previously, but the Limousin cows now heard the triumphant bellow of the new leader of the herd. Finn had just delivered death, now he would give new life.

Harry had breakfasted, and was about to take a walk down to the lake when the telephone rang. He picked up the receiver. "Hello, Harry Bainbridge here."

"Morning, Bainbridge." Harry sensed tension in the curt greeting. "Blackett here. That damnable white animal of yours broke into my pedigree herd last night and killed my prize-winning bull. He's worth a fortune you know. I'll be suing you for the value, and no doubt he's served some cows – that will be further damages."

Harry was caught completely off-guard. "I haven't seen my livestock manager this morning, but I'll send him over immediately to collect Finn." Then foolishly he tried to lighten the confrontation. "Of course, my insurers will pay the damages, but maybe Finn has left some superior genetics in the herd..."

The explosion at the other end of the line was instant. "You bloody empty-headed scoundrel! Expect to hear from my solicitors." The phone was slammed down.

Harry knew that he had committed a serious *faux pas*. The Limousin bull meant as much to Blackett as Finn did to him, and he had made light of the loss. Blackett was not a forgiving man, and Harry had notched up yet another enemy on his tally. It was becoming a habit.

Blackett would make sure he paid through the nose for Finn's escapade, and he would maximise his revenge – for that is how he would see it. Harry guessed that a compliant valuer might well put a figure of £8-9,000 on the bull, and his finances were not in the best of health at present. Finn's victory would carry a price, but little did Harry suspect how heavy the price would be.

Finnbennach's Fate 2001

Foot-and-mouth disease broke out a few miles from the estate on 19 February the following year. The outbreak of 2001 escalated rapidly into the biggest epidemic in the recent history of farming, and the Government decreed that any animals which it considered a risk should be slaughtered, whether or not they were infected. Harry took every possible precaution and effectively closed all access to the estate. The pattern of the outbreak was unpredictable. The first case of the disease in a locality would spread rapidly to neighbouring properties, causing fear, panic and despair. Those spared the tragic slaughter would regain hope as the initial spasm subsided, but then it would flare up again elsewhere. Harry lived on a knife edge. His nerves, usually so calm, were worn to tatters, but as weeks went by his fears gradually began to calm.

The phone rang early one morning in August. Harry answered.

"Good morning, Mr Bainbridge. This is your local veterinary office. I'm afraid foot-and-mouth disease has been confirmed on a neighbouring property. Your holding is now classified as contiguous premises, and all your livestock must be slaughtered."

Harry caught his breath. "Thank you for letting me know," he replied with a calmness and courtesy he did not feel. He knew from the previous track record of the veterinary services during the outbreak that he would be fighting a rearguard action. "Where has the disease been confirmed?"

"On Colonel Blackett's estate." So, this was scarcely Blackett's revenge, but maybe it was fate's rebuke for Finn's libidinous excesses?

"My cattle are a special breed that will have exemption from any slaughter order. The Ministry of Agriculture has agreed that the White Park is listed as a priority breed recognised by both the Food and Agriculture Organisation of the United Nations and by Rare Breeds International." He would pull every trick in the book to save his beloved herd.

"I'm sorry Mr Bainbridge. We have clear procedures to follow. There are no exceptions, and we'll be making arrangements for your livestock to be slaughtered."

There was no more to be said at that juncture, but Harry besieged both the local animal health office and MAFF veterinary headquarters in London with an avalanche of emails, faxes and phone calls. He demanded exemption from slaughter of such a valuable herd; he quoted the Convention on Biological Diversity; he requested that his cattle should be vaccinated rather than slaughtered. It was all to no avail. The governmental juggernaut rolled on. Harry was devastated.

The herd was not infected, but the cattle must die because the theoretical model of disease control approved by the Government deemed that it should be so!

A valuation must be placed on the herd. Harry avoided the routine valuers and those nominated by MAFF, and employed George Hastings, a man with a deep knowledge of native cattle. It was relatively easy to establish a reasonable valuation for females – cows with calves £2,600-3,350 each, cows without calves £2,350-2,800 each, the young animals an average of about £1,300 each – but Finnbennach was a bull without price. He was the result of generations of accumulated genetic merit that could not be replaced. But the MAFF valuation system demanded a value, and George Hastings pencilled in a figure.

"Harry, I know you'll regard it as an insult, but I can only value the old fellow at £4,500."

"You know as well as I do, George, that doesn't even start to recognise the special quality of Finn. Bulls like that are born once in a blue moon. Good God, man, I paid Blackett £9,500 damages for his Limousin last year, and Finn is twice the bull that he was."

"You're right, but in my opinion MAFF would be unlikely to accept a higher figure, and we must avoid arbitration at all costs. You know how it works; MAFF costs are borne by the taxpayer, and it would be foolhardy for you to run the risk of opposing them and incurring the ridiculous charges of solicitors and Arbitrators."

Harry reluctantly agreed. The total valuation for the herd probably would exceed £150,000 but that was poor reward for almost a quarter of a century of pedigree breeding. A precious part of British heritage was going to be lost because of the utter incompetence of a disinterested Government. Ten million animals slaughtered in total in the country, because the Government had kept the disease a secret in the hope that it would not break out before the election in May. He had intended that Finn would be buried on the estate with proper ceremony at the end of his natural life. Instead he would be shot and dumped in an incinerator.

There was nothing George could say. He quietly shook Harry by the hand, and drove away. Harry was beyond reason. He could not bear to watch the slaughter in the farm buildings at the west end of the estate. He returned to the Hall, went into the morning room, poured himself a large Remy Martin, and slumped in despair into a chair as far from the windows as possible.

Harry did not leave the Hall for the rest of the day. Images of his beloved cattle flashed continually through his mind. He scarcely slept that night, but it was not until he went over to the window next morning that the full impact hit him with sudden force. The financial loss and the genetic loss had been uppermost in his mind yesterday, but now the emotional loss came to the fore as he looked out at the pasture running down to the lake. It was empty. Not an animal to be seen. It was a picture of desolation – the desolation of emptiness. The background of green no longer broken by a pattern of white where the herd used to lie on the rising ground at the east side of the pasture. Tears welled up in Harry's eyes. The shock of loss engulfed him. He turned away from the window, and for a long time stood in the bedroom, silent sobs shaking his frame.

In the late afternoon he forced himself to go outside. He walked through the cattle pasture. There was all the evidence that it was the home – had been the home – of a herd of cattle, but now there was nothing. It was devoid of life. He looked for Gwenllian and Nesta, his favourite cows, but they were not there to greet him, and he missed the calm presence of the mighty Finnbennach.

"Finn, my old beauty," he thought to himself, "both of us pushed our luck too far – unable to resist female temptation. Fate caught up with you already, and I am not far behind."

He walked on through other fields, each intensifying the aching emptiness, and made his way to the top of the bluff halfway along the lake. From this elevated position he could see most of the estate, and a considerable area of surrounding land. He looked around on all sides. Fields which until yesterday had held living dynamic herds and flocks, now were still and lifeless. The hand of death was spread over the entire landscape, and the stench of death filled the air. Intense sadness, reinforced by anger, again surged through Harry. He felt that he had lost a significant part of himself, and it was almost as if he was now detached from reality. His grief exploded audibly in uncontrollable convulsive spasms. He sank to the turf and wept.

Harry's Battle at PFA 2000–2001

By January 2001 the battle lines at PFA were clearly drawn. Any obfuscation that might have been no longer existed. It was a fight on the Board for the values on which the business of the company would be conducted. Would the original concepts of artistic integrity and quality of product remain paramount, or would they be overtaken by less altruistic motivation?

In the spring of 2000, the balance of advantage had lain with Louise Crossman. As the incoming MD, she could expect the benefit of any doubt for some months, and she knew she always could count on the support of Jack Maladonis. Miles Mountjoy had begun to doubt her competence and her integrity at an early stage of her tenure, and subsequently Walter King harboured increasing suspicion of her conduct, but Peter Loder had not seen any reason to rock the boat. In those circumstances, Louise was able to carry most decisions by a majority vote.

It was not until she had been in her position for almost nine months that Louise approached a meeting of the Board with any serious apprehension. Miles Mountjoy had asked for an update report on Foreman's sponsorship at the September meeting. The Directors were disappointed to learn that Louise had failed to agree sponsorship by Foremans for the exhibition she had proposed for the following spring, but they were alarmed that Foremans had withdrawn from further discussions.

"That is a serious setback," said Miles in serious tones. "Is there some reason why Foremans have terminated our association with them?"

"I'm afraid I have no idea," she replied. Louise had no knowledge of the background to Foremans decision. When eventually she had rung Johan Barck to ask if she could submit a proposal for an exhibition of PFA's current projects, she had received a short but courteous refusal.

"There probably is a very simple explanation," Jack cut in quickly. "Perhaps I should go and have a word with Mr Barck."

"If anyone has a chance of persuading Foremans to come back on board, it's Harry Bainbridge." Miles looked round at his fellow Directors. "If I remember correctly, we rejected his proposal for Foremans sponsorship on your advice, Louise. Perhaps you would have done well to pay more heed to him."

"I can manage PFA without help from my predecessor." The colour of Louise's face deepened, and her eyes bulged. "I would prefer not to involve him, and suggest we set the Foremans problem aside for a while."

The question was dropped, but Louise was aware that her honeymoon period was at an end. There must be no more mistakes. Her negotiations with Foremans may have hit an obstacle, but she was able to report positively on English Nature.

❁ ❁ ❁ ❁ ❁ ❁ ❁ ❁ ❁ ❁ ❁ ❁

Louise had invested considerable effort to promote her position with English Nature. Jack had identified it as a priority for her to replace Harry Bainbridge in an important position. She had made an official request to Mark Hopkins that PFA should be invited to send a representative to the meeting of English Nature in December. When she received a positive response, she announced her success to the Board, and the news was relayed to the HIH Board.

The Directors of HIH had set great store by an association with English Nature. It served their purpose to be seen to be acting with a governmental body, even if it was indirectly through PFA. They were delighted by Louise's news.

Louise asked Robert Gator to represent her at the meeting. She felt that a land agent would be able to discuss rural matters with some authority, whereas she found those associated with the land somewhat distasteful. She would obtain a first-hand report of the meeting from Robert without needing to commit herself to direct involvement.

Robert called at the PFA office on his way back from the meeting in Bristol. He did not have good news. "That was a wasted journey." His opening remark did not fill Louise with joy. "Bainbridge and that Hopkins fellow are thick as thieves. No chance at all of driving a wedge in there."

"You must be mistaken, Robert." Louise's reply was sharp. "I spoke to Mr Hopkins and he was most helpful and co-operative. He responded immediately and positively when I asked for an invitation to the meeting. Are you sure you understood properly?"

Robert was dull and slow, but he could recognise a rebuke. He bristled. "If you don't believe me, I suggest you give the fellow a ring. His announcement was perfectly clear. Bainbridge is their official consultant."

The news put Louise in a quandary. Could she risk misleading the Board further while she attempted to redeem the situation? Could she somehow transfer the blame to Harry Bainbridge by implying that he was acting contrary to the interests of PFA? She was able to keep the problem under her hat for the time being, but could not delay a report beyond the February meeting of the Board. Her report was met initially with stony silence. The other Directors were concerned, not so much that she had not been endorsed by English Nature, but that she had misled them, and thereby misled the Board of HIH. She had placed them in an embarrassing position. This time she did not escape without a severe reprimand.

❋ ❋ ❋ ❋ ❋ ❋ ❋ ❋ ❋ ❋ ❋ ❋

Jack and Louise held a crisis meeting at Louise's home. They had failed to achieve their two primary targets for promoting Louise, and their attempt to discredit Harry with Ami had not materialised. A council of war was required.

"Let us look at the situation clinically," Jack opened in authoritative mode, "and see what opportunities are available to us. I think we must admit that Harry Bainbridge has tied up most UK positions rather securely. We need to regain the ground lost as a result of the Foremans and English Nature affairs, so where might we hold the advantage over him?"

Louise held her peace. Jack clearly had a plan, and she deemed it wise not interrupt his flow.

"I think I probably know Greece better than anyone in the company, and did not modern civilisation arise in Greece? An office in Athens would be a sensible extension of PFA activities, and it would give us a base outside the influence of Mr Bainbridge. I have many contacts who could obtain historical artefacts for us which would be irresistible to the American market. How does that strike you?"

"Oh, Jack, that is marvellous," she enthused. "It would be a feather in our cap, and would help to keep the support of Peter Loder. Do you think we can find enough to develop a significant trade, and can we legally import such items?"

"I've no doubt that we can. My cousin lives in Piraeus and he knows all the tricks of the trade. If we can install him as manager of a PFA office in Athens, the battle will be almost won. I would suggest that we make a visit to Greece. In April perhaps – it is a delightful month – and we can stay at the Maladonis family villa in Mikinai on the Peloponnese, just south of Corinth, while we explore the possibilities."

❋ ❋ ❋ ❋ ❋ ❋ ❋ ❋ ❋ ❋ ❋ ❋

Pamela had dutifully remained in her position at PFA as Harry had requested. It had not been easy or pleasant, but she resolved to stay as long as Harry needed her. Johan Barck had asked her again in a private capacity to organise the spring exhibition that Foremans was sponsoring, and that was a pleasant diversion.

In late February she called Harry. "Harry, how would you like to take me to Greece for a holiday?"

"Nothing I could want more, my beautiful girl," he replied with practised ease, "but might not Duncan object?"

"Mm, I suppose he might, but it would be fun. Anyway, Jack Maladonis is taking Ms Crossman, so I thought the least you could do is take me."

Harry was instantly alert. "Maladonis and Crossman on holiday together. Are you sure? Is this private or business? Have they got something going? Does his wife know?" The questions tumbled over each other.

"Steady, you excitable man," she laughed, "one thing at a time. They are planning to open an office for PFA in Athens, but haven't told anyone else. They intend to make an exploratory trip in April, and bring back some artefacts to exhibit, possibly with an announcement at the Fine Arts & Antique Fair at Olympia in June. But, wait for it, they've asked me to make all the arrangements for them."

"You are a brilliant girl! I've a very good contact in Athens – Nick Linassiades, who was at Cambridge with me. If you can work him into their itinerary at an early stage, they may find more than they bargained for."

Harry called Nick Linassiades, and explained the situation to him. In April, Customs and Excise at Heathrow, and selected national and local Oxford papers, received a tip-off regarding two travellers returning from Greece.

❋ ❋ ❋ ❋ ❋ ❋ ❋ ❋ ❋ ❋ ❋ ❋

Every year Jack Maladonis dutifully and predictably brought his wife to their villa in Mikinai for a month in the summer. It was duty rather than pleasure, but it gave him the opportunity to keep in touch with his ethnic roots while she relaxed with her novels and knitting on the veranda at the villa. They followed a fixed daily pattern, and he returned each afternoon in time to go down to the nearby restaurant for an evening meal. His step was livelier, even jaunty, as he approached Mikinai this time. It was not because of the green warmth of spring, rather than the brown heat of summer, nor was it caused primarily by the hope of giving Bainbridge a bloody nose. No, the reason was the absence of his wife, and the presence of another woman.

The realisation that she would be alone at the villa with Jack only gradually dawned on Louise. She had left the organisation of the itinerary to Pamela, and all other arrangements to Jack. When they reached their destination, and she properly understood that no one else was there, she felt a shiver of anticipation – apprehension tinged with excitement. Her first reaction was to request accommodation elsewhere, but an inner urge prevented her. She had never before found herself in such a situation. She sensed the danger, but elected not to avoid it.

"Jolly good," exclaimed Jack, opening a cupboard. "I see we're well stocked. I hope you like ouzo, dear girl, it seems there's a plentiful supply to hand." He took out a bottle and filled two glasses. "Welcome to my little Greek home. Good to have you here. Down in one, you know."

She watched him empty his glass in a single gulp. Her eyes watered and she coughed as she followed his example, but he already was filling their glasses again. Louise had neither an appetite nor a capacity for alcohol of any description, and spirits – particularly the kick of aniseed-flavoured ouzo – spelled certain inebriation. After a few glasses, cajoled by Jack to keep pace with him, she was decidedly unsteady. Jack encouraged her to two or three more, then announced that they should inspect the accommodation. Her thoughts were fuddled, her speech was slurring, and her sturdy legs were slow to obey instructions, but she followed him falteringly upstairs.

"This will be your room. Double bed," Jack indicated with a wave of his hand, and held her arm to ease her through the door and across the room. "Try it for size." It was an instruction. Her uncoordinated body fell onto the clean, smooth sheets, and he followed immediately. She lay immobile, aware of what was happening to her, but with neither the ability nor the desire to respond or resist. After he had gone without saying a word, she continued to lie as he had left her. She had never before experienced the hardness of a man inside her. She could still feel where his shoulder had pressed into her chest, and his hips had been thrust forcibly against her. Slowly she reassembled her jumbled thoughts.

Was that what it was all about? What had she done! We're here for four more nights. Will he want me again? I'm in his villa, and I depend on him to keep my position at PFA. How can I stop him? Do I want to stop him? No, he must want me. Wants me! I will go to him and show I want him.

She eased herself into a sitting position on the bed, and slowly and deliberately removed all her clothes. Jack had gone to his own room and lay on his bed. He felt a sense of triumph. He had never before had the chance of dalliance during his marriage, but tonight he had fulfilled a fantasy. He was exultant; he congratulated himself, and even contemplated further opportunities on succeeding nights.

His thoughts were interrupted as Louise came into the room and stood steadying herself with one hand on the doorframe. She was stark naked. He stared unmoving. His wife never appeared naked in his presence, and he took in every detail as if he were an adolescent. His eyes moved slowly over her small drooping breasts, past the creased bulge of her stomach to the cleft below. His eyes locked onto the forbidden zone. He had never summoned up the courage to take men's magazines from the top shelf in the bookshop, but here it was in the flesh in front of him, held in the bulk of her hips and thighs. Jack was mesmerised as he watched her standing there. She advanced slowly and deliberately with intent in her eyes. Jack swiftly got to his feet.

"It's getting late. Time we were going for dinner," he said with a forced laugh and rather desperate smile.

On the return flight from Athens to Heathrow five days later, Louise thought back over the events of the past week.

It has been more successful than we could have hoped. Jack's cousin was very little help, but how fortunate to have found a contact who can supply whatever we need. Mr Linassiades was marvellous. He did more than we could ever have expected, and made very useful suggestions. Pamela did an excellent job finding him. We have some valuable artefacts that he provided, and everything is in place to establish the Greek office. With luck we soon will have Harry Bainbridge on the run.

But it was personal matters that occupied her primarily. She looked proudly at her companion in the seat beside her, reclining with eyes closed. Her gaze moved across his broad hands, strong features, and thick, jet-black hair.

Such power and strength! He is not tall – but he is so dominant. Feeling the weight of him on me. Should I have derived some physical pleasure from our bedroom encounters? I feel that I should, but I know very little about sex and maybe that will come later. What matters is that he has taken me every night! He must have wanted me. Oh Jack, I've never been with a man before. You're my first! What a potent man. I'm no longer an old maid. I'm your woman.

"Jack, when will you tell your wife about us?"

Jack's eyes opened abruptly. He had not been asleep, but had wished to avoid conversation with Louise as far as possible. A week in her company had been enough to open his eyes to her deficiencies – intellectual, emotional and physical – and to create a growing contempt for her, but he needed to keep her on side. It would be a delicate balance to achieve. "I think it would be wise not to cause any unnecessary upset at this stage. My wife doesn't even know you've been with me, and we've enough on our plates trying to sort out the PFA situation. There will be ample time to deal with such delicate issues when we have everything under control." Jack settled back in his seat again.

"But she will need to know sometime. I mean, it's not right to deceive her. We should make it public before others discover by accident. And she'll have to know when you come to live with me."

This time Jack's eyes flew open like a startled rabbit, and he sat bolt upright. "There can be no question of that for the time being," he said sharply. "It would inevitably cause a scandal, and can you imagine the impact of that on the other PFA Directors. Bainbridge would have a field day. You must be patient." He realised he could have a problem on his hands. Did she really think that he intended to live with her?

Louise did not pursue it further. She could see the sense of his argument. She was disappointed and impatient, but meanwhile she could luxuriate in her private thoughts of their future together.

They had collected their baggage and were about to depart through the 'Nothing to declare' exit when an officer of Customs and Excise stepped in front of them. "Please step this way," he instructed indicating the other exit.

"Just our luck," muttered Jack, "when we are in a hurry. Why us? We don't even look suspicious."

The cameras were waiting when Jack and Louise finally emerged, and a small group of journalists closed in on them firing questions.

"Mr Maladonis, have you any thing to say?" asked one, thrusting his microphone in Jack's face. "Is it true that you have been questioned regarding the import of illegal goods?"

"I am from the *Oxford Daily News*," shouted another. "Can you tell me, Miss Crossman, the nature of your personal relationship with Mr Maladonis?"

"When will the office in Athens be open for business?"

Walter's telephone rang early next morning. It was Miles. "Walter, have you seen the papers this morning?" He did not wait for an answer. "PFA splashed all over the headlines. It seems that Jack Maladonis and Louise Crossman have been in Greece together on PFA business. Did you know anything about it?"

Walter struggled to grasp the significance of Miles' outburst. "No, not a thing. We have no business in Greece."

"We do now apparently. A new office in Athens. What the hell have they been up to? Listen to these headlines. 'Clandestine visit to Greece by Directors of Oxford fine arts company. Mr Andreas Maladonis, a Director of Portway Fine Arts, returned to a stormy reception after a visit to Greece with his unmarried co-Director, Louise Crossman. Both declined to answer questions, but reliable sources stated that they had been staying alone during the previous week in a villa in Greece owned by Mr Maladonis. Mrs Maladonis was not available for comment.' There's a picture of the pair of them under the headline. And here's another. 'Two Directors of Portway Fine Arts, the international art company based in Oxford, who had been in Greece to open a new office, were detained at Heathrow airport and questioned about the import of illegal goods. Officials declined to comment further, but it is believed that they are continuing their enquiries.' I want a meeting of the Board today, and they had better have some bloody good explanations!"

They were guilty of an improper sexual liaison. They were guilty of indiscreet behaviour. They were guilty of being suckered with phoney goods, but the latter guilt proved to be their saving grace. Jack was able to argue that they simply had been on an exploratory mission to test the water in Greece with no commitment, and had been bringing back some worthless copies for demonstration purposes. Their fellow Directors knew they were lying, but could not fix a charge on them. The HIH Board did not care whether they were lying, the publicity was bad news whatever the truth of the situation. Mrs Maladonis knew they were lying and doubtless she would have her revenge in good time. Jack and Louise escaped official censure by the narrowest of margins, but their credibility was severely diminished, and the damage to the company's reputation would have a severe effect on business.

Louise realised that someone had exposed them. There were very few options. Only she, Jack and Pamela had known of the visit. Pamela was handed her notice the next morning.

❋ ❋ ❋ ❋ ❋ ❋ ❋ ❋ ❋ ❋ ❋ ❋

PFA had come to rely heavily on the American market. Transatlantic trade had followed an upward path since the company was created in the mid-1980s. It was easy money. There was huge inflation of prices in the top bracket of the art market in the late 1980s and early 1990s, and the profit margin between purchases in the provinces in UK and sales in USA had led Louise Crossman to imprudent dependence on this trade to ensure company profits, and to fund her own speculative ventures.

The newsflash and images of destruction on 11 September changed everything in an instant. The disaster of the World Trade Centre caused shock-waves across the world, and the peoples of America turned defensively inwards in sorrow and anger. Grief and sympathy dominated transatlantic sentiment in the weeks that followed. Transatlantic travel almost ground to a standstill, and transatlantic trade was negligible.

Louise did not realise at first the significance of the World Trade Centre disaster. She had returned home that evening and was watching the news when the telephone rang. "Louise," it was Jack Maladonis' voice. "You will have heard the dreadful news."

"Yes, I've been watching it on the news. What a terrible thing to happen. Do you think that anything like that could happen over here?" She had become alert at the sound of Jack's voice. His wife had demanded that he leave the marital home, and Louise remained expectant that he would join her as soon as a decent interval had elapsed.

"My dear girl," he intoned, "I really haven't given that much thought. Have you thought of the impact on our business?"

"No," she replied with hesitation, unnerved by the brusqueness in Jack's voice, "Is there something I don't know?"

"I'm beginning to think there is a great deal you don't know." Jack's patience with Louise had shortened remarkably since her inept inexperienced performances in Athens, and their subsequent exposure by the officers of Customs and Excise. "Perhaps you would explain to me where you intend to find business to replace our American trade? This disaster is likely to prevent any transatlantic sales for weeks, maybe months. We will find it very difficult to generate trade elsewhere abroad because of the strength of the pound, and I suspect we will have to rely on the home market."

"Oh dear," she murmured distractedly, "maybe I'd better call an urgent meeting of the Board."

The Directors met three days later. Miles Mountjoy brought the meeting to order. "We meet in tragic circumstances. The loss of life in New York must be paramount in our minds, and our own problems are insignificant in comparison. Clearly, recent events will have an adverse effect on our business, but it is not seemly to discuss profit and loss when others are experiencing such severe sorrow. As we are here, please give us a brief summary of the situation, Louise, and then we'll close the meeting."

Louise had prepared a detailed dossier, and commenced to make a full presentation. Miles stopped her at once. "A brief summary will suffice, thank you."

She was thrown off her prepared plan, and stumbled through some points relating to the drop in the value of investments, and the increased level of borrowing. Miles noted that the liquidity ratio was dangerously low, but did not wish to pursue the point at that juncture. He declared the meeting closed.

By the time of the routine quarterly meeting on 8 October, the full impact of the disaster was evident. The loss of life was horrendous, and the possibility of global war was obvious. People throughout the developed world felt vulnerable. The impact on business was severe. The FTSE 100 was down by twenty per cent in the six months ended 30 September, and company assets had fallen to their lowest level for more than five years. Sales to America in the month since 11 September had decreased to little more than ten per cent of the level achieved the previous year during the same period. Sales elsewhere, including the home market, also had declined. At the same time, the level of borrowing had increased for the third successive quarter. Extrapolations projected to 31 December indicated that the company would not be able to service its current creditors from current assets.

Miles sat grim-faced. "Thank you for your report Louise," he began, looking directly at her, "there are two points that I wish to examine in greater detail. First, it is clear that we can not meet the interest payment to HIH this quarter, and we must determine how we deal with that problem. Second, I am concerned by the high level of borrowing. When you first requested agreement for this facility in February, you indicated that it would be short-term. Perhaps you would tell us your definition of short-term, and remind us of the purpose of your request."

Louise was nonplussed. "Mr Chairman, thank you for the opportunity to address these questions. They are indeed fundamental to the problems that we face, but I am sure that we can deal..."

"Would you please get to the point and answer my queries."

There was no answer. The borrowing to which Louise had committed the company could not be repaid because the schemes she had funded were motivated by a desire to inconvenience and embarrass Harry Bainbridge, rather than by sound principles of business management. Even Jack Maladonis could not, or would not, extract her from this mire of incompetence. The Chairman expressed his displeasure, announced that he would speak to the HIH Board, and closed the meeting.

A few days later, Miles drove the short distance from Abingdon to Wantage to talk to Walter. "I have to tell you confidentially, Walter, that I'm having acute problems with the HIH Board. My fellow Directors have little confidence in the current management of PFA, and I fear for the future. They see declining assets and declining business, and ask whether they would be better concentrating their attention elsewhere."

"I suppose I can understand their feelings, and it isn't as if we were not aware of dangers. Harry gave us sound advice just before he retired, when the FTSE 100 was not far from 7,000. He thought then that the equity market stood at more than twice its realistic value, and recommended that we should unload at least 50 per cent of our investment into cash or bonds."

"I remember well. We all felt that the bull market was unsustainable and agreed to convert 40 per cent of our portfolio. Why on earth did we allow Louïse to persuade us to restore the investment in equities soon after she was appointed? She argued we were able to buy more as the FTSE had fallen to below 6,500 at that time."

"Too late for regrets. Harry warned us more than once that we were making a big mistake, but we ignored him and believed Louise because of her background in accountancy. And didn't she crow about it in the autumn when the market rose to 6,800 or so."

"They were premature celebrations I'm afraid. The market has fallen ever since and now our investments are down by more than twenty per cent. The problem is compounded because turnover is down, and Louise has pushed up borrowings, partly because of reduced cash inflow and partly to finance her schemes. I regret, Walter, that we must take some of the blame for not being stronger in questioning her actions and motives."

Harry's Bittersweet Victory 2001

Miles Mountjoy did not have any room for manoeuvre. His expression was solemn and the Boardroom at PFA offices was filled with an air of apprehension as the meeting called at short notice on 22 October commenced in late afternoon. The Directors of HIH had become increasingly disillusioned during the past year. The English Nature embarrassment the previous December had made them uneasy; it had been followed by the disastrous damaging publicity of the Greek incident in April; finally the loss of American business as a result of the World Trade Centre atrocity had crystallised their opinion. Miles, whose own position on the HIH Board had been compromised by the failures of PFA, was the messenger.

"I take no pleasure in the announcement that I must make," he began. "Partly through factors beyond our control, but mainly through the fault of some members of this Board, the company finds itself on the brink of disaster." He paused, and looked at the faces of his four colleagues seated round the table. "My fellow HIH Directors have decided to sever all connections with PFA, and withdraw their loan with immediate effect. We are, therefore, insolvent. Unless we can raise capital to replace the HIH loan, we will cease to trade.

"However, even if we could overcome that obstacle, there is an even more serious matter which must be faced." He turned and looked directly at Louise Crossman. "Louise, I will not mince my words. You have disappointed me. You have been MD of PFA for almost two years. During that time you have dismantled perfectly good office procedures, you have removed experienced staff and replaced them with a gaggle of giggling girls, and you have alienated Harry Bainbridge who was the company's greatest asset. It might have been part mitigation if you had acquired some knowledge of the business yourself, but you have not..."

"I really must protest," Jack Maladonis interrupted. "You have no right..."

"I have every right," barked Miles, "and I have not finished yet. As serious as these matters undoubtedly are, they are insignificant compared with the conduct of two of our Directors in April this year. Miss Crossman and Mr Maladonis, you brought disgrace on yourselves and brought the company into disrepute by your unacceptable conduct in Greece. Even without the other problems, it is unlikely we would have recovered from that for several years. Your presence on this Board is no longer required." He stopped and waited. There was no reaction. "Do you wish me to put it to the vote, or will you voluntarily let me have your letters of resignation within one hour?"

If either Jack or Louise needed further evidence, a glance at Peter Loder was enough to convince them of the hopelessness of their position. Until this point, despite some misgivings, he had given Louise the benefit of the doubt. Now, his normally mild-mannered face was flushed with anger as he glared at the pair of them. They needed no further prompting. They gathered their papers and left the meeting.

The three remaining Directors examined the possibilities of salvaging the company. HIH owned 40 per cent of the shares, and these would be on the market. Harry Bainbridge and Walter King owned 30 per cent each. Maybe a buyer could be found for the HIH shares who would wish the business to continue. However, Walter was not sure that he wished to retain his shares in the circumstances, and it would be no surprise if Harry washed his hands of the whole affair. A secretary came in and handed Miles two envelopes. He opened them and glanced down the enclosed letters.

"Well, at least we have two resignations without any further trouble. I'm sure you would not wish that there should be a golden handshake to either of them, and as they own no shares there should be no complications."

The meeting closed in gloomy despondency. No decisions had been reached for action, and they agreed to meet again the following day. When Walter arrived home that evening, he called Harry to tell him the news. Much to his surprise, Harry was not angry or even downcast.

"Things may look bad, Walter," he said, "but to me they look a good deal more positive in the absence of Crossman and Maladonis. At least the remaining Directors now can act in the interests of the company, rather than being compromised by the self-interest and incompetence of those two. Look on the bright side. When I retired the company was booming. Overall it may have slipped backwards thereafter, but some sectors have not. The South African and Australian associate companies have continued to expand. Why don't you see if they have enough surplus to tide you over a difficult time?"

"You're a tonic, Harry. We have another meeting tomorrow, and I'll propose it to the others. Thanks a million for keeping everything in perspective."

Harry was a natural optimist, but he had been in depression since the slaughter of his cattle in August, especially as Ami was not around to give him support and comfort. The good news from PFA was a timely tonic. Next morning, in the absence of Ami, he rang Pamela to tell her. "Hello Pamela. Glad to catch you at home. It may be too late to be of any comfort or help to you, but I thought you'd want to know as soon as possible that Crossman and Maladonis have gone, resigned, sacked, whatever."

There was a whoop of delight on the other end of the line. "The best news I've heard in years, Harry," she said. "We did it! This calls for a celebration – you and me. Shall I come over to you?"

Harry agreed without thinking. He was too elated to quibble. "It's a long drive. I guess it'll take you more than an hour, but I'll have the champers ready for you."

"You must be kidding!" she exclaimed. "I'll expect more than drink."

She did indeed expect more than a drink. They had flirted through an office relationship for four years, she had risked – and lost – her job for him, and now she expected her just rewards. They lay in bed in tired contentment. "You know, I've been in love with you ever since I joined the company eight years ago."

"You're a married woman – what on earth does your husband think?" Harry had never met Duncan, but he knew that Pamela had married when she was young, and he wondered how she was with him. "Why haven't you started a family? I know your career is important, but better not to wait too long."

Pamela lifted her head from his chest and looked at him with a firm gaze. "Don't you understand? Sometimes you can be very slow! I want children. I want children now, but I want yours."

Harry was startled. "My darling girl, you flatter me. I'm old enough to be your father. In fact, you're the same age as my daughter. In any case, wouldn't it be more sensible to have a baby with your husband?"

"When I was first married to Duncan, we tried for three or four years but nothing happened. When we took advice and had tests, we discovered he was infertile. He didn't want to take it any further, and we have drifted along since in a meaningless marriage. When I was sacked from PFA, I told him that I wanted a baby and that I was going to try DI. He wasn't keen, but I insisted. If I get pregnant he'll not be surprised, he'll think it's donor insemination, but I want it to be yours. What does your age matter? I know I can't have you, but I can have your baby."

She lay spread-eagled on her back. What a beautiful body – firm breasts, flat stomach, gentle hillock with a thick blonde triangle, and long shapely legs. "You are gorgeous," he exclaimed reaching across to caress her. "You realise that a baby will leave stretch marks and your boobs will droop with breast-feeding?"

"You terrible man! Will you stop making excuses. Beauty is

temporary; motherhood is permanent and I want to be a mother."

She rolled on top of him and they made love again. Harry guessed that Pamela would not let him rest until she was pregnant, but he did not stop to consider whether fate might reward his libidinous weaknesses as harshly as Finn's! The thought that he still was married to Theresa never crossed his mind, and his conscience casually moved Ami aside, while he indulged his pleasure with Pamela.

PFA's fate 2001–2002

The Directors took Harry's advice. The Australian associated company did have funds available. Negotiations were opened with the Australian Chair, Rebecca Payne, a woman of formidable presence who had no need to rely on feminine wiles to achieve her objectives. She had directed the Antipodean office since Portway Fine Arts (Australia) had been established as a separate company in 1991, and had kept a close eye on the progress of the parent company in UK. It soon became obvious it was not a cosy arrangement between friends. Rebecca had sussed out the situation, and knew she held all the aces. She was not interested only in the HIH shares; she wished to buy all the shares. There was a protracted period of negotiation during the winter months, and Harry was brought into the discussions. He stated that he had no need to sell, but indicated that he was prepared to do so if the price was right.

Miles Mountjoy understood the thrust of Rebecca's offer. "You realise, Walter, that if we agree to the Australian proposal, they will become the parent company, and we will be relegated to subsidiary status."

"I suspect it may be worse than that." Walter had been briefed by Harry, who had dealt with the Australian office for several years. "Rebecca is a crusading feminist. Apparently, she formed the view early in her career that she was brighter than her males bosses, and resented the business culture at that time which required her to kowtow to them. She's spent her life correcting the imbalance, and I would expect her to make life difficult for any traditional males. We might be early casualties."

"Yes, I know, Harry told me much the same, although I think even he is surprised at the hard line she is taking. But we don't have any leverage in the present situation. I've been making discreet enquiries and can find no interest whatsoever in alternative buyers for PFA."

Eventually a price was agreed for a total buy-out. The agreement retained the company name, assumed responsibility for outstanding creditors, and took ownership of all assets including the Oxford gallery. Harry's consultancy was terminated with immediate effect. The current Directors would be retained on a nominal fee after their resignation, and the agreement stipulated that they would not become involved in any similar business in the UK during the next five years. They would be replaced by newly-appointed Directors in due course. The agreement would take effect on 1 September 2002.

Miles, Walter and Harry sat subdued and chastened. Their conversation was desultory. Harry was staying with Walter for a couple of days, and they all had met for a drink in Walter's local near Wantage. Miles told them that Maladonis had resigned from the HIH Board, and that served to lighten their spirits a little.

"One bad egg in a basket need not be a major problem, and a business can overcome one bad decision. But a combination like Maladonis and Crossman can spell disaster." When Miles resorted to the use of surnames, it was a clear sign he was in headmaster mode. "We should have seen the danger sooner. Incidentally, Harry, you were on the panel that interviewed Crossman. Just as a matter of historical interest, did you want to appoint her?"

"No, I voted for Ami Kotze, but both the others were adamant that Louise Crossman was the choice candidate."

Miles was aware of Harry's liaisons with Ami, but he was too much of a gentleman to mention it. "I'm not surprised. You may be interested to know that both Maladonis and Gator knew Crossman before she applied for the position. I have it on reliable information that they reckoned they could run the company for their own benefit if she was MD."

That nightmare had been avoided. The company had been saved, but the three chastened men knew that their own connection with it had effectively ended.

Harry's Fate 2002

Harry had been down and almost out more than once in his twenties, but he had recovered and prospered. Could he do it again 40 years on? The cottage at Chipping Campden had been his base for more than a year, but it was not home, and he felt isolated. It was the last Sunday in

January – he had been out for a brisk walk, but there was a fierce south-westerly gale, and he had retreated to the comfort of his wine and his thoughts.

His first thought was the loss of his magnificent herd of White Park cattle in the previous year – he still could scarcely bear to think of it. It had been an acute blow. He was conscious of the crushing sense of loss that fell over everything like a great greyness. He showed little outward evidence of the void inside him. It had started when Jayne removed the children from his life. Then his departure from the focal seat of power in PFA in March 2000, followed by separation from Theresa later that year, had delivered a further severe shock to his system. Finally, it was compounded and magnified by the loss of the herd. The cumulative effect was salutary. What was left for him to live for? Ami alone remained a positive light in the darkness, and she had been absent for half a year.

Even without the cattle, Highcrags had remained a very special place for Harry, but his financial position no longer permitted him the luxury of such an expensive hobby. Reluctantly, he put it on the market. In normal circumstances it would have been worth a small fortune on the American market, but that was not an option after 11 September. Nevertheless it was a highly desirable property, and sold without difficulty for more than two million pounds. The buyer, much to Harry's chagrin, was Karen Richmond. She had divorced her husband a couple of years earlier and now was a very wealthy woman. Harry had not seen her for nine years, but there probably was a certain titillation for her to own his estate.

Harry smiled quietly as the memories flitted through his mind's eye.

Highcrags! It had always been his bolt-hole – a refuge when business or personal problems became too intense, an ambience of peace and tranquillity in which new campaigns could be planned. Jayne had not liked it; Theresa had never been comfortable there; apart from Ami, his mistresses had never been invited to stay. It was his own space, miles from anywhere. No amount of money could compensate for its loss.

Harry tried to rationalise the factors that had contributed to his parlous financial position.

He ruefully mused that addiction to risk, and the tendency to spend rather than accumulate, had caused him acute financial embarrassment from time to time. First, the flamboyant purchases in Florida in the 1970s on a foundation of paper value set him up for a fall in 1983 – and what a fall that was! Second, he escaped from Lloyd's of London, comparatively unscathed, but had forfeited £150,000, and there was a potential ongoing liability. Theoretically, reinsured Names were protected by Equitas against further claims, and he hoped this would prove secure, but the threat posed by asbestosis settlements in the USA still remained poised like an executioner's blade. Third, the fall in global stock markets through 2000 and 2001 had reduced his personal portfolio by almost 30 per cent. It had been exaggerated as a result of 11 September, but not caused by it. His thoughts slipped back to 1990 when last he had dined in the Windows on the World restaurant at the top of the World Trade Centre, looking down on the Empire State building and the lights of New York. He would never be able to do that again. Maybe he would not have been able to afford it anyway. The final blow had come just a week or two ago when his contract with PFA was terminated summarily. The irony of having to sell Highcrags was not lost on him – it had given him a substantial fund, but it required the forfeiture of a place that was very special for him, and his quality of life would suffer.

Now he was facing his problems alone. It was at such times that the absence of his children struck home like the thrust of a knife.

How he missed them still – how he had missed so much of their young lives when their mother had taken them off to Switzerland and disrupted their formative years. They also had grown up rootless and itinerant. Now in their thirties they both had lives of their own on the other side of the world. He remembered the sad story of Saori, the Japanese socialite from Osaka he met on the Amalfi coast in May 1988. Hers had been the same problem in reverse.

He had travelled alone to a business meeting in Rome – Ami could not bear the thought of returning to the scene of her traumatic experiences ten years earlier – and had extended his visit for an extra two or three days at his favourite hotel high on the hill above Amalfi, a delightful place with orange blossom outside the doors of his room, which opened onto a terrace with a view eastwards down the coast. He had called the first evening at the end of an excursion for a drink at the prestigious San Pietro hotel, built into the rock face on the hillside above Positano, about twenty kilometres from his own hotel. The vaulted lounge, with hand-painted ceramic tiles and sumptuous upholstery, was empty except for a pretty oriental girl.

"Do you have a light?" She moved along the bar to join him, a cigarette poised in her elegant fingers.

"Sorry," he replied, motioning to the barman, "I'm afraid I don't smoke." The barman obliged.

She was small, but firm and rounded. "I'm Saori. Just staying here for a few days. How about you?"

"The same. Spring is the only sensible time to visit the Mediterranean. I'm Harry. Glad to meet you." She was attractive. She looked young and fresh – but it was unusual for a girl to be on her own. There appeared not to be a husband or children, but why would a single girl not be enjoying the high life?

They fell into conversation, and she asked him to stay and have dinner with her at the hotel. They dined on the outdoor terrace. She was alone with no private transport, and Harry suggested that she might care to come with him the next day. "We could go over the hill to Vesuvius and Pompeii," he suggested, "but that would mean an early start and a late return. Or we can take a leisurely circular drive to Sorrento." Saori liked her bed in the mornings, and thus Sorrento got her vote.

Harry collected her next morning around half past ten. Her tight-fitting white top revealed a full attractive figure, and her equally tight-fitting red trousers matched the varnish on her long curving nails. She wore no jewellery, and her short black hair hung straight and free. "You're not married." Harry got directly to the point as they drove westwards along the coast road.

There was a slight hesitation. "I'm divorced. I was married in Japan, but now I live in Germany with my mother." She stopped, but Harry said nothing. He knew she would continue her story to fill the silence. "I was not happy. My husband was cruel, and abused me. He beat me when I displeased him, and at last I was not able to stand it any longer. I left him, but I had a son..." Her voice faltered. She looked out of the window for a while, and then resumed. "In Japan it is the custom for children to stay with the father if their parents separate. I had to leave my son behind." Tears welled up, and spilled down her round cheeks. Harry reached over with a handkerchief. "Thank you. I'm sorry, but it still is hurtful to me. I could not stay in Japan, and I moved with my mother to Germany. She has a lot of money, and we live very well, but I miss my son."

Harry pulled over into a lay-by with a view down the coast. He put his arm around her, and she clung to him for several minutes. "I think I can understand a little how you feel," he said. "My wife took my children away when they were young, and I felt that a large part of my life was missing without them. I was able to talk to them sometimes, and occasionally they were able to visit me, but my ex-wife made it as difficult as possible. I suppose it's even worse for a mother, and I can see it makes you sad."

She smiled at him. "You are very understanding."

They continued their journey around the coast to Sorrento, with its views over the Bay of Naples to Vesuvius, and returned over the mountainous switch-back road through Gragnano and Furore, stopping for lunch at a small restaurant in the hills. When they reached her hotel, she asked him to stay for dinner again, and he was happy to oblige. She asked if he would like to take a shower before dinner, and again the answer was affirmative. They took the lift to her room which had a balcony looking out over flower-decked terraces to the sea beyond. Harry went into the bathroom and stripped down to his boxer shorts. As he came out to see if she was joining him, she was peeling off her skin-tight top. He held her round her waist and she giggled. They were still clasped in an amorous embrace when she looked at her watch. "I must call my mother," she exclaimed. "I have to call always at eight o'clock."

Harry lay back and listened to her report for the day. It was detailed, but at least he was gratified to be described as 'a very nice man' for maternal edification. When she had finished he was amused to learn that she had to check in again before retiring at eleven o'clock. He prayed they would not be in a compromising position at the appointed hour – how would her mother interpret the noises! He thought maybe he would leave after dinner.

He laughed at the memory. Life seemed to have been filled with memories of the fairer sex. Some memories were painful, many were unhappy, but he had tutored his selective memory to dwell mainly on the humour, the sex, the romance and the love. It had not been too bad on the whole. It occurred to him that Pamela had not been to see him for almost three weeks. She had been a regular visitor since October. Her absence could only mean one of two things – her husband's suspicions had been aroused or she was pregnant. In the end, what did it all mean? Jayne, Ami, Saori, Karen, Eva, Theresa, Ami, Pamela – moving seamlessly from one partner to another! Is that what life is about – an endless circuit of beautiful but short-term partners?

In retrospect, an argument with Theresa in the final stages of their time together had been a defining moment. He still remembered her exact words. 'You are a weak impulsive man, always with an eye for easy opportunity. Your strengths are your weaknesses. You have a heart of gold and your generosity is amazing, but you are easily tempted. I think you are addicted to risk and gambling in any form, whether it with women or in business. You are adored by those who scarcely know you, but those who have looked into your soul have seen a different man. You will live to regret that you have wasted those things that really matter.' Did he agree with her analysis? In part, perhaps, but not entirely.

Once again Harry had to clear away the emotional debris that had accumulated in his early life. The repressed sexuality of his youth, which he had not shaken off until university, had made him susceptible in later life to accepting opportunities whenever they presented themselves. The deprivations of his youth had elevated ambition to a higher priority than emotional fulfilment. Finally, Jayne's desertion had filled him with a deep distrust of women. He was an emotional disaster area – vacillating between excess and abstinence.

He still had an enormous reserve of self-belief, but his recent setbacks had made him take stock. His remedy for problems in the past always had been to take the initiative. *Don't wait for life,* he thought, *go and get it. That is what must be done now. The company situation is past redemption; my personal life is in tatters; I have no permanent home. Where is the best place to start again?*

7
STARTING AGAIN

Ami 2002

By the time Harry and Ami next saw each other seven months later in February, the world was a different place. The World Trade Centre had been demolished and there was war in Afghanistan. Their own world was a different place. HIH was off-loading PFA, thus terminating Harry's income from consultancy, and he had sold Highcrags. He was still under way, but lacking a firm rudder and listing badly. Ami on the other hand was under full sail. Her African project – a wildlife study – was signed and sealed, and the initial research completed. She rang Harry full of excited exultation as soon as she returned to England in February and suggested dinner. She wanted to involve him, not only because she was obliged to him for helping her out in past, but also because she still had hopes that they might have a more permanent future together.

Luigi had reserved their favourite table that had a full view of the restaurant, but was discreetly private. Caminettos was their invariable destination when they ate in Chipping Campden. They danced the lambada and the samba between courses of exquisite Italian cuisine.

She reached across and held his hand, her dark vivacity radiant in the candlelight, but her brown eyes tender and loving. "Harry," she said softly, "I understand how much you must miss Highcrags, and I miss it too. Last year at this time was a privilege I'll never forget – being alone with you and the cattle at the Hall. Thank you." She squeezed his hand.

He felt emotion rising, and tears threatening to overspill. He was becoming a sentimental old fool. "Some things in life are special. Sometimes they're taken for granted; sometimes they're not appreciated. My children, my cattle, my work – and you Ami, you are very special. My children are far away, my cattle are dead, and my life's work is negated. But you're here with me. I can't understand why. I know that I've disappointed you time and again. A beautiful young woman like you shouldn't be wasting your time with an ageing, redundant gambler like me." He was not looking for sympathy, but even if he had been, he did not get it.

"What nonsense. I'm here because I want to be. Time with you is always special to me, and I want you to be part of my new project." She told him with increasing animation of her plans and her project would be concluded with a visit to Namibia and Botswana from May to September, and the part she hoped he would play in the project before she left. She showed him an itinerary for the visit prepared by a South African called Jan Joubert, and Harry did not fail to see the handwritten note at the top, 'Everything is ready for you. It will be a wonderful adventure. Love. Jan'. He prickled briefly. Who was Jan Joubert? Ami did not notice his reaction. "You see, Harry," she concluded, "I have come to the conclusion that our very special friendship has never become more than that because we never have been on an equal footing. Now, you can be part of *my* project – somehow that releases me from feelings of obligation, and may let you see me in a different light. Maybe it finally will ignite that special spark between us."

She had not read the situation with total accuracy. There already was a spark – more than that, a burning passion – between them; it had been there ever since Egypt at different levels of intensity. What she still failed to understand was Harry's laidback approach to life. Harry took for granted the power of feeling that held them together, and accepted it as it was. Ami wanted to build on it, and fix it as a permanent relationship. It was a *grand-affaire* for both of them, but they viewed it in different ways. The brief three months until her departure for Namibia in May passed in a blur of togetherness, but when the moment arrived, they parted without any firm commitment. It did not occur to Harry to articulate his commitment because he knew it existed, not because he wished to avoid it; Ami did not put her deepest wishes in words because she still remained reticent to push too much, despite her statements at Caminettos. Once again they bid a tearful farewell at the airport; Harry full of genuine sorrow, but looking forward to hearing from her regularly; Ami still with a twinge of uncertainty, and still not fully confident that Harry was hers.

Royal Contracts 2002

Walter also had been watching Harry's situation with some interest. They were old friends and he knew that Harry would decline without action and involvement. He had been putting together plans for a social documentary to highlight the huge contrast between wealth and poverty in UK, and he rang Harry in April to arrange to discuss the project with him. They met at Harry's rented cottage after lunch.

"Harry, how are you old chap?" Walter smiled, and was encouraged to see that Harry's shoulders were still square, and his expression cheerful.

"I'm fine. Good to see you," came the confident reply.

"I hear that you and Ami are an item these days," continued Walter as they entered the cottage. "You don't waste time do you. Haven't changed that much."

"Nothing serious, really. We've known each other for a long time and she's great company." He found it difficult, even with Walter, to shed the habit of nonchalance regarding his relationships.

"I'm sure she is! Don't forget I've known you even longer, and have seen you through two wives and innumerable other women. Anyway, I don't wish to pry into private territory, but I do want to discuss an idea with you."

Harry poured drinks and they sat in the living room. Walter described his concept of a multi-media presentation of poverty and deprivation in the UK at the start of the third millennium. He planned to use TV, radio and exhibitions of photography and other art forms. He intended to contrast current extremes of wealth and poverty with those at the beginning of the twentieth century.

"You'll not believe it Harry, but the wealth gap now is wider than it was a hundred years ago. A small segment of the population owns a vast proportion of the total wealth in the country, and the Golden Jubilee this year provides an ideal opportunity to expose it." He paused, and encouraged by Harry's nodded agreement, continued. "Last October the *Mail on Sunday* produced 'The Royal Rich Report' which showed that the wealth of the Royal Family exceeded two billion pounds, all built at the expense of the British public. Despite this, the cost of the Royal Family to the taxpayer is upwards of 50 million pounds every year – quite obscene. It's expended on extravagances such as the Royal Train and the Royal Flight. Do you realise that it's used for private travel – £100,000 on a trip to the Caribbean for Charlie, or £24,000 for the Queen Mother to fly to the Castle of Mey? The Duke of York uses his title as UK's Special Representative for International Trade and Investment to soak up half-a-million pounds of taxpayers money each year jet-setting around the world to golf tournaments and racing circuits – the prince of freebies – he's a figure of fun, a laughing stock!"

Harry laughed at Walter's vehemence, but he sympathised with his views. "It would be a comedy if it weren't so serious. Andrew and Edward hoist on the petard of their inflated egos and juvenile vanities, but cost us a fortune in the process."

"The Queen is worth billions of pounds, and yet we have to subsidise her with a Civil List of eight million pounds so that she in turn can subsidise the second tier of parasites – the Princess Pushies and that atrocious Wessex couple. Then we had the full regalia of a State funeral for the Queen Mother. Why spend a fortune on a woman who owns a fortune which is free from inheritance tax – why indeed mourn a woman who dies at the age of a hundred and one years after a life of indolence and privilege! I know there are others who own indecent fortunes, but they are not maintained by the State." Walter stopped for lack of breath. The more he discussed Royal privilege, the more incensed he became. "I intend to focus mainly on the Royal Family. They surely are the final relic of a deferential society, resting on their own belief in their divine right to rule."

"Won't you be repeating the *Mail on Sunday* research?" queried Harry. The *Mail's* expose of royal wealth had raised the profile of the whole question of unacceptable privilege.

"No. I want to go much further. I want to contrast royal wealth with the harsh realities of life. At the other end of the scale, I want to show those who are sleeping rough, old people who are being turned out of nursing homes, youngsters from poor homes who don't get a fair chance to develop their abilities. What do you think, and would you be interested to be involved?"

"Yes, probably I would. I'm helping Ami with a project at present, but my input will be completed before mid-May as she'll be away after that. I sympathise very much with your sentiments, Walter, but for that very reason we must be careful not to present an unbalanced view. As it happens, I've been approached – informally at this stage – regarding a photographic commission concerning the Royal Family." He had received a telephone call just two days previously. "Anticipating that the Jubilee celebrations will boost public support for the monarchy, they'd like to have a record of the native breeds of livestock kept by members of the family – conservation is a buzz word, and I guess they hope it will show them in a good light. They must know that I kept White Park cattle. There are quite a few breeds at Highgrove alone. If I conclude negotiations satisfactorily, can I suggest I concentrate on that project, and you enlist the young Ugandan for the Jubilee work? You remember Joseph – he would have received a YPF grant if YPF still existed."

"Yes, I do. That's an excellent idea, Harry. I'll contact him. The Jubilee was his special interest. Your project sounds interesting, although I think it will take more than a few pigs and cows to maintain the royalist cause." Walter laughed. "I intend to move fairly quickly. The most intensive activity will be around the Jubilee celebrations at the beginning of June, and I'm almost ready to start now on other aspects if I can get Joseph over here, but I would be grateful for your opinion on the outline of my programme."

Their discussion of the projects occupied the afternoon and continued through the evening over a working supper. Harry was shocked by the results of some of Walter's research. Official statistics showed that the numbers sleeping rough in British cities was falling, but Walter demonstrated clearly that the opposite was true. Places in residential care homes for old people had been reduced by 50,000 in the last five years because of reduced funding and over-regulation. The poor were being penalised at every turn. Walter obviously had thought through most aspects in considerable detail, and Harry determined to pursue his own agreement on the livestock project to an early conclusion.

Next morning he contacted the agent and pointed out that spring would be a good time to photograph herds and flocks to coincide with the birth of lambs and calves. He received a very prompt response advising that the project must be completed by the end of May, and requesting a quotation for the work. In view of the time limitation, he decided to restrict the project to Highgrove, Gatcombe and the Royal

Mews. He sent a quotation, together with details of the breeds to be included, and two copies of a letter of agreement requesting the return of one copy duly signed. After a slight delay, the letter of agreement arrived in the post. He checked that it was properly signed, and filed it in the Projects folder. There was also a letter couched in pompous terms, which amused him, with instructions regarding procedures to follow to gain admittance to the properties and for conduct on the properties. Although pomposity irritated him, Harry could not help smiling at the natural arrogance of these people.

He quickly went to work. He had taken advice from the Rare Breeds Survival Trust regarding the priority of each breed, although he already knew something of genetic conservation from his own involvement with White Park cattle at Highcrags. He photographed all the breeds but made special studies of the Hebridean sheep at Highgrove and White Park cattle at Gatcombe. He also intended to give a high profile to the Fell Ponies at the Royal Mews. He had grown up with them and Dales Ponies in the Yorkshire Dales, and he still looked for the moorland herd on the Howgills in Cumbria every time he drove down the long sweep of motorway where the M6 approaches Tebay from the south. However, the Crown Equerry was particularly keen to parade the Cleveland Bays, and Harry agreed as his co-operation was essential. Harry was pleased with the completed portfolio. He ensured that it was professionally presented, and sent it to the agent with an invoice for the sum quoted. Three weeks later he received an envelope with the Royal crest embossed on it.

He opened the envelope and read the letter that it contained. A dark frown creased his brow. After thanking him for the portfolio of photographs, the letter continued: 'We note the inclusion of the breeds originally agreed, but we were disappointed that they all did not receive equal treatment. The record of some breeds was less comprehensive than we expected. Therefore, we propose to pay you £9,000, being 60 per cent of your quotation.'

Harry did not suffer fools or scoundrels gladly, and the timing in this case was particularly unfortunate. Harry was in low spirits because he had not had a letter from Ami, and conciliation was not a natural reaction. He immediately passed the letter and supporting documents to his solicitor. "Sue them," he said "for the full amount and costs." If he had not been a republican before, he certainly was now. Walter had seen the truth many years previously. It had taken a little longer for the scales to drop fully from Harry's eyes.

A cheque in the full sum demanded arrived four days later, but it was too late to influence Harry's opinion.

French Property 2002

The contracts with Ami and the royal breeds had given Harry renewed vigour and enthusiasm, but they were not long-term projects. He needed a more substantial challenge to get him fully back on track. The answer came unexpectedly in July. Miles Mountjoy rang to invite him for supper, and to stay for the weekend. Harry accepted enthusiastically. He spoke to Miles regularly by telephone, but had not seen him for a while. He would enjoy the drive across to Abingdon, and it would be good to spend a leisurely visit with Miles and Antonia.

Miles had met the Loxton brothers and they had been asking after Harry. The French market was maintaining its upward trend. Britons were rushing to escape abroad, houses were selling almost before they were on the market, and prices were rising rapidly.

"Do you remember the Loxtons?" asked Miles. "You met them met a couple of years ago. I gave you an introduction."

"Yes," replied Harry without hesitation. "They had a foreign property business based in Peterborough. There were two brothers; seemed to be decent fellows."

"What was your assessment of their operation?"

"It appeared to me to be a business with huge potential, and I recall that you were of the same opinion at the time. I was less impressed with the Loxtons' ability. They seemed to lack direction and were too casual for my liking. I suspect that attention to detail and the application of sound principles of business management would have made a world of difference."

Miles smiled. "My opinion precisely. The Loxtons are amateurs trying to run a professional business. However, they have realised their limitations, and are receptive to business proposals." Miles paused to fill Harry's glass. "How about a partnership with them? They have a business ripe for development, and we have the expertise and drive to make it successful. What do you think?

It was Harry's turn to smile. "If I know you, the deal is already agreed in principle. When do we get down to the details?"

Miles arranged a meeting for Wednesday the following week. Mike Loxton arrived alone, and explained that his younger brother had decided not remain in the business, but he remained keen to establish the partnership with Miles and Harry. It was agreed that they would focus their attention on property in France. Miles would be the partner responsible for administration, Mike would deal with promotion, and Harry's role would be to locate property for sale.

Harry was enthused by his involvement in a new business. Miles and Mike realised the benefits of Harry residing in France, but Harry had not anticipated such a move. He was aware that his responsibilities would require a considerable amount of travel abroad, but moving to France was a major life decision. However, he began to weigh the advantages. His ties to Britain were weak. He had no sympathy for monarchist privilege and decadence, and would feel more comfortable in a republic which espoused *liberté*, *égalité* and *fraternité*. He would be living on site, and that would be more effective. His contact with his aged parents, his brother and his nephews had withered through neglect. His own children were thousands of miles away, and it would not affect them whether he was in France or England.

But the deciding factor was Ami. He would have wished to discuss such a move with her – to know that she would be happy to live in France – but he had not heard from her since she departed on her African visit almost three months ago. She had left no forwarding address for him to contact her, and he began to doubt himself. He no longer exuded the aphrodisiac of power. Maybe she finally had deserted him. Maybe she had fallen for a younger man – what other explanation could there be? His thoughts flew immediately to Jan Joubert, the university lecturer who was organising her current visit and who obviously had been very helpful on her previous visit. How helpful was very helpful? Maybe his usefulness to Ami was at an end. He remembered the affectionate note from Joubert to Ami that he had seen by accident. His confidence ebbed, and an uncharacteristic depression overtook him. He knew that he must fight it, and meeting a challenge was the only way he knew. He had no reason to stay in England. Without Ami it mattered little where he lived.

Conspiracy Afoot 2002

Theresa was in limbo. Following her self-imposed exile to Herefordshire thirteen years ago, and especially since her separation from Harry more than a year ago, Theresa had missed the cut and thrust of London life, and the excitement of new challenges. Even her acrimonious exchanges with Harry had served to sharpen her senses and responses. She realised that the business experience she had accumulated in London had been wasted – hidden under a bushel, and suppressed by Harry's tumultuous career. Now, although still partially isolated in the Worcestershire manor house, she was experiencing the freedom of single life again, and she longed to get back into action – meaningful, fulfilling action. She had not been employed since she left London, and that proved a serious impediment to her ambition at the level she knew her abilities deserved.

In late June, she was intrigued to receive a letter from Australia in the early morning post. The address label read 'Mrs T. Bainbridge, Whitstone Court, Worcestershire, UK'. Clearly, the abbreviated address and lack of a postcode indicated someone she did not know well. She took out the two typed sheets. It was headed paper – 'PFA Australia' – and was signed by Ms R Payne, Chair of the Board. Well, this was interesting. She scanned quickly through the letter, and then with increasing amazement settled to read with great care and deliberation.

Rebecca Payne probably knew the twists and turns of Harry's business and personal life in more detail than any of his friends and colleagues. She made it her business to know. She was aware that the women who had surrounded Harry possessed great personal qualities. She also understood the animosity between them. As she prepared to take control of PFA, she appreciated their value to her. She knew that they would have absorbed – maybe even subconsciously – much of Harry's understanding and sympathy for the business, and her proven abilities would be applied to persuade them to work together as a team.

Her offer to Theresa was timely and welcome, and the challenge was to put Rebecca's dream into practice. Theresa wasted no time. This was an opportunity she would relish, not only because it demanded the full deployment of her skills, but also because it would be a statement for Harry to ponder – a chance for him to reflect on opportunities he had wasted. She replied immediately by email – Australia was nine hours ahead, and maybe Rebecca would pick up the message that evening. She was in luck.

Within the space of a few hours the two women had struck a deal.

Next morning the telephone rang at Pamela's home. "Pamela, it's Theresa Bainbridge. We did meet once at the office, but we've never had a real opportunity to talk." Pamela went cold with apprehension, and her hand instinctively moved to protect her burgeoning pregnancy. She scarcely knew Theresa, and was somewhat in awe of her. How much had she discovered? Theresa continued. "I know how much you enjoyed working at PFA, and you must be very disappointed by the changes that have taken place, but there are new developments, and I'd very much like to discuss them with you. Would you be interested?"

Pamela paused. Was this a trick? Why would Harry's wife want to talk to her? She replied hesitantly, "Yes, probably I would, but can you tell me a little more about the developments?"

As Theresa continued, Pamela relaxed. Theresa gave no indication that she knew anything of Harry's affair with Pamela, and Pamela had no intention of enlightening her. Theresa explained that PFA had been taken over by the Australian subsidiary headed by Rebecca Payne, and that she – Theresa – had been asked to take the Chair and put PFA back on its feet. Pamela could scarcely believe her ears when Theresa asked if she would like to resume her old job as PA to the Chair, on the same terms as before, starting in September.

Pamela needed little persuasion. She had not had a secure permanent position since her dismissal from PFA, and a salary would be very welcome, but she was pregnant and due in October. Theresa was very understanding, and Pamela was reassured. Harry no longer was a key player, and if his wife now held the reins, she was happy to change horses. The team was starting to take shape.

Theresa felt encouraged by the ease of Pamela's conversion, but she suspected that Ami would present a more difficult obstacle. Memories of the Birmingham exhibition, Harry's retirement party, and the Bonheur painting flashed through her mind. Momentarily, resentment filled her, and she cursed Rebecca for wanting Ami in the team. But as she thought more calmly, the sweetness of it dawned upon her. What a blow to Harry's self-esteem if his wife and his mistress joined forces to run his former company. Yes, the ultimate satisfaction would be well worth the awkwardness of overcoming the initial difficulty. She would offer Ami the position of Managing Director, Harry's former post, which would give her a status she would find difficult to refuse, but still leave her under the control of the Chair.

Theresa's enquiries revealed that Ami was in Africa, and would not be easy to contact. She could wait, but she was impatient to complete her task. She had accompanied Harry on one or two visits to Africa, and had not wasted her time. While Harry was attending business meetings, her Celtic gregariousness had accumulated a substantial list of friends and acquaintances, and networking soon discovered Ami's whereabouts and a contact point. She sent a fax to an office in Maun to await Ami's arrival. It was brief and businesslike:

> 'Dear Ami
> The last time we met was at Harry's retirement party. I was so pleased that you were able to attend, and it was a lovely evening. Since that time there have been great upheavals, both personal and business. Events have moved rapidly, and there now is a great opportunity for you at a senior level in PFA under new management. If you are interested, I believe we have a big job to do together. I have been offered the Chair, and I would like you to be MD. It would be a real pleasure to work with you, and I know you could bring your proven artistic qualities to the benefit of the company. Please reply as soon as you receive this message.
> Best regards, Theresa Murphy'

Ami arrived in Maun soon afterwards, her exhilaration equally matched by exhaustion after an amazing journey through one of Africa's magnificently remote areas. She often thought of Harry, and wished to share her experiences with him. But she also appreciated the chance to blaze her own trail, and break free from his powerful influence.

She was handed Theresa's fax when she called at the office the next day. Any worries Theresa may have had were not realised. Whereas Pamela had been apprehensive, Ami was thrilled with excitement by Theresa's offer. She saw immediately the opportunities of the situation.

If one thing had irked Ami over the years, it was that Louise Crossman had been appointed MD of PFA. Ami knew that she should have had the post, and suspected that Harry could have tried harder to ensure her appointment. Now maybe she had the chance to show what he had missed. He would be proud of her, would he not? Or maybe he would not; maybe he would resent her taking the post that he once held. Well, that was a problem he would have to overcome. Perhaps he should have thought more of her when he was indulging his dalliances in Budapest and Italy. She stopped thinking of Harry – the emotions were too mixed to unravel – but she immediately sent a reply to Theresa with provisional acceptance of her offer. She was due to arrive back in England in late September and looked forward to the challenges ahead.

Theresa breathed a huge sigh of relief when Ami's reply arrived. She had not been sure of the outcome, but now the path ahead was clear. It was inconvenient that Pamela would give birth in October, and that Ami's return to England was later than she would have wished, but both were a small price to pay compared with the success of her initial task. The team was complete, and Rebecca's female cohort was ready to assemble for business.

Final destination? 2002

"Same again all round, please." Harry had stopped for lunch in a small village in Lot et Garonne. David, the owner of the bar, and his wife, Linda, were British. The only other customer, Adrian, also was British.

"How d'you find life in France, Adrian?" Harry asked. "You must have formed some strong impressions after two years."

Adrian was well-educated, trim, clean-shaven, fashionably dressed and bright. "To be honest, it was a wrench at first. I'm British to the core, and always ready to defend the honour of the old country. But the Britain I knew no longer exists. The rights of criminals seem to take precedence over those of victims, and the national culture is swamped by immigrant priorities. I found it impossible any longer to identify my standards and principles with current events in the UK. It's a measure of my disillusionment that I'm happy to live in a country where the choice of President lay between a crook and a racist, rather than stay in Britain under New Labour. You've been here longer than me, David, what d'you say?"

David was a complete contrast to his friend – bulky, bearded and blunt. "Yes, you're partly right. People think I left England because of the effect of the high value of the pound on my business, or because we were being overrun by illegal immigrants. Far from it. The real reason for me was much more obvious. I couldn't stand any longer the sight of that smug bastard Blair, grinning out of the television screen and telling us that everything was under control, that there were plans to put all our problems right, that he could be trusted to see us OK. Bollocks. All I could see were longer waiting lists for hospitals, longer queues of traffic and more bureaucracy, while my pension became smaller. Plenty of cash for Tony and his cronies, but not for the rest of us. Talk about opportunities in the new millennium, the beginning of the twenty-first century will be remembered as the start of the great escape from Britain – escape from spin, smears and sleaze. Here you have fast trains that run on time, a great health service, and the food and drink – well, I don't need to tell you about that." He paused, seemed about to resume his diatribe, but thought better of it. "You thinking of moving over here?"

"Yes, I am," replied Harry. " Not sure where just yet, but I've given myself a month to find the area and the house that give me right vibes. The certainty is that I'm leaving Britain."

Harry was not an opponent of New Labour by family tradition. His political heritage gave him every option. His farm-worker great-grandparents – if they voted at all – would have supported the Whigs. His maternal grandparents remained strong Liberal supporters – a large portrait of Gladstone had hung in the parlour – although their support probably depended more on Gladstone's austere moralistic philosophy rather than on his politics. His parents voted for the Conservative party because they associated it with individual achievement. Harry's upbringing, and his own early experience, had been moulded by the principle of reward for effort and achievement, but he had never felt that any political party truly represented his interests. The Conservatives were the party of big business with a focus on profits at the expense of people; Labour were the workers' party with an ethic of rewards without responsibility; the Liberal party was an irrelevance simply held together by one or two personalities.

In the general election of 1997 he had been sufficiently impressed by the image and manifesto of New Labour to come off the fence and vote. He had not been unhappy with the state of the economy under the Tories, but he had been appalled by the antics of the Hamiltons, Aitkens and their like, and thought that a change would do no harm. *What a let-down!* He thought. *Cook, Mendelson, Byers – David's words had been spin, sleaze and smear – they beat the Tories into a cocked hat when it came to unethical politics. Their obsession with distortion and suppression of unwelcome news was making a mockery of democracy. The Prime minister was a laughing-stock. What did they call him in Italy? 'Lo Scroccone' – the scrounger. Tuscany Tony was a figure of fun, and an embarrassment to any decent Briton – in reality, was not Alistair Campbell both arch spin-doctor and Prime Minister. No, thought Harry, he was now an opponent of New Labour by conviction, and he would be very glad to leave British shores.*

The departments of Gers, Tarn-et-Garonne, Lot-et-Garonne, and Charente all had a special character, and Harry was in no hurry to conclude his search. The exploration of hidden corners of France was a reward in its own right. He would stop only when the appeal of a house was sufficient to quench his wanderlust. He had been in France for about three weeks, and was driving from Poitiers to Bordeaux one Sunday in mid-August. He was listening on the car radio to news of the disastrous flooding in Prague and Dresden, and heard that Budapest was now threatened. It seemed incredible. The sky above him was clear and blue, and there had even been a heatwave in Britain not long ago. He called for lunch at La Rochelle, attracted by its reputation for oysters, and afterwards decided not to rejoin the A10 at Saintes, but instead to continue south from Rochefort to Royan, and thence across to Mirambeau to join the A10 two junctions further down at exit 37.

The countryside of Charente-Maritime is a pattern of land and water. Towards the Atlantic coast many of the marshes, where salt was harvested until the nineteenth century, had now been converted into oyster basins. Freshwater marshes had been drained to make grazing for traditional cattle, while further inland the plain is dominated by arable crops such as wheat and sunflowers. He called at the Tour de Broue, the remains of an ancient castle standing on a low hill, which looks out over the mosaic of old salt pans and islands. Harry had lived all his life among hills, and the early imprint of the mountains of northern England still shaped his appreciation of landscape. He enjoyed the view from the Tour, but the flatness of the area held little appeal for him.

When he reached Royan, he turned east alongside the Gironde estuary, and gradually the countryside became more undulating. He drove along a range of low hills and just beyond St. Dizant reached a high point where he stopped to stretch his legs. He walked up a slope and, cresting the rise, was halted in his tracks by the view. The estuary was spread out below him, glinting in the afternoon sun. He felt a sudden sense of peace – a sense of belonging.

The local agent in Cozes pulled particulars of several houses from the files. "This is a beautiful area, Monsieur Bainbridge. It is only ten minutes from the A10 autoroute, and Paris is easy by car or train or air." Her English was excellent. "If you like wine, you will like it here. Charente Maritime is where the vines of Bordeaux meet those of Cognac. What do you think of these three houses? I think they are the style you described."

She spread out the particulars. One of them immediately attracted Harry's attention. It had an imposing yet elegant facade – full of character without being fussy. His command of French had improved during his visit, and the description further excited his interest. *'Maison de Maitre. XIXeme siecle, 650m^2, grandes dépendances, petite maison annexe, sur terrain arboré de 14,700m^2.'* It looked and sounded perfect. There were five bedrooms – three en suite – superb Charentaise fireplaces, a cellar, and about three acres of land – including gardens front and back. It was five kilometres from St. Thomas de Conac, and Harry asked to inspect it immediately.

"Ah, yes, the house on the hill," replied the agent. "I know that you will like it. I must warn you there are still some trees in the grounds that were uprooted in the great storm in December three years ago, but the house suffered no damage."

Resteulet was all that Harry could have wished or imagined. It was larger and more substantial than Whitstone Court, and it commanded views over the estuary at the front, and over the valley from the garden terrace at the rear. Hills were an integral part of Harry's being, a psychological and emotional restorative. Nostalgia stirred in him as he looked across the expansive views – it roused memories of the freedom of childhood on the bleak Pennine hills. Resteulet was his new home, and he moved in as soon as possible.

He settled into an easy chair, poured a glass of Pineau, and looked out across the valley. *Was this really home? Had he found it at last?*

How could he be sure? Did he know? Would he ever know...

With time on his hands, and an inevitable pineau beside him, Harry had ample opportunity to dwell on his past mistakes. Throughout his life, he never before had taken time to analyse himself, never tried consciously to identify or understand his priorities. His thoughts did not reflect well upon himself.

He was alone, and that disturbed him. He liked his own space, but he needed someone near him. Throughout his life, problems had seemed to solve themselves – they had righted themselves without any serious effort on his part. There had always been an attractive woman not far away. It seemed different this time. In the past there had always been at least one secure base from which he could launch himself again. But now?

He had not given enough effort to solving the problems that had arisen with Theresa. She had deserved better from him. The laws of physics state that two unlike poles attract – that had been true in the first years, but in the end the differences proved too great. Theirs had been the problem of two strong characters with conflicting ethics – could they ever become compatible without seriously inhibiting the expression of one (or both) personalities?

He guessed that Pamela was carrying his child, and about to give birth. She had always taken the initiative with him, but in the final analysis would she ever be prepared to leave the devil she knows – marriage with Duncan, unsatisfactory as he is – to settle with a man almost 30 years her senior? He felt resentment at the thought of another man raising his child, but the decision was in Pamela's hands.

But it was the lovely child-like Ami that preoccupied him. He still thought of her as the effervescent young girl that had entranced him in Egypt. He had built her up and discarded her as often as it suited his priorities. Finally, she had matured despite him and put herself on an equal footing. She was in the ascendant – an artist at the top of her profession – and he was convinced that she was no longer attracted to him, a man without power and authority. Her South African friend, Jan Joubert, probably had all the qualities of youth and charisma that she desired. He wished she could have valued him as a man for himself, but he feared he simply had been a stepping-stone on her ascent.

He was on his own; on his own until – maybe for good. Even those relationships which had been less serious had faded away. Karen decided to stay with her eccentric husband and his money, while the delicious Eva expected commitment before surrender. Maybe now he was paying the price for not making the effort that was necessary to sustain a permanent relationship?

As soon as his PC was installed, Harry sent out change of address messages by email to all his friends and acquaintances. He was aware of the potential problem of fair-weather friends and scrounging acquaintances inviting themselves to stay, but it was important to re-establish contact on all personal and business fronts as quickly as possible. Miles Mountjoy and Mike Loxton in particular would be relieved that at last their third office was operational. Harry sent a mass circulation message, but there were personal messages for others. Walter King and Johan and Sabine Barck received open invitations to visit whenever they wished. He sent Theresa a long and affectionate message describing the house and grounds and telling her how sad he was that they were no longer together. He sent Pamela a coded message which he hoped only she would understand. He asked her to let him know whether it was a girl or a boy, wished them both well and hoped to see them soon.

Harry did not send a message to Ami. He must make one last attempt win her back. He needed to talk to her, and called her at the warehouse in Narrow Street. He tried several times without success, and finally resorted to traditional mail. He rarely wrote letters – he had not hand-written a letter in decades. Nor was it an easy letter to write. He had not seen her, nor heard from her, since she left England in May to gather the final material for her project in southern Africa and the ominous shadow – Jan Joubert – was in Africa. Meanwhile he had forsaken England for a life in France. She had been in his thoughts a great deal, and slowly it had dawned on him that he should be ashamed of the way he had treated her, the woman who had been his pivot for almost two decades. He swallowed his pride and wrote as he had never written before.

> 'My darling Ami,
>
> Time passes slowly. It was springtime in England when I saw you last. I remember as if it was yesterday watching you disappear down the departure gate at Heathrow after I kissed you goodbye. My heart was heavy, and you smiled through your

tears. That was almost five months ago. You were continually in my thoughts, and I waited with growing impatience for a letter. When I did not hear from you, I thought you had deserted me – I feared that at last your youthful enthusiasm had tired of me – maybe you had found someone else. Maybe your friend in Africa had been more than that, and you were with him. It is frightening what fanciful tricks an uncertain mind can play, but in that state of rootlessness I decided to cut my ties with England, and moved to France.

It has been lonely without you, and I have had many hours to sit and picture you in my thoughts. The chance to think of our times together – the happiness of closeness, and the pain of parting – but mostly the happiness. Through my recollections I have come to understand that I have done you much wrong. I, who had the opportunity and the power to give you great happiness, failed you. I must have caused you grief and pain – maybe even more pain than others who did not love you, or loved you less. You know that apologies have never been my *forté*, but I know that I owe you many more than I can ever make.

I did not have the sense to recognise it, but I have known for eighteen years that you are the woman I wished to spend the rest of my life with, and be a mother of my children. I am empty without you. I beg your forgiveness for my foolishness and selfishness in not admitting it before. I can see now that I brushed aside your pleas with a quick quip or a smile, when I should have taken you in my arms and never let you go. My lack of commitment has wasted both our lives. You never berated me, and I never had the sense to understand that it was my responsibility to make your life complete. I pray that I can make some amends if you will allow me to.

I have a house in France that you will love. It is beautiful, but it is empty. It needs to be filled with your *joie de vivre*. The Bonheur is hanging on the wall waiting for you. It has poignant memories, but they are meaningless without you. I can not yet ask to marry you, for I am still married. I can not ask to be the father of your children, because I have kept you waiting too long. I should not ask you anything, because I do not deserve you. I have no right to ask you anything, but I do ask you to come to me. I will be yours always.

I want you, I need you, I love you, Harry.'

He sealed the envelope and sent it off with a mixture of hope and fear. He called the next day but her number was unavailable. He contacted directory enquiries, and discovered that her new number was ex-directory. He waited for her reply. He waited and his hope ebbed away.

On the eighth day after he posted the letter, he visited some properties in Saintes with Claude, a local agent. At the end of a busy day, he drove down the A10 autoroute, took the Mirambeau exit, and turned towards Resteulet through the vineyards.

The morning's mail lay scattered on the floor where he had dropped it. His composure was destroyed. The October 2002 Newsletter from PFA had brought news that he would have preferred not to have heard – Ami's appointment as MD was the tune to which any future steps must be danced. That clearly was her priority. He had been right after all to come to France. He sat with a second glass of pineau for a while, and finally took up Ami's letter. With hesitation and trepidation he opened the envelope and unfolded seven sheets of paper. He saw the ending 'With my undying love. Ami'. He closed his eyes, and drew a deep breath. If he had opened her letter first that would have been all he needed know – but now he had seen the company news. He would see everything in a different light. He started to read:

'Dearest dearest Harry,

I wanted to ring you as soon as your letter arrived. I so desperately wanted to ring you, but I decided – like you – to write a letter. I can put down my thoughts more clearly and sensibly when I write. On the phone I would be emotional and incoherent. But a letter from you! Now that is something new! My number is ex-directory because I was getting nuisance calls after my visit to Africa. Southern Africa was quite awesome. It was a funny feeling going back to the land of my birth last year, and I stayed away from Cape Town during my visit, but this year I was in Botswana and the Namibian desert. It was a great success, and

I will not bore you with the details now, but Jan Joubert had arranged a marvellous itinerary. I went to the plains of Damaraland with their huge granite mountains and the ancient San rock paintings, past Simba country to shimmering mirages in the vast silvery-white expanse of the Etosha Pan, by canoe through the swamps and rivers of the Okavango Delta among the hippos and crocs, and much more. Dear Harry, I wish you could have been with me. I missed you so much. Totally out of contact with the outside world, enveloped in the most amazing scenery and wildlife – and most of the time all I could think of was having to walk away and leave you at Heathrow, just wanting to run back and hold you. Then I arrived back in England full of hope and anticipation, impatient to hold you and share my excitement with you – and you had gone. Emigrated and left no word for me. Nothing from you until your letter. That was so cruel.

The words in your letter are lovely. They touched me deeply and they made me cry. Have you ever told me before that you loved me? I don't think you have. I knew, but you never said. I love you too – probably too much for my own good. I truly have never loved anyone but you, and I never will.

But that is only part of the story. I must go back to the beginning if we are to have any chance of understanding the paradoxes of our relationship. I was a troubled and helpless girl when you first found me, had faith in me, supported me and gave me self-esteem. You built up my confidence, and I believed we were destined for each other. I was willing to wait for you until you recovered from the hurt and trauma of the break-up of your first marriage. I knew of your affairs in Hungary and Italy. Italy! Oh Harry how could you when I was still with you, and you knew of the pain I suffered there! I was jealous – madly, insanely jealous of those other women, but I kept it hidden in order not to frighten you away. And I knew – but you did not – that I had deceived you in order to escape from my contract with PFA. Our wonderful, incomparable holiday in Egypt was based on a sham. It was a heavy weight on my conscience, and it stopped me every time I felt impelled to seek commitment from you. But still you were my best friend, and my business rock. Then you swept away my self-belief. You crushed me. You married someone else! It almost destroyed me.

I came to my senses just in time – older and a little wiser. Again it was partly due to you, and the old chemistry still was there. Remember Christmas at Bellridge Hall? I thought again, 'this is it'. But no. Once more you let if drift away. You laughingly dismissed my desperate pleas. Oh Harry, why did you let me go!

Then I grew up. At last my head began to challenge my heart. My African project gave me confidence to think that I could stand alone. I was able to stand on equal terms with you. Stand with you, not leaning on you. We reached new heights in the months before I left for Africa. A love and understanding that seemed unshakeable. Again, my hopes were raised. Again, you dashed them down. I returned to find that you had gone. Did you really think I was seeing someone else? How could you doubt me! Jan Joubert has been so helpful, but he is simply a friend. No more than that. Have I ever deserted you? Harry, am I a plaything to be taken up and thrown aside according to your mood? Do I not deserve better from you?

Now I have grown up yet again. I have a job – I am employed! You may approve, you may not. I do not know. You ask me to come to you. I can not do that. I could ask you to come to me, but I will not do that. I do not want either of us to be a planet circling round the other's sun. I want us to be locked together, entwined and circling together as we were when we danced the lambada at Caminettos.

My love, I have waited almost twenty years for you. You must not expect me to wait longer. I can not wait any longer. I am a woman now – no more a girl. I need a life in my own right, and you must show that you truly want me – more than that, you must show that you are prepared to be with me as an equal and committed partner. Can you do that? Can you make a sacrifice for me? I do not know. Only you know the answer.

How many nights I cried myself to sleep. I never told you that before. I don't tell you now as emotional blackmail or through self-pity, but simply to let you know that it can not continue that way. It should not be like that. We should be coming together with joy, not stifling sorrow because we are apart. I have wept many tears too because I do not have your child. I often wonder if I am meant not to have children – maybe it is a punishment for aborting the only child I ever conceived. But I can not believe that – I can not believe that I was meant to suffer abuse for many months and have to live with the consequences thereafter. Am I past child- bearing? I do not know, but I think not. It is very late to try, but I would try. What joy our child would bring for me. If I had known before how things would be, and if I had found the courage, I would have had your children when I was young. Then I would have them now, even if I did not have you. I should have taken my cue from the Bonheur black filly and conceived to the great white stallion! By the way, did you know that Pamela has had a baby? There are rumours that it is yours, but I know that cannot be.

I always will be yours, and you say you always will be mine. But can we be together? Is it too late? Have we exhausted all our chances? Would you forsake anything to be with me – you may think me presumptuous for being so forward, but I have been disappointed so often that I need strong reassurance from you. I ask myself whether I believe you ever will give me the happiness I crave. I hear your words, but have you really changed? If fate decrees we must remain apart – and I pray it does not – then at least the memories of our times together will help to lighten up the loneliness of my later years.

Did I say that I would be coherent if I wrote to you? Vain hope. The merest thought of you spins all reason and logic entirely out of control. I have read again what I have written, and I am not sure I understand myself what I am saying. Maybe you will see into the truth – the answer – that lies hidden in it.

I wonder if I will be strong enough to resist the temptation to catch the next flight to France. I wonder if you will be strong enough to come and show me that I matter to you above everything else. I wonder if we ever will be together.'

Harry was moved to tears more than once as he read. If her letter had arrived even one day earlier, he would have been on his way to England to see her and probably stay with her for ever. But it had not.

His mind had been swayed already by other news from PFA, and once again the spectres of female capriciousness – even infidelity – had occupied the centre of his mind. He heard not just her pleading, but also the conditions that she imposed. She wanted him to be with her, but on her terms. He was settled in France in a new home with a new challenge, and she wanted him to sacrifice it. Pamela had a child, and sooner or later she would discover it was his, but probably she would forgive him. He sat and brooded as the evening light dimmed.

Eventually he stirred. He put the letter in a drawer of the bureau, poured yet another glass of pineau and went upstairs. He took down the Bonheur painting and placed it with its face to the wall. He would hang it again when she arrived. Next week, next month, next year, the year after? Maybe never. How many glasses of pineau would drown his sorrows before he knew?

For the first time in many years the importance of his family roots sprang to the front of his mind. A powerful sense of guilt descended on him. He had been the golden boy who had rewarded the sacrifice of his parents in giving him the opportunity to escape into a wider world by effectively severing contact with them. As he revelled in the luxuries of egotistical opulence and social self-indulgence, he had shown no interest in their lives, nor in the progress of his younger sibling and his family. He had ignored their invitations to important family occasions as he followed his own selfish dreams. Now Dick had taken over the family farm, and established a reputation in his own right as a political figure in the farming world. If they ever had needed him, they no longer did so. He had forfeited his right to expect any consideration or sympathy from them. He pondered his situation with sorrow, and concluded that his guilt was too late and the rift too deep to mend. In his voluntary exile and lonely meditation, a wistful longing for the haven of his native Teesdale and a place in the Bainbridge dynasty began to assume a greater importance. Could he ever face them? Would they maybe send an invitation to celebrate his father's 90th birthday?

He sat in melancholy frame of mind – a rootless man – waiting for others to solve the tragedy of his life.

finis

LIST OF PRINCIPAL CHARACTERS

Part One: THE ENGLISH OAK

FAMILY:

Richard (Dick) Matthew Bainbridge
Harold (Harry) George Bainbridge, Dick's elder brother
Ralph Bainbridge, Dick's father
Annie Bainbridge, (née Metcalfe), Dick's mother
George and Isabella Bainbridge, Dick's paternal grandparents
Matt(hew) and Eleanor Metcalfe, Dick's maternal grandparents
Camilla Leyland, Dick's first wife
Judith Parkin, Dick's second wife
Nicholas Parkin, accountant, Judith's father
Evelyn Parkin, Judith's mother
Ralph Nicholas Bainbridge, Dick's elder son
Jennifer Simmons, Ralph's wife
Richard Alexander Bainbridge, Ralph's son
Sarah Isabella Bainbridge, Ralph's daughter
Simon Matthew Bainbridge, Dick's younger son
Angela Grant, Simon's girlfriend
Nicola Antonia (Toni) Griffin (née Hope-Clavell), Dick's third wife
Margot Hope-Clavell, Toni's mother
Stephanie (Fanny) Griffin, Toni's eldest daughter
Natasha (Tash) Griffin, Toni's second daughter
Jeannette (Netta) Griffin, Toni's youngest daughter
Susan Alderson, Dick's fourth wife
John Alderson, Susan's father

FRIENDS:

Bob Johnson, gamekeeper
Sir Geoffrey and Violet Lady de Courcy, Buckinghamshire estate
Frank Stoddart, Dick's best man

'BUSINESS' ASSOCIATES:

George Hastings, wrestler
Fred Burlinson, wrestler
Sam Forbes, owner of Dickie Ranch, Wyoming
Mo Healy, owner of Sheridan Stock Farm, Wyoming
Lt. Col. Sir Jacob Milner, owner of Cheldale estate, nr Buxton
Arthur Burns, manager of Cheldale estate
Sir Dudley Fortescue, Bt., friend of Sir Jacob
Lord (Ivor) Liffey, owner of Scargill estate and businessman
Wendy Shore, farmer with FMD
Peter Williams, farmer with FMD
James Thomson, bank official

Part Two: THE GOLDEN BOY

FAMILY:

Harold (Harry) George Bainbridge, MD of PFA
Ralph Bainbridge, father of Harry
Annie Bainbridge (née Metcalfe), mother of Harry
Richard (Dick) Matthew Bainbridge, Harry's younger brother
George and Isabella Bainbridge, Harry's paternal grandparents
Matt(hew) and Eleanor Metcalfe, Harry's maternal grandparents
Eleanor (Ella) Rachel Bainbridge, Harry's daughter
George William (Bill) Bainbridge, Harry's son
Jayne Leighton-Brown, Harry's first wife
Simon Leighton-Brown, father of Jayne
Theresa Murphy, Harry's second wife

FRIENDS:

Ami Kotze, artist
Karen Richmond, lecturer
Eva Garcia Munoz, Spanish travel guide and interpreter
Saori, Japanese socialite
Julian Duffell, University friend of Harry
James Farndale (later Lord Banthorpe), University friend of Harry
Nick Linassiades, University friend of Harry
Patrick and Christine Giles, friends of Harry and Theresa
Martin and Rose Lancaster, friends of Harry and Theresa
Michael and Norma Evans, friends of Harry and Theresa

BUSINESS ASSOCIATES:

Louise Crossman, MD of PFA
Vernon Sowerby, Chairman of HIH
Miles Mountjoy, Chairman of HIH, Chairman of PFA
Antonia Mountjoy, wife of Miles
Walter King, Director of PFA
Andreas (Jack) Maladonis, Director of HIH and PFA
Peter Loder, Director of PFA
Terry Williams, PFA Finance Officer
Pamela Croft, PA to Harry
Duncan Croft, husband of Pamela
Robert M Gator, trustee of YPF charity
Mike Loxton, partner of property company
Mark Hopkins, project manager for English Nature
Johan Barck, MD of Foremans
Sabine Barck, wife of Johan
George Hastings, livestock valuer and former wrestler
Steve Kent, owner of riding centre
Jan Joubert, South African lecturer
Rebecca Payne, Chair of PFA Australia